SECRET AGENCY

G J BELLAMY

ISBN: 9798871252062

G J Bellamy

gjbellamy.com

CONTENTS

Cast of Characters   V

1. Public outrage - Private grief   1

2. Modest beginnings   12

3. A new friend   17

4. White Lyon Yard   23

5. Sinking feeling   32

6. Foreign affairs   43

7. 1 + 1 = 2   52

8. Interesting food for thought   60

9. Country house and gardens - suitable for spies   73

10. Night falls, the games begin   85

11. Submarines with potatoes   97

12. Hide and seek   104

13. Superintendent (Inspector) Penrose   110

14. A change in direction   125

15. Calamity   131

16. Solo sleuthing   140

17. Taken up a notch   149

18. Perspectives   155

19. At the Foreign Office   168

20. 2 + 1 = 3   178

21. Of omelettes and trains   189

22. Abinger Mansion   196

23. The Wright family   204

24. Dinner   213

25. Hidden messages   221

26. Tension   229

27. Kindred and unkindred spirits   237

28. Anger and spite   244

29. Planning   250

30. Much creeping   262

31. Parties after midnight   272

32. Insistent thoughts   279

33. Disappointment   287

34. A new way of life   296

35. Future troubles   306

Also by G J Bellamy   311

CAST OF CHARACTERS

Family & Friends
Sophie Burgoyne / Phoebe King
Henry Burgoyne, vicar - Sophie's father
Lady Shelling (Elizabeth Burgoyne) - Auntie Bessie
Ada McMahon / Nancy Carmichael - Sophie's friend
Flora Dane - Sophie's long-time friend
Archie Drysdale - Sophie's second cousin

The Agency
Miss Jones, typist
Elizabeth Banks, office helper
Nick, errand boy
Mrs Barker, cook

White Lyon Yard
Hawkins, butler
Mary Roberts, maid
Mrs Lund, friend and distant relative of Aunt Bessie
Mrs Cowan, friend of Aunt Bessie
Lady Sedlescombe, friend of Aunt Bessie

Trefoil Hall
Lord Desmond Wicksworth, Defence Secretary
Lady Wicksworth
Victoria Redfern, steel industry representative
Sir Reginal Fawcett, diplomat
Butler, butler

Peters, footman

The Greek delegation
Ambassador Makri
Mrs Makri
Admiral Pavlidis
Captain Vassos
Paul Klest/Josif Abazi
Karissa Raptis
Major Theodoropoulos, interpreter

Scotland Yard
Superintendent of Special Duties (Inspector) Penrose
Sergeant Daniels, Special Duties
Inspector Morton, CID
Sergeant Gowers, CID

The Wright family
Sir Ephraim Wright, banker
Frank Wright, architect
Alfred Wright, engineer
Thomas Wright, art gallery owner
Stephen Wright
Prudence Wright, Alfred's wife
Millicent Wright, Frank's wife
Lady Anthea Manningtree (Wright)
Lord Philip Manningtree

Abinger Mansion staff
Mrs Fisher, housekeeper
Mr Reese, Sir Ephraim's confidential secretary
Mr Fenton, Sir Ephraim's valet
John Rogers, footman
Nurse Gleason
Rosina Murray, lady's maid to Lady Manningtree
Barry Chambers, Manningtree chauffeur
Mr Barstow, valet to Lord Manningtree

Chapter 1

Public outrage - Private grief

September 1920

A t six o'clock on Wednesday, 15 September 1920, Mr Frank Wright, architect, left his office in a very pleasant frame of mind. He was middle-aged, but there was a bounce in the way he descended the stairs. He had received a letter from his father and now, after all these years, the breach could finally be healed between him and his ailing, sole-surviving parent.

He shut the door behind him and went out onto elegant Adam Street. From there, it was only a short walk by the side of the Thames to the Embankment underground station. To get to the station, Mr Wright habitually walked along Adelphi Terrace - the inspired, neo-classical architectural work of the Adam Brothers. Sadly, the once magnificent buildings were falling into disrepair, and alterations over the years had disfigured the original façade. Worse still was the state of the large vaulted and arched former wharves below the Terrace. These had become dilapidated and of ill-repute - a haunt of homeless people. Frank Wright had a long-cherished idea to design something spectacular to renovate and augment Adelphi Terrace.

"Read all about it!" cried the man at the newspaper stand by the underground station. "Disarmament Day in Germany... First reports in... 'Allo, guvnor. Standard, is it?"

"Good evening, Lenny," said Frank. "Yes, and I'll take a News as well."

"There you go, guv," said the vendor as he swiftly handed over two folded newspapers to receive a penny from Frank. He began calling out once more. Frank scanned the headlines for a moment

1

before putting the papers under his arm. Then, umbrella in hand, he descended the long flights of stairs to the trains.

The northbound platform was quite crowded. Frank Wright, with many other passengers, glanced about and then peered into the tunnel, trying to gauge the arrival of the next train. The Bakerloo line was always busy. Frank worked his way along the tiled wall to stand in his usual place at the southern end of the platform. From here, he had the highest probability of getting a seat in the carriage. He recognized several people, but not anyone he knew to converse with. Frank Wright then, as regular as clockwork, began reading his Evening Standard while he waited for the train which would take him home to Maida Vale.

Within a few minutes, he felt a rush of warm air fanning his face. Pages of his newspaper fluttered. He could hear clanking noises in the tunnel - heralds of the train's imminent arrival. Frank Wright, like everyone else, prepared himself to board and, if necessary, to step left or right to get to the doors. It all depended on where the train stopped. He shuffled forward to within two feet of the edge of the platform. He looked into the tunnel and could now see the lights of the train as it approached - a sight he had seen a thousand times before.

Although the red and cream trains slowed to the sound of squealing metal, they always seemed to enter the station so quickly. Just as this one began exiting the tunnel, Frank Wright felt something around his ankle. He looked down and recognized, in an uncomprehending flash, that it was an umbrella handle. Suddenly, it was pulled hard against his lower leg and, with a simultaneous violent push in the back, Frank fell forward onto the tracks. A woman's scream and men's oaths vied with the noise of the train.

Within the hour, Lenny, the newspaper seller, had given his story first to a reporter and then to the police. The next morning, as he cried out the headlines, his voice was less strident than usual.

Families in Britain had become acclimatized to receiving bad news during the war, when an unexpected knock on the front door might presage the dreaded telegram. With the war over, that should have been a thing of the past.

Detective Sergeant Gowers of Scotland Yard and Sergeant Mansfield of 'A' division, who was in uniform, got out of the car on a quiet Maida Vale street at a few minutes past ten.

"Worst part of the job," said Mansfield.

"It is that," replied Gowers.

The two men studied the prim, symmetrical house across the road. A soft glow brightened the drawn curtains of a room to the left of the front door.

"It's a nice house."

"Yes, it is. Well, let's get it over."

The men passed through the gateway in the centre of a low privet hedge and walked up the neat stone path. They ascended the single stair and were mindful to stand back a bit from the clean doormat. Gowers reached for the knocker to give a quick, quiet, tat-tat. They stood there in silence, knowing what was coming. Gowers studied his shoes. Mansfield seemed not to look at anything. A lamp was on in the hall and light streamed through the frosted glass of the side windows and the small square pane in the door.

Millicent Wright opened the door. She was wearing a well-cut grey dress and held a handkerchief in her hand. The two men saw in her face the history of her last four hours. They saw the first hour of irritation in which the dinner was getting spoiled; the second hour in which, to her annoyance, Frank's dinner got cold as she put the children to bed, trying to explain to them their father's inexplicable absence; the third hour, in which irritation died while she searched her mind for mention of changed arrangements or any possible reason for the lateness and for the lack of apologetic phone call; and the fourth hour of imagining the worst, expecting the worst, rehearsing all that could have gone wrong - over and over. Now, the vigil ended with their knock on the door. Mrs Wright saw the police uniform and wailed, "Oh, no! No!" The handkerchief she had in her hand went to her mouth and tears started in her eyes. Her home and heart were broken.

———⋈———

It should be understood that Sophie Burgoyne is first and foremost a lady. In breeding, she can trace her Norman lineage back to the Domesday book of 1086. Before that date, the generations of her Norman forebears are lost to history. What is not lost to history is her more distressing branch of Burgoyne genealogy in which she finds herself also related to Robert I, the first Duke of Burgundy. He had the title during the period 1032-1076. Robert had the vastly understated nickname of Tête-Hardie - Headstrong. It is from this branch that her family name of Burgoyne originates. However, it is also the branch with a history about which the current family would rather not reflect because it is not exactly pleasant. Duke Robert was more than a somewhat wilful child, as his nickname suggests; he was also a murderous brigand who robbed lands and churches and took to killing anyone who got on his nerves. Had the Duke invaded another country, he might have been hailed a hero. As it was, his lack of vision made him no better than a savage bandit.

As she sat at a desk in her office, Sophie was not thinking about Robert I, family trees, or skeletons in the cupboard - she never did, anyway. Sophie gave exclusive thought to the immediate problem staring her in the face. After leaving sleepy Havering-under-Lyme, Sophie had hoped to make her new business a success. Her idea was to lift herself and her father, the vicar at Havering, out of their genteel impoverishment and to secure for them both an anxiety-free future.

On the desk to her left was an open and empty cash box. Standing before it were several neat stacks of coins. Copper predominated; silver was scarce. The sum total of her worldly wealth amounted to four shillings and elevenpence. She had counted it twice. To her right lay open a demand notice for the coal bill. It stated that, although Jos. Black & Sons very much appreciated Sophie as a customer, no further deliveries would be forthcoming until she settled her account in full. The amount owing was seventeen shillings and ninepence. Sophie did recall burning some coal to banish the chilling dampness from the office during the dreary summer. However, she could not remember a superabundance of warmth at any time and certainly nothing like almost a pound's worth.

The problems she faced were that she was thirteen shillings short, there remained but three tiny lumps of coal in the scuttle, it was chilly outside - unusually so for August - and, since the fire was nearly out, it was getting chilly inside, too. She put the remaining scraps on the fire and then composed a letter.

After typing 'Dear Sirs,' she went on to say that she could not possibly pay their account as rendered at present because of the obvious errors it contained. When a true and proper account had been presented she would be happy to pay it in full. In the meantime, if they would be so kind as to deliver a hundredweight of coal tomorrow morning or at their earliest convenience, she would be much obliged, etc. Yours faithfully, Sophie Burgoyne, Proprietress, Burgoyne's Employment & Typing Agency.

A satisfied smile appeared on Sophie's face as she read through her letter which she signed with a strong flourish. She then folded the letter into the addressed envelope, took a stamp from a drawer, put on her hat and coat, and went out to post the letter which, if she hurried, would be in time for the City of London's afternoon delivery.

―――⋈―――

The Criminal Investigation Division, New Scotland Yard, Southern Norman Shaw Building, Victoria Embankment, 16 September, 1920

"Good morning, sir," said Detective Sergeant Derek Gowers. He was reporting to his superior officer, Inspector Morton, who shared an old Victorian office with another inspector named Bygrave.

"Morning, Gowers." Morton had been writing but looked up to fix his pale blue eyes on the sergeant.

"It's about the incident at Embankment underground station."

"Tell me it wasn't a murder." Morton reluctantly put his pen down. "Let's have it."

"Here's the file, sir."

Morton took the file and looked inside. "Give me a verbal report."

"'A' Division was called in and immediately referred the case to us. I was there within half an hour. Deceased is Frank Wright, age 45, who lived in Maida Vale. He was married, wife is Millicent Wright. Two children, a boy, 13, and a girl, 9. Wright was a well-respected architect and had offices on Adam Street, which is..."

"I know where that is. Continue."

"The deceased left work as usual and walked to the station about six yesterday evening. He bought two newspapers from a stand next to the station. The newspaper seller has known the deceased for over a year. He informed me that Wright was perfectly natural and said nothing out of the ordinary. He did not notice anyone following Wright.

"The deceased reached the northbound platform three or four minutes before the train arrived. The platform was quite crowded, and Wright made his way along to a particular spot at the south end. Several witnesses said they do the same in order to get into a less crowded carriage. Of the witnesses, three recognized the deceased by sight.

"The train came in at six-nineteen. Wright was at the front of the crowd. Witnesses say a man, muffled with a scarf and wearing a large flat cap pulled down low over his face, elbowed his way forward to stand behind Wright. As the train emerged from the tunnel, the man fiddled with his umbrella, which seemed to disturb the deceased. The assailant then shoved Wright in the back very hard. The deceased fell on the tracks in front of the incoming train. He died instantly from his injuries."

"Hmm, not a suicide, then. A murder, a quarter-mile from where we are now. I don't like it. Got anything more? A description?"

"The assailant vanished, sir. He must have rushed away from the scene and nobody had the presence of mind to stop him, which is understandable. Those that could identify him had just witnessed Wright's very nasty death. Once away from the immediate area, it would have been easy enough for the assailant to remove his cap and scarf. He was wearing a nondescript old brown overcoat that he could also have removed. The crowds just swallowed him up."

"Height?"

"Five-nine to five-eleven, broad-shouldered, and heavy-set. What has been mentioned is that he looked like a very ugly customer. The passengers did not like to speak to him directly when he pushed his way through the crowd."

"Anything else?"

"Two umbrellas were found. One belonged to Wright and was dropped on the platform. It's a newish Fox with a Malacca cane handle. The other, also left on the platform, was an old one. We have reason to believe the old umbrella was used by the assailant to trip Mr Wright - to hook him around the ankle, sir, and make sure he went over when pushed. It has tears in the fabric, so it's useless as an umbrella. No maker's mark and no fingerprints. It was cleaned recently."

Morton sat back in his chair and tapped a finger on his chin. "I seem to recall a similar technique being employed before. Now, when was that?"

Without looking up, Inspector Bygrave spoke. "1917, Leicester Square. Victim was a civil servant named Draper. Worked in the Public Record Office but was seconded to the Admiralty. I never caught the blighter." Bygrave then looked up and smiled.

"Was there anything in Draper's background?" asked Morton.

"No. He was an ordinary man with no vices or disreputable acquaintances. The records he worked with were not highly classified or anything, so the Germans wouldn't have been involved. The only item of interest I recall was his life insurance policy payout of £500. I thought it was sufficient to make me look closely at his wife, she being the sole beneficiary. In the end, I couldn't find anything to connect her with Draper's death."

"Thank you," said Morton. "Gowers, get the Draper file and see if there are any similarities with the assailant in the Wright case. It may just be a copycat killing."

"I will, sir. Um, I should mention that Frank Wright is the eldest son of Sir Ephraim Wright who has a controlling interest in Frobisher Bank. Also, I'm told, old Mr Wright is rather poorly at present."

Both Bygrave and Morton stared at Sergeant Gowers.

"Then you have your work cut out for you," said Morton. "Get everything you can on the family and try to get details of Sir Ephraim's will. Report back as soon as you find anything."

"Yes, sir." Gowers left the room.

"Frobisher Bank," mused Inspector Bygrave, "has to be worth several millions."

"And the eldest son gets himself murdered when the old man is poorly. Presumably, he's in his seventies and his health is failing. I suppose I'll have to inform Penrose with Frobisher being involved. This is the kind of thing he likes."

"Yes, I would. He's probably busy with those submarine talks this weekend. Won't stop him from wanting to meddle."

"Have you ever thought about transferring to Special Branch or Special Duties with Penrose?" asked Morton.

"I always understood you had to be chosen to get in. I suppose I've been passed over, so I rarely give it a thought."

"Neither do I, really. The idea of being present at diplomatic talks sounds like nice work for a change."

"It doesn't sound bad. I'm thinking about applying to get in the Flying Squad that's just been formed."

"I wish you luck."

"You know, returning to the Draper and Wright cases, I think it's very interesting that the same unusual technique was used – the umbrella business, I mean. Let me know if you find out anything."

"I will," said Inspector Morton. "I'm sorry. I have to get on with this report I'm working on for the AC."

"Ah, you, too? He likes his paperwork, does our Assistant Commissioner. All in the name of efficiency, of course."

"Yes, Efficiency with a capital E," said Morton drily.

New Scotland Yard, Thursday afternoon, 16 September, 1920
Inspector Morton knocked on the door before entering the office.

"Good morning, Inspector."

"Morning, Morton," replied Superintendent Penrose, who was always called Inspector by everyone except his superior officers.

"Are you busy, sir?"

"Certainly I am, but come in and take a seat." Penrose was a burly, middle-aged man from Somerset.

"Thank you." Morton, a younger man, full of nervous energy, quickly sat down. "Did you hear about the death at the Embankment last evening?"

"Only what the newspapers had to say about it. Why?"

"The victim, Frank Wright, is the eldest son of Sir Ephraim Wright. You know, Frobisher Bank."

"Is that so?" replied Penrose slowly. He picked up his pipe and stared at it before looking up at Morton. "He was murdered, then, otherwise you wouldn't be here. Any leads?"

"Not yet. It's a bit early, sir. We're looking into the family, of course. What's interesting is that an umbrella was used to trip him while he was being pushed. A man used the same method in 1917 at the Leicester Square station. There seems to be no other connections between the two cases."

"A hired killer, do you think?"

"Possibly. It made me think along those lines."

"Where do you see this being of interest to me?"

"I thought the bank, sir. Sir Ephraim is not expected to live much longer."

Penrose nodded slowly. He then opened a thick file on his desk. From the top of the papers it contained, he extracted two sheets and selected one to hand to Morton.

"You've been good enough to bring me a tidbit. Now I'll show you something. Cast your eye down that list. It's the British contingent attending the submarine talks with the Greeks. Starts tomorrow."

Morton scanned the list and stopped suddenly. "Alfred Wright... the submarine designer?"

"Second son of Sir Ephraim... Now what do we make of it all? A coincidence?"

"I don't know. Makes you think, though."

"It do. It's like coming to a crossroads at night and the signpost's missing." Penrose looked at his pipe again. "You smoke, Morton?"

"Cigarettes, sir."

"I'll open the window, then. This matter bears looking into and you'll need to keep me informed about your investigation."

Thursday, 16 September

Sir Ephraim Wright was not a well man. The morning light of a September sun shone through the casement windows of his bedroom in his London house. He was in bed and on the coverlet was a newspaper cast aside. Its headlines declared the dreadful news of his son Frank's death the night before. They were to have reconciled. Frank was to have come into Frobisher Bank, taken control, been the next Managing Director. His son had ideas, would have taken the bank forward by funding revitalization projects in big cities, but particularly in central London.

Sir Ephraim grieved. He grieved, but in an extraordinary sense because his son's death had almost certainly been preventable. If only he had taken the warning seriously.

With difficulty, the old man reached over and opened the drawer of his bedside table. From it, he took out a folded sheet of paper. He looked once more at the simple, typewritten message.

Private offer to purchase
408,000 Frobisher at 8s 9d per share.
Will call to arrange.

He had known the note's arrival a week ago meant trouble when a messenger handed it to him outside his office, but he believed he could deal with what he considered a scare tactic or a poor, peculiar joke.

Sir Ephraim thought he might know who was behind the proposed transaction. He was to sell 51% of the Frobisher shares to a person with a long memory. Controlling interest of Frobisher would pass into the hands of someone who, he supposed, hated him. The price was laughable - except today nothing was laughable. The parcel's market value was close to £1.75 million while the note proposed that he should sell it for £165,000.

A telephone call giving instruction had soon followed his receipt of the note. He had been urged by the man with the deep voice, urged and warned of deadly consequences - particularly warned against contacting the police. He had defied the unidentified man, treating the matter as a prank or shallow trick, although the whole seeming charade had made him nervous enough not to bring in the police. Now the threat had been realized. His son, Frank, was dead. Sir Ephraim felt hollow, numb and barely knew what he was doing. He supposed the telephone would ring again. The deep, steady voice on the other end of the line would give more instructions and further warnings. Sir Ephraim thought of his four living children as the tears streamed down his face.

CHAPTER 2

※ ❖ ※

MODEST BEGINNINGS

MAY 1920

I t had been at the end of the preceding May that Sophie had acquired the typing agency simply by reading about one for sale in the advertisement columns of the Times. It had attracted her attention primarily because the purchase price was only five pounds. This amount puzzled her immensely, and she wondered if an error had been made. She wrote immediately requesting more information and to confirm the price.

Sophie met the elderly gentleman selling the typing agency. Its premises were situated between the thoroughfare of Eastcheap and the River Thames. Sophie soon discovered there was no real business as such, and that he was selling because he was desperate to get out of the lease.

"I'm sorry there are so few active customers left," said Mr Jenkins. "To tell the truth, it was my wife's agency, but she's that unwell now, and has been this past year, that she can no longer run it. I tried to make a go of it but I've no head for business. I was a cabinetmaker by trade. Everything here soon went downhill."

"I see," said Sophie as she walked about the unused space. Victorian furniture, Edwardian shelves and filing cabinets, and typewriters of a more recent vintage were all still in place.

"Those two Royals are in good working order. The two Underwoods need repairing."

"My concern is that the office is in a backwater, so to speak, even though the City is quite close by."

"Well, that's true. But the rents closer or in the city itself are that much higher. My wife would never have got started if she'd had to pay those rents. And we'd never have had so much space as we do here. She built up a good reputation with her clients, though," he added incongruently.

"Could you provide me with a list of them?"

"Certainly, I can."

Sophie looked out of one of the side windows at the narrow cobblestone street below. The office floor plan was L-shaped with Sack Lane on the long-stroke and St. Martin's Lane on the short one, which was also the front of the building. Sack Lane, where the entrance to the office was situated, was only wide enough for one vehicle at a time to pass through. St. Martin's was also cobbled and only slightly wider.

"The trick, Miss Burgoyne, is to find a good errand boy with a bike to fetch and carry the work to and from the customers. If you get busy, you'll need a second and no mistake."

"Thank you, I shall consider that. I see you have a telephone line."

"That's right, but I had it disconnected to save the expense. Just to warn you, it's a party line, so if you have it reconnected, you'll hear other people's conversations from time to time and they'll hear yours."

"I shall remember that. I suppose the GPO would charge a fabulous amount for a private line and take their time installing it." Sophie sighed. Her budget had no room for any telephone, private or otherwise.

"May I look over your account books, please? I need to have some idea of the running costs besides the rent."

"Of course you can. Take a seat and I'll bring them to you."

They sat together, going through the books while Sophie took notes of important facts. The office was quiet, disturbed only by the occasional clattering of cartwheels and the clip-clop of a horse's hooves on the stones. Once, a whistling barrow boy went past, pushing an empty hand cart that rattled over the cobbles. Later, a lorry inched slowly along St. Martin's, making a racket. It seemed quieter than ever after it had gone by. Then, there suddenly came a series of tremendous, dull, metallic booms from somewhere deep inside the building. Sophie jumped.

"What on earth was that!?" she exclaimed.

Mr Jenkins looked untroubled. "It's the water pipes, miss. Does it a couple of times a day. I should have warned you, but I'm that used to it now I pay it no heed. Landlords tried to fix it a few times over the years, but the noise always comes back."

———⋈———

Having caught an afternoon train, Sophie arrived back home before teatime. Their part-time cook would have some dainty sandwiches and cakes prepared; Sophie would make the tea herself. Sophie's father, the Reverend Henry Burgoyne, was a tall, spare, slow-moving, affable, erudite man. He was a widower and the much-loved vicar of Saint Bartholomew's at Havering-un-der-Lyme. Sitting with him in the vicarage drawing room, Sophie broached the subject she was so anxious to relate.

"Father," said Sophie, "I have put down a deposit to purchase a typing agency."

"Have you, my dear? That is very enterprising of you." Henry looked at her and smiled, but also raised his eyebrows questioningly.

"I'm going to make a go of it. It will be an employment agency for domestic staff as well as a typing agency."

"I wish you every success.... It's not in the village, is it? I fail to see the need for any type of agency in the village."

"It is in London."

"Oh, that's a pity. Do you need me to go up to London with you?"

"No, you have nothing to worry about and, because it's a typing agency, you can post your sermon notes to me and I will have them typed and returned to you the same day. But you must send your notes by early Wednesday at the latest to be sure to have them back in time for Sunday."

"Splendid! That is very satisfactory. I really cannot read my own writing sometimes. But where will you be staying?"

"With Auntie Bessie."

"Ah, good, good. I hope you realize your Aunt Bessie is a complete eccentric, but you were always a favourite of hers. Well, don't concern yourself about me. I survived quite well while you were away supervising in the Land Army."

"It won't be as bad as that, Father. I shall be home most weekends."

"That would be very nice." He hesitated for a moment, and a cloud crossed his face. "Dare I ask how much this will cost? I can cheerfully contribute something, but it will be a depressingly modest sum."

"You are so kind and supportive and I thank you from the bottom of my heart," she went over to hug him as she was speaking, "but I have enough saved to cover all the beginning costs... But there is something you can do to help."

"Anything. Just command me."

"I need your assistance in writing to all our friends, family, and acquaintances, telling them to send their domestic servant requirements to Burgoyne's Employment Agency. Oh, and anyone who has a connection in the city must have their express typing done by Burgoyne's."

"I most certainly will help you in that department. Yes, many of them will need staff for their London houses. Asking for business might not be the done thing in polite society, but we're going to do it anyway. It's a different age we're living in now. Where's my address book? We shall start right away!" He got up enthusiastically from his chair and then stopped suddenly to say, "Sophie, how will you manage it all? You'll need help, surely?"

"Flora will pitch in when she's not acting. She's a very good typist, too"

"Will she? That's excellent. I do like your friend Flora, although I haven't seen her in years. I had hoped to meet her again after her engagement to your brother Peter. Where has she been hiding herself?"

"In London. She's on the stage, remember? She keeps busy, but the truth is she hasn't got over Peter being killed in the last week of the war," said Sophie with a pained expression.

"Yes, yes, of course," said Henry quietly. "It will be a long time before any of us recover fully from that blow. So sad, so very, very sad... Still, when you see her, give her my warmest regards. Tell her I remember her in pigtails, running about the lawns here."

"She has changed since then," said Sophie archly, "so much so that you might not even recognize her now."

"Oh, I'm aware of that, Sophie, but that is how I will always remember her."

CHAPTER 3

— ✦ —

A NEW FRIEND

LONDON, 27 MAY 1920

A week later and having signed all the forms, Sophie paid the balance owing to Mr Jenkins and became the owner of a business with six existing customers - omitting to tell her father the exact number. She had arranged with a highly recommended sign-painter to produce an elegant hoarding to advertise the new business, the installation of which was now three days overdue. Sophie had been busy with moving up to London, settling her father so that he would not suffer discomfort in her absence, and buying things for the business. At present, she had the immediate task of cleaning to make the office sparkle. Opening the door with her own key for the first time, she surveyed all that needed doing. Sophie realized that, on her inspection tour, she had glossed over quite a few deficiencies. There was a lot to do, but she had come prepared to work.

Sophie put down her bags and parcels on a desk. She looked at her hat after she had removed it and realized that in living in Havering she had fallen behind the latest London fashions. A new hat was most certainly needed, but her coat would just about do for another year. As for her dresses? Absolutely shocking. She had one dark dress suitable for the office, but for anything else? She blushed to think that she should be invited to anyone's home because she literally had nothing suitable to wear. The economies necessary to a vicar's daughter and four years of war, much of it spent in a Land Army uniform, had paralysed her wardrobe in a dated, rather threadbare way. Sophie suddenly felt like a church mouse. Putting her best foot forward, she told herself that the work would not do itself and that she had better get on with it. She tied up her long, light-brown hair in a scarf and, wearing the oldest of all her old clothes, set to work.

As she was polishing a desk, the pipes went. The sudden, hellish thumping sound made her catch her breath for a moment, but she got back to her task and became absorbed in what she was doing.

The alarming thing she discovered about cleaning a place that has not been cleaned for a very long time was that, after an hour or two's hard work, she almost wished she had left it as she had found it. Everything now looked worse. Her first cleaning attempt had resulted only in the filth being rearranged rather than removed. Every job took about three times longer than Sophie had anticipated and the frequency with which she was changing buckets of soapy or clean water told her how very dirty a place London was. The sources of the dirt were coal fires and factory smoke which deposited a film of dust and grime over everything. Cobwebs were everywhere. Finding mouse droppings did not help, either. Being a country girl, she recognized there were no rats present in the office and for that she was thankful.

While she was scrubbing the floorboards, a cockney voice called up the stairs from the entrance on the floor below.

"Hello! Anyone 'ome?"

Sophie sat back on her heels and sagged. She was about to get up, worrying that she must look a complete mess, when she heard a rush of feet up the stairs. A small, lively looking young woman, about Sophie's age, burst into the room. She had short, dark, curly hair, peeping from under her hat and framing a vivacious face and bright blue eyes.

"'Allo, love," she said to Sophie. "Is the owner about because I've got a message for 'im?"

Sophie noticed that the newcomer was nicely dressed in clean clothes. The hem of her navy blue dress beneath her coat was exactly mid-calf, which, according to the current dictates of fashion, was exactly where it was supposed to be in 1920. Sophie got up.

"I am Miss Burgoyne, the proprietor. What is the message you have?"

"Good godfathers! I thought you was a skivvy." The young woman looked extraordinarily shocked. "I'm so sorry for making such a mistake." She really did look mortified.

"No harm done. I'm doing a skivvy's work and I *am* dressed for the part."

"Of course... Oh, yes. Uncle George, he's the sign-painter, he says the sign will be put up tomorrow without fail. What business are you opening?"

"Ah, thank you. That's a relief."

"He said how the owner was anxious for it and he really was sorry about the delay. He should have told me it was a lady running the place."

"As you can see, I'm not quite ready to open yet, so the delay has not held me up. And, to answer your question, I'm opening a domestic service employment and typing agency."

"Are you really? I do domestic work. Done it all, I 'ave, from scullery to lady's maid. I've also been housekeeper... but that needs some explaining."

"Does it? I'm taking a break now. Would you like some tea?"

"Ooh, that's very kind of you. I don't mind if I do. I'm between situations at present."

"Please, take a seat and I'll just be a moment."

Sophie felt more bedraggled than she actually looked, but she thought to wash her hands and tidy herself up a bit before starting on the tea. The young woman had sat down at a desk and was beginning to look around the place. Then she jumped out of her chair.

"I tell you what. You clean yourself up and I'll make the tea. Where do you keep everything?"

"That's very nice of you," said Sophie. "The gas ring and sink are in there. Tea and sugar are in the cupboard and the milk bottle is in the terracotta pot on the floor.

"Right you are... My name's Ada McMahon, by the way."

"I'm Sophie Burgoyne. Pleased to meet you. Oh, and there's also a tin of biscuits in the cupboard."

As Sophie composed herself, she thought it was pleasant to meet someone her own age. They soon sat down to tea.

"Uncle George is doing a beautiful job on your sign. I saw it when it had only your name on it, so I didn't know what word was coming next."

"Mr McMahon charges by the letter, as you know, so the sign will say Burgoyne's Agency and underneath, in smaller and thankfully cheaper letters, it will say 'Superior Domestic Employment and Typing Services.'"

"So, if I get on your books, would I be a superior domestic?" She had a light, giggling laugh. "Seriously, miss, can I sign up, please?"

"You're welcome to do so. I require references, though, and I'd like to hear about when you were a housekeeper."

"Of course, you'd want references and I can get some..." Ada hesitated. "I'll be straight with you. My last situation was a live-in for a lady in Epping. I did not like her and she did not like me. However, I did a very good job, but she was one of those who tries to find fault so she can deduct from your wages. The housekeeper there was very poorly, and it broke my 'eart to see her try to do her job and get more and more confused. So, I did most of her job and mine and we was managing nicely between us. The lady, who I shall not name, decides the housekeeper was not up to it anymore and gives her the sack... Isn't that funny? We're on Sack Lane! Anyway, she then says to me how I can take over the 'ousekeeping and she'll get a scullery maid to take my place. For that, she says, I was to get an extra shilling a week. The only reason I'd stayed as long as I had was because of the old housekeeper and she with no savings!

"There was no way I'd put up with that twaddle, so I gave her a piece of my mind and out I went, leaving her to reflect on what I'd said. I don't suppose she did because I'd noticed there was this big gap between 'er ears. I've told you all that because you look like a decent sort of lady. If you were to send me out to temporary situations, or a permanent one, I'd work bloo... very 'ard and be as quiet as anything, but not when somebody is doing somebody else a bad turn.... This is very nice tea. I 'adn't realized how much I was dying for a cuppa. Thank you very much."

Sophie was astonished at the flow of words. Not only because of the story itself and Ada's frankness in telling it, but also because Ada seemed to oscillate between aspirating her aitches, over-aspirating her aitches, and not aspirating them at all, depending on the intensity of her speech. Sophie did not like to ask about such a condition.

"That is quite the story," said Sophie. "I, too, have an exceptional dislike for injustice and hard-heartedness."

"That's exactly it, miss. Absolutely."

"It's Horniman's tea, by the way."

"I thought I knew it. I bet they change the name now that the company's been sold to Lyons."

"You're probably right. It's a shame to see a reliable company disappear, but I suppose I don't mind so much if the quality of the tea remains the same."

"I've got a cousin who works in a grocer's in Mile End, and you'll never guess what the cheeky beggar of an owner does with his loose tea. He has these two big tea chests. One says one-and-six the pound, and the other says two-and-six. It's the same tea in both. Can you believe that? The gentry buys the 'alf-crown tea, and the rest gets the same tea at one-and-six." Ada laughed. "I suppose everyone's happy, but if I were paying a shilling more a pound, I'd be having words with that grocer, I would an' all."

"Would you? That's very interesting. I had to have words with a grocer once about a similar matter."

"Oh, go on, miss, do tell. We can have another cup while we're sitting."

"Our grocer in Havering-under-Lyme was charging outrageous prices for delivering to our house. This was just before the war. He had put up his prices as soon as mother died, knowing my father would never notice the difference. When I took over the running of the household, I discovered what he had been doing. The wretched man showed no remorse when I confronted him the next time he brought our delivery to the door. I said I would only pay the prices he was charging everyone else, but he, being a stubborn man and not liking to have been caught out in his ruse, continued to demand I pay his inflated prices. It ended badly with him threatening court action. At least I had moved the box of groceries into the house first.

"Being the only grocer for miles around, he thought he could starve us into submission. He told his assistants not to serve anyone from the house. However, some friendly neighbours ran the blockade for us while he was out on his cart, so we didn't actually starve."

"He sounds a nasty bit of work. What did you do?"

"I had to come up with a plan or we would have been at his mercy forever. For three days I tramped the lanes around Havering, seeking out farmers who might be interested in my little idea. By Friday, Havering had its first-ever farmers' market with twelve farmers present, selling all types of fresh vegetables, bread, baked goods, butter, and a host of other things. It was very well attended. Shortly afterwards, the grocer came to terms because his monopoly was threatened. He agreed I would henceforth pay shop prices with the understanding that I did not organize any more markets. The funny thing was, the farmers organized it themselves from then on until war broke out the following August."

"That's the best story I've heard in a long while... and I 'ear some good-uns."

CHAPTER 4

— ✳ —

WHITE LYON YARD

LONDON, 2 JUNE 1920

Aunt Bessie lived at 28 White Lyon Yard, quite close to Spital-fields Market. Born Elizabeth Mathilda Francoise Burgoyne in 1859, she had, by 1874, decided to marry someone who had a title, was wealthy, and for whom she could do much of his thinking. Her rationale was founded upon her extraordinarily good looks. That, she felt, was all she needed to accomplish her goals.

Fully committed to her plan, Bessie side-stepped a dalliance with the Prince of Wales when she came out into society and was presented as a débutante at the Queen Charlotte's Ball of 1876. She did dance with him twice but avoided him afterwards as he was beginning to make his intentions unmistakeably clear despite Princess Alexandra, his wife, being present in the ballroom.

Her mother, fully aware of Bessie's plans, advised her as to who were the most suitable dance partners and then, after the ball, who would be a good catch. Mrs Burgoyne did not actually approve of Bessie's reasoning or her plan, but, as the girl was so stubborn, determined, and seemingly devoid of a loving disposition, she decided Bessie may as well make a good match according to her own selfish taste.

Sometimes, Mrs Burgoyne despaired of her children. The eldest was Determined Bessie, then came Dreamy Henry, Sophie's father, who only wanted to read ancient books, and finally Deadly Raymond who got into a duel, had to flee the country, and then came back two years later, having changed his name. He took to living in Scotland under the pseudonym of Macleod and owned a castle. In point of fact, the castle was his wife's, she being the widow of the man Raymond had killed in the duel.

Bessie married Sir Charles Shelling, Bart., who was quite handsome, an East India Company Director, a banker, and an important man in the city, extraordinarily wealthy, and smitten out of his mind with love. Sir Charles best summed up their coming marriage and relationship to one another quite early on in the proceedings. "I'll do the earnin' and you'll do the spendin'. What's money for, anyway?" This was beautiful music to Bessie's ears.

Over time, Bessie grew to love her husband for himself and enjoyed his company, quiet man though he was. He never troubled her with business matters and always took the time to show interest in what she did.

Sir Charles died in 1912, and his son, becoming known at that moment as Sir Roderick, took over the estate and the twenty-bedroom house that went with the baronetcy. Early in 1913, Aunt Bessie, tiring of country life with her son and his family, took herself off. She went not to the Grosvenor Square family home but to her own private house. The Little Bolt Hole, she called it, and it was at this hideaway, right on the northern fringe of the City of London, that Sophie would be staying.

From Sack Lane to White Lyon Yard was a distance of two miles. Sophie walked through the City to get to her new accommodation. She had already stayed several nights but had yet to meet her eccentric relative because Aunt Bessie had been away visiting her brother Raymond, the pseudo-MacLeod, at his Scottish castle of Tormodden.

This particular late Spring evening was mild, and the clouds were turned a smooth, pale gold colour by the low, setting sun. Sophie walked along, feeling the thrill and excitement of being the mistress of her own adventure. She was starting a business in London. When it was established, she thought, she would hire a manager to take her place and then she could start another business - perhaps one that was not quite so prosaic. Or she might buy property. She had not decided what she would do, but she thought she would like some excitement and glamour in the next venture.

The City's streets, as always, were busy, noisy. Sophie was still not yet acclimatized to the press of people around her or the roads filled with buses, trams, horse-drawn carts, taxis, lorries, and private cars. She saw men by the hundreds in dark suits, dark uniforms, or tweeds, and all of them wearing hats. It was a rare sight to see a hatless man. Silk toppers - she saw quite a few of those. Such impressive headgear belonged either to the liveried attendants attached to the various banks and other financial institutions or to the directors and governors of those same institutions. Other hats she saw were bowlers, flat caps, and the occasional trilby or policeman's helmet. The hat silently but effectively declared the man's social standing and class.

On her way home, Sophie had put notices in the letter-boxes of businesses that looked like they might need typing services. She had climbed many stairs. If the concern was a large one, it would have its own typing pool. Everyone else she considered fair game.

As she walked north on Bishopsgate with Liverpool Street Station ahead of her, Sophie studied the women among the crowds. She observed the clothes of the city workers very much lacked bright colour. They wore what was expected in the offices where they worked, and this amounted to a uniform of dark blues, greys, or browns. A distinguished, well-dressed woman was walking directly in front, so Sophie had the opportunity to study her clothes. She liked what she saw and concluded the woman must have a well-paid position.

Once past the station, Sophie walked with difficulty against the flow of humanity, hurrying to catch its train home. She had to give way frequently against the solid onrush of determined faces. The flow slackened noticeably once past Spitalfields Market and soon she arrived at her turning. White Lyon Yard had been built in stages between 1690 and 1825. Despite this span of years, the houses conformed quite closely in style, being of a similar, tall height. Her aunt's house, number 28, an orange-tan brick townhouse, had been built in 1810. It was large, with a full cellar, four floors, and space for eight bedrooms and three reception rooms. The garden at the back was very small, but it did give onto a narrow park shared by all the houses on that side of the street. This lent a salutary air and sense of openness to the garden.

Sophie loved the symmetry of the house. All the beautiful, old leaded glass windows were the same size. The central front door, with two large windows on either side, was surrounded by superbly squared white stone, and the entrance was reached by an elegant flight of stone steps. The next two floors were identical and had five windows each. The top floor, demarcated by a stone ledge, had the same windows. Above that, there had to be a roof, but it remained hidden from view to the street below. While looking up, she noticed a drainpipe for rainwater from the roof and thought it to be positively the longest she had ever seen.

Mounting the stairs, Sophie wondered if her aunt had changed at all in the three years since they had last met. She had to knock on the good, solid, dark blue door, using the lion's head door knocker, because the servants had not been instructed to give her a key.

After a short while, the door opened, revealing a woman in her late sixties.

"What do you want?" asked the immaculately dressed woman in a terse whisper.

"Hello, Auntie Bessie. Remember me, Sophie?"

"Sophie, of course," she continued, whispering, but she smiled now. "Come in and don't talk too loudly. It's the servants. They're having a race."

"Auntie, what is going on?" asked Sophie, also whispering once she was inside the superbly proportioned tiled hall with its regency archway.

"Don't call me auntie, makes me feel old. It was fine when you were a little girl. Call me Bessie. I came back from Scotland and the staff had slacked right off. Place was filthy, so I set them to cleaning, butler included. Only I've made a race out of it. We're whispering because I don't want to disturb them. Two of them are neck and neck. It's better than a horse race." She looked excited, almost girlish. It was easy to see that she had been very beautiful.

"The one who finishes first is the winner, I suppose."

"They drew lots for which room they got. If the room is cleaned to my satisfaction and there are no breakages, then first place gets two pounds, second gets a pound, and third ten bob. I fear Hawkins, the butler, will get no compensation for his damaged dignity. Well, that's his hard cheese. Should have kept them all at it while I was away. Anyway, Sophie, how are you, my dear? You're looking well."

"I'm very well, thanks."

"And how's Henry?"

"Father is in excellent health and sends his love. It's a pity he doesn't like London, otherwise you could see more of each other."

"It's not a pity. Seeing relations every two or three years suits me perfectly. Any more than that and they become annoying. Little Henry would take to boring me in Aramaic or something. Absence makes the heart grow fonder. Because I haven't seen him in, what is it, three years? Because of that, I love him very, very dearly."

Sophie smiled. "Do you mean that?"

"Yes, I do. Just think, Sophie. By the time you've been here six months, you'll hate the sight of me and I you. At the moment, overflowing with affection as I am, I'd like to increase the bequest to you in my will. In six months, I'll want to cut you out completely."

"Auntie, I'm not calling you Bessie... You are my aunt and I've always called you Auntie. And what is happening in six months, anyway?"

"I'll tell you what will happen in six months. I'm going to Italy, your business will have failed, you'll want to come with me because you'll be bawling your eyes out over it, I might want to marry an Italian Count or something, and you'd be completely in the way."

"I'll make you the promise that I will not go to Italy with you."

"You won't go to Italy with me? Good, then I also promise not to cut you out of my will... I like you, you've got some backbone."

"I like you... You have backbone, too."

"Ah, that's the Burgoyne spirit. Do you know I cannot stand my own son Roderick? He and his family simply bore me to tears. They don't do anything 'cept talk about crops, horses, and motor cars. The whole lot of them are about as interestin' as a bowl of stewed prunes. I had to run to my bolt hole to get away from them. That wife of his... Do you like gossip?"

"Sometimes it's entertaining, as long as it isn't harmful to anyone."

"Well, let's leave her out of it. What do you think of my chances of finding a count in Italy?"

"I think you'll find plenty of them. You're still a very beautiful woman, but I think you will scare them away by what you say."

"Beautiful woman, indeed. But you're wrong about me scaring them off. I won't. I know how to play the game. They'll be handsome, vigorous, and insincere, while I'll be revoltingly coquettish. But, my dear Sophie, I would find much of that insincerity very pleasant to hear. And I have to do something to amuse myself. Ah, I do believe we have a winner."

Hawkins, the usually regal, taciturn, and always portly butler, descended the wide staircase at his customary stately pace. He wore no jacket and looked hot and dishevelled with his sleeves rolled up. He was holding in his excitement, anticipating stepping off the stairs to stand at a respectable distance from his mistress. At that precise moment, he would deliver his message of victory. When he was halfway down, he heard, they all heard, the dull thumping of running feet coming from the back of the ground floor. Hawkins was in a positive dilemma. He swiftly calculated that while he had eleven more stairs to go at his usual pace, the briskly moving person would cover some twenty-five or thirty feet in the same time. He weighed the odds and came to a decision. He spoke while in motion on the stairs - a thing he would never dream of doing under normal circumstances.

"Your Ladyship," he began sonorously, confident he had won first prize as he was about to take the eleventh stair from the bottom.

Before he could utter his next word, a door flew open at the back of the hall and a thin, young woman ran in recklessly, calling out, "Finished the kitchen!" She almost skidded to a dead stop and, remembering her place, curtsied and said while breathlessly smiling, "My Lady."

If looks could kill, Hawkins slew Mary eleven times - once for each remaining stair. When he reached the hall floor, he turned to Aunt Bessie and said,

"As I was saying before being interrupted, I have completed the Blue room to your exacting specifications and I believe you shall find it in order, your Ladyship. I also had further to come and broke no prohibition against running in the house. Thank you."

"Well, blow me down," said Aunt Bessie. "I don't know who won. You do understand, Hawkins, Mary, that your work has to be adjudicated before any prize money is paid out? For the life of me, I can't tell who was first... What do you say, Sophie?"

"I would say Hawkins finished cleaning first, but Mary communicated her message first."

"Very diplomatic, my dear, but hardly helpful."

"The premise of the competition was to clean a room thoroughly – one drawn at random. Although I have yet to see the kitchen, I should imagine it was the more difficult task."

"Of course it is," said Aunt Bessie. "I think my niece has made a valid point. She and I shall inspect the rooms together. Hawkins, please have the others finish as soon as they are able and let us quickly return to normality. Oh, and get the name of whoever comes third."

"Yes, your Ladyship."

"Come along, Sophie, let's begin our inspection."

The two women had a late dinner, which was to be expected after the staff had been occupied in cleaning the large house all afternoon. Sophie appeared at the table wearing her best frock. She brought her aunt up to date. Burgoyne's Agency now had its sign up and would be open for business on the following Monday, it now being Wednesday.

"I can't understand why you would want to run such an enterprise," said Aunt Bessie.

"Because I want to make my way in life."

"That I can understand. But why an employment agency? It's so middle class."

"I am middle class," said Sophie. "And, if I don't work at something, I shall cease to be any class at all."

"Classless...? That's what those communist fellows are always on about. They want to sweep people like me, like us, completely out of the country. Typical nonsense of those who want to grab power for themselves. Redistribution of wealth, indeed. They mean to replace us and that's all it's about. As for the poorer classes... well, something should be done for them, but I have no idea what."

"I think most people would be happy with better wages and working conditions."

"Naturally, they would. Who wouldn't want those things? But if they can't get ahead by themselves, how is it to be managed? That's what I'd like to know."

"I'm not following you, Auntie."

"Well, supposin' there were just a hundred families who needed lookin' after. They have no skills or education. Then it would be easy. You just train and educate them so that they can find decent employment. But there are millions of them and there aren't the jobs available if they were all educated. How can the government create all those skilled jobs out of thin air? Do you see what I mean?"

"Unemployment is very bad at present," said Sophie. "I don't think I have the answer."

"Ah, well, you're not alone. I don't think Lloyd George has the answer, either. He's not such a bad prime minister as some say but, really, the government is so *full* of windbags."

"They do talk a lot." Sophie smiled. "Although they are revamping the National Health Insurance Act just now. That will provide a lot more people with a pension."

"Yes... Do you know what that oh, so noble institution of the Corporation of the City of London is doing? It's an absolute outrage. I'm so *disgusted* with them. They're making Spitalfields Market wholesale only. The change is imminent. How can they take away my local market like that...? I can answer my own question! Somebody is making a lot of money out of the new scheme. That's what it's about... And I do so enjoy going to Spitalfields. What a shame it all is."

"You do your own shopping?"

"I go once a week. It's an outing for me. Other days, I go for a walk around Finsbury Circus. But the market is special because it's so lively. I like to see all the people and the fruit and vegetables are always the freshest available anywhere. And the flowers, Sophie, look *lovely*. You should come and see them before we're refused admittance. I know quite a few stallholders and they're not at all happy about the change, I can tell you. Blasted City. It is literally taking the bread out of those people's mouths."

"I've walked past the building several times now," said Sophie. "I've been meaning to go in, but I've been occupied getting the office ready."

"Of course you have. I think we have a month or two before the change, so we can go together." Aunt Bessie was quiet for a moment. "My dear, please don't take offence at what I'm about to say... Your clothes."

"Oh, dear me. Do they look that bad?"

"You are a lovely young woman and you should be wearing lovely things. Would you allow this old lady to buy you a new wardrobe?"

"I don't know what to say." Sophie coloured a little. "I do need a few things, particularly for the office, but I don't want to be an imposition on you, Auntie. You're already helping me by allowing me to stay in your house."

"I would have said is 'Oh, yes, Auntie! A trip to Paris would be delightful.'"

Sophie laughed. "Auntie Bessie, I don't think there's an aunt like you in the world."

Later on, the kitchen and the Blue room having been examined earlier and found quite satisfactory by the two judges, both Hawkins and Mary were summoned to the drawing room and received two pounds each.

Chapter 5

— . —

Sinking Feeling

August 1920

The exigencies of running her own business and living in London produced a change in Sophie. She had always been decisive but now she had to be quick, too. Lost to her were the gentle pace of rural living in Havering-under-Lyme and the disposition that moulded itself to such a life. Being thrown into the hectic business world of the City had required her to adapt and deal with emergencies on a daily, sometimes hourly, basis. It was sink or swim and Sophie quickly had to learn to make powerful strokes. Swim she did but, despite her best efforts, her business was slowly heading towards calamity as though trapped in the outer embrace of a whirlpool.

Sophie's first month was one of popping Champagne corks. Friends and acquaintances rallied. Many of them wanted good domestic help - mostly temporary positions but a few permanent, too. It was a good start for the agency.

With great industry, Sophie interviewed many potential employees to fill the vacancies. When checking references, Sophie soon discovered that, while applying for a job, lying was a minor epidemic among the applicants. To save herself much annoyance, she had put up a sign at the top of the staircase which read, 'All references are thoroughly investigated. A false reference will be dealt with severely.' This sign hung below the one that read, 'Beware of noisy water pipes. Anyone shrieking or crying because of the sound will be asked to leave the premises.'

An endless stream of hopeful cooks, maids, footmen, butlers, and other associated professions had come through her doors.

Sophie placed about one in twenty on average. Most of the others were personally unsuited for the post in every conceivable way, as well as lacking the proper skills and experience. She was saddened in turning away so many, but at least she felt she was doing some of them a service. Those who had experience for which there was no current opening were registered in Sophie's card filing system to be contacted when a suitable position became available.

It was a puzzle to her when, almost like clockwork, a few of the same ill-suited people would come back each week. One cheerful cook insisted she had worked in some of the finest houses in the land. She had no character references, which Sophie granted her were sometimes difficult to obtain from a master or mistress. The more obvious problem was that the cook smelled faintly of brandy. Cheerfully and habitually, the cook puffed her way to the top of the stairs to ask loudly, "Anythin' doin'?" When she received the negative reply, she would say, "Thank you, I'm sure. See you next week," and then head back down the stairs, humming to herself.

Sophie felt relief and excitement when the first cheques for placements rolled in. Knowing her clients or being recommended by friends, she had yet to meet any of them in person at her office. Contributing to keeping the clients away was the location of Sack Lane. Nobody had ever heard of it or knew where it was. Although close to the City, it was off the beaten track unless one happened to be visiting The Monument, the tall Doric column with its viewing platform. Designed by Christopher Wren and Robert Hooke, it commemorated the site where the Great Fire of London had started in 1666. Hypothetically, a young man with a good throwing arm could pitch a stone from the top and just be able to hit the roof of Sophie's building in Sack Lane.

The typing agency business was very slow to get going in the beginning. By the hard work of pavement pounding, door knocking, and letterbox stuffing, Sophie believed she could now depend on twenty regular customers. Several of these were from Mrs Jenkins' old list, while Sophie had added new clients. Flora, a frequent visitor and Sophie's long-standing friend, came in to help when there was a surge in typing assignments.

A fourteen-year-old boy named Nicholas, or Nick, possessor of a reliable bike, did the fetching and carrying. In addition to his pay, he had a weekly supply of three comics for when loafing around the office. The comics were his idea and were a required bonus for him to be employed. Three comics a week do not go far. "I've read this one ten times!" said Nick. In response, he was given more edifying novels and story collections, which he declined to read because, as he said, "They 'ave too many words in them."

By the end of the first month, Ada McMahon and Sophie had become firm friends. Ada was a fixture in the office or, to be more precise, Ada was the reliable person Sophie sent out to the more important temporary placements such as dinner parties, celebrations, and other functions within the city. To Sophie, Ada was worth her weight in gold due to her cheerful disposition, as well as her being skilfully adaptable to any and all situations.

If the first month was one of Champagne and a bright future, month two, straddling June and July, proved to be one of tea. New clients began to visit the offices, but the requests for staff dwindled. At the same time, just as many would-be employees were showing up. The good ones were put on the books and waited. The typing assignments dropped off, allowing Sophie more time for tea and chatting with Flora. The domestic work dropped off, which led to more tea with Ada. There was still work, only less of it. Also, June and part of July had been unseasonably cold and wet and it required daily coal fires to keep the damp out of the office.

In the third month, it became a question of economies. This was a month when necessity suggested using the tea leaves twice. The downward slide in business continued unabated. The last week of July and the first week of August managed to produce some glorious sunshine, but the weather soon returned to being rainy and cool again. No matter the weather, the slump in work continued. Sophie wondered how she could improve her prospects. She was covering expenses but, by the end of August, while she dodged the coal merchant's demand, her capital had dwindled down to the neat little stacks of coins amounting to four shillings and elevenpence.

Despite the dilemma facing her, Sophie was now beautifully and elegantly dressed. Aunt Bessie had taken her niece immediately to the most skilled and up-to-date couturiers in London. The young woman had difficulty choosing among the artistic offerings being presented. At Gilberto's, two mannequins displayed and paraded various graceful dresses and, it seemed to Sophie, that each dress was lovelier than the one preceding it.

"It's so difficult. I just can't decide, Auntie."

"Oh, buy the lot of 'em, that's what I say. How many have we seen? Seven, isn't it?"

"Eight. But Auntie, I cannot accept such an extravagant gift."

"Well, you'll have to. I'm buyin' 'em, Gilberto here is fitting 'em, and you're wearing 'em."

"Oh, you are stubborn sometimes, Auntie. Not the peach or the gold, though. And thank you so much, you absolute darling."

"Got that, Gilberto? Get her in the dresses and properly fitted as soon as you can."

"Of course, Madame. It will all be ready in the jiffy." Gilberto snapped his fingers to summon a smartly dressed and competent looking woman who would attend to Sophie. Gilberto left, allowing the women to get on with this more intimate process.

"We'll go to Swan & Edgar's for your shoes and business wear. Do you know Harrod's is buying them out? Which reminds me, we can go to Harrod's for coats. I could do with a new one myself."

"I so very much appreciate what you're doing for me, Auntie," said Sophie. "Do you mind?"

"No, dear, not in the slightest. In fact, it is most enjoyable. I always wanted a daughter. If I had had one, I would have wanted her to be just like you."

"I think that's the nicest thing anyone has ever said to me."

Aunt Bessie looked ruffled by Sophie's comment to the point of grumpiness.

"What's the matter?" asked Sophie, while standing on a low dais as the efficient assistant pinned in place a gauzy, layered, pale blue evening dress with a yoke covered in silver sequins.

"I cannot stand sentimentality. Please don't say anything like that again."

Sophie, standing stock-still with gracious poise to avoid pin-pricks and to aid the assistant, was quiet for a moment. She spoke after a long pause.

"If I think of something nice to say to you, I shall say it, whether you like it or not. You will have to get on with it."

Aunt Bessie turned and glared at Sophie for several long seconds. Then she began to laugh, shaking her head.

———⋈———

Towards the end of August, the day after posting the letter to the admirable coal merchant, a hundredweight of coal was delivered late morning, much to Sophie's relief and surprise. However, her capital had already dwindled further to stand at three shillings and tuppence due to the urgent need of typewriter ribbons. There was always something that needed to be purchased for the agency. By her calculations and by factoring in several small cheques that were due to arrive over the next few days, she should be able to scrape together September's rent. If revenues did not increase, she would be closing her doors by the end of that month.

Sophie now realized that she had gone into business with insufficient capital and an over-optimistic outlook. She had sunk every penny she had into the enterprise, assuming she could make everything happen quickly. That assumption had mistakenly loomed large in her planning. Aunt Bessie crossed her mind, but Sophie felt she could never ask her for a loan. She believed her aunt would help but that the asking would disappoint her relative. Furthermore, Sophie would be acutely disappointed in herself for making a mess of everything. The last thing she wanted was to involve others in her downfall. These thoughts had been plaguing her for days now.

"Are we going bust, miss?" asked Nick, who had just then finished his third reading of last week's copy of Chuckles.

"I don't think so. You shouldn't ask questions like that."

"I probably shouldn't, miss, but it's bloomin' obvious, ain't it? Do you want to read my comic?"

"No, thanks, Nick."

"Quite right, miss. I'm getting too old for comics, meself."

"Seeing as it's raining and we're both at a loose end, do you fancy playing a game of cards?"

"Right you are. What shall we play? I know Rummy, Gin Poker, Newmarket..."

"Let's play Rummy, but if anyone comes upstairs, put a newspaper over the game while I attend to them."

"Right-o."

The cards came out, and the game began.

As they played, Nick said, "You know, miss, you're all right, you are. I happen to know some of the people who work for you or who you have on your books - well, my mum and dad know them - and they all say how you get good pay out of the punters, specially as money's so tight these days and jobs scarce like they are."

"Is that so?" said Sophie as she picked up a card.

"Oh, yes. I do hope things turn around for you. Maybe it's because it's summer and everyone's gone off somewhere, I dunno."

"That might be true. I've noticed fewer people in the streets on their way to work just recently."

"Gotta be that, miss."

"What are you going to do when you're older?"

"Be a docker like me dad... You see, he's got a cushy job, he has. He's a crane operator at St Kat's. He gets the best pay for the least work. Only small ships get loaded and unloaded at Katherine and it takes as much time to get a small one in and out as it does a big one, what with all the paperwork and customs clearance. But the unloading only takes a fraction of the time. So, he gets a day's pay for half a day's work. Good pay, too. That's why I don't bother meself with books or nuthin'."

"I'm glad you have some idea of what you will do in life. You're wrong about books, though."

"How do you reckon that?"

"Because through reading, you can understand so much more of what goes on around you. Stories are entertaining and have you travel to places you've never been and meet all kinds of interesting characters. I brought you in Jungle Book and a Henty story - I'm sure you would like both of them very much. But it's not just stories. Wouldn't you like to read a newspaper?"

"I don't know. They look boring."

"Well, when you're operating your crane at St Katherine's, and there's a lull in the work, what will you read? Comics or a newspaper?"

"Blimey, I never thought of that! I'd go mad if I didn't have something to do."

"A visitor is coming up the stairs. Don't look at my hand."

"I wouldn't do that to you, miss."

"Yes, you would."

"All right, I won't look, I promise."

"Make sure you keep it."

The visitor entered the offices.

"Archie! How lovely to see you!" Sophie rushed towards the tall, debonair man. He had fair hair, a monocle dangling on a thin ribbon around his neck, and was carrying a Homberg hat. They embraced affectionately.

"Soap, my most radiant cousin. Let me have a good long look at you." He had a pleasant voice, pitched just a shade higher than one would have expected from a man his size. It made him sound boyish and ineffectual.

"How long has it been? Four years, I believe." Sophie could not stop smiling.

"Yes, and me, a lieutenant, about to go to the front for the first time in his spotless uniform. My God, I was so scared." There was a hollowness in his laugh.

"Were you, my poor dear? You hid it well... You did look smart, though. I think I fell a little bit in love with you."

"My goodness, a bit early for the confessional, what?" He was smiling.

"We always did tell each other our secrets," said Sophie.

"So we did, and I've missed our long rambles around the estate. You always brightened up the ancient pile."

"That's nice of you to say... and reminds me why it seems so strange, seeing you here out of your natural habitat, as it were. But where are my manners? Find yourself a perch and I'll make some tea."

"I'll help you. I've got quite a knack for that sort of thing nowadays. By the way, I left my umbrella downstairs in the vestibule. It won't get pinched, will it?"

"I shouldn't think so. Come along, Archie. It's delightful you're here."

She took him by the arm and led him to the kitchenette. They passed Sophie's office to get to it.

"Hello, who is this young gentleman?" asked Archie as he paused at the doorway.

"Nick, sir," said the young man.

"As you were. Reading the newspaper, eh? Sorry to bother you." Archie had noticed the peculiar position of the newspaper on the desk. He could tell it was concealing something rather than being read. As he turned to continue on to the kitchen, the smile left his face and a furrow appeared in his brow. He was twenty-eight, but he suddenly looked much older.

"Well, my dear old Soap, how's the jolly old business doing, anyway?"

They sat in Sophie's office with their tea. Nick, the newspaper, and the deck of cards were all out of sight now.

"Let us just say it is having some growing pains. I believe we're in a summer slump."

"Ah, quite likely. And what a deuced, miserable old summer it's been. I really do think it's extraordinarily game of you to have come to London to take on a business as you have. I wish you every success."

Sophie looked hard at her childhood friend as well as second cousin. She was five years younger than Archibald Drysdale, but they had always been the best of friends. They had often sought each other's company to talk or to get into childhood scrapes and adventures at family gatherings and during long summer holidays. Sophie had enjoyed extended stays at Parklands, the large estate of Lord Bledding. The old lord had since died and Archie's older brother, Neville, had the title now. Neville also had two strapping young sons and so Archie would never be a peer of the realm.

"Are you ever up at Parklands?" asked Sophie.

"Once in a while. It's Neville's place now... Listen, Soap, I won't beat about the bush. Please excuse my manners for not coming to see you earlier. My feeble excuse is I've been very busy lately. Connected with that business, I'm afraid I've come to see you today with an ulterior motive."

"Oh, that sounds very mysterious. What on earth can it be?"

"Let me ask this first before I get to the other thing. Can I help with the business at all?"

Sophie sighed. "You could take me out to lunch and lend me a fiver."

"Both of those things are very easily accomplished."

He reached inside his superbly tailored jacket. To Sophie's astonishment, Archie took out his notecase and from it deftly produced a large, new £5 note. He handed it to her.

"There are strings attached to this money," said Archie, becoming serious. "It is not mine, but belongs to the Foreign Office. We're having a spot of bother and I immediately thought of you as a person who might be able to help us out. If you accept, there are six more of those for you to keep."

"But I thought you had a soft job with the government. And now it's handing out five-pound notes... What are you up to, Archie?"

"My job is fairly soft most of the time. Once in a while, I chase around after people to see what they're up to and to catch them or spoil their game if we think it's something bad."

Sophie hesitated for a moment. "Spying?"

"Keeping an eye on someone, yes. Most of the time, we work with the police. Scotland Yard mainly. Other times... we'd rather they weren't involved."

"Are you saying the Foreign Office breaks the law?"

"I wouldn't say that because I'm not a lawyer."

"You're evading my question, Archie. Please speak plainly."

"I admit it, yes. It's a very bad habit of mine. But you see, although we are having this conversation, at some future date, I might need to deny all knowledge of it."

"This sounds extraordinarily serious. You're not pulling my leg, are you?"

"Unfortunately, I'm not. Let me explain the general situation. The war either toppled or weakened many of the prevailing power structures in Europe. Before then, certain clandestine groups were at work. They were and are numerous and ardently dedicated to their various causes. They range in size from small groups of local amateurs to large organized international networks that are extremely well-financed.

40

"Since the war, these groups have become bolder. The government has to stop or disrupt their activities and that work is incessant. The local bobby cannot arrest them. Scotland Yard, exceptional institution though it is, does not have unlimited resources to collect information or effectively counter the activities of these hidden groups. The aim is pretty much the same for each outfit - overthrow or subvert our elected government and install their own regime. The government has instituted some measures and there are in place several departments to deal with known threats. I'm attached to those departments. I, and a few others, chase after the more nebulous, more insidious threats before they become a problem."

"Good grief... This is what you do as a career?"

"Odd, isn't it? You never know how things will turn out. I won't be doing this forever, but it is what I'm doing at present."

There was a long silence in the office.

"That fiver can be from me if you do not agree to what I'm about to propose. However, if you do accept, I'm authorized to pay up to thirty-five pounds in total for the little job we have in mind."

"Thank you for the help, Archie. I very much appreciate it and it is timely... You'd better tell me what this is all about. As you have observed, I need capital to survive. I must confess, I'm loath to borrow money, particularly from you, Sweet Boy."

"It's a long time since I've heard that name... Yes, well then, a certain gentleman will be visiting a certain country house and, we believe, will attempt to acquire a certain set of documents that do not belong to him. We can get you into the house as some sort of domestic. If you went as a house guest, he would be put on his guard because he knows who's expected and on the guest list. A late arrival might tip him off.

"I know you're a good actress. Remember those plays we used to put on? I do, and the tricks we played on the staff. You also know the ways of country houses upstairs and downstairs... and in my lady's chamber, what?" He smiled again, for the first time in some minutes. "I thought you would be perfect for this little job. Oh yes, the job is this. Should this gentleman actually acquire the documents, you are to re-acquire them, substituting another set in their stead before he leaves. Any interest?"

Sophie's lips compressed into a thin line as she thought hard. She picked up a pencil and asked, "Where is this house?"

"Yes, Sophie, we tend not to write things down at the FO unless it is super vague and relatively meaningless. We don't like to give away our real intentions." Archie tapped the side of his head. "Commit it to memory. Say yes, and we can go to lunch and have a good old chinwag."

She sighed. "Very well, then."

"Good girl, Soap. I hoped you would accept.... I do most abjectly apologize to you."

"Oh, why?"

"For not being the fun and careless Archie of yesteryear... That, and for catching you at a weak moment with your business and everything. It was very unsporting of me."

"Archie, you need never apologize to me for anything. I understand perfectly the difficult situation your work must put you in on occasion. But let us be absolutely clear, I want to do this and it's not just for the money. It sounds rather exciting. Also, I detest the idea of hidden groups messing about in our country's affairs."

CHAPTER 6

— ⟡ —

FOREIGN AFFAIRS

SEPTEMBER 1920

On the evening of September fifteenth, Sophie met Archie in the Foreign Office on King Charles Street.

"I had no idea what a splendid place this was," said Sophie as they climbed the main staircase. "I've read about the Foreign Office in the papers but, my word, inside and out, the place is so extraordinarily beautiful."

"We have to impress the foreign potentates, don't you know? But wait until you see my office. That will bring you down to earth quickly enough."

"Where is your office?"

"One more flight and a hundred yards down the corridor will bring you to my little cubbyhole. Until recently, it housed the London office of the Cairo Intelligence Department, but they're all getting pensioned off or moved around."

"You mean Lawrence of Arabia?"

"He's been here, of course."

"Hmm... What is your department called?"

"That is a very good question. No one has come up with an official name as yet. What it should be called is The Bureau Without a Specific Reason for Existence."

"I don't like that," said Sophie. "What about, The Invisible Hand Department?"

Archie smiled. "Very lurid, but that might give the game away."

"I'm sure it would... but then foreign spies are hardly likely to consult a directory to find where the British spies are working."

"That's a very practical observation. Should you meet some of the people to whom I report, you will notice that displaying a sense of humour anywhere in their vicinity proves to be a liability rather than an asset."

"I see. Must I be sober-minded, too?"

"I think you must, but only while the game's afoot."

They settled in at Archie's modest but serviceable set of offices, which really should have been redecorated after the former occupants had vacated.

"You have three telephones on your desk. Is that to make you look important?"

"I only use one. The others are lines leftover from the Arab Bureau days. I had a call on that one from a fellow speaking in Arabic. I had no idea what he was saying, so I had to get a translator in here on the double. It turned out the man was telephoning from Syria and wanted to know if I would buy his goats. He said they were very plump and there were none finer within fifty miles of Damascus."

"What did you do?"

"I got his particulars and then I had someone go through what he had said, looking for a coded message. Waste of time. He was, in truth, only selling goats as far as we could tell. It was a shame to disappoint him... And that is a fine example of the important work we do here on any given day."

"I'm sure it is not. Let's get down to business, shall we?"

"I suppose we ought to," said Archie. "I gave you an outline of the proposition when we went to lunch. Now we must get down to brass tacks. Do you know Trefoil Hall in Bedfordshire?"

"I know of it. That's Lord Wicksworth's country seat, isn't it?"

"Yes, it is. Being the Defence Secretary, Lord Desmond Wicksworth is hosting an important meeting this weekend with the Greek Ambassador, Dimitri Makri. As you know, Greece and Turkey are at war over former Greek territories which had been seized by the Ottoman Empire. We're backing Greece to regain those territories and we wish them to have our newly developed submarine. An NX class prototype has already passed its sea trials. The submarine is a small, highly manoeuvrable vessel with improved depth control and is well-suited for operations in the Mediterranean and the Black Sea. This weekend's get-together is for the Greeks to decide whether or not they will take delivery of eight subs. To facilitate their deliberations, the NX designer, Alfred Wright, will be on hand with actual drawings to explain the finer technical points to a gentleman named Admiral Pavlidis. He will be assisted by several Greek naval gentlemen who will interpret the usefulness of what is being explained to them. They will not be given copies of the drawings to keep, as they are considered top secret.

"Now, if the list had stopped there, we would not be having this conversation. Unfortunately, it did not stop there. Attached to the Greek delegation will be a civilian engineer named Josif Abazi from Macedonia. He is acting as an independent advisor to the Greek government. His real name is Paul Klest, fifty years old, Austrian by birth, a first-class marine engineer, and an international spy for hire. He worked for Germany during the war. The Greeks are not aware of his former spying activities. This is he." Archie handed Sophie a grainy photograph of a smiling, solid, middle-aged man.

Sophie looked at the picture. "Can I stop you a moment, please? Why not simply tell the Greeks all of this?"

"Wouldn't that be the simplest way? Of course it would. We cannot mention it to our Greek counterparts for several reasons. The first is that we do not actually know who is after the plans. We suspect the Russians or the Turks, but have no evidence. Secondly, there has to be an intermediary agent working inside the Greek government who arranged to have Klest included in the talks. There are people trying to find out who that intermediary is. If we go blurting out that Klest is a spy, we will never know who. That's why we wish to switch the plans and watch for the reactions of several persons whom we believe are less than solidly committed to the Greek cause and whom we have under observation. Finally, if we inform Lord Wicksworth the Greek delegation has a spy in its midst, then he'll probably give the game away by glaring at everyone he meets."

"Oh, dear me. What a devious muddle. So it's left up to you to sort it out?"

"Yes, and now, more precisely, it is up to you to solve the problem."

"But if this Abazi-Klest person walks off with the plans, surely it would be noticed? Then action could be taken against him."

"That is not how the plans will be stolen. Do you know how to use a camera?"

"Only a Box Brownie. I think my family snaps come out rather well."

Archie opened a drawer and took out a very compact looking camera.

"Ever seen one of these?"

"It's a Minnigraph, isn't it?"

"Yes. It's a Levy-Roth from Austria. It uses 35mm film. Klest has one of these, but his camera has a modified lens, suitable for photographing documents. This is what he will be using."

"How do you know that?"

"He came through customs and is in the country as we speak. A Minnigraph, identical to this one except for the lens, was the only camera he had in his possession."

"Ah, that's very clever of you."

"Thank you. I accept your compliment on behalf of others who actually earn their keep."

"Don't do that, Archie. When did you become so self-deprecating?"

"Shortly after you saw me in uniform for the first time and we'll leave that subject undisturbed where it lies."

"Yes, yes, very well, then."

"Let me show you how to load and unload the film from the camera."

Within ten minutes, Sophie was fully conversant with the camera's operation. Archie had her repeatedly unload and reload the film cassette. Soon, she could repeat the action with her eyes shut in less than a minute, despite some trickiness with the catch.

"Very good. That's all you have to do." Archie reached into his drawer again. "In this paper bag is the cassette you will use as the substitute. Keep it safe. It contains submarine drawings, but they are based on an old A class vessel with some significant errors. The thought is this: should Klest deliver the dummy film to his paymaster, his reputation as a spy will be torpedoed. If, once he leaves Trefoil, he develops the film first, he will see what has been done and will be similarly sunk, though with considerably less drama.

"To the practicalities of this little job. In all events, Klest must not leave with the drawings or with photographs of them. So substitute the film cassette only if there is opportunity to do so but destroy his camera and film if no other course is available to you. Here comes the difficult part. He will have someone with him. She will be presented at Trefoil as his assistant. I doubt if there is anything between them, but you never know. Her name is Karissa Raptis. She's Greek and, like Klest, a spy - but with a more minor reputation. No cameras were found in her luggage. She is twenty-nine and speaks English fluently, having lived in London for five years up to the age of fourteen. She will be the one photographing the plans. That is our assumption, otherwise there is no real reason for her presence. Klest sets up the opportunity and Raptis photographs the plans."

"Which of them will have the camera afterwards?" asked Sophie.

"Ultimately, Klest, although Raptis will have it in her possession for a time."

"This is much more complicated than when you first explained it. You realize that my going as a lady's maid confines me almost exclusively to whatever rooms the lady is given in the house?"

"Yes. You'll have to dodge the staff, the Klest-Raptis combination, as well as all the other guests."

"If I should fail, do I still get paid?"

"Yes, you will. However, if another little enterprise were to present itself, you would not be considered for it."

"Ah, ha. Excellent. Should I fail, and, Sweet Boy, I'm telling you now I will *not* fail, what would you do if Klest got away with the drawings?"

"I am only at liberty to divulge information pertaining to your own circumstances."

"I believe that's Foreign Office speech for mind your own business. I'm beginning to get the hang of it."

"To continue," said Archie, "Trefoil Hall is a large place. The main house has fourteen bedrooms available for family and guests. That is where the Greek contingent will be bedded down for the night. The home-grown guests have mostly been pushed out to both the East and West Pavilions, which boast six bedrooms apiece. These symmetrical buildings are each connected to the main house through a bow-shaped corridor. I've never seen the place, but I'm told it is a remarkably elegant Queen Anne period house."

"Being in a pavilion puts me even further away from where I should be."

"It does, but there's a silver lining in these arrangements. From your second-floor bedroom in the East Pavilion, you can see both Klest's and Raptis' bedrooms on the second floor of the east side of the main house. Take these binoculars with you. They might come in handy."

"That's rather off, isn't it?" Sophie's face clouded over.

"They shouldn't be trying to pinch our plans."

"No, they shouldn't. Very well, then."

"If you use them, don't go right up to the window or they'll spot you. Stand back in the room."

"I'm glad you mentioned that. Who else is going?"

"Nobody you know. It will be all military and civil servant types who think they might be missing something if they don't attend.

"Your travel arrangements are as follows. On Friday, leave St. Pancras on the 8:55 train, platform 2, and that will take you to Bedford. From there, hire a taxi to Trefoil, which is on the outskirts of the village of Oxley. It's a drive of about five or six miles. Oh, yes, keep your receipts and stubs and the dear old government will be happy to reimburse you."

"I'm glad to hear it," said Sophie.

Archie paused for a long time.

Sophie asked, "I believe there's a little more I should know, or do I just knock on Trefoil's front door and ask if anyone needs a lady's maid?"

"Yes," said Archie slowly as he rubbed an earlobe. "I'm coming to that. Do you know the Staffordshire Redferns?"

"Only what I read in the newspapers. I know they're wealthy and some of the children are a little wild... Wait a moment... Archie, what have you been up to?"

"The least wild of the children goes by the name of Victoria. You'll meet her at St. Pancras. She's twenty-six and she and I have an understanding that one day..."

"You're getting married!?"

"We will probably announce our engagement at the end of this year or early next."

"How wonderful...! Why the hesitation?"

"There are two reasons why I hesitate. The first is that old father Redfern - he's an invalid, by the way - does not approve of me because my prospects are rather dim. He believes I'm a fortune hunter and a middling kind of civil servant without the redeeming merit of having a title."

"It would be good to get his consent, but that's not as important as it once was. I could give you a character reference," said Sophie with a sudden smile.

"That would be nice, but it's gone beyond that now. He's threatening to cut Victoria off without a penny should we marry."

"Oh, I see. That is a problem... But his eldest son and two other daughters are always in court or making some public display of themselves."

"Yes. I believe he enjoys their notoriety, but with Victoria, who is quite normal, by the way, he takes an entirely different position."

"Ah... Do I deduce that I will be lady's maid to Victoria this coming weekend?"

"Yes, ah, yes, that is correct."

"Archie, explain yourself properly."

"This is my second reason for hesitation. You have to understand that the work I do is known only to a few highly placed and influential people."

"You mean Victoria doesn't know you're a spy?"

"I hate that word, but, to put it simply, she has no idea what my work is."

The ticking of the office clock became audible.

"Let me understand this correctly. You're sending me off on my first..."

"Mission."

"On my first mission. I have not one but two spies to tackle. I have to retrieve top-secret submarine plans from experienced international agents and foist on them some dummy plans. I'm not in the main house, but some outhouse at the end of a corridor. I'm going as a servant and, therefore, I will not have free access to all areas. The only support I'm getting is a pair of binoculars with which to play peeping Tom. Then, to top it all, my entrée into the house, brimful of foreign dignitaries and spies, is through your fiancée-to-be who hasn't a clue why I'm there. I suppose I have to put on an act in front of her, as well."

"It would be immensely helpful if you could. There was no other way I could get you into the place. Victoria doesn't really want to go. It's only because of old man Redfern's steel interests that she's there at all. You see, she knows the steel business and often represents her father at meetings."

"I wonder what you will say to Victoria when I'm invited to your wedding? Victoria, you've already met my dear old second cousin, Sophie. She likes to pretend to be a lady's maid whenever she gets the chance."

"Well, you know, something will be managed at the time."

"How is it that Victoria came to be invited?"

"I convinced old Redfern to send her. I told him it would be good for his business - because of the steel for the submarines - and for his international reputation. For a moment, it warmed relations between us to something approaching ice-cold."

"And Victoria? Specifically, what did you tell her about me?"

"I said, because these talks are an obligatory part of the Anglo-Greek treaty and with the Greeks and Turks at war, that for security purposes, it was necessary for all personal attendants to be supplied by His Majesty's Government."

"Is that true? Because if there are contracts in the offing, I would like my agency to have a crack at them."

"In actuality, it is a partial truth. You, yourself, are the evidence of that."

"Oh, Archie, and to your fiancée-to-be, as well." Sophie sighed and compressed her lips. "So, as far as she understands the matter, you and I have never met."

"That is the assumption she has and that I wish to maintain. If Victoria had been unable to attend, then we would not have been able to act in the matter."

"You haven't made this very easy for me, have you?"

"If there is anything I can do, I shall do it. There will be another person at Trefoil who is aware of your mission. This person will remain incognito but shall be ready to extract you from any difficulties, should they arise."

"Will this person be in the carriage on the train when Victoria asks me about myself or talks about you? Of course not... So what are these difficulties you're talking about?" Sophie sounded extremely suspicious.

"Hard to say. I only want to reassure you that, should anything go wrong, help is at hand."

"And how, exactly, should I contact this person if things do go wrong?"

"You don't. I can't explain the matter to you, but this person has a great deal of experience in difficult situations. That is all I can say. Is there anything else you'd like to discuss?"

"Yes. Have you a pseudonym for me?"

"I've had a couple of ideas..."

"Good, you haven't chosen one yet, then. Well, I have. My name shall be Phoebe King. Please commit it to memory. Oh, and I shall want your telephone numbers here and at home."

Chapter 7

— · —

$1 + 1 = 2$

At 7:30 a.m., Thursday morning, Sophie was having breakfast downstairs in the breakfast room at White Lyon Yard. She normally ate alone because Aunt Bessie always had breakfast in her room and rarely appeared before eleven. Today, surprisingly, Aunt Bessie joined Sophie before she left for the Agency.

"Good morning, dear. What a perfectly revolting hour of the day this is," said Aunt Bessie, as she entered the room.

"Good morning, Auntie. But it's lovely outside."

"So you say. This is just too, too early to be decent. Bring me an egg, Iris. Oh, yes, and send Hawkins to me." She sat down. "I kept waking up... Things on my mind, you know."

"Nothing serious, I hope?" enquired Sophie.

"Serious...? Extremely serious. I forgot to tell you earlier, it's Chinese Night tonight because it's the third Thursday in the month. It's September and the new season has started. You don't need to fret because I got your measurements from Gilberto and I've had something made up."

Sophie was about to take a bite of toast, but stopped. "What are you talking about?"

"It's just a little get-together. Can you use chopsticks?"

"I've never even had Chinese food."

"You'll have to acquire the habit quickly, otherwise you'll starve." Aunt Bessie smiled. She was about to continue when Hawkins silently entered the room.

"Ah, here he is. I'll tell you everything in a moment, but I must talk to this man first."

"You wanted to see me, your Ladyship." Hawkins had newspapers under his arm.

"Yes, I do. You brought them, I see. Well, what has your research produced?"

"I have been studying the matter with great diligence and have concluded that this is an auspicious day."

"I'm glad to hear it. Very glad."

"I believe it is a Union Jack day."

"Eight trebles, eh? Excellent. And which gee-gees do you propose?"

"Funny Face for the centre, my Lady."

"Jockey?"

"Titch Williams, a London jockey."

"Yes... I like him. Uses the whip sparingly. Funny Face, though... What are the odds?"

"Three to one. The favourite, Genial Host, is five to four on.

"It's risky... We'll go through the others with a fine-toothed comb when I've had my breakfast. Where are they running?"

"At Kempton, as are two more. The others are at Doncaster and Aintree." Hawkins very quietly cleared his throat. "I've taken the liberty of calculating the payout on the estimated starting prices."

"Well, don't keep me in suspense."

"For one pound bets, should they all win, the profit on the day will be £242 17s 6d."

"Hm, not bad... But do I recall Funny Face is a three-year-old?"

"That is correct, my Lady. I believe that Mr Williams is the jockey who will be able to get the fastest time over the distance. My informant tells me the horse is in the finest condition and will make a race of it against the four-year-old Genial Host. The going is firm, the wind will be light out of the north-east, and there is no rain in the forecast. These are perfect conditions for just such a spirited animal."

"Right-ho, here's what we'll do. Ten pounds each way on the Union Jack. Twenty on Genial Host to win and we're going to Kempton, so get the car out. Yes, and get Colonel Lockhart on the phone. I know he'll want to tag along."

"The race is at two, my Lady. I believe the Colonel is an early riser but as it is not yet eight, I fear it may be too early to place a call to his residence."

"I'm having to be up early. He can blasted well answer his telephone, Hawkins."

"Yes, my Lady. I will convey the urgency of the situation to him." Hawkins left the room as silently as he had entered.

Sophie had forgotten to eat during this exchange.

"Don't look at me like that. Put the toast in your mouth."

"Auntie, you're gambling."

"Is this the vicar's daughter in you coming out? I suppose Henry is against gambling."

"I doubt it has ever entered his mind... What on earth is a Union Jack?"

"Eight trebles, dear. If you don't know what a treble is, get Hawkins to explain it to you. Now, about tonight..."

"No, Auntie. One thing at a time. Hawkins said the winnings on a one-pound bet would be two hundred and forty-odd pounds. You said ten pounds."

"With eight ten pound bets that accumulate, we stand to win nearly two and half thousand. More because they're each-way bets, which means they can come in first, second, and maybe third. As per our arrangement, Hawkins will get half that sum. His having a vested interest keeps him sharp. Usually, he's a very good racing form advisor but our last Union Jack fell to pieces and it was a great disappointment to him. Funny Face... where do they get such strange names from?"

"Excuse me, Auntie, I have to go to work."

"Of course you do. Before you go, I think I'll make Mary your maid while you're here. She's a very pleasant sort until she laughs. Then she sounds like a donkey, so be warned."

"I can manage..."

"Don't be difficult. And get me a replacement between-maid, you must have one on your books. Just make sure she can get along with the housekeeper."

"Does Mrs Todd need getting along with?"

"Not really, but she's a treasure and I don't want her upset."

"I'll bear that in mind. Goodbye, Auntie."

"Goodbye, Sophie. Be back by six, sharp."

Sophie hammered away on a typewriter. Three jobs had come in by the early post. One was a sales contract that required her close, undisturbed attention as several of its clauses were phrased in the most arcane and convoluted language Sophie had ever encountered. As she began typing, hopeful domestic service applicants began appearing at the rate of one every ten minutes or so. She had those who could write fill out their particulars on a card. The rest she interviewed, extracting information from them with such speed that, by the time the exchange had finished, the applicant was unsure what had just happened. Sophie began by saying something like, "Take a seat. I'm very busy. I want precise and complete answers to my questions. Name?" Her brevity was born out of necessity. Sophie now had sufficient experience to know that some applicants liked to talk and, given the chance, would take minutes to say what could be said in five seconds.

It had been a productive morning for the young proprietor, but not a particularly lucrative one. At just before noon, Ada arrived unexpectedly.

"I'm so sorry, miss. There was nothing I could do," she said as she was taking off her coat. "Mrs Brimley suddenly brought in this local girl, permanent. She looked half-starved. She paid me to the end of the week but said the rates you arranged for me were too high for temporary. She didn't want to pay your fee on top, and she certainly didn't want to pay the permanent fee."

"Too high! She doesn't know what she's talking about. Our rates are competitive and you do excellent work. Too high, indeed. I'm striking her from our register."

Ada smiled. "Quite right, too. Do you know, when she paid me my money, she was wearing a diamond ring with a stone the size and shape of a baked bean? Bloody cheek, that's what I say."

"Not in the office, Ada."

"Sorry, miss, but I'm that put out for you as well as for me, that I am."

"We're both put out. There's nothing to be done. What are you having for lunch?"

"I was thinking about getting a Cornish pasty from the baker's around the corner. They're quite good and he don't get 'is meat from the knacker's yard, neither."

"That's very reassuring. I'll come with you."

"If you don't mind my asking, where did you get your coat from? It's beautiful."

"A gift from a very kind aunt who took me to Harrod's to get it."

"'Arrod's, eh? I've never been inside. It's supposed to be very expensive."

"It is, but it's like an Aladdin's cave, full of wonders. It was my first visit and I could not believe the Food Hall. There were so many new and interesting things. They had small jars of Beluga caviare for twenty-four shillings."

"Over a pound for fish eggs! Who can afford that?"

"Obviously someone can. I've never had caviare," said Sophie wistfully. "They say it's an acquired taste."

"I've had some. There was a little bit left over from a very 'igh-class dinner I was working. So I tried it."

"What was it like?" asked Sophie.

"Oh, it was disgusting, miss. Made me want to heave. One nibble and I had to throw it away."

"It sounds like I'm not missing anything, then. Let's go and get our lunches."

The two young women chatted while they sat together, eating their lunches, back at the agency. When they had finished and cleared everything away, Sophie asked Ada to come with her to her private office, as she wanted to discuss an important matter. She had been turning over an idea in her mind throughout lunch.

"Shall I put the closed sign up?" asked Ada.

"Leave it be. Shut this door and take a seat."

If Ada was puzzled she did not show it.

"We've known each other for about four months," began Sophie. "In that time, I have come to depend on you in several areas. I also believe we get on very well together."

"I think so, too, miss."

Sophie smiled before continuing. "One thing I have noticed is that, although you tell a lot of stories about your various experiences, you never maliciously gossip about people. In fact, I would not be able to place the actual person in your stories because you never name them. Your love of story-telling is mixed with discretion. I wonder, how discreet can you be?"

"Well... I would say," answered Ada in a very precise tone, "that if you asked me not to repeat something, I wouldn't tell the police what it was even if they used thumbscrews on me."

Sophie smiled again. "I'm sure it won't come to that... What I will tell you next falls under the heading of things never to be repeated to anyone... Where to begin?" She stared at Ada for a moment. "This weekend, starting tomorrow, I will be working as a lady's maid."

"A lady's maid?" Ada was shocked. "Well, I never... Why is that, miss?"

"I've been recruited as a spy."

Ada looked even more shocked, her eyes opening as wide as they could go. Finally, she said in a low tone of repressed disbelief, "Not like Mata Hari?"

"Ah, no, no, nothing like her. This is a respectable form of spying... Well, semi-respectable, anyway."

"Oh, thank goodness for that... But a lady's maid?"

"Yes. Unless you are willing to help me in the matter, I cannot explain anything more than this - the Government fears that an item of great importance is going to be stolen this weekend. My job is to retrieve that item."

"Oh, I see... So, you mean, would I like to help and be a spy an' all?"

"That about sums it up."

"Well, I don't know. You'll 'ave to tell me a bit more."

"As I said, I'm to retrieve something of importance should it be stolen by a certain foreign person. This will all take place at a conference held in a large house outside of London. As it stands, I fear I might fail to retrieve the article because the arrangements are very awkward indeed. Should you refuse to accompany me - and I would completely understand if that were to be your decision - I will do what I can on my own. I would very much like you to come with me, though."

"Have you been a spy for long?"

"This will be my first mission."

"Blimey... You *are* working for *our* government?"

"Of course, Ada."

"That's all right, then. If you were working for any of those foreign powers, I'd be saying no straight away. As long as it's our own people... What's the pay like?"

"Supposedly, I will be reimbursed for my expenses, but I won't be for yours. I will receive a total of £35 for three or four days' work. The way I see the division of that sum is that you receive half the amount, but you'll have to pay your expenses from it. The principal expense will be a return train fare of some seven or twelve shillings, depending on whether you travel third or first class."

"So, let me understand this situation," said Ada seriously. "I'll clear nearly seventeen pounds for three or four days' work...? That's a *lot* of money... I'll travel third class, if you don't mind. What do you want me to do?"

"Be a lady's maid in my place while I will be - I'm altering the original plan, by the way - a Domestic Staff Manager sent by the government. You see, the person who recruited me has attached me to a lady who has no idea that I will be spying. It's too, too awkward for words."

"Oh, I see. Yes, that's right awkward. That would be like breaking into a jeweller's with people looking on. If it's any help to you, I can pick locks. I know somebody, not mentioning any names, who's a locksmith - only he's having an 'oliday at the moment, if you take my meaning. Well, I've known him for a long time, since I was a little girl, and he showed me how to pick all types of locks. He said I had a real talent for it. I've never done anything criminal with that knowledge, but I absolutely can get you in anywhere you like."

Sophie realized that Ada was undoubtedly talking about a family member.

"A week ago, I would have been shocked and dismayed at such a revelation. Today, however, I think your lock-picking skills might prove to be very useful."

"You won't tell anyone, will you, miss?"

"Not even if they use the rack as well as thumbscrews. Starting tomorrow, my name will be Phoebe King."

"Can I make up a name for myself?" asked Ada, whose eyes were dancing with excitement.

"Of course, you can."

"I'll be... Nancy Carmichael. Would that be all right, miss?"

"I think that sounds splendid. Now, let me explain what it is we shall do and who we are up against."

CHAPTER 8

— . —

INTERESTING FOOD FOR THOUGHT

S ophie's large bedroom in the house at White Lyon Yard was an extraordinarily pretty room. Although the style of furniture and decoration was of the Belle époque, which, by 1920, was considered passé, it was that very look that Sophie had admired in magazines while growing up. Her room had a dark mauve damask wallpaper with a design of trailing vines and overflowing urns of flowers. What particularly engaged her was the painting by John William Waterhouse entitled Cordelia, which hung over the bed. It was of a sad and beautiful woman who, standing in the stern of a ship, stared back at Sophie from the painting. It usually made her pause for thought, but not tonight.

"Good evening, Miss Burgoyne," said Mary, who was waiting in Sophie's room for her charge to arrive. She spoke very cheerfully and seemed eager and excited to begin her new duties as lady's maid to the niece of her mistress. "I'm to be your maid, miss."

"Good evening, Mary. Yes, I'm very happy with the arrangement."

"If there's anything you want me to do, please tell me."

"I will be certain to do so. Is Mary your actual name or one given to you?"

"It's my real name. Mary Roberts, I am."

"Ah, good... Is this your first time being a lady's maid?"

"Yes, it is, miss, and I want to do my best."

"I'm sure you will. The first thing you *can* do for me is to explain what on earth is going on this evening?"

"Oh... um, her Ladyship instructed me to say nothing to you about tonight. She said it was to be a surprise."

"Where is it we're going? Can you tell me that much?"

"They was strict instructions, miss. I'm that sorry I can't tell you, even though I want to."

"You have nothing to apologize for if you are doing what your mistress instructs. Did she say anything else?"

"Yes. She says I'm to draw a bath and help you dress, to be ready for seven-thirty. Your new clothes have arrived. I've laid them out for you to see." She pointed to the bed behind her.

"Perhaps the clothes will give me some clue."

Sophie approached the bed and was greatly surprised by the Chinese costume she saw. Laid out was a Cheongsam dress in dark red silk and embroidered in even darker red and black thread to form large butterflies and flowers. It had a high, plain collar and three-quarter-length sleeves. A pair of black velvet slippers, lightly embroidered with golden dragons, lay on the floor.

"Good gracious. I'm to wear this?"

"Yes, miss. There's a little bag to go with it."

Mary handed the bag to Sophie. It was a tiny A-shaped embroidered purse decorated with gold cranes on a black background. The frame, clasp and chain were of chased silver.

"This is exquisite," said Sophie, after briefly studying the bag.

"Shall I run your bath now?"

"Ah, yes, please do."

While Mary was out of the room, Sophie gently drew her fingertips across the silk dress. She sat on the bed, tried on the slippers and smiled, wondering what they would say in Havering-under-Lyme if they could see her now.

———⊠———

Sophie ascended the staircase to the fourth floor of the house. Her slippers were comfortable, but the strangeness of the cut and feel of the Chinese clothes made her rather self-conscious. Mary had tried to style Sophie's long hair to match a photograph of a young Chinese lady from about 1910. The attempt failed so, between them, Sophie and Mary settled on a centre-parting, with a loose strand of hair hanging down on either side of her face while the rest, meticulously swept back, was restrained by a large, pearl-studded clip.

"If your hair was black, miss, you'd pass for a Chinese lady," said Mary, very proud of her efforts. Sophie had looked at herself in the mirror and decided that she did look very well indeed.

At the top of the stairs, she approached a pair of ornate, black lacquered doors. She opened one of them and went inside.

"Here she is," said Aunt Bessie, seated at a table with three other women. "Apologies for there not being any gentlemen on hand to escort you in, but it is ladies-only tonight."

Sophie did not take in her aunt's words. She stood with her mouth open. The room was huge, occupying half the floor, and was full of Chinese people except for the table where Aunt Bessie was sitting. The well-appointed room was, to the minutest detail, a replica of a Hong Kong restaurant, circa 1900. Its ornate ceiling was heavily gilded, the pillars red, and the walls adorned by a diverse array of Chinese artwork. The smell of unfamiliar foods and tobacco smoke hung heavy in the air. Tall potted plants stood on the white-tiled floor while bright flower arrangements adorned white tablecloths. It was too much for Sophie to take in all at once. The room was one astonishing issue. The unaccountable presence of so many Chinese people eating dinner, talking, or smoking surprised her even more. The patrons did not acknowledge her arrival and continued laughing and talking in Cantonese.

"Come and sit down," said Aunt Bessie.

"Yes, Auntie," said Sophie in a vague way. She saw the empty chair and sat down on it. The four ladies at the table were also dressed in Chinese garb. Aunt Bessie looked beautiful in a pale blue dress with a dark blue, lightly quilted jacket edged in silver. She had a beaming smile on her face.

"Bit of a shocker, eh?"

"Yes, very much so... Why?"

"A good question. I must say you look quite superb, my dear. I see Mary had trouble with the hair, but she's done tolerably well. Now, I want you to meet some dear old friends of mine. On my right is Lady Sedlescombe. We went to the same finishing school. This is my niece, Sophie."

"Pleased to meet you, my dear. Were you born in Hong Kong?"

"No, Lady Sedlescombe, I was born in Winchester."

"Then who are your people?" continued her Ladyship.

"Me, Baggie. I'm her blasted people," said Aunt Bessie. "She's a Burgoyne. I just told you, she's my niece."

"Oh, then that's why you're here. I assumed you were Eurasian. I know you said she was your niece, Needle, but I thought you might be drawing a veil over a delicate family matter."

"We dress up in Chinese clothes," said Aunt Bessie, "because it's Chinese Night. We have it every month. Sophie is joining us, that is all it is."

"Don't be testy, dear. It was a simple error on my part." Lady Sedlescombe turned to Sophie. "Please forgive my mistake."

Sophie smiled and nodded in return.

"Sophie, this is Mrs Lund," said Aunt Bessie. "She's a distant relative of yours by marriage. One of the Drysdales."

"A pleasure to meet you, Mrs Lund," said Sophie.

"Likewise... Burgoyne... Havering-under-Lyme. Correct?" Mrs Lund looked very gruff and formidable.

"Yes, Havering-under-Lyme is my father's parish."

"I recall you're the lot who went to Parklands every year. I think I met you when you were five or six. I don't suppose you remember me."

"I'm afraid not... unless you were the lady who gave me Liquorice Allsorts."

"I was she. You have a good memory." She smiled briefly. "I still have a weakness for them, by the way."

"And this is Mrs Cowan. Unfortunately, she hasn't spoken since 1916, but she understands everything you say."

"Good evening, Mrs Cowan," said Sophie.

The fourth lady, a war widow and blank-faced up until the introduction, suddenly smiled warmly at Sophie.

"Cowie, dear," said Aunt Bessie, touching the lady gently on the arm. "This is Sophie Burgoyne. She's my niece, who's staying with me. Please show her how to use her chopsticks. There's a pet."

With quick movements and gentle smiles, Mrs Cowan picked up her set to demonstrate how the sticks should be placed in the hand. She closed her hand around them, snapped the sticks together a couple of times and, with a deft movement, picked up a napkin. Mrs Cowan nodded for Sophie to try. Her first attempt was awkward. Mrs Cowan patiently helped while Sophie continued to practice.

"We can order while you two are mucking about," said Aunt Bessie. "Menu's on the wall. It's in Chinese, so I'll order for you, Sophie."

"I must say, I'm delightfully puzzled by all of this. You have a Chinese restaurant on your top floor? I've never heard of such a thing. And where did all these Chinese people come from?"

"I have an arrangement with the owner of the Pearl Garden Restaurant that he comes here with his staff to do all the cooking. A few of the people at the other tables are his friends and relatives, the rest are his best and most regular customers. We always have a full house."

"But why, Auntie?"

"One of my silly little follies. In 1901, Shelling and I went out to Hong Kong. He was there for business reasons. We stayed in the Hong Kong Hotel for two months. The only restaurant that Europeans frequented was Gripps, inside the hotel. The fare was good, but it soon became very samey to Shelling and me. We decided to ask a Chinese waiter to recommend an authentic Chinese restaurant. Well, he did. So we took a rickshaw to a place just below Pedder's Hill. We found the restaurant upstairs above a flower shop.

"Of course, the first thing we discover there is that no one speaks English. And Shelling and I had no Cantonese, or so little it was laughable. We just pointed and ordered from the menu on the wall without any idea what we were doing. Suffice it to say, my husband and I were rather astonished at the sheer quantity of food they served us. There must have been enough for at least twenty people.

"Shelling went down to the street and shouted at the top of his voice, "Anyone speak English?" He returned with a Chinese man and, through his broken phrases, we invited the whole restaurant and staff to partake of the food. Oh, my goodness, what a fuss they made of us, praising us to high heaven - although, of course, we had no idea what anyone was actually saying. It cost Shelling a packet, but it was such fun. We laughed about it for years. I thought I would like to replicate that restaurant and what you see here is the result. I had photographs taken, and this room is very nearly an exact copy of the place. I always invite Chinese people to the house once a month. It cheers me up no end. Oh, by the way, the Union Jack blew up again. We only made three pounds on the day even though Funny Face won."

Life with Aunt Bessie was proving to be quite the adventure, and the delicious Chinese food took Sophie's imagination to the Far East. As she looked around the room, fascinated by what she saw, she decided that she, too, would go to Hong Kong one day.

"Mrs Lund, I met Archibald Drysdale the other day," said Sophie.

"Did you? That's right, he works in London. Something in the Foreign Office."

"So he gave me to understand. Have you seen him recently?"

"Summer of last year, he came to visit us. Although, as with all young un's, I think he just came for the riding. Sits a horse well but then he always has. Do you ride?"

"I know how to ride, but life in a vicarage does not lend itself to such pursuits."

"Ah, pity that."

"One does not readily associate the clergy with horse riding," said Lady Sedlescombe, "but you'll never guess who I saw sitting uncommonly well on a hoss this June. Taking difficult fences, too."

"And who was that, dear?" asked Aunt Bessie.

"The Bishop of Cirencester."

"Old Beaky? Good heavens... Was he riding a shire horse? It would take an animal of that size to support his girth!"

"No, it was a hunter, but it was a monstrous animal. The Bishop really should do something about his condition."

"He should read his Bible," said Aunt Bessie. "The passage about fasting forty days and nights would be a good start for him."

"He has a touch of the gout, you know," said Lady Sedlescombe. "He makes a lot of fuss and noise over it. I thought I heard him swear at one point, but I must have been mistaken."

"We can't have our bishops swearing," said Mrs Lund. "I trust you *were* mistaken."

"Yes, let us agree that I was mistaken."

"What does Archibald do at the Foreign Office?" asked Aunt Bessie, addressing her question to Mrs Lund.

"I'm not sure. I think they make it up as they go along, but pretend it to be frightfully important," said Mrs Lund. "He's not very highly placed, which is a pity because the lad has a brain. But if he makes a career out of it, I'm sure he'll get on."

"Is he married?" asked Lady Sedlescombe.

"No, but he's hanging around one of the Redfern girls. Bound to end badly."

"I think it's Victoria Redfern to whom you're referring," said Sophie. "I've been informed that she is the least afflicted of the family and is quite normal, with no penchant for notoriety."

"Ah," said Mrs Lund. "That is good news, indeed."

"That family has too much money," said Lady Sedlescombe. "I think it has warped their outlook on life. I suppose I more particularly mean the younger generation."

"Speaking of excess wealth, what do you make of Lord Stokely, hm?" asked Aunt Bessie. "He's the darling of the press at the moment."

"I've met him several times," said Lady Sedlescombe. "He's handsome, certainly, but he strikes me as a very calculating man despite his veneer of good manners and winning ways. I've also heard one or two disturbing stories concerning him..."

"Excuse me just a moment. Cowie, dear, we're going to have China tea." Aunt Bessie smiled at her friend. "Would you like that or would you rather something else...? China it is, then. Sorry, please continue, Baggie."

"There's been nothing definite brought against him personally, but it is said that he can be very vindictive amongst other things."

"How do you mean?" asked Mrs Lund.

"Well, as I say, there have been several stories, but one I have heard mentioned concerned a former partner in a Jamaican sugar cane venture. It was some years ago. The man was found in Jamaica, brutally murdered shortly after Stokely had pulled his money from the business. It is said, but there's no proof, you understand, that it was his doing through his agents. Having met Stokely, I can quite believe it of him."

"But you have no evidence," said Mrs Lund.

"I don't. I realize that. I'm thinking more of the man's psychology. I cannot accuse him of anything, of course, but he seems capable of such an act."

"I've never met him," said Aunt Bessie, "but I've been watching his progress. All I know for certain is that he seems to be an up-and-coming man. He has a lot of money and makes more all the time but, above all, he wants political power. I have observed he is being wined and dined by people of influence. That worries me. Sometimes, I think, political ambition allied with capital can go too far."

"Yes, I agree. I hope he never gets into high office," said Lady Sedlescombe.

"I can only go by what I've read in periodicals," said Mrs Lund. "I must say that I've agreed with many of his views."

"But that is the charm of the man," said Aunt Bessie. "He says so many sensible things, but what he leaves out is how they are to be accomplished. Jobs, cheaper food, improved trade are his calls, couched in very reasonable terms. He's campaigning, but for what and for whom? He never explains it. Because he does not state *how* he will do those things we so desperately need to be done, I fear we might detest his policies if we knew them thoroughly."

"I have only ever seen photographs of Lord Stokely," said Sophie. "What I see is a man who is being accepted into all levels of society and one whom the newspapers and magazines are willing to exalt."

"That is just the problem," said Aunt Bessie. "What has the man actually done except talk about himself and his ideas, his 'Renewed Britain'? MPs fall over themselves to shake his hand and be seen with him."

"Hmm, I'd never considered those things before," said Mrs Lund. "Quite the eye-opener."

"In future, I'll pay more attention to Lord Stokely," said Sophie. "Do you think he's a danger to the nation?"

"Oh, yes, my dear. When you get to be my age, you will have seen his type with their thirst for power many times before. Most of them come to nothing or eventually find a suitable place to exercise their useful qualities without harming others. Stokely's problem is that he has no restraining influences upon his ambition. He's not beholden to anyone, as far as I can tell."

On Friday, the imposing edifice of St. Pancras Station, containing the Midland Hotel, reminded Sophie now, as it had before, of the certainty and solidity of all British institutions that went to support the workings of the capital, the nation, and the empire. She alighted from the cab outside the main entrance, paid the fare, and looked up. Rich, red-bricked and creamy-stoned Gothic architecture soared upwards to the roof and beyond, into spires and towers high above. She saw many detailed and decorative features in the brickwork and wherever she looked, she found something delightful or satisfying. Sophie went inside.

In the Booking Office Hall, Sophie negotiated, through the window set in good Victorian panelling, the price of a first-class ticket - an unheard-of luxury for the Burgoyne's of Havering-under-Lyme. In a sudden moment of additional extravagance after a lifetime of economy, she reserved for herself a seat with its back to the engine. She justified the extra expense by convincing herself of the necessity of protecting her beautiful new business attire from the steam engine's soot smuts. The last thing she wanted was to arrive at Trefoil Hall looking like a wreckage. She hoped the Treasury would view the matter in the same way.

In the station, the slightly peaked, single-span roof of steel and glass created a space beneath that dwarfed passengers and made the rolling stock seem like playthings. Sophie saw Ada waiting under the clock by the wall. They had previously agreed that they should remain in character for the entirety of the mission.

"Good morning, Miss King," said Ada.

"Good morning, Carmichael... Eight-forty." Sophie checked her wristwatch against the station clock, which was difficult, as they were directly beneath it. "I hope Miss Redfern is not the type to be fashionably late."

"What will we do if she doesn't show up?" asked Ada.

"We'll go on without her."

"This must be her coming now. Blimey, look at the luggage. Is she staying for a month?"

"She'll have to change at least three times a day, so she'll have ten outfits or more. Let's remain in character. You and I will not speak to each other except on business matters."

"Yes, Miss King."

Victoria Redfern approached the area under the clock. She was wearing a grey, fur-trimmed cloak, negligently open, and a matching hat with a thin veil. Sophie thought her whole outfit, down to the soft brown ankle-high boots and silk stockings, had to be French. It occurred to her that Archie would never be able to afford such an expensively dressed wife.

Following Miss Redfern were two porters, each with a hand-cart loaded with a steamer trunk. Bringing up the rear was a uniformed chauffeur weighed down with several cases and two hat boxes. The entourage slowed to a crawl as Miss Redfern hesitated. She was uncertain as to which of the figures under the clock was her lady's maid.

"Tally-ho," said Sophie under her breath. Ada and Sophie both picked up their single suitcases. Sophie raised a hand to attract Miss Redfern's attention. They then walked towards her as she had come to a stop.

"Why are there two of you?" were the first puzzled and slightly imperious words from Victoria's cultured red lips. She had a faint northern accent.

"Good morning, Miss Redfern. Government regulations require my presence. Miss Nancy Carmichael will be your lady's maid while you stay at Trefoil Hall."

"Good morning, Miss Redfern," said Ada at her cue. She bobbed prettily.

"I am failing to understand something here. I've been saddled with a strange maid, as well as all the other inconveniences connected with this weekend, but I cannot see where you fit in, Miss..."

"King," supplied Sophie promptly. "As a supervisor and manager of domestic staff on behalf of His Majesty's government, it is my duty to accompany all staff on assignment to smooth over any issues that may arise. Usually, there are several servants in the complement. On this occasion, we have the highly unusual circumstance of there being only one. Nevertheless, I am required to be present at Trefoil Hall as long as Miss Carmichael is present."

"Government waste! This is absolutely absurd."

"The train will be leaving in eight minutes," said Sophie. "On the way, I can explain how I can be useful as your assistant."

"Assistant? Why would I need you as my assistant?"

"Everyone else of any distinction, class, or office will have an assistant at Trefoil. I can detect no secretary or similar person in your retinue, Miss Redfern. Therefore, if you so desire, I can take notes or draft letters for you. I'm sure there is a typewriter at Trefoil and I am conversant with Pitman's Shorthand. Failing a typewriter, my penmanship is passable."

"Well, as I have little choice in the matter, let us board the train."

After the train had lurched and puffed into motion, Ada, in a half-full, third-class carriage, settled herself down to read the latest edition of Woman's Weekly. She looked at the cover and smiled to herself over the way Miss Burgoyne had handled Miss Redfern. Ada further smiled as she considered that she was now a spy in the pay of the British Government.

In the open first-class carriage, Miss Redfern was irritated. Miss King had her back to the engine while she did not, having neglected to arrive early enough or remember to reserve a seat at the Booking Office.

From each of their comfortable, plush chairs, a section apart, the two women could see one another, but an onlooker would never have guessed they were travelling together.

"Mind if I open the window, miss?" asked a florid-faced gentleman from Birmingham once the train began picking up speed. "I'm finding it a little close in here," he added as he began to reach for the window.

"I do, actually," answered Miss Redfern.

"Ah, I see," said the gentleman.

He sat down again and, although he had not meant to, he scowled. He began to read his newspaper, holding it like an immense barrier between them. Miss Redfern did not think it close in the compartment at all. The train rattled on for several minutes.

"I fear I must insist," said the man suddenly. It was apparent he had been thinking of little else while trying to read. "I think it's the scent you're wearing."

"My scent...? But if you open the window, the soot will come in."

"Like as much, it will, and I'm sorry to be a bother, but, er, I need some air."

"I'll agree to the window if we exchange seats," said Miss Redfern.

"Ah, I can't do that now. I paid extra for it."

"Perhaps I can be of some assistance," said Sophie. She had approached Victoria's section.

The two disputants looked up.

"I have a seat with its back to the engine. Perhaps the gentleman and I can make an exchange and resolve the issue."

"Well, that's very kind of you, miss. And I'm sorry to cause trouble, but it's my sinuses, you see. Where are you sitting?"

"In the next section. I'll get my things."

"I'll be right there with mine. Excuse me," he said to Victoria as he got up.

The exchange was effected on the swaying train. Victoria stared at Sophie, who, smiling, sat down. "Would you like something to read, Miss Redfern? I have a Tatler or a Country Life."

"Oh, the Tatler, if you don't mind."

"Not at all... Personally, I think your perfume is delightful. Shalimar, isn't it?"

"Yes, it is... And thank you for your intervention."

"Oh, I'm happy to help, Miss Redfern."

The two women, behind their respective magazines, wondered about each other. Sophie believed that, if she could strike the right note of helpful care and indispensable attention towards Victoria Redfern, she might in turn achieve closer proximity to Paul Klest and his assistant Karissa Raptis. This would increase her opportunities to observe them or retrieve the film. The budding spy also wondered about Archie and Victoria. She recalled Mrs Lund's prediction that their relationship would end badly.

Victoria was frankly puzzled. Accustomed to getting her way in so many things, she recognized a similar spirit in Miss King. The woman from the government was efficient, competent, and decisive, while being annoyingly pleasant at the same time. She dressed well - quiet and business-like. Pretty, too, in her way. Victoria wondered what her background was and decided she would have to have a word with Archie. Somehow, Victoria felt, Miss King needed to be explained.

CHAPTER 9

— • —

COUNTRY HOUSE AND GARDENS - SUITABLE FOR SPIES

L ord Wicksworth's country estate, Trefoil Hall, proved to be
magnificent. It met Sophie's expectations in every way. The
pavilions were extremely large and imposing structures in their
own right. A sweeping, fully glazed concourse on either side of
the beautiful house connected each of the outlying pavilions and
rendered the complex a study in symmetry. The main building -
the Hall - consisted of three floors and would have been a byword
for refined taste and excellence even if the pavilions had not been
added. No expense had been spared when the house was built,
added to, or when the gardens were laid out.

Even though it was September, the gardens had yet to divest
themselves fully of all their summer trappings. Beds of dahlias
and asters provided colour amongst the immaculately trained
and pruned bushes and shrubs while the carefully mown lawns
were a marvel of perfection.

No car had been sent from the Hall to collect Victoria Redfern.
She, with half of her luggage, had gone ahead in one taxi while
Sophie and Ada followed in a second with the other half and their
own. The spies were being scrupulously careful and spoke about
only the most mundane or necessary matters in the cab. Their
aged taxi driver, in his aged and wheezing taxi, had very large
ears. The two young women were concerned that he might have
large, loose lips to match. However, this circumspection did not
prevent them from loudly praising, as schoolgirls would, Trefoil
Hall for its unusual beauty, remarkable size, and setting.

The taxi went partway around the large, circular driveway and stopped in front of the ivy-covered front entrance to let out Sophie. It then proceeded along one side of the building to the servants' entrance to let out Ada. For Ada, the question of accommodation and acceptance in the servants' hall was a simple one. For Sophie, it was not yet settled.

After she had rung the bell, a footman promptly opened one of the double doors for Sophie to enter.

"Good morning, m'm. Whom shall I say is calling?"

At that moment, she came perilously close to saying Sophie Burgoyne.

"Miss Phoebe King. I am Miss Redfern's assistant. Please have my case taken to my room."

"I will certainly do so, miss. If you would kindly wait here a moment, m'm, I will inform them of your arrival."

The footman left the large hall. Sophie knew that he had gone to fetch the butler and, perhaps, inform the housekeeper that someone had arrived who was not on the list. This would cause a minor dislocation of their carefully prepared arrangements. Sophie assumed there would be a spare bed somewhere, perhaps several. Where she would be placed would be entirely dependent upon her interaction with the butler. As she well knew, butlers could be difficult. An old doddering majordomo and she should be able to choose her own room; a supercilious creature, and the outcome was much less certain. The question was, how ladylike and imperious could Sophie pretend to be?

The footman returned with a spry, tall butler, nudging fifty.

"Good afternoon, madam," he said when he had stopped at a respectful distance.

"Good afternoon. As I have already explained, I am Miss Redfern's assistant. Am I to understand that you were not expecting me? I find this most disturbing. "

"I'm sorry to say, madam, that is exactly the case. Neither myself nor the housekeeper had been made aware of your coming to Trefoil this weekend - undoubtedly an oversight, for which I apologize. We shall remedy the matter immediately."

"I suppose the choice of rooms is limited with all the Greeks staying."

"A suitable and comfortable room shall nevertheless be found for you. Might I suggest, madam, you wait in the library while we prepare your room? It will be a matter of some minutes."

"Very well, I suppose I must. What's your name?"

"Butler, madam."

"Thank you, Butler. Please show me to the library."

"If you would be so good as to follow me, the library is this way."

And so Sophie Burgoyne, alias Phoebe King, followed Butler the butler to the library. At least now she was assured of a bed for the night and that made it a matter of so far, so good in terms of her mission.

⸻ ⋈ ⸻

Sophie was shown to her room, which was in fact a small apartment. It was situated on the third floor of the main house. She deduced the rooms had formerly been those of a governess or nanny but, because the Wicksworth children were now all grown to adulthood, that office and these rooms had fallen vacant. Some mild transformation had taken place. The pictures on the wall were mainly attractive, scenic prints or amateur artwork probably executed by a family member. The space was clean and bright and the glorious feature that Sophie appreciated most was the tremendous view over the beautiful gardens. Sophie looked out of the window and wondered how many governesses had stared at the same scene over the last three centuries.

If she had been left to herself, Sophie might have gone to the library to find a volume, returned and put several cushions on the very wide windowsill, to spend her afternoon reading and dreaming a little until going for a stroll in the garden below. The room and the view made her realize how busy she had been over the last few months. This particular return to the countryside dramatically threw into relief the changes that had been wrought in her life. She loved her new life and business in London, but realized what she had given up in exchange. Sophie momentarily felt how Cordelia looked in the painting at Auntie Bessie's house.

Her reverie was brought to a halt when she suddenly remembered she was on a spying mission.

———⊱✠⊰———

Ada was enjoying herself. To be a lady's maid accorded a domestic servant a level of distinction beyond most of the other household positions. A lady's maid was little inferior to either the butler or the housekeeper and, in truth, commanded her own domain in a domestic sense. The downside to such an elevation could be resentment and jealousy among the other servants, depending on the character of the lady's maid. Because Ada was lady's maid to a socialite of a prominent and extremely wealthy family, she was of interest to the rest of the staff. That Ada was also friendly, talkative, could listen to others, did not put on airs, and knew what was going on in London brought her quick acceptance in the servants' hall. As was to be expected, neither the housekeeper, Mrs Vaughan, nor Butler took any particular interest in her beyond common courtesy. Butler, a keen observer of domestic staff and with vast experience, quickly understood that Ada was as competent as they came and privately wished there were a couple of Adas on the staff in Lord Wicksworth's London house.

The young cockney spy went to work immediately on Miss Redfern's wardrobe in a bedroom in the West Pavillion.

"Miss, may I ask you something?"

"What is it?"

"I have studied the schedule for the weekend and there are two formal dinners. Are you wearing your black evening dress or the red one tonight?"

"The red I think... Your name's Carmichael. I know some Carmichaels in Yorkshire..."

"Oh no, miss. That wouldn't be possible, now would it?"

"No, of course not. It just seems an unusual name for a servant."

"I didn't know that, miss. But I do come from a very big family and they mostly work on the docks or the railways. A lot of the women work in factories. Come to think of it, miss, I must be the only one in the whole family who is in service."

"I see."

"What shoes will you be wearing tonight?"

"The ones with the silver buckles."

"Those haven't been worn before, have they?" They might pinch a bit round the toe, and I didn't see any shoe stretchers. Shall I go and find a pair in the 'ouse?"

"Oh, yes... How would you do that?"

"I'll ask around the household domestics first and if they haven't got nothing to spare, I'd go after the Ambassador's wife's maid. She looks like she knows what she's doing. I bet she has a set even though she is Greek. She'd give them to me on account of keeping up good international relations."

"How extraordinary... What if she doesn't speak English?"

"She does speak it a little bit because I heard 'er in the servants' hall asking for a few things and when she asked for some olive oil, they sent her to the kitchen and she understood that, all right."

"Well, see what you can do. Was there anything else?"

"Ah, yes there is, miss. You'll have to explain your undergarments to me. You have a lot of them and I'm not sure what you want to wear and when you want to wear them.

"And another thing, do you want your clothes cleaned and mended here or save them for when you get 'ome? A lot of what you've got is very beautiful and I wouldn't trust the laundress here yet until I know her work and I doubt we'll be here long enough for me to get acquainted with 'er ways. I can clean, press, goffer anything you like but I wouldn't give nothing to the laundress at the moment, in particular as the house is so full and she so busy or will be."

"Have you spoken to her?"

"I did, and she's a bit on the surly side, so I don't think she'll do me any favours. Plus, she's got 'elp who I doubt is trained properly. I fear you'll have stuff shrunk in the wash when only a spot cleaning is needed."

"If I need anything cleaned, you're to do it. The rest can be seen to when I go home."

"Very good, miss."

"We'll go through the lingerie together. I'm quite particular about it."

At about three o'clock, Sophie went on a tour of the house and grounds by herself. The house was beginning to fill up with new arrivals. Because most of the people she met inside were British men and she had yet to be introduced to anyone, she passed them with a slight nod of acknowledgement but without speaking. The Ambassador had not yet arrived but was expected at five o'clock. There was no sign that Lord and Lady Wicksworth were in the house. Sophie presumed that Butler would mention to her Ladyship that an unexpected extra guest had arrived - a Miss Phoebe King, assistant to Miss Redfern, who was representing her father's steel interests.

Sophie let herself out through some French windows in the drawing-room and onto the terrace with its southern exposure. It was pleasantly warm outside in the sunshine. Sitting at a table at the other end of the terrace were three smartly uniformed Greek naval officers. She noticed they looked preoccupied, speaking without smiling, but then their nation was at war, so their dour demeanour was to be expected.

As she descended some steps onto a garden path, Sophie wondered what the Greek Navy would do with eight submarines if it had them. She realized she knew very little about international politics and military considerations beyond the brief summaries found in newspaper articles.

The path led her through a stone archway in a wall and then into an Italian-style formal garden, dotted with fountains, statues, and benches. Two older men in black morning dress were walking slowly along one of the gravel paths, deep in conversation. Sophie took them to be senior civil servants or diplomats. She went in a different direction so as not to disturb them. The path led her towards a similar archway on the far side, but this one, cloaked in Virginia creeper, looked so ancient it seemed as though it belonged in a Roman landscape. She learned later that it was a reconstructed entrance of a nine-hundred-year-old monastery that had once stood in the area.

When Sophie was halfway across the gardens, Paul Klest alias Josif Abazi, accompanied by Karissa Raptis, emerged through the archway. Klest glanced towards Sophie but made no acknowledgement. Klest looked very much like the photo Archie had shown her. He was a tall, solidly built man with fair hair. Miss Raptis was also quite tall, but dark-haired, with a dark complexion. Klest was speaking rapidly while Miss Raptis listened without comment and they walked at a smart pace. Sophie wondered what they were discussing with such great urgency, for that was the impression they gave. With her quarry sighted, the game had begun.

She continued her ramble and went through the arch. Here she found three gardeners at work on a series of oval flowerbeds. One was a large man with a beard who tugged at his flat cap when he saw her looking his way, but immediately went back to his work. They were clearing out spent annuals and cutting back perennials with care. Seeing summer being packed away after its days of glory always made her wistful.

Beyond the beds, the gardens transitioned into a tamed and beautiful woodland area with a stream, pools, and even a small waterfall. The path led to a curving wooden and very pretty bridge over a pond. Past the bridge, the vista opened up and, beyond some willow trees, she saw a small lake with boats tied up to a dock. But on the bridge itself, a man in a grey lounge suit stood at the railings and stared into the depths. He was quite tall, on the thin side, and in his mid-forties, with thinning dark hair. He had a sad air about him, but was completely absorbed in his contemplation. The reflected light from the rippling water illuminated his face. He was wearing a black armband, signifying a recent loss.

To get to the lake, Sophie had to pass him on the bridge.

"Oh, excuse me. Am I in your way?" The man came out of his reverie, straightened up, and stood close against the railing to let her pass. "I was watching the carp."

"That is a very pleasant pursuit on such a beautiful day," said Sophie.

"Yes, it is," said the man quietly.

"I'm sorry to have disturbed you... Where are the carp?" Sophie approached the railing to look.

"Directly below. There are several, but there's one big fellow who shows up now and again."

Sophie looked and saw the fish. She had hoped the man might introduce himself, but as he did not and she should not; she let the matter be.

"Charming. I think I'll return at another time with some bread to feed to them."

"That's a good idea." They both fell silent.

"Goodbye," said Sophie.

The man managed a weak smile and said goodbye, too.

As she walked off the bridge, Sophie believed she had just met Mr Alfred Wright, the submarine designer. She wondered, as she walked, whether he was sad because of his loss, or was it that he had just spoken with Klest and had been upset by that? Should engineers from opposite sides of the negotiating table even be conferring with one another before the talks begin? She sighed, not knowing the fine shades of etiquette in such diplomatic negotiations. But, to her, it did not seem to be correct behaviour.

At four o'clock, tea was served in the drawing room, and it was a busy affair. The room was full of old tapestries from the Gobelins factory in Paris; they even covered the Chippendale chairs. Hanging on the walls were tapestries up to the size of carpets, displaying a variety of colourful classical or French romantic scenes. Very carefully, Sophie set her delightful Sèvres cup and saucer down upon the snowy white tablecloth. It had been a long time since she had been to tea in so sumptuous a room. She looked around at the unusual collection of people. There were eight ladies present - all seated around the table. Several older civil servants of high rank were also seated. Every other man in the room was standing. To Sophie's mind, the group of twenty or so men, as a whole, looked as though it had been transplanted from a Naval officers' club, the members of which would have been much happier with chunky glasses of whisky and soda than with the dainty cups of tea provided by their hostess.

Although they looked out of place, the general, moderate buzz of conversation indicated the seriousness of their discussion. Servants moved quietly and deferentially among the throng. At the island of femininity in the sea of masculinity, Lady Wicksworth presided over the table. Sophie observed her Ladyship, a strong-featured woman in her mid-fifties. She watched as Lady Wicksworth looked at the men and saw an expression cross her face that Sophie interpreted as "I'm not inviting this lot to tea ever again." Lady Wicksworth turned back to the table and caught Sophie looking at her. She smiled.

"It seems we are to be ignored," said her ladyship.

"They are busy, I suppose," replied Sophie.

"If it were me, I'd have the business settled in an hour. What do you say, Miss Raptis? Are men as efficient as they pretend to be?"

"I believe some are, your Ladyship. It depends on the man," she answered. She had an educated, precise voice with only a slight accent.

"Yes, I suppose that's true. I'm very heartened by seeing you and Miss Redfern present at these negotiations. I think it's about time women were included in such deliberations and you are both so young. Most heartening."

"There's still a lot of work to be done," said Victoria Redfern. "I am not permitted to vote until I'm thirty. That is a law that must be changed."

"I quite agree," said Lady Wicksworth. "But I should imagine it will not be so very long before the change is made."

"If the pressure is kept up on our elected officials, your Ladyship. If there is any slackening off on our part, they'll slacken off on theirs."

"I see," said Lady Wicksworth. "How is your father, Miss Redfern? I've met him twice, I believe, but that was before the war."

"He is well in himself, thank you, but he's confined to a wheelchair these days."

"That must be so trying. I should imagine it's quite a relief for him to have you represent his interests. Tell me, do you know much about steel-making?"

"I do. I was thirteen when an Ironmaster taught me how to pour my first heat. That's a batch of steel from a Bessemer converter dropped into ladles before moulding." Victoria Redfern's usually slight north country accent deepened as she spoke.

"Good heavens... And what is it like in the steel mill?"

"Hot and hellish. The rivers of molten metal grab your attention like nothing else in the world. They glow in the dark like liquid gold and fire. If you have ever seen that painting hanging in the Tate of Pompeii by John Martin, that's what it's like."

"The next time I'm up to London," replied Lady Wicksworth, "I shall look out for that painting. It sounds very dramatic, as does steel-making itself."

Sophie heard the passion in Victoria Redfern's voice and gave her a sideways glance. She accepted a second cup of tea when it was offered to her and thought again of Archie and Victoria's prospects.

"Miss Raptis," said Lady Wicksworth, "I am very curious to know how you came by your excellent command of English."

"My family owned a shipping line and maintained an office in London. My father ran the London bureau for six years, so part of my education was done in England."

"Ah, I see. That explains it. I haven't been to Greece for years and would very much like to go again. I do hope this war ends quickly so that life can return to normal in your country."

The conversation around the table drifted into other matters and Lady Wicksworth began talking to the wives of three civil servants and a friend of hers. The three younger women, left to themselves, remained more or less silent, except for helping each other to cakes or making ordinary observations about the room and its furnishings.

Sophie now knew where she stood in the mind of Lady Wicksworth. Clearly, she had been advised of Sophie's sudden appearance and need of a room. Sophie was, then, the overlooked assistant, sufficient in breeding for her Ladyship to talk to directly in her drawing room, but not highly placed or interesting enough that she would enquire into Sophie's antecedents. Something above a governess, Sophie supposed, and that would have been Butler's estimation of her as he informed Lady Wicksworth. She decided that was about as perfect as it could be for the mission. Sophie would be dining with the dignitaries later. Invited to tea as a house guest meant she would be invited to dinner, too.

About half-past four, Lord Wicksworth arrived home, which event emptied the drawing room of all the British men except for a few older gentlemen seated in armchairs. Sophie saw the look of displeasure on her Ladyship's face, but made sure she did not catch her eye again.

"I suppose I must accept such poor manners under the circumstances," said her ladyship. "I notice the Greek gentlemen are not similarly afflicted. If you will excuse me, I shall go up to my room."

The tea party broke up almost immediately after Lady Wicksworth's departure.

At five o'clock, the Greek Ambassador and his wife arrived. They were accompanied by a Greek army officer and an extraordinarily large and athletic looking gentleman in a dark suit. Mrs Makri did not speak English, and the officer acted as her interpreter. The diplomatic welcoming committee was punctilious in receiving the official representative of the Greek nation. Lord Wicksworth was on first-name terms with the Ambassador but presented his wife formally with much smiling to the Makris. Lady Wicksworth attempted a warm welcome with Mrs Makri and, although the officer interpreting was charmed and delighted, Mrs Makri seemed somewhat less pleased to be at a country house. Whatever Mrs Makri's deficiencies may have been, the Ambassador, Dimitri Makri, more than compensated for them by being extraordinarily delighted by everything and everyone around him. He expressed himself in the friendliest and most genial of terms.

From a semi-concealed vantage point at the top of the massive cantilevered stone staircase, Sophie watched all these proceedings in the hall below. She heard a door being closed and then someone approaching from the bedrooms given to the Greeks. Sophie hurried in the opposite direction along the carpeted corridor towards the servants' staircase. She peeped around a corner. Where she had been standing just moments before, Karissa Raptis now stood to observe the scene below. *A penny for your thoughts.* Sophie would have liked to have known what was on the foreign spy's mind at that moment. She used the servants' staircase to get to her room on the floor above, where she attended to her clothes after her walk. While occupied with that, she decided to speak to both Ada and Miss Redfern before dressing for dinner.

Chapter 10

Night Falls, the Games Begin

Sophie knocked on the door to Miss Redfern's room in the West Pavilion. Ada dutifully answered it.

"If Miss Redfern could spare me a moment, please, I would like to speak to her."

"Yes, Miss King. I'll ask if Miss Redfern is receiving visitors."

"Show her in," called out Victoria from inside the room. She was seated at her dressing table, wrapped in a long yellow silk dressing gown, and carefully powdering her face.

"Please, come in," said Ada, holding the door open wide.

"Miss Redfern, I have just come from the dining room. It is about tonight's seating arrangements."

"What of them?" Victoria answered, studying her work in the mirror.

"There are two tables for tonight's dinner. You are seated at the main table close to Lord Wicksworth but are opposite the Ambassador's wife who does not speak English. Would you prefer another seat?"

"Who is either side of me?"

"A Greek, Captain Vassos, is to your right. On your left, Sir Reginald Fawcett, whom I believe is one of the elderly civil servants we saw at tea."

"Does the officer speak English?"

"I cannot say, as I have not been introduced to him."

"What a bore it all is. You may as well leave it because who knows who I'll be stuck with if you move me? I doubt her Ladyship would be pleased by such a request."

"I did think of requesting a change, but there is a simpler and more expedient method."

"Oh, how do you mean?"

"I would simply re-arrange the cards more suitably."

Victoria stopped what she was doing and spoke to Sophie's reflection in the mirror with a slight frown on her face.

"Would you?"

"Yes, Miss Redfern. My idea is that Admiral Pavlidis would be seated on your left instead of Sir Reginald, and Mr Josif Abazi would sit opposite.

"I'd be surrounded by Greeks."

"Although fifty, Admiral Pavlidis is a very distinguished-looking man. He speaks English, as does Mr Abazi. I have seen both of them conversing with Lord Wicksworth without assistance. These would be the men to convince about the steel contracts for the submarines, as I believe they are the chief negotiators and appraisers of the submarine project."

"But they'll be manufactured in Britain."

"Yes, that's true. But no manufacturer will be present tonight. You will have a clear field, Miss Redfern, to persuade the Greeks that your father's steel is the best for this project. Of course, Mrs Makri may have proved to be very entertaining, but I fear that likelihood to be remote, especially as her interpreter is seated at the lower table where I am also seated."

"Ah... Well, yes, see what you can do, Miss King."

"Certainly... May I ascertain if the service you are receiving is to your satisfaction?"

Victoria thought of how Ada had energetically attended to her new shoes and laid out everything perfectly and now the enigmatic Miss King was about to rearrange the table place cards secretly to further her father's business interests.

"Yes, I have no complaints."

"Very good, Miss Redfern." Sophie retired from the room.

On her way out, Sophie slipped a folded square of paper into Ada's hand. They would meet after dinner at ten-thirty in the summer room on the ground floor of the East Pavilion. The note also said 'Get her to talk about A.' A stood for Abazi.

Sophie returned from the West Pavilion and approached the main entrance of the dining room. As it was past seven o'clock, she hoped Butler had completed his final inspection of the table and all its accoutrements. She had no time to stop and marvel at the beauty of the neoclassical room, pale blue and white with its heavily moulded ceiling split into quadrants, each possessing a painting of Greek mythological subjects. Sophie bypassed the smaller table set for twelve and approached the long table that was ready to receive twenty-four diners. She quickly rearranged five place cards so that Victoria Redfern would be surrounded by Greek decision-makers, with one of them being a spy.

As she approached the door to leave, she heard a voice outside. Sophie ran to the entrance near the kitchen. She got out in time and hurriedly returned to the hall so that she would not look out of place near the servants' areas. Sophie then demurely ascended the main staircase of Trefoil Hall.

The building was rectangular. Three bathrooms occupied the centre of the first floor, with doors facing south, east, and west, but presented a blank wall on the landing side to the north. A corridor ran around the block of bathrooms and connected with two short spur corridors on the southern end. Ranged along the outer wall of the corridor were all the bedroom doors. These continued along the short northern corridors that extended out from either side of the landing.

There were twelve bedrooms in all. Sophie observed from the landing that several principal rooms were very large, which meant some bedrooms had to be quite narrow to allow them all to fit into the space, extensive though it was. She would have taken a quick tour of the area but preventing her was the large, athletic man who had accompanied the Ambassador. He was sitting in a chair, stationed just inside the left-hand corridor, reading a Greek newspaper, and keeping watch over the Greek-assigned section of the house. Sophie did not pause to look at him as she climbed the stairs, but realized now that the bedrooms belonging to Klest and Miss Raptis had to be two or three doors along from where the guard sat. She supposed he would stay at his post while the Ambassador was in his rooms.

Despite Greece being at war with Turkey and despite the reason for the dinner being far from anything like a social gathering, the military, political, and business types gathered around the tables managed a modest degree of conviviality. The men outnumbered the ladies by a ratio of three to one. The gentlemen were in evening dress except for half a dozen naval officers - three from each navy - in their dark blue dress uniforms, colourfully relieved by copious amounts of gold braid, shiny brass buttons, and medal ribbon bars.

As if by common consent, nearly all the ladies were dressed in white or off-white evening dresses. Amongst these, Lady Wicksworth took the hypothetical prize for the best-dressed woman at the table. She wore a long, ivory-coloured costume with many narrow pleats and much delicate beadwork. She was very noticeable at the end of the long table, for she also wore a bandeau which secured a curving grey feather.

Going against the safe, diplomatic choice evidenced by most ladies present were two noticeable trend-setters. Miss Redfern wore a sleek and somewhat daring maroon Paris creation with the longest string of expensive pearls Sophie had ever seen. Victoria was undeniably attractive and turned several heads.

The other who bucked the trend was Sophie, and she was very annoyed with herself for doing so. Being new to spying, she had excitedly packed two evening dresses in her case without considering the effect they might have. Gilberto's work was superb and, although the two dresses she had brought were not the showiest in her wardrobe, they certainly did not permit her to blend into the background. Tonight she wore a jade green, silk crêpe Georgette dress, and the colour suited her perfectly. Her jewellery was very modest, but its inherent restraint elegantly enhanced the wearer.

Sophie, too, was turning heads and that was not what the spy wanted to happen. Also, she was unused to such attention, being always one of the poor relations at most upper-class family gatherings. She now felt uncomfortably on display and this heightened her colour, which rendered her more attractive still. At least, the Greek interpreter, Major Theodoropoulos, sitting next to her at the table, plainly thought so.

He was an entertaining and handsome young man in his army dress uniform. The Major monopolized Sophie's attention almost to the exclusion of those around them. It got to the point where Sophie feared he was going to be indiscreet. More frustrating for her was that, while she wished to guide the conversation around to the topic of submarines and, eventually, to the characters of Klest and Miss Raptis, the unmarried major insisted upon talking about all things beautiful - places, art, music, literature. So enthused by his subjects, he would soon, Sophie imagined, become lyrical over moonlight, perfume, and romantic situations. As a reader of romantic literature rather than from personal experience, Sophie had the distinct impression that a walk on the terrace in the mild night air was in the offing. She would not have minded, but she knew she had more important things to do.

In sharp contrast to Sophie, Karissa Raptis, seated three diners away on the opposite side of the smaller table, was very quietly dressed. Her pale fawn-coloured costume, while attractive and complimentary to her, would be unlikely to elicit rapturous comment. During dinner, Sophie slyly observed the spy while the Major's attention was briefly diverted elsewhere. She noted that Miss Raptis only spoke in answer to something said and did not seem to initiate any conversation herself. Sophie knew that she should have adopted this same demeanour. It annoyed her that she had got it so wrong.

Soon after the main course had been served, there was a noise and commotion at the main table, somewhere about the middle. All heads in the room turned to see what was the matter. It quickly became apparent that Sir Reginald Fawcett was indisposed, afflicted by a fit of coughing. The old man stood up and tried to make an apology, but his coughing would not permit him. He was expediently helped from the room by a footman. There was almost complete silence as he went out and then arose an intense murmuring as soon as he had gone. Within a few minutes, it was as if the incident were forgotten.

For the ladies, the after-dinner niceties were kept to a brief minimum. They sat in the drawing room for half an hour and discussed neutral topics. To mention Greece was to mention the war. Since the gentlemen would not be joining them and since Lady Wicksworth was finding the presence of a mute and uncomprehending Ambassador's wife rather trying, she soon departed, claiming that she needed to rise early the next morning.

However, had she known that Miss King was a Burgoyne, she would have been immensely interested and stayed longer. Her Ladyship would have pressed Sophie for information because of the connections other branches of the Burgoyne family enjoyed. Her interest in Sophie would have been more specific because Lady Wicksworth and Aunt Bessie, when much younger, had once been bridge partners. After a charity dinner, Lady 'Bessie' Shelling, and Lady Wicksworth had played bridge. Their opponents, whom they soundly thrashed, were Lord Curzon before he became Viceroy of India and the Duke of York, who later became King George V in 1910. This was one of Lady Wicksworth's fondest memories.

The gentlemen also had to rise early, for that was when the official talks would begin. However, over their after-dinner port and cigars, their conversation was exclusively about the war and the part the new submarines could or would be playing. Deep discussions about the intentions of the French, the Russians, and the Bulgarians circulated the room. The more specific naval talks progressed to a point where they could almost get the plans out and have at it there and then. But, because they conversed in smaller groups, each with its own specific interest, the progress was piecemeal. The plans remained safely locked inside Lord Wicksworth's safe.

Around the table in little cliques, Josif Abazi and Alfred Wright formed an engineering nucleus, Wicksworth and Makri formed the decision-making nucleus, and the naval officers formed a third party. The more numerous English civil servants spoke to their Greek counterparts. Sir Reginald Fawcett was still absent and indisposed. Major Theodoropoulos was in great demand for his services, as was a British interpreter. The Major had expressed the sincerest of regrets at being parted from Sophie when she left the room with the other ladies.

On her way back to her bedroom, Sophie noticed a footman in the hall who did not seem to be doing much of anything. She did not notice him because he was a footman in livery; she noticed him because he did not look like a footman. In fact, to her, he looked like a policeman, and a large one at that, pretending to be a footman. He also seemed unsure what he was supposed to be doing. Sophie could have told him. She would have said, "Stand still or disappear and come back when called for." She found it amusingly quaint. Her amusement was almost doubled when she found another footman, almost as large, on the first floor. He was in the right-hand corridor and seemed to be slowly patrolling the hallways.

Sophie climbed the stairs to the top floor and could not resist stopping to take a peek through the balustrade. She observed the British policeman-cum-footman approach the now vacant chair of the Greek bodyguard and then turn around abruptly as though turned back at a frontier post between two nations. Stifling a laugh, she stepped quietly away, wondering how many of them there were in the house. She stopped laughing when she realized that these various guardians of the peace might interfere with her activities at some future critical moment.

———⋈———

Once back in her room, Sophie exchanged her evening gown for a dress more suited to her supposed station. She quickly removed the light cosmetics she had worn and went downstairs, carefully avoiding all sentinels and staff by using the servants' staircase. She had to be careful because some of the staff lived in the house on the top floor and they could be retiring to bed about then.

She arrived in the summer room of the East Pavilion without difficulty and thought to leave the room in darkness so as not to attract attention. The spacious apartment was cool and functioned as a huge lounge on summer days. Sophie had seen it in daylight and found it filled with rattan furniture and many soft cushions. It had the feel of the Empire and of India, being decorated with many objets d'art from that land. The southern wall overlooking the lawns consisted mainly of a series of glass doors that, when opened, would make the room very airy and feel as though it were a part of the outdoors.

From the bag she had brought with her, she took out the binoculars to use. They did not help her in the slightest. The light was on in Miss Raptis' bedroom - it had a single window and was, therefore, a narrow room. According to Archie's explanation, Abazi's bedroom was next to it but nearer to the lawns. It had two windows, but the light was off. She put the binoculars away, intending to give them to Ada, whose bedroom was on the floor above the summer room.

The waxing crescent moon had risen in the clear sky and, although the lawns were moderately illuminated, little could be seen inside the summer room. The dark forms of large potted plants took on a menacing look while Sophie waited and her eyes adjusted to the darkness.

Ada was late, not surprisingly because she was subject to her lady's orders. While waiting, Sophie looked towards the lawns, as there was little else to be seen. While she looked, a barely perceptible shape flitted across the first glazed door to her left. The shade hid behind a doorpost. This shadow among shadows slowly crouched down to peer into the room through one of the lower lights. Sophie stood motionless, hardly daring to breathe. Something akin to fear rose inside her. She should not be where she was and the figure outside should certainly not be where he was. The figure continued to look in and Sophie felt a sudden exhilaration. The person, she was certain it was a man, moved on stealthily and rapidly, crouching low as he went until he passed the last door. Sophie walked quickly to a side window, but, look where she might, she did not see the phantom again. He had vanished into the gloom between the pavilion and the house.

"Psst!" said a whispered voice by the door. "Are you in here, miss?"

"Yes, Carmichael," whispered Sophie. "Don't turn the light on. Someone's outside."

"Who is it?"

"I don't know."

"I'd better not come over 'cos I'm bound to bump into something."

"I know the way. I'll come to you."

Sophie returned to the door.

"I think he's gone. Somebody is creeping about very suspiciously. It might be a thief."

"Oh, I dunno. No thief would try it on in an 'ouse full of people. Could it be another spy?"

"I have no idea, Ada. Do spies creep about in gardens?"

"I would think so. Not all the time, mind you, but when they have to. Do you think 'e's one of our'n or one of their'n?"

"That's a good question. I thought it was one of theirs, whoever they are. As far as I know, there's another person present on our side, but I don't know who it is. When I asked, I was essentially told I didn't need to know."

"Oh, that's very 'elpful, I don't think. I tell you who else is in the house. Just before tea, I passed this police matron dressed as a maid and she's as big as an outhouse. And she don't know what she's doing. She looks everyone full in the face like she wants to arrest them for vagrancy. First rule of a maid is to avert your eyes. What is the world coming to, I ask you?"

"She's not the only one. I've seen two different footmen who can be nothing but policemen."

"What's the Old Bill doing here?"

"Well, the Greeks have a guard over their corridor or for the Ambassador. I'm not sure which it is. I suppose the powers that be are doing something similar."

"Only they've turned it into a music hall act. Footmen and maids, indeed. They won't fool anyone."

"Yes, but enough of them. What happened to Sir Reginald Fawcett?"

"The old gent taken poorly? I don't know. Nobody does. A doctor was called in, but he pushed everyone out of the room so none of us know."

"Let's hope it was nothing serious. Has Miss Redfern mentioned Abazi?"

"Yes, she did. And it didn't take much to get her going. He must be some kind of talker, because I think she's taken a shine to him. But it's not what you might think. It's all about steel and engineering so I didn't learn much about 'im. But, miss, 'ow can a woman be so mad about steel? I know I'm her maid and everything, but it's unnatural. Her face lights up when she starts talking about it. She sent me cross-eyed with her alloys and carbons. Oh, yes, you should hear 'er talk about heat treats. Anyway, with her, Abazi is the cat's whiskers. The Admiral will probably recommend her steel, and the other navy officer backed both of them... What did you think of the dress she was wearing?"

"You turned her out very well... and it was a stunning dress."

"Thank you, but wasn't it just? All her knickers and camisoles are French or American. Top to bottom, inside and out, whatever she's wearing, it's best quality and imported. I hate to think 'ow much she spends on clothes. And, miss, she's got dresses like you wouldn't believe."

"Is that so?"

"Yes, and there's a problem an' all."

"What is the problem?"

"Me putting two and two together, I think Miss Victoria Redfern would like to know how Miss King manages to afford such a beautiful, jade-green, silk dress on a government-hired domestic's pay. She remembered what you was wearing right down to the colour of your eyeshadow, and I never saw you dressed for dinner, did I?"

"Oh."

"Yes, 'Oh', Miss King. Reading between the lines, I think Miss Redfern was getting all the attention until one of the Greek gentlemen must have mentioned the lady in the green dress at the other table. I think they got all poetic about you after that. Well, Miss Redfern is not in a poetic mood about her assistant at present."

"I must do something to calm her down. We have enough on our hands without her being upset into the bargain.

"Now for the itinerary. Miss Redfern will be in meetings between nine and eleven, in which there will be general explanations about the submarine and its capabilities. She will be asked to speak about the supply of steel and the ability of British industry to get the vessels built on time and within budget. From then on, the two sets of negotiators will thrash out the details between them. That will be done in separate meetings for technical and financial matters. Sunday is for finishing up all business and, by the end of the day, a deal will be struck and a memorandum of understanding drafted and signed.

"I believe Abazi and Miss Raptis will have direct access to the plans from twelve tomorrow and onwards. I think they will take the earliest opportunity to photograph them and get their mission completed."

"How do you think they will manage that, miss?"

"I've thought it over, and I believe Abazi will cause a diversion. You said Miss Redfern thought him a good talker - so, perhaps, he will engage Alfred Wright in conversation and suggest to him, and anyone else in the room, that they step outside for a smoke or a walk. That would leave Miss Raptis alone to take the photographs under the pretext of writing out notes or something similar.

"When the party returns, Miss Raptis will still be working and the drawings are exactly where they left them, but she has the photographs. Her mission is accomplished."

"So you'll want to pinch the film Saturday afternoon or night?"

"Ideally, yes. I would like to make only one attempt, but that may not be possible with the Greek guard sitting where he does. I think I shall have to excuse myself from dinner tomorrow to get in her room, but first, I must find out if the guard follows the Ambassador wherever he goes. I haven't seen him anywhere since early this evening."

"That's the big Greek fella in civvies. He was in the servants' hall 'elping himself 'andily to everything that was going while you was all at table."

"Ah, excellent. Then I'll follow the Ambassador and his guard to see where they go and once they're out of the way, I can get in the Greek rooms. Allowing time and opportunity for Miss Raptis to take the photographs and then remove the camera from the meeting room... I shall make my attempt around teatime. Karissa Raptis will most certainly continue working in the morning room while the Ambassador will just as certainly be present at tea. By the way, how do you find the servant's hall?"

"Very nice, indeed. Very liberal. Lovely food and as much as you want. It's funny, the butler's name being Butler, but he seems to be a good sort. Strict and kindly at the same time. The sort of butler you wouldn't want to disappoint. I was presented to the housekeeper. She's quiet and looks like she won't stand for any nonsense. It's a well-run house, miss."

"That's the impression I have. I'm happy you've fitted in so quickly. I thought the dinner was excellent. Tell me, how are you getting along with Miss Redfern?"

"She's easy to handle. She's not what you call chatty, but I've had her laughing a couple of times and that always 'elps. No complaints."

"That's reassuring. We have to keep her calm throughout this. Hopefully, I will be able to explain why that is so important one day, but I can't at the moment."

"I understand. Do you want me to do anything particular to-morrow?"

"Just keep your eyes and ears open, which you do anyway. If anything happens my end, I'll contact you. We will meet again here at the same time, regardless.

"I'm uneasy with this man creeping about the grounds... I don't think we can tell anyone without drawing unnecessary attention to ourselves. We'll just have to ignore it for the moment and keep our own goals in sight... I must say, despite that, I'm very much enjoying all this."

"Oh, me an' all. It's gettin' right exciting. I think I'd better get going, though. I've still got to tuck 'er in. Good night, Miss King."

"Goodnight, Carmichael. Oh, yes. Take these binoculars and give them a try. I've no idea what we're supposed to be looking for. Miss Raptis' bedroom has a single window in the middle and Abazi's, with two, is immediately to her left. Don't stand too close to your window with them in case you're seen."

CHAPTER 11

───── ❦ ─────

SUBMARINES WITH POTATOES

I t was a day of closed-door meetings. Many rooms in Trefoil Hall had been reserved for the deep, convoluted discussions that were coming. These discussions would be conducted by small knots of men, determined to keep secret their real intentions while, at the same time, seeming to be full and frank in their speech. Superficially, the impression given to everyone present was one of devotion. Greece and Britain were devoted to each other's well-being, as no two nations had ever been devoted in the history of mankind.

What the Greeks wanted were eight cheap submarines. They also wanted the Royal Navy's presence in the Eastern Mediterranean and the Black Sea to continue indefinitely for the purpose of keeping in check the predations of Communist Russian or Turkish vessels, as well as supporting Greek land operations. What the British wanted was to reduce the Royal Navy's presence in the region to save money and have the Greeks pay full cost price for the submarines. The submarine fleet represented a cheaper alternative to such presence and would be an effective deterrent to enemy vessels. Representatives of the two governments diplomatically haggled over price, payment terms, and how long the Royal Navy would be floating about in the area. Slowly, cautiously, they edged nearer to the point where both nations might grudgingly say they had a deal.

The general meeting on Saturday morning was held in the ornate, mirrored, and lavishly painted ballroom - not too dissimilar to the blue, pink and gold ballroom at the Palace of Versailles. Like many general meetings, its purpose was to explain everything everyone already knew and also to build a sense of historical importance into the coming days' deliberations. The interpreters were kept extremely busy. Lord Wicksworth, Defence Secretary, made the longest speech of anyone who addressed the assembly. He stood at a podium behind and to one side of which was a row of seated speakers yet to speak. Listening to his Lordship, one was led to believe that if he could be anything he liked in the world, he would be a Greek, living in Greece. When the Greek Ambassador spoke effusively, he implied that the nearest thing to heaven on earth was Britain, and the British people were like angels in disguise.

The other speakers tended to drone on about significant yet obvious details more narrowly related to their sphere of expertise. Last on the list of speakers was Victoria Redfern. Sophie sat in the audience with a pad and pencil at the ready to take notes in shorthand should anybody say anything particularly noteworthy. When Miss Redfern began speaking, Sophie witnessed her transform into a zealot, an ardent believer in British industry and, most pointedly, the steel industry. Sophie found her performance compelling and scribbled down a few notes, even though she had no interest in steel whatsoever. Sophie also noticed a gradual change in Miss Redfern's voice. Her educated, upper-class accent began to disappear, replaced by the voice of the steel mill. Her mother's family being from Leeds, her father's family from Wolverhampton, and her time spent in foundries and in northern English boardrooms, combined to produce an incisive directness that could not be challenged. She was polite and earnest, but the undercurrent of her message was this, "If you don't buy my steel or have your boats built in Britain, why, then, you're nothing but a complete fool." The room responded with a round of applause.

———⋈———

Once the general meeting was over, the ballroom occupants made a rapid movement to other designated rooms to get on with the real business of negotiation. The engineering committee had the morning room to itself. The committee consisted of Wright,

Abazi, Pavlidis, Miss Raptis, and three other naval officers - two British and one Greek. The Greek diplomatic headquarters was established in the lounging area of the billiards room while their British counterparts were in the conservatory. Between these two strongholds, necessary meetings would be held on the neutral ground of the library. Much of the work would not actually be accomplished face to face - that was reserved for the knottier problems. Instead, flurries of folded, diplomatic notes would pass between the strongholds, carried purposefully by the most junior of the diplomats. In this way, the work of the day would grind on.

Miss Redfern was now effectively unemployed. It was unlikely she would be called upon by either side for the rest of the day. The Ballroom had emptied, leaving just herself and Sophie present. The Ambassador, accompanied by his bodyguard, had repaired to his suite. Lord Wicksworth had headed to his greenhouses where he would remain until luncheon. The negotiators would have sandwiches, tea, and coffee sent in to them. They were expected to work through every meal, except dinner, until a conclusion had been reached. Miss Redfern now had time on her hands and, as Sophie could plainly see, a question in her mind.

"That was a very effective speech, Miss Redfern. I believe the Greek delegation was quite impressed by it."

"Like as much, they were. So, Miss King, there's something I want to know." Miss Redfern's voice had not fully regained its upper-class aplomb.

Sophie did not reply and could see that Victoria was having difficulty framing the question.

"I don't wish to seem impertinent but I am persuaded that you are more than just a civil servant."

"Well, civil servant I am. Would you be more specific, please, then I might be able to answer your query?"

"Well, that's it right there. You just did it. Your words are those of a middle-class domestic manager, but your voice and mannerisms are those of a lady."

"Partly that's my training and partly my background, Miss Redfern. Also, I have been hired because I am decisive by nature and I suppose it shows in my manner."

"Hmm, I'm not convinced. If it were just that, I probably wouldn't have spoken. But that dress you wore last night. It's the latest fashion and had to have cost you a couple of months' salary. I know the price of such things!"

"It was a gift from someone special."

"Ah, was it...? I see... I suppose it's none of my business, then."

"I'm happy to answer any of your questions."

"No, forgive me for poking my nose into your private life."

"No offence taken, Miss Redfern... I tried taking some notes, but really there was little said this morning that couldn't have been found in any newspaper."

"Yes, I agree. You could do something for me, though. I need to send a note to Admiral Pavlidis. He asked for the deformation characteristics of our three-quarter inch plate steel, and I didn't have them to hand last night."

"You can use these," said Sophie. She offered her pad and pencil.

Miss Redfern took them and began writing. "I had to telephone my father. What he doesn't know about steel isn't worth knowing."

"May I ask you something?"

"What is it?"

"Why are you so passionate about steel?"

"I am, aren't I? Passionate, I mean. It's business and a hobby for me." She handed the pad and pencil back to Sophie. "The main thing that drives me now is showing the men that I, a woman, can compete with them at their own game."

"I can fully appreciate that. That must be difficult for you sometimes."

"It has been. I have no illusions. I know my success is not just through my own efforts. If company directors, steel buyers, and material suppliers did not have the respect they do for my father, I wouldn't get on at all in the business. But because they do, I'm making the most of it and making them sit up and take notice. A little at a time, all the time, and we'll have equality one day."

"Very well put, Miss Redfern."

"There you go... I liked your dress, by the way."

"Thank you. I much admired yours. A Paris creation?"

"It was... Miss King, are we chums?"

"I think so, but I must observe the proprieties, Miss Redfern."

"Of course, you must."

Sophie knocked on a door to the morning room. She waited a moment and then entered. Immediately, she saw plans laid out on a long mahogany table. Alfred Wright and Josif Abazi, alias Paul Klest, were examining one of them together. Karissa Raptis had been discussing something with a British naval officer, but looked up when Sophie came into the room. As she turned to shut the door quietly, Sophie could feel Miss Raptis' gaze fastened upon her back. Abazi, ignoring the intrusion, was still looking at the plans with Wright.

Admiral Pavlidis was seated with his chin in his hand, studying another plan at the end of the table nearest the door. Sophie approached quietly and then waited a moment to one side of the Admiral. While appearing to be looking at nothing in particular on the opposite wall, she was actually taking in exactly what was on the table. She saw there were seven large sheets of paper laid out end to end. The other men in the room stood in discussion by the French window that led to the terrace. Karissa Raptis was still watching her, but less intently than she had at first.

After a few more seconds, Sophie cleared her throat in the time-honoured manner of the British servant, who dare not speak first to a superior but wishes to gain his attention at once. The Admiral looked around and was surprised to find her there. He stood up.

"Madame, you wish to see me?"

"Thank you, sir. I have a note from Miss Redfern." Sophie held out the note to him.

The Admiral took it. It consisted of a brief line of text and two short columns of figures, followed by a signature. He read the note and nodded to himself.

"Will there be a reply?" asked Sophie.

"No, except to give my thanks to Miss Redfern."

Sophie smiled, turned, and left the room. On her way back to Miss Redfern, Sophie noticed a third footman who was likely to be a policeman. He passed her in the corridor coming from the West pavilion. A nondescript man, he was not quite as large as the others, but he was more active - almost running in fact. *He definitely should not be doing that*, she thought. *It must be something very urgent!*

—⋈—

Having eaten lunch, which was a perfunctory affair with no other gentlemen present except Lord Wicksworth and Ambassador Makri, Sophie had little to do for the next several hours. As the weather remained fine, she decided a walk in the gardens would be pleasant to while away the time before entering the rooms of Miss Raptis and Abazi. She supposed Karissa Raptis would remove the camera from the morning room as soon as was convenient once she had taken the photographs. Her excuse was likely to be that she needed to obtain something from her room.

It was warmer than the day before and the air balmy. Sophie thought it would be pleasant to take a boat out on the lake, but such a pastime would be better in the company of a friend. She toured the Italian garden and then went out through a different archway than the one the day before. This path led one past a series of hedged-in areas containing flower beds and ultimately to a true English garden. It must have been glorious in high summer with the large beds, a riot of tall, colourful flowers, sailing like galleons amid a green sea of grass. But now the beds had begun to furl their myriad tiny sails while only chrysanthemums bloomed and the first leaves were turning colour on the surrounding trees.

Beyond the English garden, she entered a large, walled kitchen garden - always a favourite area for Sophie. The wall and gates were about as old as the house itself. She shut the black iron gate behind her and it closed with a trembling, nearly musical squeak and a heavy clank. Two of the three gardeners she had seen yesterday were at work here. The taller of them, the one with the beard, was carefully lifting potatoes with a fork. Sophie watched the men from a short distance with that generous sense of well-being that comes from watching others work. Sophie lifted potatoes in the vicarage garden. She had lifted tons of them during her time in the Land Army before she became a supervisor. The man with the beard had a slight limp as he walked between rows. He worked hard and well, like one born to the land. Once more, he found her watching him. He pulled at his cap again and smiled.

"Are those King Edwards?" asked Sophie.

"So they be, miss." The bearded man looked to be about forty and had a weather-beaten face. He was dressed shabbily in an old tweed jacket and brown corduroy trousers. One of his worn boots was tied with string and he sported a round, wide-brimmed felt hat that had seen better days.

"I prefer them to Majestics," said Sophie. "More resistant to blight as well as for the flavour."

"That's true, that. We had a few Majestics earlier, but they be finicky. Can't stand a frost no matter how light." He had the slow, rolling speech of a countryman. She thought his accent sounded close to that which was heard in her own area of Winchester. "But if you don't plant so many, then the blight can't seem to take a-holt the same way."

"Oh, I know exactly what you mean. I was in the Land Army and we lost part of a large field to blight in seventeen."

"And just when you didn't need it."

"Unfortunately, yes. Sorry to have disturbed you."

"Not to worry, miss, but I best be getting on. These taters are wanted for tonight"

CHAPTER 12

━━ ❖ ━━

HIDE AND SEEK

T ea time came. The Ambassador and his wife were in the drawing room drinking tea while his bodyguard sat outside. Abazi and Miss Raptis were in the morning room. A poorly disguised policeman was walking through the first-floor bedroom corridors. Sophie, observing from the stairs above, was judging the timing of his patrol. She waited for an opportune moment to get from the staircase and into the Greek corridor while his back was turned as he walked towards the southern end.

A nearby door closed on the second floor, which caused Sophie to make it appear she was simply going upstairs. A maid started down from the top, stopping to let Sophie pass her by. When she had gone, Sophie returned to her vantage point to begin her timing process again.

Sophie calculated she had twenty seconds while the man walked away with his back turned and off the landing from which he might see her on the stairs. She looked through the balusters and saw him turn at the end of the landing to begin walking to the far end of the right-hand corridor.

As noiselessly as she could, she descended to the landing, keeping her eye on the man's retreating back. She made her dash. With a few seconds to spare, she passed the right-hand corridor and reached the Greek gentleman's chair. She carefully looked around the corner into the Greek hallway. It was empty.

At that moment, she did not know which was Karissa's bedroom. She picked one in the middle. There was no light coming from under the door, so it boded well. She waited a moment, just in case the policeman traversed the southern corridor to peer into the Greek hallway. He obligingly coughed in the right-hand passageway. She darted for the door.

It was unlocked. Once inside, she quickly scanned the narrow room. The room felt as though it had been empty for some time. Sophie went to the dressing table to begin her search for the camera. Instantly, she realized she must be in the wrong bedroom because she saw a man's set of hairbrushes and a man's pair of gloves. Sophie opened the wardrobe to find the white uniform of a Greek naval officer hanging up.

Opening the door slowly, she glanced cautiously up and down the corridor, having lost track of the policeman's current position. She tried the next bedroom door to the south and went in. A mild, blended scent of perfume and creams hung in the air. She began searching Miss Raptis' room. It almost came as a disappointment when the first drawer she opened contained the Minnigraph camera. The lens was indeed a different shape from the one she had seen in Archie's office.

Sophie could see that, according to the dial on the back of the camera, twenty-three photographs had been taken. She re-wound the film and then opened the camera. Quickly, she removed the cassette, putting it into her pocket. From the paper bag Archie had given her, she took out the substitute cassette and slotted it into place. This camera's catch was stiff, and she had to press hard to get it closed again. She advanced the film until it reached the twenty-fourth position so that everything appeared exactly as it had done when she found it. It was a matter of seconds to put the camera away and carefully slide the drawer back. On top of the dressing table was a bottle of perfume of a brand she did not recognize. Sophie picked it up and sniffed at it. She thought it smelled quite nice.

It was silent in the hallway but, when Sophie looked, she was shocked to see the back of the footman-policeman who was now sitting in the Greek guard's chair. For her to get out of the corridor unseen was impossible. She rapidly sought a solution to her dilemma.

Although she knew no Greek, Sophie had overheard a few words of greeting. She mouthed them in silent practice as she approached the man's back.

"Yasou, navarchos," she said brightly, while passing by the policeman.

"Good afternoon, ma'am," said the policeman, rising out of his chair.

"Ahh, Anglos. Sorry, my mistake. Good afternoon." Her pretend accent would not have fooled a Greek national.

The man smiled and nodded. He sat down again while Sophie gaily began descending the stairs with the film in her pocket, blithely unaware that her greeting had elevated the policeman to the rank of admiral.

As tea time had not yet ended, Sophie visited Miss Redfern's room in the pavilion to inform Ada that the mission had been accomplished. However, Ada was absent from the room. Sophie could not leave a note so she returned to the main house. On her way, she met Ada returning to the West Pavilion through the curving corridor. They were alone in the passageway so they stopped to talk.

"Carmichael...," Sophie looked behind her to make sure they were alone, "I've got it!" Sophie looked so pleased.

"Have you, miss?" replied Ada, just as excitedly. "Good for you... Was there a problem?"

"No. If anything, it was too easy."

"Can't complain about that."

"I have to call in the code word now. It's all so thrilling."

"It is. I have to go because she'll be back from tea at any moment. But miss, there's a bit of something going on. The word is, Sir Reginald is recovering, but a second doctor and a nurse come up special from London and are in with him. They've just arrived, and that's not all what's arrived. There's a Scotland Yard detective with them. That's all anyone knows about it at present."

"Really? How very odd... I wonder why Scotland Yard wishes to see Sir Reginald? I'll find out what I can. We shall meet later, Carmichael."

"Yes, Miss King."

There are several variants of any sensational news item that can circulate about a country estate at any given moment. Above stairs at Trefoil, His Lordship would have the most complete knowledge on the subject, her Ladyship would know almost as much, while the guests would know the least, if they knew anything at all. Below stairs, the butler and housekeeper would know as much or more than his Lordship and most of the staff would know as much as her Ladyship. On Saturday, Sir Reginald Fawcett was indisposed - this was common knowledge. For once, his Lordship knew more of the matter than did his butler. The night before, Doctor Ridley, the local man, had been called in immediately to attend to Sir Reginald in his bedroom in the West Pavilion. When the doctor arrived, the elderly gentleman had been helped to bed by the man assigned to him.

"My name's Ridley. How are you, sir?"

"Thank you for coming to see me so promptly. My coughing fit has passed," said Sir Reginald. He addressed the valet. "You can go now."

The doctor watched him go out and close the door. He turned back to Sir Reginald with his eyebrows raised.

"Don't want the servants listening. There was poison in my wine."

"I beg your pardon!" said the doctor, frankly astonished.

"Sounds incredible, I know. I have a lung condition that makes me sensitive to smoke and chemicals. I took wine and, near the bottom of the glass as I drank, I felt something gritty hit the back of my throat, causing me to cough. I believe I expelled most of it, but I also think I swallowed some. My stomach's been very uneasy, but that's all there is to it. I've been lying here wondering if I'm going to die in the night."

"Do you feel dizzy or have a headache? And how large a sip did you take?"

"A large but not indecorous one. I was hoping for a refill." Sir Reginald smiled wanly. "Head aches but nothing extreme. Took aspirin for it."

"Allow me to examine you, sir."

"Go right ahead."

The examination was conducted quickly and efficiently.

"Your blood pressure is a little high, but your heart is strong and beating regularly. I find no discolouration in your eyes. Did this substance have a taste to it?"

"Not that I recall. What do you think it was?"

"I would have said it was indigestion if you had not mentioned poison. The grittiness and lack of taste suggest arsenic. But that's only a guess. It's nine-thirty now. Was your glass preserved?"

"I didn't think of it. They will have cleared everything away by now. I was rather concerned with my own mortality. I'll be gone soon enough, but I would like to stay for my full innings."

"I think you have a good few years left to you, Sir Reginald... Have you mentioned your suspicion to anyone?"

"No. I don't know if you're aware of it, but important talks are being held here this weekend. The Greeks, you know. I didn't want to disturb anyone... The thought of mentioning it to his Lordship... Well, I didn't like to."

"I think, as a precaution, I shall have to pump your stomach, sir. I shall need the help of a servant to do so."

"Really? I didn't even start my dinner... I suppose you must."

Dr Ridley recalled the manservant, and they attended to Sir Reginald. Afterwards, the doctor decided, as a further precaution, that more specialized help was needed in the matter. As it was a suspected case of poisoning, Dr Ridley knew of a good London specialist to bring in. He also informed the authorities promptly by telephone.

A local police inspector visited Sir Reginald at about eleven-thirty and took down his statement. Privately, the Inspector was inclined to dismiss the whole incident as an unfortunate and untimely fit of choking or food poisoning rather than view it as a deliberate attempt on Sir Reginald's life. However, because of the diplomatic meeting and the weighty positions of those in attendance, the local man could not ignore Sir Reginald's assertions. So, it was later with great relief that he handed over the diplomatic nightmare of an enquiry to Scotland Yard.

Lord Wicksworth was made aware of the situation and, for once and for some hours, knew more about the matter than anyone else in the household. He kept the news from her ladyship. He merely remarked to her that Sir Reginald was comfortable, needed complete rest and quiet, and would be attended by a specialist the next day.

After the general meeting on Saturday and after his return from his tour of the estate, his Lordship reluctantly mentioned, in a private conference with Lady Wicksworth, that some men from Scotland Yard would also be accompanying the specialist from London. To this statement, her Ladyship responded in various outraged ways. She stated that if 'Wickles' was going to treat her like a simpleton, she would make his life so thoroughly miserable that he might as well end it. He hurriedly told her everything. She had difficulty at first comprehending what he was saying. Then the full enormity of the truth sank in. Finally, Lord Wicksworth cautioned her to keep quiet about the matter and, on this point, she immediately and fully acquiesced. For Trefoil Hall to gain the notoriety that one might be poisoned during dinner was not something to be relished. And the last thing either of them wanted was for the Greek delegation to find out. Everything, they agreed, must be managed discreetly.

CHAPTER 13

— • —

SUPERINTENDENT (INSPECTOR) PENROSE

There were two telephone lines in Trefoil Hall. One terminated at a telephone mounted on the wall in a separate sit-in booth under the stairs. This was now effectively in possession of the Greek party. Lord Wicksworth, while sitting in his study, wondered what his telephone bill would be for the month and wrote a memo to himself to remember to charge their calls to the Treasury. As he wrote, a call came in on the other telephone line and, as the instrument was on the desk in front of him, he picked up the receiver to answer.

"Wicksworth here... Drysdale at the Foreign Office...? Yes, operator, put him through."

"Good afternoon, Lord Wicksworth," said Archie Drysdale.

"I remember the name. Have we met?"

"Once, during a dinner at the American Embassy. Lord Bledding is my older brother."

"Yes, yes, I can place you now. Well?"

"I've been informed that you're having a spot of bother."

"Dash it all! How can you possibly know?"

"I'm the gentleman who takes care of the stray cats and dogs."

"Oh, I see... Who else knows?"

"One other person. We shall be discretion itself."

"Relieved to hear it. What will you do?"

"I would like to remove the bother you're having. If you permit me, I will need the use of your telephone for about half an hour. After that, there may be other small requests, but I hope to get everything clean and tidy without any disruption to your household."

"I would be grateful if you could. Specifically, what would you like me to do?"

"If you could give the following message to Inspector Penrose. Tell him, For a thorough cleanse, use Soap."

"Is that all? I hope that means something other than the obvious or I shall sound like an utter twerp."

"I'm certain he will say nothing but only smile."

"Very well. I suppose you want to play your game right away. I can only surrender my study for the half-hour you're requesting. We are very busy here, you understand?"

"I do, sir. And I apologize for the peculiarity of my request."

"Life is full of peculiarities, Drysdale. My regards to Bledding when you talk to him next."

"I will pass your message along. Thank you, sir. Goodbye."

As soon as he had hung up the receiver, Lord Wicksworth pressed a button on the wall. A minute later, a footman entered the room.

"Peters, where's Butler got to?"

"He's attending to the Greek Ambassador at the moment, my Lord."

"What do you know about detectives being in the house?"

"Would your Lordship be referring to the gentlemen from Scotland Yard?"

Lord Wicksworth sighed. "Yes. Find Inspector Penrose and tell him to see me here at once."

"Very good, my Lord."

Earlier, Sophie had telephoned in the codeword for a successful mission to a Foreign Office operator. Later, she decided to talk to Archie directly, in case there was anything else she needed to do. Now, she found three Greek men outside the booth waiting for the phone to ring. Each of them lounged in an attitude of bored resignation, waiting for the operator to call back to tell the lucky winner his call had been connected. If Aunt Bessie had been present, Sophie thought, she would be wagering on who got their call connected first. Sophie decided to try again later because another long-distance call might overwhelm the local operator, who was already dealing with several long-distance or international calls to the same number.

"Miss King?" asked Peters, the footman.

"Yes."

"Would you be so kind as to accompany me to his Lordship's study? A gentleman by the name of Penrose wishes to speak with you. He asked me to say there is a telephone for your use in that room."

"How extraordinary. Penrose? I don't believe I know him."

"I understood it to be an urgent matter, Miss King," said Peters.

"Then, lead on."

"Thank you for coming, Miss King," said Inspector Penrose as he got up from his chair in front of the desk when Sophie entered. Peters held the door open for her and then closed it after her as he left the room. Inspector Penrose was a west countryman by look and by a noticeable trace of Devon or Somerset in his voice. He was a solid man, about six feet tall, with a tanned face.

"I don't believe we've met," said Sophie.

"I've not had the pleasure, miss." He spoke slowly and lightly rolled his Rs. "Please, sit down. You're probably wondering why I've asked to see you." As Sophie sat in a plush chair in front of the desk, he took out a little leather wallet. He put the open wallet on the desk in front of her. "That's who I am."

Inside the wallet was a plain rectangular silver token. At its top was an embossed small crown and the words, 'Metropolitan Police, Issued to:', followed by the engraved words, 'P D Penrose, Superintendent of Special Duties.'

"I call myself an Inspector mostly," said Penrose. "It doesn't make people as fidgety like my full rank does."

"And what if I'm feeling fidgety now?"

"Well, you see, Miss King, I might know what was giving you the fidgets... If you have them."

"I see. You have the advantage, Inspector."

"I don't mean any harm. That there phone should ring in a moment. A Mr Drysdale will be on the line. I've an idea you should talk to each other. I don't exactly know what your particular business with that gentleman might be, but I could make a good guess. I'll leave the room if you wish, but I must come back as soon as you've had your conversation, for we've a matter to discuss."

"Oh. This is very unexpected... and it sounds ominous. What shall we talk about while we wait? The weather?"

He smiled readily. "It's nice out. I understand they have pretty gardens here."

"They most certainly do. It's a pity Sir Reginald can't enjoy them just at present. Have you news of him?"

"Resting comfortably. But let's not jump the gun," he said, with a twinkle in his eye. "Mind if I smoke a pipe? My tobacco's not particularly stinkful."

"Please, don't let that stop you. I like the smell of tobacco. My father smokes a pipe."

"I much prefer a pipe to cigarettes," said Penrose. "And I don't care for a cigar." He took out his pipe, which was a large, pendulous briar. "Do you smoke, Miss King? More and more ladies seem to be acquiring the habit these days."

"I tried a cigarette once, and I thought it vile. I coughed like anything."

"I believe everyone does that to start." He had taken out a pouch and was packing the bowl of his pipe. "It's a filthy habit. At least, my mother says it is. And once you've started, it's mortal hard to give it up. Still, I find it aids in contemplating things, so I don't think I'll ever be parting with my old reliable."

He lit his pipe with a match. The phone rang.

"That'll be 'ee. Shall I leave?"

"Please stay, Inspector."

Penrose picked up the receiver.

"Trefoil House, Penrose speaking." He sent a cloud of smoke into the air. "That's the party we're waiting for," he said to the operator.

"Afternoon, Mr Drysdale. The lady is right next to me." He passed the receiver to Sophie, got up, and went over to the window. He stood still, square-shouldered, and sent the occasional cloud of smoke upwards as he surveyed the vista.

"Hello, my dear," said Archie. "I hear you went shopping today. Did you buy exactly what you wanted?"

"I did... It was quite the bargain in the end."

"I'm so very pleased for you. Now, I believe the gentleman in the room is an old friend of mine. Just to make sure, if you ask him where his favourite beer is brewed, and if he happens to mention Devizes, then we can be certain it is my friend."

"I shall do so."

"That being the case, he will be suggesting some very entertaining pastimes for you to consider while you stay at Trefoil."

"Will he, dear? That sounds most delightful and I'm anxious to hear what he will suggest by way of entertainment. But, after my shopping excursion today, I'm running rather low on funds."

"Not to worry, everything's laid on, I should think. Probably best to ask, though."

"Then there's nothing for me to worry about?"

"Not in the slightest. Make sure you enjoy yourself and I'll see you very soon. Goodbye."

"Goodbye," said Sophie, and then she hung up the receiver. "Do operators listen in often?" she asked of the Inspector.

Penrose turned around and puffed out a cloud. "All the time, Miss King. And what with extensions, and such, there's no telling which ear your words might be tickling."

"Are there no secure lines?"

"A few, but not out in the sticks like we are."

"Mr Drysdale said that you prefer a particular type of beer."

"I'm a Taunton man and we have good cider but, to my mind, the best beer is brewed in Devizes."

"Having established that praiseworthy fact, you and I are free to speak."

"Very good." Inspector Penrose came over and sat down. His pipe had gone out, so he put it in his jacket pocket. "All of that rigmarole may sound silly, but I've known it to save lives before. Now, let us come at the business in hand. I have no idea what you've been up to at Trefoil, but I'm sure it was for King and country. I'm a policeman. I'm here on police business. It's me who's here because of the delicate situation we have with the Greeks being present. I'm persuaded that somebody tried to poison Sir Reginald Fawcett. I doubt it were an accident, so it was deliberate. What can you tell me?"

"He was poisoned!?" exclaimed Sophie. Inspector Penrose said nothing but put his unlit pipe back in his mouth and stared at Sophie.

"Oh, dear... Well... I was at a different table at dinner last night. I hadn't really noticed anything... not until he started coughing."

"What did you think had caused him to cough?"

"I would have said a bone lodged in his throat or something similar to that."

"On his way out of the room, did you notice anything or anyone that was out of place or doing something out of the ordinary?"

"Ah, no, I don't believe I did. We all looked towards him, of course."

"What about the servants? Any of them become noticeable to you?"

"It was the footman who was just here who helped Sir Reginald."

"Peters is his name. I know about him. Anyone in the background making a sudden move?"

"No... There is something I should tell you, Inspector. I switched some of the place cards just before dinner."

"Did you? Which ones and why?"

"I moved five of them. I don't know how much you know, but I'm accompanying Miss Redfern. She is not aware of... what I'm doing here. I moved the cards with the object of improving her company's prospects of supplying steel. If she were surrounded by Greek decision-makers, I believed the conversation would help her build a rapport. I moved Mr Abazi..."

"Paul Klest, you mean," said Penrose.

Sophie sighed. "That makes it so much easier. Yes, I moved him and Admiral Pavlidis next to her. I left Captain Vassos where he was because he was about her age. I think he has an engineering background, too. To do this, I had to move Mrs Makri, the Ambassador's wife, and Sir Reginald. I realized that where I had put Sir Reginald had him opposite a Greek diplomat, whom I believed to be his exact counterpart on the Greek side. I thought it best to do a swap. I exchanged Sir Reginald's card with that of the man next to him. So, in the end, Sir Reginald was sitting in Alfred Wright's original place.

"You don't say," said Penrose intensely. "That makes a world of difference."

"In what way?" asked Sophie.

"Alfred Wright had a brother, Frank Wright. He was murdered this last Wednesday evening. Pushed onto the tracks of the Embankment underground station in the path of an oncoming train."

"Oh, how awful... That must have been the death I saw reported in the newspapers."

"That's right. It was on the front page the next morning. Only they were saying suspicious circumstances. Truth is, we've had a murder like that before, a couple of years back. An umbrella was used to trip the victim as well as him being shoved in the back. A couple of witnesses say they saw bits of what happened before Frank Wright fell, but can give no usable description of the man who did the tripping and the pushing. At least, by the size of the individual, they *believe* it was a man. He was heavily muffled, with a scarf around his neck and a cap pulled down. He left an old umbrella at the scene, but we can't trace it. Manufacturer went out of business a couple of years ago."

"Oh, my goodness. Then what I have told you makes a significant difference."

"It certainly looks that way, Miss King. I believe I should now be concerned for Mr Alfred Wright's safety. I think I shall go and look in on him."

"You should find him in the morning room."

"Can you point me in the right direction? I don't think I have the lay of the land just yet. And when I've seen him, you and I will have a further talk. That'll be somewhere else, as his Lordship is anxious to have his study back."

"I'm on the third floor here. Just send me a message when you're ready."

"Very good, miss, I will."

———⋈———

Inspector Penrose found he had to observe the protocols prevailing in the house. He extracted the engineer from the morning room by means of a signed note conveyed by a footman. When Alfred Wright joined him, they seated themselves in the ballroom.

"Thank you for coming so promptly, Mr Wright," said Penrose. "Let me first say that I'm very sorry for your sudden and tragic loss. And, er, please excuse me for taking you away from your meeting, but I do have to ask some questions. They're in connection with your late brother." Penrose had his notepad ready.

"I see, Inspector," said Alfred Wright. He was nearly the same height as Penrose, but much thinner. He wore a grey suit and gave the impression of being a grey, sad man. "I did speak to an officer named Williams the day after my brother's death." He spoke evenly with little inflexion in his voice which made him sound bored, or boring, but his black armband suggested some measure of life had drained from him instead.

"Did you? I've asked for some reports to be sent, but they'll be a while coming. I'm present at Trefoil about another matter, so I apologize if some of my questions cover the same ground. I'll be brief because you're busy. Did your brother, Mr Frank Wright, have any enemies?"

"I don't believe he did. He was an architect... I suppose there was rivalry with other firms, but he never spoke of such things. I can't think of anyone who bore him ill-will."

"Very good. And yourself, do you have enemies?"

"Me? Why would you ask that?"

"We'll go faster if we stick to the questions, Mr Wright."

"All right. Well, no - no more than anyone does. If your question is to find out whether there might be anyone willing to kill both Frank and myself... It's absurd."

"Absurd it might seem, but your brother was murdered, and that's a fact." Penrose leaned forward in his chair. "I don't wish to upset you unnecessarily, but a bit of news has come to my attention. Last night, were you aware that your seat at dinner had been changed at the last minute?"

"No, I was not... Such things are never explained to guests."

"You were originally seated where Sir Reginald sat. Now, sir, can you keep a secret? I'd like this to go no further at present, but it's necessary for you to be informed."

"This sounds rather serious. I will, of course, not say anything... Do I require a lawyer?"

"Ah, no, no, it's nothing like that. In all likelihood, Sir Reginald was poisoned. He's recovering nicely, though, because he coughed most of it up. A sample of his stomach contents has been sent for analysis, so we will know for certain very soon. I've an idea the poison, arsenic most like, was meant for you. Sir Reginald took it only because your place had been swapped with his."

"Oh, good heavens! This is..." Alfred Wright seemed rendered speechless.

"Isn't it just, Mr Wright? In a way, it was a good thing it were Sir Reginald. He has a chest condition and is sensitive to things in his throat. Made him cough violently. Probably saved his life, that did. Now if it had been you sitting there, well, I don't rightly know what would have happened. Do you see the point I'm making?"

"I do, Inspector... I do, indeed."

"Could this attack be connected with the new submarine at all?"

"I hardly think it likely. If I were killed, the submarine could still be built and, with a little preparation, another engineer could have taken my place at these negotiations."

"That's interesting... The Greek gentlemen in the morning room. How do you find them?"

"That suggestion is preposterous. They're all engineers and professionals. Why, even Miss Raptis has a good level of professional acumen."

"There's a lady in there? They seem to be getting everywhere these days. I do think that if all the governments were entirely composed of ladies, we might not have any more wars to speak of. But you never know. Be that as it may, does anyone in that room strike you as antagonistic, overly friendly, quiet and brooding, or the like?"

"I have noticed none of those things among the people present. We are entirely absorbed in resolving technical issues. The submarine has been accepted as it stands and only outstanding ancillary issues are being discussed at present."

"Fine. I have to ask this question. Have you been approached confidentially by anyone present?"

"Confidentially? I fail to grasp your meaning."

"Well, to be blunt, have you been asked to work for a foreign power or been offered money?"

"Certainly not...! Certainly not...! The very idea."

"Well, the idea is not so far-fetched because I know it does happen once in a while. Now, I must caution you about your safety. Do not accept food or drink from anyone but a servant who will be designated by his Lordship. Do not obtain your food and drink for yourself from any place. Do not remain in a downstairs room alone or with only one other person. It would be wise to lock your bedroom door at night. I'll have a constable posted outside your room. During the day... please keep out of the gardens and you may as well stay off the terraces. Furthermore, keep our little discussion under your hat. It serves no purpose to tell anyone, and it might serve us better if you don't."

"This is ridiculous. Am I to be a prisoner? I'm not even convinced by what you say."

"Ah, I disagree with you there. Rationally speaking, you know I'm correct in instituting these measures. It's the basic premise you're having difficulty accepting and I can appreciate that.

"You're free to do as you please, of course. I believe it would be very unwise not to take precautions while the matter is being investigated. I will proceed with the arrangements I've outlined. You have to keep in mind that somebody in the house put arsenic in a wine glass meant for you. Somebody in a crowd shoved your brother onto the train tracks. You and I don't know what will be tried next, and it's better to be safe than sorry, I always say. I think that's all for now, Mr Wright. My apologies for having taken you away from your meeting."

———✂———

"If I lived in a house as big as this 'un, I'd never be finding my spectacles or my pipe." Penrose had his fists punched into his waist and was surveying the interior of the summer room and the lawns outside. "What a beautiful place," he added.

"You would never lose a thing," said Sophie. "Your servants would know exactly where everything was. You would say, 'Bring me my pipe,' and it would be brought to you."

"There is that... I doubt I could ever bring myself to say such a thing to another 'uman. And I highly doubt I'll ever be in that type of a situation."

"What should I call you?"

"Inspector Penrose is good enough. Now, Miss King, we're nice and quiet here. I'd be interested to hear of anything else that has come to your attention."

"I can relate an interesting event. First of all, I would like to clear up a little matter. What have you been told about me? I seem to have an exemption from suspicion in the matter of the poisoning but surely, as a police officer, you would regard me as a potential suspect until my innocence could be established."

Penrose smiled broadly. "I think I'll have a pipe, if you don't mind." He took the article from his pocket. "You know, Miss King, it's few people as could grasp a situation as readily as you have done. It's even fewer who'd be bold enough to state the matter as plainly as you have. You should hear some of the things I have to listen to at times. It tries one's patience.

"I don't think I'm talking out of turn if I say that, as soon as you agreed to do some work for the government, you were put under observation."

"I was? By whom? You?"

"I can see why you were hired. No, it wasn't me personally doing the observing, of course. Lady Shelling has a very fine house in White Lyon Yard. Keeping well, is she?"

"Well, *really!* You've been checking up on me... Who asked you to do this?"

"Mr Drysdale, naturally. He and I work together off and on. We have similar interests, you might say. But it's a standard procedure to enquire into a person's background for the type of government work you're doing."

"Hmm. When I spoke to Mr Drysdale on the telephone, he gave me to understand that you might ask me to do some other work."

"Yes, that's right. It concerned Sir Reginald, but that's not needed now."

"Oh, that's a pity."

"Instead, would you be willing to help in keeping an eye on Mr Wright and watching for any of the household as seems to be acting out of character?"

"Yes, I can do that."

"That would be you and Miss McMahon."

"You know about Ada?"

"We saw you off at St Pancras. We already had her name, so it wasn't hard to see what was being done. Trustworthy, is she?"

"You tell me. You seem to know everything. I firmly believe she is."

"We'll say she is, then." Penrose smiled.

"I think there is a matter that needs to be settled first, Inspector Penrose. I would naturally aid the British government and the Metropolitan Police in any way I can and at any time. However, what you are asking of me is a little beyond what I would volunteer to do as a private person. I am also a woman of business. Bills do not pay themselves, unfortunately."

"Well, Miss King, we do make small payments of appreciation from time to time."

"If we are talking about sums of money, it would be best for you to be specific."

"Payments are made according to a scale. It's 18s 6d per day or part thereof."

"And how much do the men get paid?"

"The men? Well, they get more because they have families."

"How much do the single men get?"

"Ah, yes, well, they get two pounds and ninepence."

"Then that's the rate Miss McMahon and I will be paid."

"Both of you...? Excuse me for a moment. I'll have to give this some thought." Inspector Penrose got up and went over to the row of doors. Then he unlocked and opened one of them. He lit his pipe and stood in the entrance, puffing clouds of smoke outdoors. After a while, Sophie joined him.

He took his pipe out of his mouth and pointed with it. "This would be a great place to have some dogs."

"Yes, it would. Retrievers or setters, for me."

"Yes, them's good. That lawn is so flat, I'd love to see a greyhound tearing across it. That'd be a sight to see... Three pounds ten the pair of you the day. I have a budget and can get in hot water over this."

"Then we have a bargain, Inspector Penrose."

"Ah, that's good. What else has been going on in these parts?"

"Last night, about a quarter to eleven, a man crept past these doors right from one end to the other. He stopped at the first door to peer into this room."

"Did he now?"

"He peered in and I thought he saw me. Then, after some seconds, he worked his way along, crouching all the way. I lost him in the darkness between here and the house."

"You had the lights off... Let's go and have a look."

They went outside, and Sophie watched as he examined the ground. He found nothing on the flagstones. On the turf, by the side of the pavilion, he found several slight depressions. He looked up.

"Came from the gardens through that archway." Penrose turned around abruptly and headed in the opposite direction. Sophie was about to follow when he stopped at the corner. "You'd best stay where you are, Miss King. We should not be seen together."

"Of course, how stupid of me. But I'm fascinated by what you're doing."

"I'll tell you if I find anything."

Sophie went back inside and watched through a window as the Inspector scoured the ground, working his way up to the terrace. He then examined the terrace and more carefully around the entrances to the house and by the stone stairs which led down to the gravel paths. He came back and, because Sophie had the impression he was a slow-moving man, she was surprised when he walked so quickly at first and then broke into a brisk jog.

"What did you find?" asked Sophie.

"Rubber-soled shoes. Most impressions are indeterminate. Biggish chap and didn't smoke or stand about. He climbed the steps to the terrace this end and went down the ones at the far end. Walked on the gravel for a few paces because he had to and then took to running on the grass to be quiet. Has a long stride, so he was running at a fair clip. Curtains must have been drawn downstairs, otherwise you'd have continued to see him from here against the light from the house. This prowler has his wits about him. If you hadn't seen him, I'd not have found what I did find."

"This is what I don't understand," said Sophie. "He was not here to burgle the house, not with so many people present."

"Unlikely, but not impossible. One thing he's not, and that's a poacher. What exactly does that leave us?"

"Um, I suppose, a murderer or a spy."

"Not a spy. You know where they're to be found, don't you, miss?" Penrose smiled. Sophie thought he was joking, but he continued. "It doesn't make sense for one of them to be out here running about, not when they're already on the inside."

"Unless he was chasing or following someone."

"That's more in keeping with the evidence I've just seen of his activities. Let's go back inside."

They stood facing each other. "If that man knew the house was so full, which I believe he would, why would he be outside just then?" asked Sophie.

"That's a good question, that. Why indeed?"

"Especially if he happened to know the police were on the inside."

"Maybe he didn't. They're in disguise."

"No, they're not," laughed Sophie. "They stick out a mile."

"Let me tell you, they're not officers under my charge and it was his Lordship's idea to dress them up. Didn't want to alarm the guests so I've been given to understand. They should have been in uniform, to my mind."

"Of course they should. Perhaps the prowler spotted one of them through a window."

"Possible. No need for him to run, though."

"Perhaps he couldn't stop laughing and had to get away before someone heard him. Really, Inspector, his Lordship's wishes should have been overruled. Police uniforms are smart enough and I would have thought everyone would be glad of a police presence."

"I agree. Still, there were only the three, so it's not like anyone was tripping over them. One poor fellow had to shave his moustache off for the part."

"I saw him. But there were four of them, including the police matron."

"The matron I know about, but there were only three of them."

"No, you're wrong, Inspector. Miss McMahon has seen the matron, and I saw three footmen who knew very little of the duties or usual conduct of a footman."

"Describe them to me, please."

"The largest was in the hall. I think it might be he who had shaved off his moustache."

"It was a beautiful object. Good rugby player, too."

"I saw another fellow, almost as big as the one on the first floor, patrolling the corridors. I have seen that gentleman many times."

"I know that one. Those two were doing what they're supposed to be doing. You see, the Ambassador has a bodyguard with him and his Lordship felt the British should do something similar. Silly, really, but go on."

"There was a third man in the West corridor coming from the pavilion. I noticed him because he was running. Although servants are never to run in a house, I dismissed it as an exception because I thought he might be delivering an important message. However, he also had the look of a policeman about him. He was the smallest of the three and seemed active and purposeful."

"He's the odd man out. That's very interesting. As his Lordship's so busy, I'll have the butler bring all the male domestic staff to me. You'll take a look at them from behind a door while I interview them. If you see the fellow, you'll let on quietly and we'll find out all about him."

"Now it makes me think he might be the prowler."

"Can't put the cart before the horse, Miss King."

CHAPTER 14

— ✦ —

A CHANGE IN DIRECTION

Ada required convincing before agreeing to help the police. In the neighbourhood where she had grown up, to be a police informant was to be a squealer, tout, snout, snitch, rat, narker, or a snake in the grass. Ada used all of those terms in explaining how she would never be one of them - never, ever. So ingrained was her antipathy for such work that she did not realize she was actually being asked to look out for and then observe a murder suspect and potentially prevent someone from being murdered. When the obstacle to her understanding had been surmounted, Ada said,

"Well, I don't mind that, then, miss, now I've got it straight. But why does the Government pay so much more than the Rozzers? It's good money, I s'ppose, and I'm not complaining, but spying pays much better."

"Yes," said Sophie, smiling. "I wouldn't mind a spying job once or twice a month. I was thinking of having it painted on my sign."

"Oh, go on, miss, you're pulling my leg."

"A little, but wouldn't it be hilarious to have it say, 'Burgoyne's Secret Agency'?"

"That would be so funny... Yes, yes, and underneath it could say 'Superior Sleuths and Domestics.'"

"Well, isn't that just us? I have to go, Carmichael. I have a lot to learn from Inspector Penrose. I'm watching everything he says and does."

The rounding up and interviewing of the various men and lads employed on Lord Wicksworth's estate took a considerable time. For over an hour, a parade of grooms, chauffeurs, gardeners, farm-workers, footmen, a chef, and an odd-job man filed in and then filed out of the estate manager's office in an adjoining building. While they did this, Sophie watched through a gap in the door as Inspector Penrose, aided by Detective Sergeant Daniels, kept each individual a few moments, asking for name, age, occupation, and any other detail that seemed pertinent. Frequently, Penrose asked about the extra footmen that were in the house, but if the person did give a description, it was always of a known policeman.

The Inspector had begun the interviews with the two policemen pretending to be footmen. They both categorically stated there were just the two of them assigned to footman's duty and neither had seen the individual the Inspector was looking for but would keep an eye out for him.

Working down a list of names, the employees presented in all shapes, sizes, and ages from a wizened seventy-eight-year-old groom who had no thought of retiring as long as he could work, to a brawny fifteen-year-old lad who was good with a scythe. After twenty-seven interviews, there was no one left to see.

"Well, that's that, Daniels," said Penrose to the other detective, after finishing with the last employee. "We've seen the lot. You can carry on interviewing the staff now about Sir Reginald."

"Not one of them came close to the man I saw," said Sophie, after she emerged from a small adjoining room and Daniels had gone. "If they were a similar size, they were too old. There was one person missing, though. I've noticed a gardener both yesterday and today. He has a beard and stands about six feet tall or more so he couldn't be the running footman... He even has a limp and he's older. I would say he's a real gardener from Hampshire or West Sussex - definitely from a southern county, that I do know."

"You spoke to him, then? I'll make a note to ask the estate manager where that gardener has got to. Perhaps he went home and the manager's forgotten to mention him to us or put him on the list."

"What do you think, Inspector?"

"The footman and the gardener need to be found. It's likely the footman's an interloper. He seems a more likely suspect now. I wonder..."

"One of the visitors dressed up?" interjected Sophie.

"Very good. That'd put him at risk of being recognized, though."

"Yes, it might," said Sophie. "But just suppose, if our man had come in as a visitor and changed into the livery of a footman - he would be mistaken by other visitors for one of the servants, by the servants as one of the police, and by the police as one of the servants."

"He might have done just that. That indicates a deal of intelligence and a lot of daring. You have to be able to think you can get away with it to try it, but you have to be confident, too, so as not to lose your nerve. Why dress up today, though?"

"To get access to the kitchen, perhaps... Oh, no, that wouldn't work - he could only manage that while a meal was being served." Sophie paused for a moment. "I know. He was coming from the West Pavilion so we should get a guest list for that part of the building. Butler or Mrs Vaughan would have the names."

Penrose began pointing with the stem of his pipe. "You're thinking he was coming from his room or he had delivered a message to someone in that wing? Hmm, that bears looking into." He was about to walk away, but stopped. "Butler the butler - what be the chances of that? He must get tired of people's faces while they're a-grabbin' holt of the obvious."

"I'm sure he's used to the reaction. I must go and dress for dinner, Inspector. I'll take a look at the cards, but I'm not sure that I'll rearrange them again."

———✖———

Dinner, a buffet, was a lacklustre affair. That was how Lady Wicksworth saw it. She had made a vow that there would be no more military conferences at her house while she had breath in her body. Wickles would be hearing her elaborate upon the causes for her simple vow later on.

Although knowledge of the poisoning was confined to Lord Wicksworth and herself - she did not know that Miss King also had this knowledge - she could not help but feel that many were acting as though the food had been liberally sprinkled with strychnine and arsenic. In reality, many negotiators had spoiled their appetites with demands for sandwiches and snacks during the day. As a consequence, nearly all the diners seemed to be picking at their food. Several places at the tables were empty as the absentees wrestled with difficult negotiating points in other rooms. Sir Reginald stayed in his bedroom. Alfred Wright did not put in an appearance, either.

The conversation was less than scintillating. Mrs Makri looked bored because the interpreter, Captain Vassos, was not present and every British person merely smiled at her without speaking, which proved very tiring for both parties after a while. At Lady Wicksworth's end of the table was a senior diplomat from each country who, being determined not to say anything that could be construed as a commitment by the other, tacitly agreed to say nothing. Lady Wicksworth, therefore, had to do all the conversational heavy lifting. She ran through her list of 'safe subjects for the table' and both diplomats declined to say very much about their families, the weather, wines, automobiles, horses, dogs, gardens, music, theatre, and past and future notable social gatherings. Conversely, at the other end of the table and towards the end of the dinner, Lord Wicksworth, Ambassador Makri, and Admiral Pavlidis were loudly swapping golfing stories with great mirth.

The underlying reason for this joviality was that the delivery schedule and price of the submarines - their costs, spares, repairs, and training - had been agreed upon. The one sticking point was where to put the submarines when they were not in use. This issue did not trouble Lord Wicksworth or the Ambassador, but was of extreme importance for the representatives overseeing the finances of their respective nations. The Greeks were for modifying existing docks by extending their facilities at Salamis near Athens. The British thought there should also be auxiliary facilities in or near Thessaloniki in the north-east of the country. The Greeks liked the idea, but not the cost. The British loved the idea and wanted British firms to design and build the extra facilities. They could have settled the matter in five minutes and enjoyed a celebratory dinner as some others were already doing, but these financial johnnies did not feel that was what the negotiations were for. The announcement was to be made Sunday afternoon, and they thought they may as well continue negotiating up to the deadline just to show how difficult it had been to work out the final deal.

Sophie had discovered that one British diplomat had been a member of the Board of Trade, so she rearranged the seating once again to have him sit next to Victoria Redfern. While quickly moving the cards, she also discovered she would be seated opposite Karissa Raptis. She left that arrangement as she found it, thinking it might prove interesting.

During dinner, Sophie spoke to Karissa Raptis. The two women developed a slight rapport, although they only discussed neutral topics. Karissa mentioned her times in Greece and Britain while Sophie embroidered a personal history, loosely based on life in Havering-under-Lyme, but was careful to move her dear backwater over by several counties. She invented fictitious names for family and friends. Sophie thought she was doing quite well, but what perversely kept coming to mind was to ask Karissa about the perfume she had found in her bedroom. The subject was on the tip of Sophie's tongue a couple of times. To mention Karissa's perfume would imply it was too strong a scent, and that Sophie could smell it a broad table's width away would be tantamount to a personal observation of bad taste. Nevertheless, the image persisted of the interesting and foreign-looking scent bottle on Karissa's dressing table.

Sophie discovered the excitement of possessing knowledge one is supposed to keep secret while conversing with the very person from whom you are supposed to keep it. She found it far more exciting than keeping a birthday surprise a secret, which was the only type of espionage with which she had been familiar.

She did wonder how Karissa had become a spy and supposed her story might not be so very different from her own recruitment. Sophie further wondered whether she, herself, would ever cross the line and actively spy for her country in a foreign land. To conjecture who it was Miss Raptis and Paul Klest were working for would not get Sophie very far. She decided that it was a question for Archie to answer.

Between dinner and midnight, Sophie took frequent walks through the house and pavilions, hoping to observe some irregular or unusual activity among the guests and staff. At all times, Sophie knew where to find Alfred Wright. Most of the time, he was in meetings. On two occasions she had seen him in the company of others - once in the hall and once in the drawing-room. Wright seemed to be quite relaxed. In those around him, she could read nothing, although, if she put her mind to it, a sinister design could be imputed to each and every one of them. She found it odd that what she once took for ordinary conduct could now, simply because she was watching, be readily invested with evil intent - an odd look, an off-hand gesture, a whispered comment - these things had her embroidering sinister plans and scrutinizing the most inoffensive person for signs of malevolence.

Between her duties, Ada tried to glean what she could from the servants, but learned nothing new. Everyone appeared to be behaving normally. The only person who seemed to Ada to be thoroughly out of place and suspicious was the police matron. She told Sophie this when they met at ten-thirty in the summer room.

They both found it curious - they said as much - that, although the exchange of camera film had been successfully concluded, there was a distinct and annoying lack of immediate progress in their new mission. The latter had robbed a little glory from the former.

CHAPTER 15

— ⁑ —

CALAMITY

T he night was quiet and uneventful. Sunday morning produced a change in the household arrangements. Lady Wicksworth, accompanied by a small entourage, went to church, as did many of the servants. The negotiators went back to work at ten. Such guests as were superfluous to the negotiations and had a mind to do so also went to church. The village of Oxley had two places of worship - a small, ancient Church of England sanctuary and a Congregationalist chapel.

As Trefoil was next to Oxley, Sophie chose to walk. The grounds of Trefoil were so extensive that by the time she had left the estate, she was nearly halfway to the church.

Her return walk was peaceful, and Sophie took her time because it was so pleasant. Although not sunny, the clouds were bright and the air mild and sweet. The scents and colours of a declining summer and burgeoning autumn resided in the tall hedgerows. As she walked along the leafy lane, Sophie came to an open patch and surprised a small charm of goldfinches, feeding on dry stalks. They took off to fly about close by, uttering their distinctive tinkling twitter until she had passed.

Near the main gates, Lady Wicksworth's Crossley Manchester overtook her. The car slowed down to turn into the estate. Sophie was close enough to hear the chauffeur working the gears. By the time she had entered the beautiful wide drive, lined with magnificent elms, the car had sped away. Beneath the large, spreading trees on either side, the shaded grass was sparse, thinner and taller, requiring less frequent cutting. As she proceeded along the drive, her attention focussed on the superb façade of the house ahead. After a while, she looked to her right where the lawns led to screens of trees and, beyond them, to the rising land where lay the fields of the home farm. She noticed two female deer, browsing in the middle distance in front of some trees and undergrowth. They looked up suddenly, ears pert, but not in Sophie's direction. Then they slowly moved into the copse.

As she neared the house, Sophie decided to enter by the back, crossing the terrace to do so, to prolong her enjoyment of the countryside and Trefoil's park. As she began her detour around the West Pavilion, the sharp crack of a rifle came from some distant trees to the southwest. Birds took flight, and a crow cawed noisily.

She stopped and turned to look. The lawns were empty, and the only movement in the scene was the wheeling of the dispersing birds. She searched the trees whence the sound emanated and waited, expecting to see a deerstalker come out - even though hunting on Sunday was illegal. After some moments, Sophie saw the gardener to whom she had spoken, running athletically towards the place from which the shot had seemed to come. He did not run in a straight line but weaved, turning this way and that. He had a large revolver in his hand.

Sophie watched him progress quickly across the lawns, making use of the sparse cover available. She realized he, like a trained infantryman, was attacking an enemy position while endeavouring not to make himself an easy target. She stared, unable to take her eyes off the now diminishing figure, and unable to make sense of the unfolding scene.

The man went in amongst the trees and disappeared from view. In the quiet of the countryside, she detected the distant sound of a car's engine being started. Moments later, there followed two quick shots, then a long gap, followed by a third - all pistol shots this time. The quiet returned and everything looked as though nothing had happened, that there had never been any disturbance in the tranquil landscape. She remained where she was for a few moments, expecting the gardener to return to view. It occurred to her suddenly, forcibly, to go to the house and find out where the rifle bullet had gone and what had been the reaction there to all this shooting.

As soon as Sophie was on the gravel path and had a view of the back of the main building, she could tell something was grievously wrong. A small knot of men clustered on the terrace. Inspector Penrose was one of them; another was the largest policeman, dressed as a footman. Penrose finished speaking to him and the footman then went inside through a French window. The police matron came out, carrying a blanket. Sophie hurried. She had seen death before and could recognize in the attitudes of the people that death was present on the terrace. But who? She feared who it was, but she wanted to see - before the anonymity of a covering blanket made that person no longer one who was recently alive but turned him into a corpse, someone who had gone for good.

She rushed up the terrace stairs and, between the group of people, saw a huddled form in a grey lounge suit. It looked as though Alfred Wright had curled up and gone to sleep on the flagstones. As she approached, Inspector Penrose noticed her and came forward, screening the body as he did so.

"Nothing that you should see here, Miss King," he said quietly. There was kindness in his voice. "We need to get on with our work..."

She stopped. "It's Mr Wright, isn't it?"

"I'm afraid so."

"That poor, sad man," she said in a mournful voice as she remembered her brief conversation with him. "He was watching carp..." Sophie felt a sudden surge of anger. "Who did this?"

"We don't know anything for certain. Let us worry about all of that. Why don't you get some tea in the house? The other ladies are sure to be having some to calm their nerves."

"I don't want tea, Inspector. I want to find the murderer. I was in the drive when a rifle was fired... and then the gardener..."

"Miss King, I strongly advise you to say nothing to anyone. Do not mention the gardener to another soul. Do I make myself clear?" Penrose spoke quietly, but all kindness was now absent. It was an order.

"Yes, you do. I'll get some tea, then."

Sophie left the terrace the way she had come. Her emotions and thoughts were in a riotous muddle. Half of her wanted to sag and weep for Alfred Wright, a comparative stranger. The other half of her wanted to slay his killer. She wondered where Lord Wicksworth kept his guns. What came as a surprise to her was that, although her stomach turned over at the thought of this sudden loss of life and she felt very agitated, she did not feel afraid.

When the first rush of anger subsided, Sophie more coolly thought about what had happened. The gardener had to be a policeman or something similar - perhaps a secret agent. The Inspector had been adamant about not mentioning him; therefore, he knew him. The killer had fled by car; the gardener had gone after him and had fired his revolver. She wished she knew more and was determined to get everything she could from Inspector Penrose later on.

———⋈———

Initially, the household was stunned, subdued by the occurrence. But, because many of the men present were decisive, and some used to danger, the progress of the negotiations was barely interrupted. However, Wright's death helped bring a quicker conclusion to the discussions than there would otherwise have been.

Lord Wicksworth was worried about the ramifications of a killing on his property. He worried over the newspaper reports and the effect on the government. He worried about the Greeks and what they would think. He worried and so he made important phone calls.

Lady Wicksworth was told the news by Butler as she sat in her dressing room. She swallowed hard and went limp - dismay written on her face. For a moment she sat, lost, then she rallied.

"Butler, inform the staff that luncheon shall continue as planned. We shall observe a moment of silence beforehand, so please ensure that *everyone* in the house is present in the dining room. That includes all the Greeks."

"Yes, your Ladyship. I shall attend to it at once."

Penrose commandeered Lord Wicksworth's study. The peer was literally and figuratively put out, but had no choice in the matter since a guest in his house had been murdered. He had already telephoned several people and was now waiting for a particular reply. He instructed Penrose to inform him as soon as his important call was returned.

"'Scuse me," said the gardener to a policeman in the hall, "but the Scotland Yard man is a-wanting to talk to me. Know where he be?" He stood, hat in hand, revealing unruly blond hair.

"He's in his Lordship's study. Back of the hall, third door on the right. You'll have to wait your turn, though."

"Thank 'ee."

The gardener did not wait; he knocked on the door and opened it. Two men were in the room.

"Sorry to be a-botherin' you."

Penrose looked up and paused for a moment. "Daniels, you'd better start interviewing the Greeks. Find out who was with Wright the whole morning up until the time he was shot."

The gardener waited awkwardly and nervously until Detective Sergeant Daniels left the room. Then his attitude changed completely.

"Sorry we're meeting under such awful circumstances, my dear Penrose. I haven't seen you in a while. Keeping fit? And your family?" The man nonchalantly stepped forward to sit in a chair. His voice was pure public school.

"I am, sir, thanks. The missus and the little ones are all in good health. And yourself, sir?"

"Excellent. Drop the sir business, there's a good chap."

"I don't suppose you got him?" Penrose took out his notepad and began writing.

"Unfortunately, no. He was about five-ten, a solid fellow, wearing a green tweed jacket, brown trousers, and a flat, light-brown cap. The car was a black Morris Bullnose, registration number AC 438. There's a bullet hole somewhere in the rear right paintwork. He was headed for the Bedford Road so he could be going to Bedford or Northampton."

"That's a London registration number and a recent model. I'll get them on it."

"Yes, it was a self-starter, more's the pity. If he'd had to crank it, I'd have caught him."

Penrose placed a call to Scotland Yard and got through immediately. He described the man and the car.

"Well, we'll see what happens," said Penrose. "Car's probably stolen. Did you see the rifle?"

"No, I didn't. He was already at the car and had it stowed when I was close enough to have seen details. He was parked on a very short track and I saw him standing next to the car, but not the rifle. I got his number as the car moved. Then, I started firing. There were trees and bushes in the way, so I don't believe I touched him then. I got out on the road and tried a longish shot as he was going around a bend. I heard that one hit."

"That was a good effort on your part. What put you on to him?"

"I'm up here on private business, as you must realize, and I was keeping an eye on things. I came last Monday and, on Tuesday afternoon, I saw a johnny who looked out of place. He was not the same man as today's visitor. The Tuesday man was about fifty, with silvery, close-cropped hair, and wearing a morning suit - he has a good tailor. I didn't see his car, but he must have parked it by the gates. I took a squint through my field glasses. The man was either sizing up the back of the property or just taking a look out of innocent curiosity. He left a minute or two later, but I have no idea how long he'd been standing there. It made me think that any funny business while the Greeks are here would come via the back of the house. So I did night patrols but, to be honest, I thought I was wasting my time and just missing my beauty sleep. Still, the last thing we want is the Greek Ambassador to be assassinated. Instead, some other poor blighter takes a bullet... How do you like my outfit?"

"Very convincing, and you certainly look a lot older. If it hadn't been for the colour of your hair, I wouldn't have recognized you."

"I shall remember my old thatch is a give-away. Apologies if I smell a bit ripe, but I missed my weekly bath yesterday. Where was I? Night patrols, yes. So, I've been on the alert ever since. I spotted a man creeping through the grounds late Friday night, so I followed him. He met another person on the terrace just before eleven. I didn't see the inside person, but they opened the door and the two of them had a very brief talk. I tried to get close, but the door closed before I managed it. Then I legged it after the outside man only to lose him in the dark... I do hope this is not becoming a habit of mine. Very disheartening, don't you know?"

"You'll catch the next one, I reckon," said Penrose. "Were you wearing rubber-soled shoes Friday night?"

"I was, o most observant one. How did you manage to divine that?"

"There was a lot of creeping about on Friday. A person saw you peering into the summer room in the East Pavilion."

"Did she indeed? A lady standing with the lights off - so she spotted me. I assumed she was there because of an assignation and, being a gentleman, I removed myself quickly. I hope I didn't alarm her."

Penrose smiled to himself. "Not unduly... I'm here because of another matter - the poisoning of Sir Reginald Fawcett. Turns out it was Alfred Wright they were after. Sad to say, I've had a right slap in the face with this here shooting. What distance do you put it at?"

"Attempted poisoning, hmm, very interestin'. I'd say it was three hundred yards, give or take. On the way back, I found his shooting position - it was pretty obvious where he had lain prone to take his shot. I left a marker by it for the constables to find. He took the spent cartridge with him."

"Must be a good shot and probably used a scope. The bullet went straight through Wright's heart. Sounded like a .303 to me, although I was inside at the time."

"That's what I think. So we have a marksman in a stolen car who decides to take a potshot at Wright on a Sunday. Add that to an attempted poisoning and my question is, why?"

"Blowed if I know. To my mind, the poisoning was an amateur affair. You see, the arsenic hadn't dissolved properly in the wine, so most of it was collected at the bottom. Sir Reginald choked on it as he came near to draining his glass and spat most of it out. That type of handling of arsenic smacks of the amateur, it does. Now the shooting, on the other hand... that gentleman knows what he's about."

"Perhaps he's an adept in one and a neophyte in the other."

"Perhaps... I'm not partial to that idea. I would say there were two of them. One inside and one outside. The inside one could be an extra footman we apparently had running about the place and can't account for. We've only got a brief description of him and, as far as we know, only one person clapped eyes on him."

"Let us say there are two of them, then, and that does fit in neatly with the two on the terrace on Friday night. These two are determined that Wright should die this weekend. What is significant about Alfred Wright that two people wish him dead all of a sudden? His death would have no bearing on the negotiations."

"His older brother, Frank Wright, was murdered Wednesday evening. Pushed in front of an underground train, he was. They come from a wealthy family."

"Oh, my, my, we *are* in deep waters. I hadn't heard about that. Being a gardener here isolates one from the London news. Alfred Wright and Frank? Not Sir Ephraim Wright's sons?"

"They are, as it happens."

"Ah, I see. There's a less obvious purpose behind it all, then. I'm beginning to see the hand of an old friend of ours in this. Sir Ephraim has a bad heart, among other things and is in decline. Can't have more than a month or two left, so I've been told."

"You're up on the family, are you? Wouldn't happen to know about his will?"

"Inspector Penrose, that is not the kind of detail I usually get to hear. All I can say for certain is that there are five legitimate children and possibly two or three others, according to rumour. Naturally, only the five would inherit. Sir Ephraim is a very wealthy man. At a guess, I would say his estate is worth about three millions, perhaps more."

"That's helpful. Five children and two are now dead. I still need to see the details of his will. CID is working on the case, but it'll be awhile yet before they collect everything. They should be talking to Sir Ephraim today. Poor old fella, two bits of bad news like this might take him off. It's a certainty this case at Trefoil will be handed to them as well, so they can combine the two investigations."

"I've had dealings with Frobisher's so, if I think of anything, I'll let you know. Should I make myself scarce before the big wigs arrive? I can't see myself doing anything useful here now."

"Might as well. Did anyone see you?"

"Possibly from the house, but I didn't notice them. A young woman was coming around the side of the West Pavilion. She had a grandstand view of me running about like a lunatic. What will you say to her?"

"Oh, I'll think of something, don't you worry."

The telephone rang.

"That'll be for his Lordship," said the Inspector.

"Trefoil Hall, Penrose speaking... Yes, put him through." Unconsciously, Penrose straightened his tie.

"Good afternoon, Prime Minister... I'm Superintendent Penrose of Scotland Yard... His Lordship is not in the room, but I'll fetch him immediately. Please stay on the line."

Penrose put down the receiver and got up with alacrity to find Lord Wicksworth. As he passed by the other man, he paused to say quietly,

"If you want to tell him how to run the government, now's your chance."

The seated man smiled broadly. Once Penrose was gone, he drummed his fingers on the arm of the chair, then got up quickly to leave the room and the estate.

CHAPTER 16

— ◆ —

SOLO SLEUTHING

S ophie Burgoyne believed her alias, Phoebe King, was not doing what she was being paid to do. The riot of emotion she had experienced after the first shock of Alfred Wright's death had now passed or, at least, had settled to a controlled disquiet. She sincerely wanted to do something to avenge the man. Regarding her situation in another light, she realized that if she did not soon produce results, there would be no good reason for Inspector Penrose to hire her ever again. She looked at her wristwatch. Luncheon was in fifteen minutes, leaving her very little time.

On the dressing table lay her notepad. In her hand was her pencil. She stared at the blank page, willing ideas to come to mind. At first, there was nothing. No clear thought presented itself. Sophie reviewed each person she knew in the house. She considered conversations she had heard. Then she wrote names and put questions beside each of them.

Ambassador Makri, are you in political danger? Does someone wish to embarrass you?

Mrs Makri, do you understand English, despite the pretence of not doing so?

Josif Abazi, you have done very little to earn your pay. What more are you up to?

Greek bodyguard, where were you this morning?

Alfred Wright, why were you walking on the terrace? Who was with you?

Victoria Redfern, I like you, but I need convincing of your innocence. Were you involved in the poisoning or the murder? Why do you want to marry Archie?

Having made her list of names and questions, Sophie memorized them and could now craft a plan of action. She tore the page from her notepad. The newly minted spy noticed indentations from the impress of her pencil on the next sheet. She ripped it out, too, lit a match and set fire to the pages in the grate. When they had burned, she stirred the ashes with a poker. With three minutes to spare, she went downstairs.

As she went, she kept thinking of the murder of two brothers at two different places. She did not doubt that the two events were connected. Who was behind it all, though? Could it be a family member?

After the sombre lunch, Sophie could soon cross one person off her list. She had seen Mrs Makri rise from the main table, so Sophie hurriedly left the room by the servants' door. She rushed along the outside passage to intercept the Ambassador's wife while the interpreter was not present.

Sophie, wearing a look of consternation, had stepped into Mrs Makri's path to say in a low, alarmed voice,

"Mrs Makri, there is a giant *spider* on your shoulder."

"Ah, sorry, I have no Inglis." Mrs Makri concluded her statement with a smile.

Sophie then smiled at her. "Such a pity. I wanted to know if the rumour is true about your children being cross-eyed."

"No, sorry, I don't understand."

"I must apologize for having so rudely imposed upon you." Sophie held out her hand, and Mrs Makri shook it. They smiled politely at each other before parting.

———◁∅▷———

Before lunch, the police and medical professionals had arrived from Bedford, and by three, police officers arrived from London. A guard got to his post at the gate only minutes before a journalist tried to gain admittance to Trefoil. Bedfordshire's Chief Constable and County Coroner were informed of the death of Alfred Wright. Despite it being a Sunday, they both promptly put in an appearance.

With the house in an uproar, the negotiators felt the mounting urgency and made a sprint for the finish line. The deal was completed by 3:20 p.m. Diplomats communicated with their respective national leaders, followed by the closing meeting. Together, the Greeks and British crafted a joint communique suitable for the public.

During the meeting, the visitors, both Greek and British, were eyeing the clock with particular train times from their Bradshaws etched in their minds. They each calculated it might be possible to catch a train from Bedford to wherever it was they were going at around six o'clock. The timing depended on Lord Wicksworth and the length of his concluding speech. If he spoke for too long, an epidemic of polite despondency would afflict his audience. Nearly all of them wanted to avoid getting embroiled with the police.

For once, Lord Wicksworth was concise. However, at the very end of his speech, a police officer handed him a note. He read it and said,

"Finally, I have been requested by the Chief Constable to ask you to remain for a while to assist the police as they pursue their inquiries into today's tragedy. I am informed that the delay in your travel arrangements will be kept as brief as is humanly possible. Thank you so very much for your patience."

Instead of despondency, a thorough, grey gloom became palpable in the room as thoughts of missed trains to heavenly places elsewhere arose in the minds of the hearers. Although the Chief Constable had written the note, the inspiration for it was pure Penrose.

———✄———

"I can't believe this." Victoria Redfern's scowl made her look quite ferocious. She lay propped up against pillows on her bed. A discarded novel and an open box of Terry's chocolates lay on the coverlet beside her, while Ada was carefully packing up her clothes. "A brute killed poor Mr Wright and everyone's been avoiding the police like the plague until they're *asked* to stay. Of course, they're all falling over themselves now to be first in line to talk to them." She punctuated her speech by stabbing the air with a half-eaten chocolate. "And the Greeks have got in first. If I had known they were going to play it that way, I would have got in ahead of them."

"I'm very sorry to hear that, miss," said Ada. "Shall I see if I can get you in to see them?"

"What can you do, Nancy?"

"Well, my nan always used to say, you never know what's possible until you try. What I should do is book an appointment for you."

"What are you talking about? An appointment with the police?"

"It was Miss King's idea. She said that I should go to the police officer that does all the thinking and say you want an appointment because you have a train to catch. Then, if he says 'No', you can say I'm going to so and so and you can reach me there. Then he'll agree to the appointment because 'e won't want the bother of travelling. Miss King said that if you was to say it, he'd take advantage of your good nature and insist you stay and take your turn. But if I was to say it, as though it were coming from you, then it would sound like a hultimatum. Whoops, sorry, miss. Ultimatum. That way, you'll get your appointment. Where is it you're going tomorrow?"

"I'd like to leave tonight because I have to arrive in Manchester about lunchtime. Then I return to London in the late afternoon... Hold on a mo, Nancy. Do you really think you can swing it?"

"No 'arm in trying, is there?"

"Very well, then. Give it a go... Have a chocolate... Take two, but not the coffee ones. They're my favourite and I leave them till last."

Ada went to find Inspector Penrose. As Ada left the corridor to the West Pavilion, Sophie passed her, heading in the opposite direction. It looked as though they ignored one another, except for the virtually imperceptible hand signals passing between them.

Sophie knocked on Miss Redfern's door, opened it, and then called in a gentle voice,

"It's Miss King. May I disturb you for a moment?"

"Come in, you'll have to take me as you find me."

Sophie entered the room. Victoria was still lying on her bed.

"I am so distressed," said Sophie, "that this outrage occurred during your stay at Trefoil."

"It is extremely shocking, but it's not your fault." Victoria fixed her gaze on Sophie.

"You seem to take it well," said Sophie. "Many ladies would not."

"That's true, although you're dealing with it pretty well yourself."

"Going through the war trained one to expect bad news at any moment."

"It certainly did that. I lost a brother, two uncles, and so many workers from the mills. We have one mill from which five hundred and sixty-three men enlisted. Do you know how many of their names are on our Roll of Honour board in that mill? Two hundred and seven. We lost forty-four in one morning on the Somme. I can recite those names to you if you want me to."

"And I would like to hear them," said Sophie, who then sighed. "I come from a small village. We lost eighteen, and I knew each of them and their families. My brother was among them. He was only twenty-four."

"It gave little time for tears."

"Mr Wright's death has put me right back in that atmosphere where you cannot collapse, no matter how you feel."

Both women were quiet with their thoughts for a few moments.

"You came to see me."

"Yes. I've been turning over a matter in my mind. Why did you come here this weekend?"

"I was invited, of course... It was an odd request, but, as I'm in business, I could see the opportunity it presented. When I found out I was the only industry representative to be present, I didn't think so much of it. It has turned out all right in the end... You helped with that."

"It was little I did. I'm sure you would have made a success of it in any event. May I ask who it was who extended the invitation?"

"A gentleman by the name of Drysdale."

"Ah, yes, will you marry him?"

"What did you say?"

"Sorry for the abrupt nature of my question. I know Mr Drysdale; I'm a distant cousin of his. I know this is a personal matter, but I worry there will be trouble for you in the future."

"Miss King, your question and your thoughts seem quite impertinent, even if you are a distant cousin."

"They are, but I am concerned for both your happiness and his."

"I don't want to discuss the matter."

"I understand your opposition. We do not know each other, and etiquette requires we confine our conversation to polite, general topics. There is one matter, however, that needs to be aired. Allow me to state it as it strikes me. I cannot see how you will ever get on and be happy outside of the steel business. I am aware of your father's threat."

"Has Archie told you this?"

"Yes, but not willingly. It was because I pressured him about the arrangements for our working here. More to the point, it is you who have told me of the difficulties you will face in the future. I've seen your passion and drive. How can you set those aside and expect to be happy?"

Victoria looked quickly away without responding. Instead, she deliberated as she stared across the room. At last, she turned back to Sophie.

"It's me Da... He says Archie is after the money. But he isn't, because that's not in his nature. He's willing to marry me without a penny... Ha, but Archie's no fool and has seen what you've noticed. It worries him a lot, I can tell. Oh, the whole thing's a muddle. I love Archie and would give up everything for him but, I suppose you're right about my happiness... It's strange, being able to confide you... but I'd rather we spoke no more on this matter at the moment... There's more to this visit of yours, though. You've not come just about Archie and me. I'd say you're crossing me off a list of suspects... And I'd really like to know why you are here at Trefoil in the first place."

Sophie looked at her and, with an expression of half-smiling reluctance, gently shook her head.

"You know, one day, Phoebe King, I'll get it out of you why you're really here. And Archie, he needs to explain himself. He's convinced I take him for an ordinary civil servant, but he's not and neither are you... You had me fooled, though, with your domestic manager story. I won't ask questions now because I can see it's related to what's going on in the house. I suppose it's important business for the government and I shouldn't pry."

"Thank you for understanding. I'm sorry for my rudeness, but I had to clarify where you stood. Perhaps your father will come around eventually and I do hope he does. I thank you for your candour. You will be leaving tonight, so I'll say goodbye now and not trouble you again."

"Before you go, answer me one thing. Is Nancy in on this?"

"Miss Carmichael is an excellent and very discreet lady's maid who reports to me in all domestic matters. She is also loyal to you, as someone in her position should be, even though the arrangement is temporary. We are here because you are here, but you are not the reason for our being present."

"You could have just said 'yes'."

"I could have, but I thought the situation required clarification."

"Well, I suppose it did... It's funny, but the pair of you are like a double-act. I never can tell what either of you is going to say or do next... Goodbye, Phoebe, best of luck."

"Goodbye, Victoria, I wish you the same."

"Oh, hold on, take a chocolate. The coffee ones are the nicest to my mind."

Meanwhile, Ada had gone to the Estate Manager's office to speak to Inspector Penrose.

"Good afternoon, Inspector," said Ada. "Miss Redfern would like an appointment as soon as you're ready because she has to be in Manchester first thing in the morning."

"Thank you, Miss Carmichael. What time does she prefer?"

"I think in about half an hour."

"A quarter to six, then. Bring her here and Sergeant Daniels will take down her statement."

"Yes, Inspector... Er, if you don't mind my asking, any ideas who done it?"

"I do mind."

"Oh, I see. Makes you wonder what he was doing on the terrace at that particular time. I'd be looking into that, I would. I'll tell Miss Redfern you'll see her, then."

She gave a slight curtsey before leaving. When she had gone, Penrose smiled to himself and reached into his pocket for his pipe.

"How did it go, miss?" asked Ada. She spoke to Sophie alone in the summer room while Miss Redfern was being interviewed elsewhere by Daniels.

"It was very satisfactory. She's an intelligent woman and suspected we were up to something. Her suspicions about us had to be allayed. Miss Redfern understands we are both here on another matter. I doubt she'll mention it to you, but say nothing if she does."

"Do you think she had anything to do with the murder?"

"No, I don't. The police may find something, of course. Personally, I'm convinced she's not involved. And there was another matter that I can't yet mention; I'm far more settled in my mind about that, too."

"Oh, that's good. Now, you was asking about the Greek bodyguard. I got them talking in the servants' hall and, if betting was opened on likely suspects, he'd be the favourite. They've all taken against him for some reason. The truth is, he's 'ardly moved his great big self all day. He just follows the Ambassador like a puppy. So, I say, it couldn't 'ave been him outside with a rifle, now could it?"

"No, we can cross him off the list."

"What's next, miss?"

"Let me see... Oh, did you drop the hint about Alfred Wright being on the terrace?"

"I did an' all."

"What did the Inspector say?"

"I couldn't get 'im talking. It was just like you said, so I made the suggestion and left him to it."

"I'll follow up on that later. We have two people to investigate. Ambassador Makri - does he have any enemies in the house?"

"Blimey, that's an awkward one. I'll see what I can do, but I have me doubts I can help much there. Who knows anything about Greek politics, I ask you?"

"Keep off politics and find out if anyone has noticed an unpleasant atmosphere or nasty behaviour - that kind of thing."

"That won't be a problem because servants are always very sensitive to atmospheres."

"Josif Abazi is, of them all, the hardest to fathom. He's the spy, Paul Klest, yet it seems to me he's hardly done a thing. Karissa Raptis took all the risks in taking the photographs. Although Abazi may have contributed to stealing the plans by providing the cover of a marine engineer, he has done nothing that makes him appear like a master spy. He must be involved in something else. Naturally, I'm assuming it is to do with Mr Wright's death."

"Well, I'm not sure I can do anything about him, miss."

"I'm also having difficulty in deciding what to do. The presumption is that Klest is a clever, calculating man. If we make a move that looks obvious, he'll spot it and think we're on to him. We have to be careful."

"If you spill wine over him, I could take care of his suit; then he and I could have a chat."

"Wouldn't he see through that?"

"Well, why should he?"

"We may need to do something like that despite the risk. We'll hold your idea in reserve. What are the dinner arrangements for tonight?"

"They're all in a dither because the number of guests keeps changing. A couple have left already and more are likely to, but then there are the new arrivals, the Chief Constable and what 'ave you. There's plenty of food but, for the life of me, I would not go near the chef at the moment. If there was another murder, it would be in the kitchen."

"It is such an awful pity about Alfred Wright. I wonder, are you still enjoying yourself? I ask because I find I am despite the frightfulness of it all."

"Oh, I'm the exact same. I can hardly remember what I used to do with m'self before this weekend."

"We both seem to be cut out for this type of work. But we'd best be getting on."

"You go first. You know, Miss Redfern has the loveliest chocolates. She gave me a couple. Very, very nice they were."

"I also had one, and it was delicious. I've never tried Terry's before... Shall we get a box for the train journey home?"

"That is a lovely idea." Ada's face brightened at the suggestion.

CHAPTER 17

TAKEN UP A NOTCH

Among the crowd in the hall was Paul Klest, wearing a grey suit. Sophie decided it was not so dissimilar to the one worn by Alfred Wright. As the spy stood talking to a British diplomat, she studied Klest in profile - he was a heavier man than Wright and about an inch shorter. Close up, they had these dissimilarities; at a distance, Wright and Klest could be mistaken for one another.

Sophie could not imagine what the diplomat and the spy were discussing. Should either turn and notice her through the open door, they would assume she was writing at the desk. Instead, through sly glances, Sophie drew quick, full-length profiles of each man, accurate enough for them to be recognizable. Klest seemed preoccupied. She had now seen him a few times, and he smiled often, although she thought it a restrained, controlled type of smile. He had not laughed, but that did not mean he never laughed.

Knowing how British gentlemen behaved, Sophie knew the diplomat would discuss anything or everything except the murder of Alfred Wright. Klest might talk of it, but the diplomat, after having acknowledged the awfulness of the tragedy, would steer the conversation away to other matters. They might both treat the submarine negotiations the same way. Once concluded, there was little need for discussion. An engineer who spied for Germany during the war and a British diplomat - she found the combination a fascinating one. The diplomat would not be seen dead talking to Klest, not if he knew his history. Or was the diplomat colluding with Klest? It seemed unlikely. They would neither speak in public nor be seen together, if that were the case. The diplomat would also avoid Klest if both had prior knowledge of Wright's assassination.

Ambassador Makri, followed by his bodyguard, joined the two men. At least he was smiling. The diplomat perked up to return a perfunctory smile to the Ambassador. They spoke to one another. Klest now looked sullen. The joint conversation lasted for a few moments before the Ambassador moved away.

Sophie was deciding what to do next about Klest when she heard a disturbance. Its cause was out of her sight, but she assumed it emanated from near the front door. The commotion gave her the impression that some dignitary had arrived. Klest brightened to the point of smiling while looking towards the newcomers. The diplomat turned and also looked delighted. Their behaviour intrigued Sophie. Who was producing this electrifying effect? She got up, putting her notepad into a pocket. It was six o'clock on the dot by her wristwatch. Sophie had decided the matter needed investigation, so she left the room by a circuitous route to avoid Paul Klest.

He was famous because he was never out of the newspapers and newsreels. Almost everyone knew who he was. Lord Stokely was a handsome man. He was charismatic, too. Before his arrival, men had filled the hall, forcing conversation out of boredom while awaiting their turn to be interviewed by the police. The engine of police work may have been purring along, but its fuel, the disgruntled inhabitants of Trefoil, resigned itself to waiting. Sophie had seen this. Now, she would have said that some spontaneous, joyous festival had begun.

"Where is Lord Wicksworth?" Lord Stokely's fine, distinctive voice rose above everyone else's. He stood so that he showed to good advantage. His clothes were immaculate, and he presented a picture of all that was manly, upright, and honourable. He waited by the entrance for Wicksworth to come to him. Before her eyes, Sophie witnessed the formerly taciturn and reserved men, both British and Greek, transform into a willing and expectant audience for Lord Stokely. She witnessed a Royal Navy officer doing the work of a footman by hurrying away to find Lord Wicksworth. This brought rushing to her mind the conversation between Auntie Bessie and Lady Sedlescombe. Sophie, quite intrigued by what would happen next, wanted to stay to watch, but she hurried away, propelled by a sense of urgency, to find Inspector Penrose.

"Sergeant Daniels, I need to see Inspector Penrose at once. Is he free?"

"Only if it's very important, Miss King."

"Is he with someone?"

"No. He's thinking and doesn't want to be disturbed."

"I see. Well, when he's ceased thinking, please tell him Lord Stokely has arrived."

"Oh, lor, why's he here?" said Daniels in a tone of sinking, incredulous dismay.

The sergeant's few words conveyed volumes of information to Sophie. His honest outburst of complaint went far beyond the annoyance of another unwanted dignitary's arrival. Stokely was the last person Daniels wanted to see.

"I have to tell him he's here," said Daniels. He recovered his composure. "Follow me."

Daniels knocked on the door and entered without waiting for an answer. Sophie followed and saw Penrose, leaning back in his chair, remove a handkerchief from off his face.

"What is it?" asked the Inspector. He had not been asleep because he looked alert. "Oh, Miss King. Has something turned up?"

"Someone, Inspector. Lord Stokely has just arrived. He's in the hall with everybody dancing attendance upon him."

"Uh," said Penrose, who then puffed air out and shook his head. "Well, Daniels, make yourself scarce. Keep an eye on him, but stay out of sight if you can. Don't talk to anyone... Now, lad!" Sergeant Daniels left the room.

"Miss King, go up to your bedroom and lock yourself in. Don't come out. Keep well away from his entourage. There's bound to be a slack handful of them knocking about the place. You can trust them about as far as you can throw them. They mustn't know you're here. Miss McMahon... she's probably safe at present, but tell her to get Miss Redfern off the premises and onto a train as soon as possible. No, better still, you hop over to the West Pavilion and expedite matters. Then go to your room. Tell

Miss McMahon to meet you there as quickly as she can. I'll get a chauffeur to drive Miss Redfern to the station. What is it?"

"I'm astonished by your reaction."

"A certain mutual acquaintance didn't explain matters to you very thoroughly. At the time, I doubt it was necessary. Be that as it may, that man out there is an enemy to our country. Few people see it like that. I'm certain he's got his hand in this or I'll be... That's all for now, my dear. Off you go and look sharp."

"Do you really mean for me to lock myself in?"

"I believe I was plain enough, Miss King."

"Has something happened?" asked Miss Redfern.

"No, nothing has happened," said Sophie. "We wish you to catch your train on time."

Ada was packing the last things away. Sophie was helping her fold or rounding up stray articles.

"Hold on, you're bundling me out of the house. The train doesn't arrive until gone eight. I had hoped for a bite to eat before I left."

"I can get a sandwich from the kitchen while Miss Carmichael gets help to carry your luggage to the car."

"No. I'm staying here until you tell me what's going on. I'll leave tomorrow if I want." Her face took on a stubborn look.

"Lord Stokely has dropped in and it's thrown the household into disarray."

"What's he doing here?"

"Nobody seems to know, but his presence has dislocated everything."

"I've met Stokely. I think he's a time-waster... Thinks too much of himself. Judging by your looks, there's more to it than that."

Sophie stopped what she was doing to straighten up and look Victoria in the eye. She kept silent, signalling nothing.

"Right then, I best be going. Come to think of it, I'd like a sandwich. Chicken and thin-sliced tomato if they have it, beef with horseradish if they don't. Plenty of butter on the bread, please, and leave the crusts on."

"I'll get it at once." Sophie hurried from the room.

After she had gone, Miss Redfern said to Ada,

"She's quite the character. Do you like working with her?"

"Oh, yes, miss, I do. I trust her, you see. She always does right by people. It doesn't matter what their background is or nothing."

"That's good... Here, tuck this in your pocket. Don't spend it all in one shop."

Victoria gave Ada a sealed envelope.

"Oh, thank you very much, Miss Redfern. Your kindness is much appreciated. It's been a pleasure doing for you, that it has."

"I'll tell you straight, Nancy. I have a maid and I'm happy with her. If I hadn't a maid, I wouldn't think twice about offering you a job. I mean that. But I would have pumped you until you told me everything. I'd like to know what's been going on here."

"Thank you for the compliment, miss. I always try my hardest to give satisfaction. About the other thing. I gave my word I would never tell another living soul."

"Oh, did you...? Then it would have been right interesting."

Victoria looked out of the window. A curious smile spread across her face. Ada, while bending over to fasten a strap on a trunk, similarly smiled.

The hall became Lord Stokely's salon - only lacking comfortable chairs.

"My dear, dear Wicksworth." Stokely's well modulated voice carried through the hushed room. They shook hands. "I am so inexpressibly saddened by what has happened here. I was close by when I heard the news. Wicksworth, if there's anything I can do, name it."

"That's kind of you, Stokely..."

"It's nothing, don't mention it... Ah, your Excellency. It is such an honour to meet you again. And your excellent lady? Does she travel with you?"

"Lord Stokely, this is a pleasant surprise under these unfortunate circumstances. Yes, Mrs Makri accompanies me. She is quite distressed by the occurrence."

"I'm sure she is. Please tell her of my regret at not being able to meet her... Gentlemen, I have a photographer travelling with me. Shall we pose for a quick photograph or two? I'm sure your talks have reached a satisfactory conclusion."

A cameraman began setting up an Anschutz camera on its tripod.

"We should have something for posterity," said Ambassador Makri.

"Of course, of course," said Lord Wicksworth.

"Perhaps one of you both, shaking hands?" suggested Stokely. He smiled, laying a guiding hand on each man's shoulder.

The cameraman adjusted his camera, composed his subjects, and took several photographs, accompanied by the smell and slight thump of ignited flash powder. The photograph to appear on the front page of the next morning's National Chronicle, a newspaper owned by Stokely, was of the Ambassador and Lord Wicksworth shaking hands while Lord Stokely stood in the centre behind them. It gave the powerful impression that Stokely had overseen and moderated the talks between Britain and Greece. The Chronicle scooped all the other papers on this story. However, relegated to a small article on page two was the report of Alfred Wright's demise. It failed to mention the circumstances of the event occurring at Trefoil, leaving one with the impression that the untimely death had been as a result of an accident.

CHAPTER 18

— ∙ —

PERSPECTIVES

Sophie and Ada locked themselves in Sophie's room after having successfully seen Miss Redfern off to the station.

"Why lock the door?" asked Ada.

"Inspector Penrose was quite adamant that we should. He mistrusts Lord Stokely and his staff. I presume it's in connection with our work here. If our identities are compromised and we're employed again elsewhere, it could land us in trouble."

"Oh, I see... Would Lord Stokely's men snoop about the house with everybody about?"

"I wouldn't have thought so. The Inspector is more familiar with him than we are."

"If they try our door, we don't want them coming in 'ere with us in it, do we, miss?"

"No. I believe that would be worse than if we went about our business openly."

"I'll fix the lock so they can't get in."

"That's a good idea. I'd like to watch."

They approached the door.

"Right, so look here, miss. All the gubbins are on our side. We've left the key in the lock. He'll try the handle first and find the door locked. He'll look through the keyhole for the key. If it's how it is now, he'd know someone was in the room and had locked the door from the inside. We don't want to give them that much satisfaction. Excuse me, miss."

From somewhere under her dress, Ada produced a small roll of canvas.

"Tools of the trade... Not my trade, though."

Ada knelt down to untie and unroll the canvas. A row of curi-ous-looking tools tucked into pockets was revealed.

"Would you like a cushion for your knees?" asked Sophie.

"That would be a 'elp, thank you."

While Sophie brought over a cushion, Ada selected a screw-driver from the roll. Once settled, she unscrewed the lock cover and removed it.

"Not much to it, is there? That's the deadbolt. Door's locked at the moment. If he uses a skeleton, it will move that lever there and the bolt will move to its unlocked position. So, all I do is jam this little strip of metal... against the lever... like so." Ada tried to unlock it, using the key gently and then forcefully. "No, that's not going anywhere. I'll put the cover back on. When he looks, he'll find the door was locked from the outside. When he tries to pick it, 'e'll reckon he's losing his touch. Serves 'im right."

"That's ingenious. We should keep out of his line of vision from the keyhole. I'll clear away anything that makes the room look occupied."

"Good idea."

They sat in chairs on either side of the door. Anyone spying through the keyhole would conclude the room was unoccupied. The third floor was quiet while they whispered together. Once, someone entered a nearby room, doing so with a natural amount of noise. At seven-thirty - Sophie could barely make out the time on her wristwatch - a door opened along the hall. There followed a murmuring of voices, and the sound of the door shutting. Another nearer door opened. Within ten silent seconds, it closed again.

Sophie and Ada stared at one another in near-darkness. They held their breath, their gaze riveted upon the door handle. Almost imperceptibly in the gloom, it moved. It moved again, followed by stillness. A few moments later, they heard a key being inserted into the lock. Then there came some muffled scratching sounds, followed by the handle wiggling. The visitor tried the handle again. He gave a sharp thump near the door handle and repeated the whole process. It became quiet after that. They heard the door opposite being opened and closed again within a few seconds. Further away, a door opened and closed. The floor returned to silence.

"He's looking for someone," said Sophie. "He didn't have time to search those rooms for an object."

"Us, do you think?" asked Ada.

"It's possible... Me, perhaps, if they've discovered I switched the film cassette."

"Don't see how they could, miss."

"I don't, either. If it isn't us, it must be... well, it has to be the running footman, I suppose. He's the only missing person. It's dinner now and someone in Stokely's party is touring the rooms hunting for the footman. If that assumption is correct, it connects Stokely with the attacks against Alfred Wright. But why? Why would he do such a thing?"

"That's beyond me. What I still don't understand is how his nibs guessed the rooms would be searched... It was funny, though, wasn't it?"

"Yes, I found it rather thrilling. We had the enemy at the door and you thwarted him. It was a gratifying moment."

"Yes, it was, an' all. Oh, by the way, I owe you £2 10s. Miss Redfern very kindly gave me a fiver. That's the biggest tip I've ever 'ad. Such a nice lady. She might be a bit tricky in the future, but very, very nice."

"Oh, no. Your offer is generous, but you have earned that money."

"In a way, yes, I did. But so did you. You helped, and you got me the job and, God bless you, you've split everything down the middle like a saint. I don't know anybody who does that. So, fair's fair; I owe you £2 10s and you can't possibly refuse me."

"Ah, as you put it so kindly, I accept. Thank you. And I'm glad Miss Redfern appreciated your work for her."

"That's settled. Only I've to break the note first. How long do we wait now?"

"That must be it for this evening's entertainment. We won't know when they leave. I should imagine the Inspector will tell us when they've gone."

"If 'e remembers. So what's the matter with Lord Stokely?"

"A few weeks ago, I would have said there was nothing wrong with him. People I respect, and now Inspector Penrose and

Sergeant Daniels, have given me to understand that Stokely is plotting something on a large scale. It seems he wants to control the country. We should consider him an enemy of the state. We are at war with him."

"Blimey, and him so famous and popular. But what's he done?"

"I don't really know - we'll have to ask the Inspector. But we do know that he tried to break into my room. At least, he sent someone to do so. That is a concrete fact. What person of rank does such a thing?"

"Well, miss, I've been told stories, but they was mostly domestic troubles, if you take my meaning. But spying and sneaking about? Never, not once."

"Oh, dear. Does that sort of thing happen often?"

"More than it should. Now and again, a gentleman will forget 'isself. Often it's because of the drink. I had to warn one off with a hat-pin. I told him, if he put a hand on me he'd feel how sharp the pin was, and that I'd fly at 'im like a wildcat, and 'e could forget about ever 'aving children. He lost interest soon enough."

"I'm astonished."

"Once they go for your backside or whatever, you 'ave to turn on 'em right away. Then they know to leave you alone."

"Well, of course, you do. What do you say to them?"

"You'll have to excuse me first, miss." Ada spoke in an intense whisper. "I shout 'Keep your bloody hands to yourself or I'll go straight to the Master!' Or Mistress - it depends who 'as the biggest say in the house, you see. That usually works. Once it was the Master hisself so I left the 'ouse and never went back.

"Yes, I've had it happen four or five times and that's because I usually work temporary, which means I've been in a lot of houses and worked at a lot of big dinners and what 'ave you. But most gentlemen are gentlemen."

"I'm so sorry you've been subjected to such appalling behaviour. Among the women I know, the matrons caution the younger ones not to remain alone in a room with certain gentlemen. It used to be any man not so long ago, but that's changed. Those gentlemen, once identified, can be avoided. We all know who they are, so we circumvent the unpleasant circumstance of unwanted attention. However, I had an altercation once."

"Did you?"

"It was while I was in the Land Army. Out of the blue, an officer started saying the most outrageous things. He began pawing at me. I punched his nose."

"Well, I never."

"His nose was bleeding profusely when I left the room. I don't think I broke it, though. Doing physical work in the field had made me quite strong and, while growing up, I had often watched my older brothers boxing, which gave me a rough idea of what to do. I hit him harder than I meant to."

"I wouldn't worry about that. Good for you. It's one thing if you 'ave an understanding with a gentleman and he gets a bit carried away, but it's another thing entirely when someone in the house reckons they can make themselves free with your person."

"Hmm. Returning to Stokely, I've been told he's vindictive to the point of killing a former business partner, but I'm not sure how reliable that information might be. What is certain is his hunger for position and power."

"I never knew that."

"He's come here with an ulterior motive. It is not the done thing to turn up with a party of people on a Sunday, especially near dinner. I wonder why he did?"

"Maybe he was hungry... He's very good looking... If he was ugly, I'd 'ave no trouble believing he was wicked. Because he looks so nice, I dunno what to say. Why is that?"

"That's an old, old problem. We're easily distracted and when that happens, we think less critically about people's motives. The best looking apple might contain a worm and one never knows that unless one inspects the apple carefully."

"You know what's worse than finding a worm in an apple...? Finding half a worm."

"Oh, Ada, really... My goodness! I said your name!"

"Good job it's just the two of us, miss. But I had a similar moment yesterday. Miss Redfern called out 'Nancy', and I thought to myself, 'Who's she talking to?' I assumed she was having a turn. Then I remembered it was me who's Nancy. Brought me up right short, that did."

There came a soft knock on the door. The women looked at each other as well as they could in the nearly complete darkness. Sophie got up and spoke in a fairly accurate Scottish accent.

"Who is it? I dinna want to be disturbed."

"It's Sergeant Daniels from Scotland Yard." His voice was quiet and careful. "I might have the wrong room, though."

"No, you don't," said Sophie in her usual voice. "Please be patient. We need to fiddle with the lock."

When they had switched the light on and opened the door, Sergeant Daniels informed them that Lord Stokely and his party had departed from Trefoil. He also mentioned that Inspector Penrose wanted to see Miss King.

On her way to meet Penrose, she found herself thinking about the man digging potatoes. It suddenly occurred to her that he must be the one who Archie had said would get her out of any difficulties had they arisen. It had certainly been he who had given chase to the sniper. And, she concluded, it would have been to him that the task would fall of preventing theft of the submarine plans, had she failed in her mission to switch the cassette or destroy the film. Her step quickened, and she smiled. Spying was proving to be much more dangerous and much more exciting than she had anticipated.

"Please, take a seat, Miss King," said Penrose. "You probably have a few questions."

"It's more like a dozen," said Sophie, as she and Penrose sat down.

"Likely you do."

"I'll give you my report first."

"Very good." Penrose looked at her quizzically and then moved his notepad so that it was in front of him.

"Mrs Makri does not speak English. I verified this. It means that she could not have been the one to persuade Mr Wright to walk on the terrace because he spoke no Greek."

"Good," said Penrose, as he made notes. "I specifically told Wright to keep off the terrace, but that's where we found him. Before you go any further, Paul Klest and Miss Raptis were the last to see him alive. They were working in the morning room while Wright was taking his stroll on the terrace. It was outside the ballroom that the sniper got him."

"So they must have tricked him somehow. That means they were here for two reasons."

"Looks that way. We've no proof they did anything and their statements tally perfectly. It's their word against nobody's. Both of them are very cool customers."

"Ha. Klest was wearing a grey lounge suit similar to Mr Wright's. I had wondered if the rifleman made a mistake and shot the wrong man?"

"That's possible as a theory, but it's unlikely. Why kill a spy at a high-level conference? They're normally found dead in alleyways or in a rooming house with the gas on."

"Oh, how sordid. So, to continue, Ambassador Makri might have political enemies, but I'm unable to inquire into that."

"You mean the assassination attempt was to embarrass him somehow?"

"That, or blackmail him, or frighten him. There seem to be several possibilities along those lines."

"Again, that's a theory that could have some legs, but it's also unlikely. Too heavy-handed and... oblique, to my mind. I'm not partial to it."

"Oh. The Greek bodyguard. According to the servants, he didn't leave the Ambassador. Therefore, he could not have been outside with a rifle."

"That's excellent. We haven't been able to speak to him yet."

"Are you in charge of the case?"

"Oh, no. That's all for the local force and the two CID men from London. They're welcome to it, although they'll keep me up to date on their progress. It's this way, Miss King. I'm what you might call a floater. I stay out of everyone's way and let them do their jobs. They keep me fed with information and I guide them a bit once in a while. I only came up because of Sir Reginald, although I had a prior interest in the Wright family. Sir Reginald hasn't sworn out a complaint because he doesn't want to make a fuss. He prefers to call it an accident. There you are... I'm just a busybody, after all." Penrose smiled to himself.

"Well, I'm glad you're here," said Sophie. "The investigation would be going nowhere if you weren't."

"That's kind of you to say. What else have you got?"

"One more item. Miss Redfern; I consider her to be above suspicion. I've spoken to her extensively and reviewed her conduct while at Trefoil and at no time has she evidenced a suspicious interest in Alfred Wright or Sir Reginald. She does not hold extreme views. In fact, I like her."

Inspector Penrose emitted a rich, shaking laugh that mildly affected his whole body. "That's very good. Do you know why, Miss King? I'll tell you. It's because, without regard to station or wealth, you suspected Miss Redfern might be complicit in the murder. As she's your excuse for being here, you could have overlooked her. There's many a seasoned detective who might have done just that."

"Oh, well." Sophie was a little embarrassed by the expansive compliment.

"You also made a terrible mistake. One you shall never repeat."

"Oh, did I? What was it?"

"You had a private telephone conversation with the man you're working for. That was none of my business. I stayed and listened. I asked if you wanted me to leave the room. You didn't take me up on my offer. Even if I hadn't spoken, you should have said the call was private and insisted I leave. When on the job, you must stay in character all the time, no matter what. It's your upbringing getting in the way."

"Yes, I suppose it is. You're right. I shan't do it again."

"Stokely's entered the picture. That makes life a lot more difficult. How do you know I don't work for him?"

Sophie paused for a moment. "Because you gave the code word."

"I did. How do you *know* I don't work for him? There's a difference."

"I would say your reaction, and that of Sergeant Daniel's, to the news of his arrival was so thoroughly genuine, I could not be mistaken in your antipathy for the man."

"That's better. Let's say he hadn't arrived. You wouldn't have seen my reaction. In any event, that occurred later. At the time of your allowing me to listen in on your call, you didn't have that assurance. Do you see what I'm saying? Trust no one. Even people you trust now might switch allegiance in the future. You cannot

162

assume anyone is trustworthy unless you have vetted them and you continue to do so regularly. If you have doubts about the spy business, leave now. Once you're in, life will never be the same again."

"I'm in, Inspector Penrose."

"Ho, that's quick."

"I can see this type of work could be difficult and dangerous, but I'll take the risk. Now, tell me about Stokely."

"In a word, he'd probably like to rule the world. To do that, he needs to rule Britain first. To get there, he'll tear down the government and the nation's institutions if he has to. Stokely wants money and power; he also wants a following, and heaven help those who stand in his way. He'll do anything to achieve his ends."

"Why not arrest him?"

"He's untouchable at present. Anything that happens as shouldn't is carried out by agents of his agents. Through them, he uses money, blackmail, and threats of violence to achieve his objectives. If anyone crosses him, their careers are finished. A few have disappeared."

"Would that include a Jamaican sugar plantation owner?"

"You know about that? That was years ago, but, yes, it was him behind it. In fact, it was that case which first brought him to our attention. I say 'our', meaning the few people who aren't bedazzled by the man."

"So it's just the people in the Special Branch who are monitoring him?"

"You'll need to ask them. I have some dealings with Special Branch but, as I've said, I'm a floater. Daniels works for me permanent and I can bring in others if needs be, but I'm not attached to any department."

"I see. I suppose, Stokely arriving here out of the blue means he believes himself to be secure. My guess is that, even if he ordered the killing, he can come here safely, knowing the crime does not trace back to him."

"That's right. He thinks differently. You or I would stay as far away as possible. Not 'ee... I'd like to know why he came. It was not only for the publicity photographs. I've an idea a plan backfired, and it needed his personal touch to move it forward."

"You could be right," said Sophie. "It puzzled me why you had us lock ourselves in our room. Do you know somebody tried the lock on my door?"

"Yes. It was Klest. Daniels followed him and saw what he was about."

"Klest...? Yes, that makes sense now. He was definitely looking for someone rather than an item because he spent no time searching the rooms. I'm sure he was seeking the missing footman."

"That's an excellent idea. I'm partial to it because I had the same thought. Here's how I view the thing. Stokely has taken against Sir Ephraim Wright. The old man's ailing and Stokely decides a couple of Wright's children should die before their father. There's definitely a reason behind that, but I don't know what it is.

"On Wednesday, someone kills Frank Wright, the eldest son. It was a daring murder and I would say carefully planned. Mr Frank had been followed and his daily habits were observed beforehand. That, and the way it was carried out, smacks of professionalism.

"On Friday, the first attempt is made on Alfred Wright, but, by a sheer fluke, Sir Reginald receives the poison. Before dinner, the footman puts poison in Alfred Wright's glass according to the place names. He did this right after Butler inspected the table, but before you switched the place names around. I can't see it happening another way. The glass with poison was on the table before anyone sat down to dinner. Once they're all settled, the footman goes around the table, pouring wine for guests and ensuring Sir Reginald is one of them. Only he believes him to be Alfred Wright. That means he didn't know Mr Alfred by sight. I don't doubt our man did this because another servant might have seen the white powder in the glass."

"Inspector Penrose, I can't tell you how relieved I am that Sir Reginald suffered no ill effects because of what I did."

"Don't you worry. Sir Reginald has recovered and can add an interesting story to his repertoire. I've said this to others. It was a good job you changed the places around, for it saved Alfred Wright's life. Him being killed later doesn't bear upon it. I'll also say this: had the poisoning been successful, we'd never have closed the case. Nothing to go on, you see. The footman would have escaped on Friday and we'd never have known to connect him to the poisoning. As it is, you saw him on the Saturday and that gives us a sporting chance."

"That's kind of you to say... I interrupted your narrative, please continue."

"Sir Reginald takes ill. Our footman poisons the wrong man and panics. That puts him in a lather. He checks up on Sir Reginald yesterday, which is when you see him. You'll be happy to hear one of the Greek gentlemen observed the same footman about the same time you did. Only found that out an hour ago.

"Our footman disappears. He's an amateur, and he's jumpy. If we say Stokely's also involved, then perhaps the footman's scared because he's now in trouble of a different kind. Just conjecture at this point. So he hides somewhere.

"Going back to Friday night. We had a trespasser about the grounds, did we not, Miss King?"

"We most certainly did."

"As it happens, the 'trespasser' you saw had a right to be there because he was actually following a real prowler. A rendezvous took place on the terrace about eleven o'clock. The prowler met a person from inside the house. Who would you say that was?"

"Klest?"

"Right. I also think that the real prowler might be the man with the rifle. He and Klest arranged the rendezvous in advance of this weekend as a backup plan in case the poisoning failed. Klest and his paymaster obviously plan for all contingencies. Now, why would they risk such an amateurish first attempt? Why even try such a thing at, of all places, a high-level, crucial diplomatic meeting? I'll tell you why. Stokely. Again, we wouldn't dream of doing such things, but he would. He's obviously, for some as yet unknown reason, got a bee in his bonnet about the Wrights. For another unknown reason, he employs an amateur poisoner.

"So, I ask myself, what does he get out of all of this? He embarrasses the government, which is something he enjoys. He successfully removes another Wright from the world. As for the footman who bungled his mission, all I can think is that Stokely wants a hold over him. He gets him to commit a murder or attempt it, then he has him in the palm of his hand.

"It's Sunday and poor Alfred Wright gets shot. He was always going to be killed. I can't fit the similar grey suits in anywhere unless Paul Klest somehow used the device to get Alfred Wright onto the terrace. It might have been a coincidence. What else happens on Sunday? Lo-and-behold, the footman has gone missing, then Stokely arrives, and Klest goes looking for someone - the scampering footman, we believe. That means they expected to find him still in the house."

"It looks like they've lost him," said Sophie. "I have a question. You talk of a single paymaster, yet Klest was here for two reasons..."

"Don't compromise your mission... You were originally here for the Foreign Office, weren't you? But continue being careful what you say."

"Are there two paymasters or one?"

"Take a wild guess."

"Oh, dear me... You mean Stokely is behind the other thing, too."

Penrose smiled. The warmth of it was for Sophie's guess, not for the substance of her answer. He continued,

"And it seems it's vitally important for them to find the footman. Either there'll be another death or the footman is critical to Stokely's plans. I should imagine Klest had some very hard words spoken to him for having lost control of the situation."

"When Stokely arrived," said Sophie, "I saw Klest uncharacteristically beaming at him as though he had seen a vision. It was extraordinary. Another thing that has puzzled me, Inspector, is why did you think they would search the rooms?"

"Stokely's agents are a tricky lot - determined and resourceful. It was possible they'd ask awkward questions, and I didn't want them taking an interest in you and Miss Carmichael. I wanted you out of their way and it meant Miss Redfern had to go home."

"That makes sense. When Klest tried my door, he could not see the key in the lock because we'd removed it. With the key gone, Klest could have picked the lock and found us."

"Indeed, he would have. How did you get around that?"

"You can thank Miss Carmichael for some quick thinking there. We jammed the lock and took the key away. He could not get in."

"Very resourceful of you both… I'm going to recommend your name to someone. I've an idea you could assist him with domestic staff. Are you available for a few days?"

"I can certainly fit it in. What is this person's name?"

"I won't know for certain until I get back to the Yard. They might reassign the case with everything that's happened. The detective will look at certain aspects - to whit, solving the murders. He will not be privy to everything we've been discussing. Can you keep the Stokely and Wright matters separate?"

"I fully realize that I am only at liberty to divulge information pertaining to the detective's own case and circumstances. That is all he shall receive from me." Sophie finished with a prim smile on her face.

Inspector Penrose began laughing again. "That's very good, that is. That's Mr Drysdale's Foreign Office way of speaking to a tittle."

CHAPTER 19

—— ∘ ——

AT THE FOREIGN OFFICE

On the train back to London early Monday morning, Sophie forsook first class to travel with Ada in a third-class carriage. They sat on a bench seat with an open box of chocolates between them.

"Inspector Penrose said there might be more work for us in the next two weeks. He's going to suggest our services to a CID detective who's working on the Wright case. Are you interested?"

"I should say so! I want to know the end of all these doings," replied Ada excitedly.

"So do I. You should understand there are some risks. The next time someone tries our door handle, they might mean to do us harm."

"I'll have a few hat-pins with me at the ready, then."

Sophie laughed. "That's a good idea. We will take steps to defend ourselves if we have to. A life preserver might be useful. Or is it called a blackjack?"

"Oh, a cosh. Yes, miss, those would be right handy. You can buy 'em, but you can make one cheap out of a bit of garden hose and sand."

"We should do it properly and buy them... How do you make one?"

"You cut off a foot of 'ose or a bit less. Tie one end with wire so it's pinched flat. Wrap it so nothin' comes out the end. Pour sand in the other 'ole, almost to the top. Then pop a bit of lead in the end, tie it off, and wrap it. There, Bob's your uncle, you have yourself a cosh."

"That's quite simple, really. Where did you learn that?"

"My dad always carries one. Where we live, the Old Bill only arrives to pick up the pieces after it's all over. Specially at night. I mean, you have to protect yourself, don't you?"

"Yes. I wonder if the police would let us carry a revolver?"

"Godfather's, miss, that's goin' it a bit."

"Oh, it was just an idea. You see, with a revolver, you could shoot them or hit them with it as the circumstances warranted. It just seems more convenient to me. We'll purchase suitable blackjacks, because I don't like the thought of sand leaking everywhere. We have friends in Christchurch. They have a lovely place and we always go swimming in the sea. It seems for a week afterwards, I am forever shaking sand out of things."

"I know what you mean. We'd go down to Southend for the day and bring back half the beach."

"Half the beach," repeated Sophie, looking out of the window. "Half the beach or 'Alf the beach?" She was silent for a moment. "It's rude of me to ask, and you needn't say anything..."

"You mean my haitches? You've lasted about the longest of anyone before asking."

The train rattled. Ada spoke.

"January this year, my friend and me got given tickets to the Aldwych Theatre. We was right up the back in the upper circle. Could have done with them binoculars, really. It was beautiful, though. I loved the theatre, and the turnout was so lovely. All kinds of gentry were there. Oh glitterin', it was. For once, I felt like I was a part of it. Though me and Winnie was dressed nice, we was nothing like some of the ladies.

"We get in our seats and we're all a-tremble with excitement, waitin' for the play to begin. That lovely actor, C. Aubrey Smith, was the leading man - he's the cricketer an' all. And Mrs Patrick Campbell was the leading lady. I'd 'ave said she was too old for the part, but once she was on stage, it didn't matter. Lovely they were. I 'ave nothing against them. I 'ave nothing against the theatre management because it was all so beautiful. It's the playwright I want to have a word with and I will one of these days.

"Pyg-bloody-malion. I'd like to take a blackjack to that 'enry 'iggins, I would. Henry Higgins. First of all, why does George bloody Bernard Shaw call her Doolittle? Doolittle! I bet the poor girl was up at five in the morning picking them violets. You can't do that year-round, neither. And she 'as to stand out in all weathers trying to flog 'em... In competition with others, I might add. 'E missed that bit. It's barely above begging, selling flowers like she was, but that poor girl is doing what she can to keep off the streets. Doolittle, I ask you.

"All he does, that Higgins, is run her down and run her ragged like a slave or plaything. I call 'is behaviour disgusting, that I do. Well, I won't go on but what 'appens at the end? Nothin', that's what. Disgraceful, I call it. Does he behave any better at the end than he does at the beginning? No, 'e does not. Why would she want to 'ang round such a surly, pompous old geezer as that? He doesn't even know the meaning of the word tenderness.

"Anyway, enough about the play. I don't blame the actors, no, I don't. No, I blame 'im, Mr Shaw, with his mug in the papers all the time. I'd like to pull that beard of 'is. I'll tell you why, seeing as you asked.

"I came away from the Aldwych crushed. I'd spent an evening listening to people laughing at the way I speak. That's not nice. I went out for a lovely night and I came back in tears. So I decided I would try to improve my accent, I did an' all.

"Well, I started on me haitches. But I can't do it! I 'ave to think to haspirate me haitches, otherwise they've gone somewhere. Aspirate, I mean. A chatterbox like me can't remember 'er haitches all the time. And now I'm stuck like a good 'un. I can't drop 'em anymore without feeling bad about it and I can't say me haitches like I want to - they always come out funny. If it were just me, it wouldn't be so bad. I've met two other girls with the same affliction. My tears have dried but I'm so angry with him. It's all 'is fault. His fault."

"Pygmalion is based on a Greek myth," said Sophie.

"I know that, miss."

"I doubt very much that Mr Shaw ever considered the possibility that people with cockney accents would attend his play... I can't excuse him. I've never seen a performance, but I have read it and I didn't care for Higgins, either. He is a pompous ass, but I think his character works in terms of the story. It all centres upon Eliza's transformation. It's a pity Higgins didn't transform as well. There are many Higginses in the world. Eliza is purely fictional, something springing from a Higgins-like mind. She has never existed. You are not her."

"I suppose not, miss... It was people like me being laughed at that hurt."

"It wasn't a personal attack; it was short-sighted indifference. I always wanted to see a production. Now, I shan't... What will you do about your aitches?"

"Thank you for that kind word... I don't know what to do. I have enough pluck not to care most of the time what people think. But not always."

"I have an idea! You hold a five-pound note I have a half share in. Let's go to 'Arrods and spend the lot on ourselves."

"Oh, miss. Should we?"

"If you want, I don't see why not."

"I wouldn't mind.... It is a lovely idea. But it's Harrod's, miss, you know that."

"Not today, it isn't. Today it's 'Arrods... Ada, you must call me Sophie. Without a doubt, we are comrades in arms. I also consider you my friend."

The train rumbled on for a minute.

"My friend Sophie." She said the words as though they were foreign to her. "I like that very much. But I'll only call you Sophie for today, miss..." Ada nearly doubled over in laughter. "Ha, ha, Sophie and me, we're off to 'Arrod's, on a nice spree!"

They both laughed and ate more chocolates.

———⋈———

The shopping expedition was a delightful success. The young women could have stayed longer, spending more, but Sophie had to return to Sack Lane. There, she issued a flurry of notes because she needed help with the typing work that had arrived in her absence.

On Monday evening, Sophie visited the Foreign Office to deliver to Archibald Drysdale her report concerning the weekend's activity. In Archie's office, she carefully explained the events at Trefoil and handed over her written report.

"Well done, Sophie. Mission accomplished. I'm very saddened by Alfred Wright's death. That was an awful thing to happen. Has it affected you?"

"It has. In several ways. It's so disturbing because that poor man was entirely innocent of wrongdoing. I've been really puzzled by it. For the life of me, I don't understand why he was killed. That is, until Lord Stokely put in his appearance. Now I realize it was part of a larger plot... I have an intense dislike for that supposed peer. What's going on, Archie?"

"It's difficult to tell at present. It's interesting that Stokely visited Trefoil. He's sending a message to someone, but it escapes me what the message is or who it's meant for. The obvious connection is the Wright family and, by extension, Frobisher Bank. By the way, the sniper used a stolen car which was recovered in Uxbridge. There the trail goes cold. We've lost him."

"Hmm, pity. What will happen to Paul Klest?"

"He will probably go into hiding once it's discovered the submarine plans are not bona fide. A certain Greek politician is playing a dangerous game, and, I suppose, will be very annoyed."

"Is not Stokeley behind this?"

"I'm sure he is, but I'm not convinced it is entirely his show."

"And Karissa Raptis?"

"It's a risky business, and she did her job well. She has that in her favour. Miss Raptis will probably make herself scarce for a while."

"No firing squads or anything?"

"Oh, definitely not. That only happens if a person switches sides. Even then, they can be used as a double agent. Good quality spies are hard to find. If a spy was shot every time a mistake was made, there would be no spies left at all."

"My goodness, that's a relief... Now, there are several things I wish to address."

"Let me give you this first." Archie took an envelope from his jacket pocket and slid it across the desk.

"Thank you, Mr Drysdale. I cannot tell you how timely this is."

"No, thank you. Sorry, I interrupted."

"If you wish to interrupt again like that, please feel free to do so."

Archie smiled. "You haven't changed at all, really. Grown-up, of course, but you're still the same Soap. It's so refreshing. Don't ever change."

"I'm glad you're refreshed because I hinted to Victoria that I was working on secret government business. I had no choice but to explain a little of the situation."

"I know you did. Victoria called from Manchester. It was a long call. We had quite the wide-ranging discussion. All's well that ends well, so you needn't worry. I also learned of a lady's maid named Nancy Carmichael."

"I was about to mention her... You're not angry with me?"

"Not in the slightest... Truthfully, I was at first. I came to realize, in my dense way, that you were in a bind and I had put you there. Victoria, as you have seen, is an intelligent and forceful woman. I knew you would work it out, and you did. She likes you, by the way." Archie smiled. "What do you make of our Superintendent Penrose?"

"He's a very amiable person with a mind like a steel trap."

"Yes, that sums him up admirably."

"Archie, could you explain all this spying business to me? I mean, who does what, exactly? And where do you and Inspector Penrose fit in?"

"It's funny him having everyone calling him Inspector. He's quite sensitive about it. Now, the espionage business. To put it simply, Police do police work. Based at Scotland Yard, Special Branch does special police work that comes much closer to being characterized as spying. Special Branch works in conjunction with MI5. Those two confine their efforts to domestic problems. You've obviously heard of the Special Branch in connection with their work in Ireland. What a thorny, ugly issue that is. I hope it's settled peacefully one day.

"Special Branch has a wider mandate than Ireland. The trouble is with the politicians who often shape that mandate, narrowing its focus to larger domestic problems and with a continual eye on finances. Should a new subversive group become active, MI5 and Special Branch may be aware of them, but the bureaucracy can slow them down or hold them up completely in dealing with the new threat. That's where people like Penrose and I come in. There are a few more of us scattered about. We have the responsibility of reacting quickly to awkward situations as they arise.

"A perfect example was when the name of Josef Abazi appeared on the list of attendees at Trefoil. Records revealed he was none other than Paul Klest. We had a few weeks' notice to put an operation together. That's too short a time for some departments, particularly since MI5 has been scaled back so heavily since the war."

"Fascinating... Then who deals with the foreign powers? You at the Foreign Office?"

"Yes. That's C's group, though. C standing for Sir Mansfield Smith-Cumming. It's called the Secret Intelligence Service. C can be difficult to deal with sometimes. The Service is presently obsessed with the spread of Russian Bolshevism. That means smaller, nimbler groups are being overlooked. Some in authority felt a loose network of individuals such as ours could attend to such groups.

"Much of this is public knowledge. Our little network, of which you are now a fully paid-up member, is unknown to the public. Only a few cabinet ministers and such like are aware of our existence."

"Lovely," said Sophie. "I find it exciting, being a spy. The more clandestine and invisible it is, the better I like it. Now, who does the gardener work for?"

"Gardener?"

"Oh, come on, Archie, you know exactly who I mean. He was shooting at the man who shot Alfred Wright. I want to hear what happened."

"I didn't see mention of further shooting in any report."

"I see. Well, I had spoken to him earlier and then I saw him charging across the lawn with a revolver. I was certain he was the person you sent to help if any difficulties arose."

"I do not know to whom you are referring."

"So it was him, then. I was right." Sophie smiled with satisfaction. "I have to be going, Sweet Boy. Business is picking up and I need to start early tomorrow. If you run across any little matters needing attention, please consider me and my agency first. I will drop everything, reassign the office work, and be ready to attend to any peculiar difficulty in which you may find yourself."

174

They said goodbye and Sophie went home to White Lyon Yard.

Half an hour later, a Rolls-Royce, a new, dark red Silver Ghost - an all-weather, Mulliner-built tourer - drove slowly along Horse Guards Road. As it drew level with the lake in St. James's Park, the occupant in the rear spoke.

"Stop the car. I'll jump out here and walk the rest of the way."

"As you wish," said the chauffeur.

"Be a good fellow. If anyone follows me going in or coming out, jump them, will you?"

"Of course I will."

"Excellent. I'll be at the Red Lion in about half an hour."

The man got out and walked along Horse Guards. He limped slightly. His thick, plush overcoat was exceptionally well-tailored and a small red rose added a splash of dark colour in his button-hole. Wearing a bowler hat and a white silk scarf about his neck, he carried a walking stick, which he swung in a jaunty way.

From one end of King Charles, well-lit by street lamps, the chauffeur kept his employer under observation until he stepped under the arches to enter the Foreign Office building. The car sped away to park near the pub. As soon as he had brought the Rolls-Royce to a stop on Parliament Street, a police officer approached.

"You can't park here. Your best bet is to..."

"Sorry for interrupting," said the chauffeur. "Please look at this. I only need half an hour."

He handed the constable a small leather wallet which, when opened, revealed a note signed by Sir William Horton, Metropolitan Police Commissioner. It stated, 'The bearer, the Honourable Ralph St. John Walter Gossuin Yardley, shall be rendered such prompt assistance as can reasonably be given by the Metropolitan Police as and when requested.'

"He's inside the Foreign Office and I've to mind the car," added the chauffeur, when the constable had read the note with the aid of his lamp.

"The Commissioner, eh?" said the officer. "I suppose it's all right, then."

"Thank you, constable. Here, get yourself a drink. It's chilly this evening." The chauffeur handed him a shilling.

"Ah, very kind of you. You have a good night."

The constable continued on his beat. The chauffeur got out of the car, proving to be an enormous man, some six feet four inches tall with a barrel chest, thick neck, and massive arms and hands. He wore a smart, long, brown trench coat over his chauffeur's uniform. With a smile, he pushed back his cap and opened the door to the Red Lion.

"Sinjin! What are you doing here?" asked Archie.

"Passing by, old man, so I just dropped in," said Ralph 'Sinjin' Yardley, now carrying his bowler. No longer in the guise of a weather-beaten gardener and with thick, yellow hair, he looked younger, more like his actual age of twenty-six. As with many men who had been through the war, Yardley had acquired a hardened look. His rugged features would have been handsome if he smiled more. With the false beard removed, the red line of a scar was now visible along his left jaw.

"Anyone notice you come in?"

"A cleaning lady and a porter who must be ninety. You have my report, but I wanted to see you. This Wright business is not over. What can I do?"

"Nothing at present. You're correct, of course, but it's a police matter now so I can't do anything... unless called in."

"And the likelihood of that?" asked Yardley.

"Low to non-existent. No foreign powers involved, you see."

"Dealing with these matters piecemeal is very irritating. I like to see things to a conclusion... Who's handling the case?"

"An Inspector Morton is now in charge."

"I don't know him. Any good?"

"Penrose says he's competent," replied Archie.

"Very well, then. I see I'm out of the blasted picture. One day we'll get Stokely, but I don't see how that's possible at present. He's too slippery and the longer his popularity builds, the more difficult the situation becomes."

"Unfortunately, he is in the ascendency. But he'll make a mistake one day."

"What does that say about us? Are we so weak that we have to wait upon our enemy's mistake? We should seize him now."

"You seem more anxious about this affair than others we've been through."

"It's the sheer, arrogant boldness of the man that gets under my skin. We have to content ourselves with combatting his agents while he sits in perfect safety. Also, I'm annoyed with myself for missing that ruddy sniper."

"Ah, so that's more to the point, I think. You had no warning an assassination was in the offing. You can't be everywhere at once. Besides, he's eluded the police and could be anywhere by now."

"Yes, he knew what he was doing, that one... Archie, tell me about Phoebe King."

"I can't do that."

"Why not? I think she's charming. I'd like to meet her. You could introduce us. Come on, old man, what do you say?"

"That expressly contravenes policies concerning the conduct of agents. She works for me now." Archie was emphatic.

"Well, I found her delightful, and she knows her potatoes. That is a rare and, to me, fascinating combination. I'll have to work it out on my own... Going to the club later?"

"I'll drop in, I think... Potatoes, indeed... How is Viscount Ranemore?"

"Father's doing fine, thank ye. He's jubilant at present because of a cabbage cultivar he's selectively bred. It matures faster, stores longer, and is more resistant to disease, or so he tells me. It's going into commercial production next year. At present, he's tinkering with root vegetables and the long-term storage of apples, that and pottering around yet another greenhouse he's had built. Visit us when you get a chance. Take that as an open invitation. I'm down most weekends."

"Thanks, Sinjin. I'll take you up on that, if I may. I'd like to visit those greenhouses again. The old schedule permitting, of course."

"We'll get some riding in, too. Au revoir."

CHAPTER 20

— · —

2 + 1 = 3

On Wednesday morning, 22 September, at 9:15, Detective Inspector Morton sprinted through traffic with a hand securing his bowler hat. He reached out for the rear railing of a number 21 bus. He caught hold of the rail to swing easily onto the platform. The conductor scowled at him. Morton, smiling, showed him his warrant card. The conductor nodded indifferently in response. Morton ran quickly up the stairs. It was a dry, sunny day in London. The weather, possibly ashamed of its noticeable failure during the height of summer, seemed now to be trying to atone for the widespread disappointment it had caused.

Morton got a double seat to himself on the open-top bus. A bachelor, in his early thirties, he generally had a breezy outlook on life. He sat, stretched out his long legs, pushed the bowler to the back of his head, and unbuttoned his jacket. He selected a Player's Navy Cut from a packet and lit it with a match. The bus crawled along the Strand between the Courts of Justice and Fetter Lane before the traffic ahead opened up sufficiently to allow the bus to move a little faster. Along Fleet Street, he finished his cigarette.

With his arm on the railing, he abstractedly smoothed his moustache with his finger. Penrose had visited him late the night before. That wily bird had suggested a unique course of action, although Morton had initially rather resented the intrusion into his investigation. After Penrose had gone, the more he considered the proposal, the better he liked it.

As far as Morton understood the matter, he was supposed to see some old maid who ran a domestic servant employment agency. She would hire out three or four servants who had their wits about them. They would go to Abinger Mansion, near Dorking, to work while reporting to him on any unusual circumstances. And Sir Ephraim Wright certainly needed watching. Five staff had left on account of the murders in the family. How they had assumed that, Morton did not know because both inquests had been delayed while the newspaper reports had downplayed the deaths, particularly that of Alfred Wright. He thought that if he could get a few old sensible biddies inside the mansion to keep their eyes open and their mouths closed, they might pick up on something that would give him a lead on the murderer. Morton was sure it was one of the family. He became conscious that he was playing with his moustache and stopped himself, concentrating instead upon the view about him and upon St. Paul's Cathedral in the near distance.

———◆———

"Sophie, if you say 'Where's all this work come from?' once more, I shall scream." Flora, Sophie's long-time friend, was trying to type. Since Monday afternoon, and after Ada and Sophie had been deliriously oblivious in Harrod's, work had come in - a deluge of work, amounting to twenty-seven typing assignments. Sophie could talk while she typed. Flora preferred absolute silence.

"Sorry, Flora. I won't do it again. I'm just amazed, that's all. Amazed and relieved."

"Enough! Away with your chatter."

"And off with your head!"

They both laughed and continued typing. A few moments later, laborious steps sounded on the staircase.

"Hello, Miss Burgoyne. Anything doin' for a cook?"

"Not at the moment, Mrs Barker," said Sophie, who continued typing. "Perhaps next week. But stay off the brandy and perhaps I can find you something."

"How do you know I haven't already given it up?"

"Have you?"

There was a loud sniff. "I'm tryin'."

"Try harder, my dear. It will be better for you."

"You don't know the trials I go through. A nip once in a while is a great help. Anyway, you have a lovely day and I'll see you next week. Coo, you look right busy. I won't disturb. Tat-tah."

"Goodbye and take care of yourself," said Sophie. She looked up, smiled at her, and quickly resumed her typing.

"There, finished it, and no mistakes... despite numerous interruptions." Flora took the letter and carbon copies from her typewriter. "That was the most boring letter in all of human history. I kept getting the urge to spice it up. What's next?"

Flora was undeniably a beauty with her long raven black hair, dark brown eyes, and dark complexion. As an actress, when there was a part in a play for a foreign princess, a gipsy, or an adventuress, she got it, but only if it was a minor role. In acting, as in many other walks of life, it was who you knew that counted as much or more than anything else. The acting profession in London was brimful of established, leading ladies. A young actress, such as Flora Dane, could wait many years before she got her break - her chance at a lead or an important role. The pay from a succession of intermittent small parts was not very good, hence she was now also a typist.

"Does she come every week?"

"Every single week. I don't even know if she can cook."

"I thought I could smell drink on her from here," said Flora. "How does she survive...? She even looks happy. Perhaps I should take to the bottle."

"Don't be stupid, Flora. You have no need of that."

"How do you know?"

"You are almost quoting Mrs Barker. It might numb the pain for a while, but it will wreck your life."

"Does that matter?"

"Of course it does. I will never let you harm yourself. Now stop slacking and start typing or we'll never get through it... I just remembered something. My father sends his best wishes to you and, do you know, he still thinks of you wearing pigtails?"

"I love Mr Burgoyne... Not my buck teeth, as well?"

"He didn't mention them. They were never as bad as you thought they were."

"So you used to say. Pass one over."

"This one looks exciting. It's for a sales letter about a revolutionary purgative called Buloji. It cures pimples, haemorrhoids, enteritis, sallow complexion... insomnia... there's a dozen more... Oh, giddiness. That's interesting. Are you feeling giddy? This one's for you."

"Don't be so revoltingly bright. What is giddiness, anyway?"

"I don't know. It sounds very serious. You do realize you have in your hands the cure for a quarter of the world's ailments? That is a tremendous responsibility."

"What are you working on?"

"Private correspondence from a banker to the manufacturer of one of those home Turkish steam baths. You know, those peculiar cabinet things one sits in? I believe this may be the opening salvo before lawyers get involved. The steam bath blew up."

"With the banker in it?" exclaimed Flora.

Sophie laughed. "If that were the case, he could not have written the letter, could he? I can barely read his writing... No, it blew up on its own... and the door of the steam bath smashed through the bathroom window to land in a neighbour's ornamental pond... He, the banker, is looking for five hundred pounds in damages."

"Five hundred, my goodness. You can buy a complete house for that. If I had five hundred, then I would be giddy." Flora smiled at the thought.

"Me, too, and I wouldn't take Buloji for it, either."

"What do we have here, then?" Flora glanced at the handwritten pages and proceeded to speak in a slow, sepulchral, stage voice. 'Pimples, boils, and coated tongue... vile scourge, thine end hath come. The dawn of Buloji hath begun!"

Sophie stopped typing and laughed. "I could never watch you deliver lines like that from the stalls. I wouldn't be able to control myself."

"Is that so? If you were in the audience, Sophie, I would do it deliberately just to annoy the producer. Away with such pettifogging, unenlightened creatures. The earth should be swept clean of them."

"Come on, I have to concentrate now. I'm getting to the part where the banker's wife had hysterics."

"Sounds like you have material good enough for a play. Put the explosion in the last act, though. That stare doesn't frighten me, but I will be a good girl now."

Inspector Morton walked along Sack Lane. He climbed the stairs and read the signs warning of false references and water pipes. He opened the door and entered the office, hesitating on the threshold.

Flora and Sophie were busy typing. Neither looked up when he came in.

"Good morning," said Sophie, still typing. "If you can write, please fill out a card. They're to your left. Return the pencil to its place when you've finished. If you cannot write, I will be with you in a moment."

"I'm here to see Miss Burgoyne. Is she in?" he said, holding his bowler hat.

"I am she. Just one second more... There." Sophie finished. She got up and bestowed a pleasant smile upon the visitor. "You must excuse me. We have a lot of work and deadlines to meet. Are you looking for domestic staff or typing services?"

"Domestic, actually."

"Ah, very good. Let us go to my private office and you can explain your requirements. We have many well-qualified persons on our books and I'm sure we can find exactly what you need. It's this way, please."

Sophie had not failed to notice the intense stare of Morton's pale blue eyes.

"After you, Miss Burgoyne."

They went to Sophie's office and settled themselves.

"Do you mind if I shut the door?" asked Morton.

"Yes, I do. Please, leave it open. My assistant is trustworthy, and she's unlikely to hear us in any event."

Inspector Morton was nonplussed. He had imagined he would meet an aged spinster. Instead, he was in the office of a young, attractive, smartly dressed, and decisive woman who would not let him shut the door. Also, her assistant was a beauty dressed in arty, colourful clothing.

"Oh. I'm Detective Inspector Morton from Scotland Yard. This is my warrant card. Inspector Penrose gave me your name."

"Did he, indeed?" She read the warrant card. "You're from the Criminal Investigation Department... If you would just push the door to... Thank you. How may I help you?"

"It was explained to me how you were present at Trefoil Hall this past weekend. You're aware of the Wright investigation, I understand."

"I was current with the information as of Monday morning. If anything has occurred since I am not aware of it."

"You mean Penrose confided in you?"

"Up to a point, yes."

"Oh, I see. Perhaps you wouldn't mind telling me what you know... To save time."

Sophie knew she had to restrict her statements to the murder case. She also recalled Penrose's caution about trusting people.

"I was at Trefoil for the negotiations. Sir Reginald was poisoned, but Alfred Wright was the actual target. I know that Alfred Wright was shot. The sniper used a rifle from a distance of some three hundred yards. I am informed that Frank Wright's death on the Underground was a murder. It is probable that all three events are connected."

"That's handy, your knowing all that. It makes my explanation easier." Morton settled himself in the chair. "Inspector Penrose spoke highly of you. A plan has been worked out and we need lookouts inside a house. This would be Sir Ephraim Wright's house, Abinger Mansion, just the other side of Dorking. He's failing but still has his full faculties. He won't be with us by year's end, I'm told."

"I understand he is Frobisher's."

"Just so. He has a lot of property and usually lives in London. Abinger Mansion is the family home. It's like he's gone home to die. Now here's the problem as it stands. Because there have been two murders, his London staff won't go out to Dorking. It's the distance and the upset, I believe. Some of them have handed in their notice. A few have gone down with him, but they're short-handed there. I'm in contact with the housekeeper, who's now at Abinger Mansion. She's given me all the details and is being very helpful."

"What is the usual complement for Abinger Mansion?"

Inspector Morton consulted his notebook.

"I'm told the full complement is fourteen. There are only six at present. Four from London, including the housekeeper. There are two local women - a laundress and a cleaner. Another two locals can come in for kitchen duties."

"Is there a butler?"

"No. Sir Ephraim has a valet who sees to him. Mrs Fisher, the housekeeper, she runs everything."

"She doesn't need fourteen for one gentleman."

"It's a large house with ten bedrooms for guests and family. And she does need the staff because, this coming Friday and Saturday, his immediate family will be visiting. Sir Ephraim has summoned them. They'll all go because he's worth a fortune and none of them will want to cross him just now. He has three remaining children, two sons and a daughter. She's married to the Earl of Manningtree and he'll also be present. No doubt they'll be bringing a couple of servants. Plus, there'll be the two widows and four grandchildren. I make it at least twelve visitors, including the grandchildren and visiting servants."

"What does Mrs Fisher require?"

As Sophie was listening, she was thinking of her card files and who could possibly go to Dorking. At that moment, there was only Ada and herself. The piles of typing assignments also came to mind, and she considered how more might come in daily.

"She desperately needs a cook or a chef, otherwise she'll have to do the cooking herself. Mrs Fisher can't find anyone available who'll go so far out of London. She needs three maids capable of serving at table, occupying the children, and doing some light cleaning."

"In other words," said Sophie, "they not only need to be competent but very adaptable."

"Exactly. And for my requirements, they need to report on the family's activities because our investigations are strongly leading us in that direction. I need people with intelligence who can keep their eyes and ears open."

"I see. Then whoever goes must also know when to keep what they found out to themselves. What of Sir Ephraim in all of this? You don't seem to have mentioned him very much."

"You noticed that. Yes, well, here's the difficulty. Sir Ephraim refuses to have the police in the house. He also refuses to believe his two sons were murdered. It's as simple as that. He's convinced he's cursed by misfortune all of a sudden and nothing more. You should know that he was estranged from his eldest son for some years. They argued over Mr Frank's wishes to be an architect, whereas the father wanted him to go into banking. There was bitterness between them which had only been smoothed away in the last few months."

"That is very suggestive," said Sophie. "You came to me for staff and I can fulfil your requirements. Four ladies shall be present at Abinger Mansion, hopefully before noon on Friday, train timetables permitting."

"That's excellent. Let me explain to you what it is I will..."

"Excuse me for interrupting, but I, too, have requirements, and I believe you need to hear them before we go any further."

"Requirements?"

"They are these. Burgoyne's Agency shall bill - Scotland Yard, I suppose - for the full complement of staff. The rate is twelve pounds per day each day or part thereof that my staff is present at or travelling to or from Abinger Mansion. In addition, all travelling costs will be reimbursed and any incidental expenses deemed necessary shall be itemized, receipted, and similarly refunded.

"I'm going to Scotland Yard on another matter tomorrow, and I think I should see you in your office. You can give me more complete particulars on every person in the house.

"We must have a system of communication if another incident occurs in the Wright family or for any other reason where the police are needed. I trust you will have a detective or two posted nearby. We cannot rely on the local bobby."

"All that part is under my supervision. But this billing by Burgoyne's, um, the Metropolitan Police usually pays according to a fee schedule."

"I'm aware of that fee schedule. I have no interest in it. If you want this job done properly, then you would naturally choose Burgoyne's. In this field of endeavour, we are second to none. If it is a question of cost savings, and I understand there may be budgetary constraints, I wish you good luck. If you want the best, then you pay the rate. It's as true in this matter as it is in any area of life."

"I'm a detective," said Morton. "Financial matters such as these are outside my purview. I'd have to get it approved first."

He was very curious to know why Sophie was going to Scotland Yard. He speculated whether she would tell him her reason for going.

"Why are you going to Scotland Yard?" he asked.

"A private matter. Will you be in your office in the late morning?"

"I will, as it happens. I'll be talking to my superior this afternoon about the other thing."

"That's good. Can I get a firm commitment from you now, dependent on your superintendent's blessing? I must organize for this weekend and it would be a great help to start immediately. Any later, and I might have difficulty keeping my promise." She smiled at him.

"Ah, yes, it is short notice, I suppose. Let's say it's a go, shall we?"

"Excellent. I shall begin organizing at once."

Flora smiled at Inspector Morton as he made his way out. Once Morton had left the agency, Sophie emerged from her office in a slow, thoughtful way. She looked at Flora. She returned her gaze with her eyebrows raised.

"A special friend of yours? I don't think he is, yet. I saw no adoration in his eyes."

"Sorry? Um, no, no. Flora, can I ask you something?"

"Has he upset you?"

"Nothing like that. Would you like to be a spy for Scotland Yard? It's only temporary."

"A spy? Oh, come on, Sophie. Are you saying the gentleman with the bowler was from Scotland Yard?"

"I'm serious. He's an inspector, and it's a vitally important job."

"Oh, do tell."

"Not unless you agree to the work first."

"You really are serious. Spying for the police? I'm not sure I like the sound of it."

"How about catching a murderer while acting out a part? There is actual work involved. You'll be a maid in a house. There will be four of us going."

"Acting? And in a troupe of spies? Oh, yes, yes, sign me up! Do I write my name in blood?" she asked eagerly.

"Only if you want to."

"What is the pay for such peculiar work?"

"That's up in the air. If it lands where I hope it does... Two pounds a day for four days plus travel expenses."

"Two pounds? How marvellous! That's eight pounds! Wait a moment. You mean to say that the police just wander in here off the street to offer jobs and money like that?"

"You are my friend, but there are some things I cannot tell you. This work can never be a topic of conversation at parties. No one must ever hear of it."

"You know I can keep secrets... When does it start?"

"This Friday morning."

"Ah, I'll have to dump Freddie, then. He wanted to take me to a dinner dance on Friday evening. He's getting boring, anyway. I'm all for it. How ripping."

"That's a relief. Thank you."

"Who else is going?"

"Ah, now therein lies a problem. I'll explain everything about the mission later, but I have to get busy. We have a mountain of typing to work through and we can't do that and spy at the same time. When Nick comes in, don't let him leave on deliveries without seeing me first."

Among her card files, Sophie had the name and address of a rather intimidating office manageress. She wrote a note to Miss Jones, asking her to come in immediately to manage the typing and the office. Miss Jones possessed a hatchet-like face and the disposition to go with it.

The second note was for Ada, asking her to finish a newly begun assignment with an elderly lady, as a replacement would be taking her place. Sophie ended by saying there was other special work requiring Ada's personal attention.

The third note was for Ada's replacement, giving her instructions about the job she was to start.

Before she wrote the fourth note, Sophie checked her cards for a cook. She already knew the answer, but she irrationally needed to confirm her fears. She pulled open a wooden drawer and reached into the divider marked 'Culinary - Cooks' and took out the single card it contained. For Sophie to fulfil her word to Inspector Morton, there was only one cook she could call upon. She held in her hand the card for Mrs Barker, the weekly visitor.

Sophie took down her address and wrote out her fourth note with deep misgiving. She asked Mrs Barker if she would submit to a test of her cooking skills because an urgent situation had arisen in her line of work.

CHAPTER 21

───── ❖ ─────

OF OMELETTES AND TRAINS

Inspector Morton cleared the Burgoyne expense with his superior officer. To his surprise, the matter was approved without argument. Sophie visited his office the next day, where he supplied her with many details about the Wright family members. He did not tell her everything, only what he thought she needed to know. Her pertinent questions strengthened his feelings of the sagacity of having hired Burgoyne's.

Afterwards, when Inspector Bygrave returned to their shared office, having absented himself while Sophie was present, he chafed Morton over his charming visitor to the point that Morton scowled and asked him to 'Knock it off'.

Nick, Sophie's office boy, protested he was being run ragged and was only mollified by an extra shilling for delivering notes on top of all the other work. He performed prodigious feats on his bicycle. Later on, he suggested he be made boss of the courier department when he brought in a 'mate' to help. Sophie agreed to this in principle and for a trial period.

Miss Jones successfully completed her trial run. The lady proved to be a harsh, productive dynamo and came with impeccable references. She took over and typed furiously. Two temporary typists assisted her and had to keep up to the pace she set. Miss Jones also dealt with prospective job applicants and requests for domestic servants. Sophie could not tell if Miss Jones liked her work, temporary though it was, but the severe woman gave every sign of being whole-heartedly invested in running Burgoyne's efficiently during Sophie's coming absence.

Mrs Barker lived in a slum. She would not allow Sophie to enter her abode, and so the cooking test was conducted two streets away in a near-slum dwelling belonging to a friend of Mrs Barker. The kitchenette there boasted a gas ring. Just as importantly, the gas had not been cut off.

The slum had smelt awful; the room in the near-slum house smelt musty, and Mrs Barker still had a faint aura of brandy about her. Sophie had purchased the ingredients for a French omelette, deciding that this would be the simplest and most effective method of testing Mrs Barker's skills.

"Here you are, Miss Burgoyne, Omelette de la mère Poulard." Not standing on ceremony, Mrs Barker brought a sizzling frying pan, black as pitch, over to the table and served the omelette onto the best china plate with its chipped rim.

"You know the correct name," said Sophie with some surprise. Mrs Barker smiled and nodded.

The omelette looked good to Sophie. She picked up her fork, which, for safety's sake, she had cleaned scrupulously. Separating a tentative forkful, she ate it.

"This is delicious. It's so light and fluffy... It's obvious you can cook. Oh, Mrs Barker, please sit down and tell me what happened."

"An old story, miss. A broken heart and then drink until it interfered with my work. But I swear to you, I am trying. I just need another chance to put me back on me feet."

"You'll have your chance. This is only temporary, but pays well. Would sudden money be a problem for you?"

"It might, unless you hold on to some of it for me, please. And pay me out when I need it?"

"I can do that."

"Are there many people staying in the house?"

"It's a big house past Dorking. The family and guests number about a dozen, but the resident and visiting staff might bring it up to almost thirty people staying there. The pay is two pounds a day for four days, plus travelling expenses."

"'Streuth! How much? Well, I never! I don't know Dorking, but I can cook. I haven't lost me touch, as you can see. I'll need two full-day helpers for that many. And a third in a pinch if they want a big dinner."

"That should be no problem. I've been told there's local help for the kitchen when needed. Now, about your uniform..."

"Can I stop you there, miss? I have everything from before. I've not sold it, I've never pawned it and never will. It's all packed away nice. It's in mothballs, so I'll take it out directly, give everything an airing and get rid of the creases."

"That's wonderful. We are to meet tomorrow morning at Waterloo station under the clock at a quarter past eight. I'll have your ticket. Can you get there on time?"

"I can... but I've got nothing," she said awkwardly.

"I'll give you a five-shilling advance as soon as I've finished my omelette. Now there's a reason the pay is so high. You need only concern yourself with feeding the household. The rest of us will work as domestics, myself included. We will be present in the house to gather information for the police. It is in connection with a murder investigation. If this issue presents an insurmountable problem for you, I must make other arrangements."

"Ooh, that's unusual, but I don't mind helping the police. Seeing as I'll just be cooking... No, I can't see a problem. Whatever you have to do is your business. Because you've been so kind, I'll be more than happy to go along with whatever you ask of me. I can keep me trap shut, if needs be."

"I'm so glad. You're helping me immensely in this. Now, let me give you your money."

Sophie held out two half-crowns. Mrs Barker took them. They looked at each other.

"I won't touch a drop, I promise you. On my life, I won't."

"I know you won't." Sophie gave her a reassuring smile. "I must go because I've a hundred things to do. So I'll see you under the clock, Waterloo Station, at fifteen minutes past eight tomorrow morning."

"I'll be there bright and early, just you see. Goodnight, Miss Burgoyne, and thank you."

After Sophie had gone, Mrs Barker sat down and cried.

Sophie hurried along the grimy streets in the fading light. She thought over the way Mrs Barker had risen to the occasion. Her manner had changed, as though old mannerisms and attitudes had undergone a sudden revival. The cheery visitor to the agency was disappearing as the proud, professional servant reasserted herself. Sophie walked on and the unfamiliar, run-down area became potentially threatening as the day waned. She kept a tight grip on the new blackjack in her coat pocket as she walked towards better lit and better frequented areas.

It rained on Friday, 24 September. The first person to arrive under the clock at Waterloo station was Mrs Barker. She was half an hour early with a grim, determined look on her face. Her clothes were clean - very respectable - but dated to circa 1910 and topped by a round, brimmed hat. At fifty-five, she was that type of solid British cook who believed that eating could overcome any illness or ailment. As long as a person ate dinner at the proper time, then everything would be all right, no matter how dire the news in the papers. For her to say, "He's hardly touched a thing," gave the flavour of her thoughts, which were more closely aligned to, "He'll be dead by morning." Failing invalid or champion prizefighter - it did not matter - if they did not eat, they were as good as gone already.

When Sophie saw Mrs Barker, an intense relief washed over her.

"Good morning, Mrs Barker. Any sign of the others?"

"Good morning, Miss Burgoyne. I haven't seen them."

"You must call me Sophie from now on. Remember, I'm to be a maid like everyone else. It will be Flora, Ada, and Sophie."

"I'm not sure I can do that, miss."

"Among us, you are the senior servant and we will treat you as such. Should it be an issue, you could try calling me Miss Burgoyne and I will represent myself as the manager of our little group, but in Abinger Mansion, I will have no oversight of your work. I'll just be a maid."

"Very good, miss... Burgoyne."

"Clapham Junction is huge!" said Ada, looking at the numerous tracks and platforms. "I've never been so far south before."

The train stopped at the platform with a lurch. Other trains arrived or departed. The four women travelled together, third class, on the London & South Western Railway.

"Where're you from?" asked Mrs Barker, who sat opposite Ada.

"Poplar, off the High Street."

"I'm from Bethnal Green... I've got family in Poplar."

"Oh, yes? What street? I might know them."

So began the friendship of Ada and Mrs Barker as they sought to find a common relative or acquaintance somewhere in Bow, Limehouse, Stepney, Whitechapel, or Hackney. In their search, they brought out details of their respective families, their occupations, and a host of associated facts both relevant and irrelevant but which they both found immensely absorbing.

"Isn't it funny, listening to them?" said Flora. "How many times have we heard, 'Who are your people?' So we do exactly the same."

"True. Though I've never heard it done street by street through the whole of East London before. I'm glad they're getting along." Sophie paused and then raised eyebrows enquiringly. "Is Freddie terribly upset?"

"He says he is, but then he puts Brilliantine on his hair. That makes me doubt his sanity."

Sophie laughed. "Well, I can't say I care for that slicked down, oily look, either, but how does his sanity come into it?"

"We were at a little Soho restaurant and he was, I suppose, being romantic. There was a candle on the table. As he leaned forward, I thought, 'What shall I do if his head catches fire?'"

They both laughed.

"What did you decide? Does Brilliantine even burn?"

"I don't know. I decided it would be the water in the flower vase first, followed by wine."

"Poor man. You didn't tell him, did you?"

"Of course not. But I completely missed everything he was saying. I think he thought my smiling was because of his ardour. I hope I didn't encourage him."

"You are terrible, sometimes."

"Perhaps. My face is worth thirty or forty dinners a year. Some men waiting at the stage door want to marry, but most don't.

Letting them take me to dinner...? My conscience is clear. I never lead them on. They do that for themselves. At least, the ones I seem to attract do so... How is your love life?"

"Pshaw! Non-existent. Buried in a small village or covered in mud from fieldwork is not where or how one finds a marriageable man."

"Oh, yes, that would make it difficult... I was reading an article and, do you know, there are now nearly two million more women in the country than there are men?"

"I think I knew there was an imbalance. I had no idea it was so large."

"Perhaps I should marry Freddie while I can. What do you think?"

"You'd make both him and yourself very miserable."

"He has pots of money so I wouldn't be that miserable... Maybe I'll pay attention to what he is saying next time."

"I knew it! exclaimed Mrs Barker. "I told his mother that little Georgie Roper would turn out wrong."

"Oh, do tell us," said Sophie, intrigued by her outburst.

Mrs Barker turned a triumphant smiling face towards Sophie.

"Oh, excuse me, Miss Burgoyne... You say it, Ada."

"Mrs Barker knew this family called the Ropers who lived in Bethnal Green. Every last one of them has red hair. She knew Mrs Roper, she who was Susan Friday before she married, and her second-born was Georgie."

"He was a little monster at age four. That was when I last saw him," said Mrs Barker. "It was in 1891. I said to Susan, 'He's going to land himself in trouble one of these days, you mark my words.' Go on, Ada."

"And he did, miss. I don't live far from All Saints Church in Poplar. It was a Thursday night in August last year. About midnight, there was all this shouting going on. Nobody could tell where it was coming from. It sounded like it was coming from 'igh up somewhere. Not heaven, though, 'cos there was a lot of bad language in it. All the doors on our street was opening, with everyone coming out their front doors to see what the racket was about. And we're all in our nightclothes. Turns out there are two men on top of All Saints Church 'aving a fight. They're both drunk and bellowing like bulls.

"All that noise brings the coppers. The police have got their lanterns out and keep blowing their whistles 'til there's a crowd of them and there's a big crowd of us. We're all staring up at the church roof, watching the performance. After a while, the two fellas on the roof get wore out, so they just sat on the edge while the police get the ladder back up and persuade 'em to come down peaceable.

"Between us, we put the story together because there are tools, ladders, and strips of lead everywhere. After a session down the pub, the two fellas had decided to do a bit of climbing to nick the lead off the church roof. Only one great brain knocked the ladder over while they're up there. It was like three ladders tied end to end. They're stuck on the roof so they took to fighting about it. Oh, it was such a laugh, 'specially when they almost fell off.

"Well, they go to court, get six months a-piece and one of them is none other than little Georgie Roper, now age 32, him with a carrot top an' all, who Mrs Barker knew as a little sprig of four. And she warned his mother about him."

"I was right. I always knew little Georgie would turn out wrong," said Mrs Barker, triumphant in her quiet satisfaction at finding her prophecy fulfilled.

"That is fantastic," said Flora. "I wish I had seen it. Although, Ada, you paint such a vivid picture, I almost feel I was there."

"Thank you, miss."

"You must call me Flora. We have the same rank in the Burgoyne army."

"It's a bit hard to remember, Flora."

"Don't worry. If you muck it up, I'll call you Miss Ada. What's your first name, Mrs Barker?"

"Muriel, after my grandmother on my dad's side."

"I like that name. I believe you're the first Muriel I've ever met."

CHAPTER 22

———— ✦ ————

ABINGER MANSION

"Next stop is Leatherhead, so we're getting close. Ada and Flora, how do you like your uniforms and lace caps?"

"Very comfortable and quite stylish," said Flora.

"The stitching on the uniform is very good and the cap's pretty," said Ada.

"I was agreeably surprised because of their reasonable cost and quick delivery. They look smart, I think." The three maids wore identical dresses under their coats.

"Now, assignments. We are to shadow and note everyone in the house as and when we can. The highest priorities are the three remaining children. The youngest, Anthea Wright, is married to Lord Philip Smythe, Earl of Manningtree. She is to be called Your Ladyship or My Lady. Likewise, he is only to be addressed as your Your Lordship or My Lord. They will arrive with a lady's maid, a valet, and a chauffeur. I do not have their names. As there are two of them, we will divide surveillance of them between the three of us. The housekeeper, Mrs Fisher, will tell us which rooms will be occupied when we arrive.

"Anthea has brains. Of the remaining children, she is most likely to continue on in Frobisher Bank. She's not trained in banking, though. So, like her two brothers, I think she might sell whatever shares she receives.

"Ada, you are to pay specific attention to Stephen Wright. If he needs a maid for something, you are to attend to him. He is thirty-four and the youngest son. Stephen is a bit of a rake, continuously in debt, and unmarried. All that makes him the last person one would want to run a bank.

"Flora, you are to attend to Thomas Wright, aged thirty-six. He's married but his wife is expecting in two months and cannot accompany him. She has had two miscarriages, so it's easy to understand why she does not wish to travel at present. Thomas owns an art gallery in Kew. He has no interest in banking... You'd think he would have when it's given him everything he has but, no matter. I suppose he is a businessman. He also paints.

"For myself, I get to look after Sir Ephraim. He is not being helpful. I'm sure he has a secret, otherwise he would talk to the police. No one, and above all Sir Ephraim, must find out we are reporting on the family. I will be in contact with a detective daily or by telephone if necessary.

"According to Inspector Morton, Sir Ephraim is on the brink of changing his will. His current will contains a roughly equal division between four of the children and had a much-reduced bequest going to the eldest son, Frank. He was forty-five when he died. There was a severe breach between father and eldest son because Frank insisted upon being an architect, whereas Sir Ephraim wanted him to go into Frobisher. Lady Wright died of the flu last year.

"Since that time, both father and eldest son have worked at reconciling their differences. They had been successful. It is conjectured that Frank would have received much more under a new will. The lawyer was not instructed in the matter, so nothing is known for certain of what might have been. What is strongly suggested is that after this weekend, there will be a new will. Sir Ephraim has hinted at this, but has given no details.

"What is definite is Sir Ephraim has 63% of the shares in Frobisher. He has always wanted the family to retain a controlling interest in the company. There are more details but we need not concern ourselves with them. I said that so that if anyone under surveillance expresses a need for money or a wish to sell shares, we should pay attention to it, because it contradicts Sir Ephraim's wishes.

"I didn't know this until yesterday, but Sir Ephraim's confidential secretary, Matthew Reese, may visit the house or stay the weekend. If he stays, we should remember that he reports to Sir Ephraim. Also, bank couriers are likely to come and go. Mrs

Fisher knows them as they routinely visited the London house. Are there any questions so far?"

"This is all quite fascinating," said Flora. "So, we are definitely looking for someone who will gain under a new will or someone who would prefer the current will to remain in force. Is that right?"

"I don't know the answer. I would assume that if the murderer is one of the three remaining children, his biggest threat has gone. The settlement with Frank has been averted by his murder. Also, their share increases even more with Alfred's death."

"Do you think they will kill anyone else?" asked Ada.

"I sincerely hope not," replied Sophie. "All right, then. I think we should have a system of hand signals, as it will be difficult for us to talk sometimes."

"Crossed fingers," said Ada. "Left hand means the housekeeper is out for blood, right hand means it's the butler. Thumbs up, we're ready for the master and mistress, thumbs down and there's a problem. So, thumbs down before dinner says, if you've forgotten to do something, you'd better do it right now."

"I know about the thumbs," said Mrs Barker, "but I've never seen that crossed-fingers business."

"You wouldn't because you're in charge of the kitchen. You don't really come under either the butler or the housekeeper."

"No, I suppose not. I've had interfering housekeepers occasionally, but no worse than that."

"We shall adopt those signs," said Sophie. "If we need more, we'll sort them out as we go along. We're all learning here. Our thumbs down will signify that there's danger. As there's no butler, right fingers crossed shall mean a difficult situation ahead. Let's practise them. You, too, Mrs Barker."

They practised, making them as subtle as they could.

"What are we looking for?" asked Flora. "Someone acting out of character?"

"Abinger Mansion will be a house of mourning. Any person not mourning or, at least, feigning grief will be interesting to us. Let us assume that Sir Ephraim writes a new will based on discussions with his three children. I'm sure that could produce some odd behaviour among them... I'm not sure what form it will take."

"Where there's a will... there are relatives," said Flora. Ada giggled. Flora smiled at her.

"If we are discovered, I think we must keep as many of us as we can in the house as long as possible. That's the main thing. If, for example, Sir Ephraim believes I should leave, you three are to stay until Monday, as agreed."

"Very good, Sophie," said Ada.

"Yes, Miss Burgoyne," said Flora in a demure voice, with downcast eyes.

"'Ere, Ada," said Sophie. "I 'ope you don't 'ave no trouble wiv your young gent. 'E might take a fancy to you. Know what I mean?"

Ada stared at Sophie in astonishment for a moment, but then grinned broadly.

"I doubt he'll be coming with an offer of marriage, so 'e better watch himself or 'e'll get what for," replied Ada.

"I don't believe my ears, Sophie Burgoyne," said Flora in amazement. "That was pure Whitechapel... The cadence, timing, delivery... everything."

"Whitechapel... Maybe. I'd have said Limehouse, myself," said Mrs Barker. "But it sounded natural."

"I doubt I could keep it up for very long," said Sophie.

The train arrived at Dorking station. The four women stood under the overhang outside because a light rain was falling. A large, new Sunbeam limousine rolled along the station approach and stopped in front of them. The navy blue paintwork glistened, beaded with raindrops. The driver leaned across and asked,

"You the party for Abinger Mansion?"

"Yes, we are," said Sophie.

"Right. Bring your cases round the back and I'll get 'em tucked away."

The man got out promptly. He was about thirty, with a small, black moustache, and dressed in an immaculate, grey chauffeur's uniform of jackboots, a peaked cap, and a double-breasted jacket with brass buttons. The chauffeur opened the boot.

"Look sharp, girls. Don't want to get wet, do we?" His tone was familiar, accompanied by a smile.

They began handing him the cases and getting into the back of the car. They set off soon afterwards.

"Star and Garter... Looks like a nice pub, that," said the driver over his shoulder through the partition.

"It's pretty wiv all the plants outside," said Flora, in an East End accent. She flashed a quick look at Sophie.

"Yes. My name's Barry. I'm Lord Manningtree's chauffeur. I came early to bring the big luggage. Lord and Lady Manningtree will arrive by train this afternoon at four."

"I'm Ada... I know you can't turn round and look, but there's Sophie, Flora, and Mrs Barker back here."

"Nice to meet you all. Mrs Barker? You must be the cook. I'll take special care of you. If there's anything you want for the kitchen, let me know and I'll run into Dorking to fetch it. I got to keep on your good side, haven't I?"

"You're setting off the right way about it, young man," said Mrs Barker, pleased by his deference.

"What's the 'ouse like?" asked Flora.

"It's big, old... Victorian... but it's up to date. Electric light and telephone."

"What are the quarters like?" asked Ada.

"I don't know, I haven't seen them. I've only been here a couple of hours. My digs over the garage are nice. Very snug and no complaints from me. Your kitchen looks brand, spanking new, Mrs B."

"That's Mrs Barker if you please. And I'm very thankful to hear it."

"Sorry. No offence. That's how we get on at Brayston Hall."

"Ah, that's in Suffolk. I was at the Chattisham estate several times. Brayston is quite close by. That was a while ago, though."

"Is that so? I've been over to the Duke's a few times myself."

"Have any of the guests arrived?" asked Sophie.

Because of the way she spoke, Barry hesitated, suddenly aware that this female was from a different class.

"I'm a manageress with our agency," said Sophie. "We had short notice, so I'm pitching in as a maid this weekend."

"Oh, yes, of course," said Barry, who nodded his head and smoothed his moustache. "No, I believe they're all arriving this afternoon. I'll be going back and forth as they'll be coming by different trains."

"Is it far, then?"

"No, just a few miles. It's hard to find, though. Right out of sight, it is. There are woods everywhere around here, as you'll soon see."

As the car travelled, Mrs Barker smiled to herself because she was getting a kitchen. Ada looked pleased because of the excellent pay, and excited because she was spying. Flora looked forward to the challenge of acting her part. Sophie was wondering how she would recognize a murderer among people she did not know. From the back of her mind, the thought of Stokely kept trying to intrude itself into her musings.

After Abinger Hammer, the Sunbeam turned off the main road, and the chauffeur reduced their speed to suit the bumpiness of the lane. The rain was heavier now and puddles were forming. Trees enclosed the road. To one side, beyond the trees, a few cows grazed in long green fields. On the other side was a thick forest of mostly newer growth with some larger oaks, ash, and hornbeam in the midst, and the occasional stand of pine trees. Once, the forest opened up to where a long, bare hollow, lying among beeches and yews, invited the eye to follow along until the track disappeared into the damp gloom.

"They've let the forest go," said Sophie. "Old ways are disappearing. This was all coppiced along here once and now it looks so dark and uninviting."

No one in the car quite understood what she was saying. They saw trees while Sophie saw a forest that was no longer managed or cut back as it would once have been.

The car passed through a wide, open gate between a pair of stone pillars topped with round stone balls. The long metalled driveway was finished with large stones and tar, but in good repair for its age. This smooth surface wound through flat woodland. The further they got from the road, the more the forest opened, becoming airier, until they drove through a small grassy park of fine oaks, elms, and beeches. Upon rounding the last bend of the driveway, the house came properly into view.

"Who'd 'ave thought this would be buried out 'ere?" asked Flora.

It was a big house of dark red brick and very wide, surrounded by lawns and well-tended bushes. Whoever had designed it had also designed commercial buildings for city and town centres because such influences had been unconsciously transferred into the plan of Abinger Mansion. The quality of the construction was undeniable and, even if the house was plain, it gloried in its simplicity of line. Over time, it had settled comfortably into its surroundings as much as the dark red brickwork allowed. The main building had two floors with attics and dormer windows in the roof.

"I suppose we're up in the roof," said Ada.

"Look, there's an addition to the left," said Mrs Barker. "We might be in there."

"You might," said Ada, "we'll soon know if we are."

They entered through a side door in the large addition and found themselves in a small, separate hall. Their entrance set a bell tinkling above the door. Two passages led away from it, and they could see a staircase and two offices.

"That's nice. It's lovely and warm in here," said Ada.

They heard someone walking briskly along a passage, advancing towards them.

"Coming!" she called.

A thin woman in her late fifties wearing a plain black dress strode purposefully into the hall and came to a sudden stop. The relief was apparent on Mrs Fisher's face.

"I'm so glad you got here safely. Welcome to Abinger Mansion."

"Good morning, and thank you, Mrs Fisher. We're glad to be here. I'm Sophie Burgoyne. Although I'm a manageress at the agency, while I'm here, you must treat me like any other maid. This is Mrs Barker."

"Good morning, Mrs Fisher."

"Good morning, Mrs Barker."

"This is Ada..."

"Good morning, Mrs Fisher," said Ada, who bobbed.

"And this is Flora..."

"Good morning, Mrs Fisher," said Flora, who bobbed, too, mimicking Ada exactly.

"Good morning, girls. You will want to know about your sleeping arrangements. Don't worry, the attic is comfortable and heated by radiators. Your room is ready. Go up those stairs to the top. First door on your left. As soon as you're settled, come back here and wait if I'm not in that office there."

She pointed to the room next to the side door. Ada and Flora both bobbed and took their cases upstairs.

"Mrs Barker, your room is in the annexe, but I'm sure you're eager to see the kitchen first."

"Yes, I am, Mrs Fisher."

"Lunch is prepared. If you could take charge of tonight's dinner, I would be so very thankful. It's turbot and beef and I had thought to have something simple for the staff, perhaps shepherd's pie, but nothing's started yet. The larder is well stocked and you can send out for anything you need. The local shop in Abinger doesn't have much besides the basics and shuts at half-past four. Several shops in Dorking are open to half-past six tonight."

"You leave it all to me, Mrs Fisher."

"Excellent. Now, Sophie, I had thought to put you in the annexe. Since you wish to be treated as a housemaid, you can take the room next to Flora and Ada. You must get it ready yourself. You can't miss the servants' linen cupboard - it's right at the top of the stairs."

"I'll get settled and come straight back down, Mrs Fisher." Sophie bobbed and followed the others upstairs.

"As soon as I get my coat off, I think I'll put a kettle on," said Mrs Barker.

"That would be most welcome," said Mrs Fisher. "Let me show you to the kitchen."

CHAPTER 23

— ∗ —

THE WRIGHT FAMILY

"I have worked for Sir Ephraim for the last four years," explained Mrs Fisher to Sophie as they sat in her office, drinking tea. It was just after one. "He has always given me a free hand in domestic matters and everything was straightforward while he lived in London."

"How often would he come down here?" asked Sophie.

"Three or four times a year... for holidays and birthdays. It was his family home while growing up."

"I can understand that attraction, but being here now puts him beyond easy reach of medical specialists, doesn't it?"

"That was my chief concern. Sir Ephraim was adamant, though. First, he had a stroke, but he's recovered quite well from that. Now it's his heart, and I try to keep him as quiet as possible. He had an acute attack and recovered, but I know he's had some minor ones, too. He's come back here to die. I could not argue without it putting his heart under stress and he doesn't like to be thwarted or opposed."

"Hmm... How has he taken the deaths of Alfred and Frank?"

"Honestly, I feared the news would finish him. It didn't. He attended both funerals and, just before Mr Alfred's funeral, he stated he wanted to come here for good. Of course, that put the settled domestic arrangements in London into uproar. Two deaths coming so close together had a disturbing effect on the staff. There was a general reluctance to come to Abinger Mansion. Several staff, including an excellent cook, have left. Despite all this going on, Sir Ephraim seems calmer now than he has in some time. I've formed the impression that this weekend is of immense importance to him."

"I can appreciate that it would be. The future of Frobisher Bank must weigh heavily upon him. I understand he built it up quite considerably."

"Yes, he did. It was his life. There are also his London properties. His estate is very valuable, as I'm sure you have heard."

"Inspector Morton informed me that Sir Ephraim refuses to consider the deaths of his two sons as anything but accidents."

"That's what he says... I don't believe him, though. With Alfred, I thought he was expecting bad news... I mean, the news hurt him, but it was as though he was expecting it and was braced for it." Mrs Fisher shook her head in puzzlement.

"He's a clever man," she went on. "He sees far ahead in any financial matter. Something is troubling him, although he does not speak of it. I don't see how it can be to do with the business - he'd know what to do for the best if it was that. I suppose he will keep his secret... And yet, as I say, this coming weekend has almost cheered him up, as if he's relieved."

"I saw two wreaths on the front door as we drove past," said Sophie. "Such an unusual sight... Tell me about his other children."

"It seems peculiar to call them children when they're fully grown. There isn't one of them who can replace him at Frobisher. He's close to Lady Manningtree. Thomas he likes, but they have very few interests in common. He tolerates Stephen, the youngest. Sir Ephraim despises his spendthrift ways, but he also perversely enjoys making Stephen beg for money."

Mrs Fisher stopped herself from saying more. Sophie assumed she had come close to commenting on Stephen's character and relationship with his father in unflattering ways.

"When I attend to Sir Ephraim, is there anything I should know about his habits?"

"Don't touch the curtains unless he requests it. Just recently, he's wanted them drawn at all times. It's best to humour him as and when you can.

"You should be aware, Mr Ephraim might be quite playful on occasion. He's seventy-six, has a bad heart condition, has tragically lost two sons, but those things will probably not stop him. He's been harmless as long as I've been his housekeeper, but not so in the past. Particularly the long past. There have been incidents - with repercussions. They were hushed up and dealt with. I'm aware of three such incidents. I can't say if there were others."

"Are the police aware of these children?"

"Oh, yes. They knew before they interviewed me. I believe they know more about them than I do."

"I'm sure they do. Shall we meet him, then?"

"We can try. He tires easily. He might be asleep."

Abinger Mansion was airy and spacious inside. It was furnished with heavy pieces of the best quality furniture from about 1860. They were of un-ostentatious design and, after sixty years of careful polishing, had developed a rich patina. Sophie had seen little of the house so far, but a few glimpses had informed her it was a comfortable place to live. When she encountered the main hall, she found the long marble staircase to be very attractive and the whole downstairs area light, spacious, and tastefully decorated.

It was a complete contrast upstairs. The bedroom corridors were wide enough for three people to walk abreast. The expensive, hand-woven carpets muffled the sound of footsteps. These long, dark red runners, the dark patterned wallpaper, and the dim electric light gave the long passageways a sombre, closed-in feel despite their width. Sophie was surprised by the difference - as though two minds had chosen the design and decoration of the different areas.

Mrs Fisher opened the door to Sir Ephraim's separate apartment. It revealed a small ante-room with several doors leading off it.

"Office," said Mrs Fisher in a hushed tone as she pointed, becoming economical in her speech because of the proximity of the master of the house. "His secretary uses that room when he's here. Dressing room, which leads to a bathroom and the bedroom. The bedroom."

Mrs Fisher knocked gently, then opened the bedroom door. Closed heavy curtains darkened the room. A small lamp shed a pool of subdued light by the bed. A woman was sitting close to it. When she got up from a comfortable chair, she put down her book. Sophie could see, by the silhouette of her dress and small nursing cap, that she was a nurse. She came over to speak to Mrs Fisher.

A voice came from the bed. "Don't say I'm asleep, Gleason, because I'm not." The voice was frail. An elderly man's voice, but there was a residual strength in it.

Nurse Gleason smiled and nodded before leaving. The light from the anteroom revealed she was in her forties.

"Sir Ephraim," said Mrs Fisher, "I have your new maid with me. I wanted to introduce her to you so that you're not surprised by a strange face in your rooms."

"Why? Is she hideous?" Sir Ephraim had been on his side, facing away. He turned back and said. "Step forward into the light so I can see you... My word! You're not hideous at all. What's your name, girl?"

"Sophie, sir." She bobbed.

"Very well, Sophie. You may dust my rooms. They need dusting three times a day, but don't bring the vacuum cleaner. I hate the thing." He was a small, fading man with thin, short white hair, an aquiline nose, and skin like parchment.

"The rooms are cleaned daily, Sir Ephraim." Mrs Fisher went over and began arranging his pillows to make him more comfortable.

"Cleanliness is next to godliness. They need cleaning more often. Why can't I have Sophie dust my rooms when I want?"

"They were cleaned while you were asleep." Mrs Fisher almost smiled.

"You're becoming devious, Fisher. Perhaps I should get another housekeeper."

"If you do that, sir, I can put my feet up for once." Mrs Fisher finished arranging the pillows.

"Do you see what I have to put up with, Sophie? I'm a prisoner in my own home and Mrs Fisher here is my jailer." He looked at the housekeeper. "Reese could arrive this evening. When he does, find a bed for him and send him in right away."

"Certainly, sir. Do you require anything else?"

"Yes. Health, strength, and my two sons back. Ha. You can leave me now." There was bitterness in his voice.

Mrs Fisher inclined her head, and the two women left the room. They met Nurse Gleason in the anteroom and there followed what was obviously Mrs Fisher's routine and frequent enquiry into the status of Sir Ephraim's health. The nurse reported that he was comfortable, continuing the same, but his breathing laboured sometimes.

The staff's supper was at six in the servants' hall in the basement. Mrs Fisher presided over the table and declared Mrs Barker's beef pies, garnished with pastry rosebuds and leaves, to be a great success. Sir Ephraim's valet, Mr Fenton, and the young footman, John Rogers, both seemed morose and ignored each other. Lord Manningtree's valet, Barstow, and Lady Anthea's maid, Rosina Murray, were quiet and aloof, and it was easy to impute to them a condescending attitude. Mrs Fisher had to maintain the bulk of conversation otherwise, by convention or disposition, they would all have eaten in near silence. There were several occasions when Sophie nearly spoke without first being addressed. Also present at the table, besides Flora and Ada, were Barry the chauffeur, another housemaid, and a hall boy. Mrs Barker, the kitchen maid, and two scullery maids were busy in the kitchen and had eaten earlier.

At 6:30 p.m. in the lounge, Lady Anthea Manningtree and her brother, Thomas Wright, sipped sherry while they chatted. Anthea, a slim woman with bobbed, dark curls, wore mourning and Thomas, a thin, ordinary man, wore a dark blue suit with a black armband.

"Hello, hello, here you all are," said their brother, Stephen, as he entered the large room. "One not so big happy family all getting together again and so soon after the funerals. Where's his Lordship?" Stephen had features that were once fine but were now becoming coarsened through late hours and too much to drink. He wore well-cut tweeds, but his flamboyant red tie and silk handkerchief demanded more attention than was usual. His entire ensemble was out of place at Abinger Mansion just then.

"Lord Manningtree will be down for dinner," said Anthea. "He felt we should have some time alone together to discuss matters."

"Jolly decent of him. Thank you for reminding me what his title is. What's this pow-wow about?" Stephen sank into a leather armchair and lit a cigarette.

"Stop it, Stephen," said Thomas. "We're here because of Frank and Alfred."

"No, we're not. We buried Frank on Monday and Alfred on Wednesday. The only reason we're here is because we're scared father might give all his money away to charitable causes. We've all come to ingratiate ourselves to make sure we get ours. That's why I'm here. I assume that's why you're here. Personally, I would rather drown my sorrows in London."

"Why do you always act this way?" asked Anthea.

"To get attention... and to annoy people. It's a pity poor old Alfred has gone. He always got so irritated with me. It was delicious. Are you drinking sherry? Filthy stuff. Bring me a whisky and soda."

"Stephen," said Anthea, "you know very well Father only permits sherry before dinner. Have a sherry; it's very good."

Flora walked over to him and moved an ashtray stand next to his armchair. "Your ash, sir," she said in a voice of reverential quietness, full of solicitude. She believed she was striking the right note.

Stephen stared at her. "Thank you," he said, and flicked the ash off the end of his cigarette. "I'll have sherry, then."

"When you've served the sherry, you may go," said Anthea.

Flora poured out a glass and served it to Stephen. The Wright siblings were quiet until she left. On her way out, she closed the door without shutting it. Outside in the hall, Flora waited for them to start talking again. She tried several positions until she found a comfortable one where she could both clearly hear their conversation and see anyone approaching her.

"Stephen, stop grasping for attention or we will get nowhere," said Anthea.

"All right, truce, pax, etc., etc.," said Stephen.

"We all know that father will never choose one of us to run his precious Frobisher Bank," said Thomas. "We were discussing what he could have in mind. It can't be the case that he's turned maudlin enough to forget our deficiencies, the ones he has so candidly pointed out to us our entire lives.

"I spoke to him earlier and, although he's weaker and slower, his mind is just as sharp as it's ever been. He's up to something, though. There's no doubt in my mind about that."

"We all need money," said Anthea. "Brayston is a veritable money pit. The estate's income is barely enough to pay for its upkeep."

"Sorry to hear that," said Thomas. "I'd like to move my gallery from Kew to the West End. I don't want to be messing around with third rate artists for the rest of my life. There's no money or future in it. If Father is going to do something absurd... I mean, we're his flesh and blood! He can't be giving it away."

"He wouldn't do that, would he? It isn't right... What makes you think he will?" asked Stephen.

"Why all the mystery?" asked Anthea, shaking her head. "The terms under the current will suits all of us. If he's making a change, we can only be worse off, not better. Look, I don't mean this how it sounds but, if he were to die peacefully tonight, we would be certain of our futures. Who knows what he's about to do?"

"Oh, come, come. What are you two suggesting? Perhaps he's had a new will drawn up already."

"No, he hasn't," said Thomas. "I slipped a quid to a clerk at his lawyer's office. He told me Father has not made a new will. Neither have they received instructions to do so."

"I see. Very enterprising of you. What is being proposed here?"

"We can't wait," said Anthea. "Instead of us being in competition and reacting to something we don't like, we must present a united front and take the initiative. All three of us must become ardent believers in continuing the Frobisher tradition. To do that to good effect, we shall act preemptively."

"This about-face - he'll think it fishy," said Stephen.

Thomas leaned forward in his chair. "Yes, he might. Why don't we do it, anyway? We'll say he should put the shares into a testamentary trust... With us as beneficiaries, of course. The trust-johnny will make sure everything runs smoothly, the shares will be secure until we eventually get them, and Frobisher can hire managers to run the place while we wait. We will receive a proper annual income from the trust. But it can only work if we all pull together. The way Father will view it is that he gets his beloved bank to remain in the family.

"I'm sorry about Frank, but look, what a near miss we've had. If they had reconciled, the lot would have gone to him. Father wanted him to control the bank. He's always wanted that. I believe we all recognize these things as fact."

"It was a possibility," said Stephen. "I'll grant you that much. Frank was good with figures and business... So, the old man is in the mood for a change and we're to guide him in the right direction." He sipped some sherry before swallowing the whole glassful. "How are we to pull this off? Walk into his bedroom and deliver an ultimatum?"

"Don't be absurd," said Anthea. "I'll suggest the idea of a testamentary trust at dinner. Thomas will second the idea. He'll do so as though he's unfamiliar with trusts and how they operate. What we have to impress upon Father is the notion of the family keeping control of Frobisher Bank. We must make him see that his empire will remain intact. Surely, he'll be pleased by our stepping into the gap left by Frank. We have to consider this situation from his point of view."

"Sounds plausible. Then, I suppose, I chime in like I've found a new religion?" asked Stephen.

"Exactly," said Thomas. "After that, we'll be sweetness and light this whole weekend. We must try something because there's no telling what he'll do otherwise." Thomas sighed deeply. "I am so tired of scraping by on the paltry allowance he gives me."

"You're complaining! He cut me off. Although, I believe I'm about due for a reinstatement. Anthea, what about his Lordship? Will he go along with this?"

"He will think it a splendid idea because I will tell him it is a splendid idea. All he needs to know is that regular money will come to Brayston."

"Are we all in agreement?" asked Thomas, looking at his sister first, who nodded, and then at his brother.

"'All for one and one for all,' type of thing?" said Stephen. He shrugged his shoulders. "It's worth a try."

"Look at the time," said Anthea, glancing at the clock. "I have to dress for dinner."

Flora moved quietly and quickly away from the door. Anthea left the lounge to stride down the long, wide empty hall.

"Did you see that maid?" asked Stephen.

"One could hardly miss her. But, ah, Stephen, let us not lose sight of what we need to do here."

"I suppose so. Do you know, for a moment, I thought you were suggesting we bump Father off?"

"You really are the limit sometimes. As if any of us would think of such a thing."

CHAPTER 24

—— ❖ ——

DINNER

The low cloud brought night on early while the rain still fell. The woods were wetted to the darkening of tree boles and swelling of streams. In its small park within the close forest, Abinger Mansion blazed with light. From many of the rooms on the ground floor, bright yellowy bars streamed across glistening lawns, picking out long, slanting raindrops. The air was mild but wringing wet.

A hundred yards to the left of the house, a figure emerged from a neat line of bushes. It began moving slowly, deliberately keeping to cover. The shadowy figure's course followed a wide, shallow arc across the front of the building and avoided the streams of light from the windows. It paused often, blending into the gloom whenever it stopped. Having traversed the front, the figure halted before cautiously moving closer. Finally, the figure hid behind a bush not fifteen yards from the house. Had it stepped into the light from the dining room, the shadowy figure would have resolved itself into a man - one wearing a long waterproof trench coat and a broad-brimmed oilskin hat that dripped rain. He carried a small pack at his side. Across his back was slung a canvas bag suitable only for a gun.

The figure studied the house, staring into the dining room's interior, watching Ada draw the curtains across the room's three tall windows. As she drew the last curtain, the figure disappeared.

"Sophie," whispered Flora, beckoning her friend into an empty bedroom along the passageway from Sir Ephraim's suite from which Sophie had just emerged.

"What is it?" whispered Sophie, as she shut the bedroom door behind them.

"All three are after Sir Ephraim's money. It was disgusting hearing them talk."

"Oh, how awful... What did you hear?"

"They're trying to make him think they're going to work together to keep control of Frobisher Bank within the family. I don't understand it very well, but they were talking about putting the bank shares into a trust."

"That won't help," said Sophie. "Estate duty for large estates is now up to 40%. They'll have to sell some shares or property to pay it."

"You don't say?"

"My Auntie Bessie was talking about it the other day. Actually, she was talking about ways around paying estate duty. It sounds quite easy unless the property is entailed. What did the three of them sound like - their attitudes?"

"Other than reminding me of Macbeth, I think they are just obnoxious people. But at one point, I thought they were about to plot the killing of Sir Ephraim. Perhaps I misheard because they, Anthea, really, never mentioned it again. Instead, it came out that Thomas and Anthea had already decided on a trust, and they convinced Stephen to join them. Together, they mean to convince Sir Ephraim to go along with their plan. They're anxious about being cut from his will or receiving reduced bequests. That's my report. Once one gets over the initial frightfulness of listening at a door, it is really rather fun. Even when the people are disgusting. Do you think it's habit forming? I must go because I'm looking after the Manningtree girl."

"Well done," said Sophie, smiling. Flora smiled back.

They left the bedroom and headed in different directions.

Sir Ephraim's journey to the dinner table was a long, laborious process. Against the advice of his physician and the more immediate protestations of Mrs Fisher, Sir Ephraim insisted he would sit at his own table with his family about him one last time. He had dressed for dinner but also wore slippers.

The main staircase had many stairs. Sir Ephraim stopped on every one of them. He insisted Sophie support his right arm while he ineffectually held the rail with his left. The footman went before him while Mrs Fisher followed behind. Nurse Gleason waited with a wheelchair at the bottom.

"I used to slide down this bannister." Sir Ephraim's breath came in brief gasps. "I don't think I shall tonight."

"That must have been quite the slide, sir," said Sophie. "Just a few more steps."

"It's not worth me putting in a lift... You're too educated to be a maid."

"While I'm here, I am a maid. Usually, I'm a big cog in a tiny domestic servant agency."

"Big cog... That's good. I'm a big cog, too, but now look at me."

"You're doing very well under the circumstances, Sir Ephraim."

"Yes... I like you. You don't chide me like Fisher does."

"She has your best interests at heart. What would you do without her?"

"Run amok... You're a good sort, Fisher," he called over his shoulder. "Dependable... and you put up with me. Do you hear?"

"I do, sir, and thank you," replied the housekeeper.

"Yes. I know I can be difficult sometimes... Sophie, I think I'll have to be carried back after dinner. All right, let's try this next one."

As this difficult descent was being accomplished, in the children's bedrooms, Arthur, Viscount Manningtree, aged eight, and his sister, Lady Mary, aged six, were being read bedtime stories. Lady Anthea's maid, Rosina, read to Arthur, who soon fell asleep. In another bedroom, Lady Mary was wide awake and giggling almost hysterically. Flora and the little girl were pretending to be rabbits while they read a Peter Rabbit story together.

Once safely at the bottom of the stairs and seated in his wheelchair, Sir Ephraim was taken to the dining room by his nurse.

There were only five to dinner. After the turbot, the main course had been served and as the dishes were being taken away by Sophie and a footman, Sir Ephraim spoke to his son-in-law.

"How are things at Brayston?"

"Oh, everything's fine in the main," answered Lord Manningtree. "We had a poor harvest this year. The wheat came off without difficulty. The root crops and fruit trees," he shook his head, "it was one problem after another for both home farm and tenants."

"Are you still growing sugar beet?" asked Sir Ephraim. As he spoke, and it was difficult for him, he took short, frequent breaths.

"Yes, but the price is awful."

"A government subsidy is what's needed," said Sir Ephraim. "You'll never have price stability until you can compete with sugar cane imports. Sugar beet was fine during the war, but not now."

"Should I get out of it?"

"Not for me to advise you. You're the farmer, Philip. What I would do is look into commercial greenhouses for greater profits."

Lord Philip nodded.

"I believe there are a lot of sound investment opportunities at present," said Lady Anthea. "The car industry, for example. Particularly the distribution of petrol and the establishment of vehicle dealerships."

"Hmm, Anthea, that is quite perceptive of you," said Sir Ephraim. "It's a growing industry, and that growth requires financing."

"I've been thinking Frobisher could take a lead in such financing," she continued.

"Ah, yes. But that's for others, now," said Sir Ephraim.

"I know, Daddy. But we can carry on with your work."

"How is that possible?"

"Well, I don't like to discuss business at table, but we're all family here, after all. And facts need to be faced. No, I was thinking, Frobisher's shares could be put into one of those trust things. Then the family could continue your work."

Sir Ephraim said nothing while he stared at his daughter.

"Trust?" queried Thomas. "How would that work?"

"A trustee administers entrusted property as specified in a legally binding document." Sir Ephraim's breath came faster and shallower.

"Oh, I see. If it means keeping control over the direction of Frobisher, I'm all for it," said Thomas. "I mean, we should be realistic. I'm not exactly an expert in bank financing and I would think such help would be jolly useful."

"The shares are a simple issue," said Sir Ephraim. "The management of the bank is not. No trustee could help you there."

"Couldn't we find a competent manager?" asked Lady Anthea.

"That's not so easy," said Sir Ephraim. "It would require someone with vision and a sound background. They'd want a lot of money and a share of the business. Frank had the vision. He wanted to redevelop run-down areas of London. That's solid thinking. Safe and profitable thinking."

"But, Father," said Stephen. "Couldn't we do that through this trust business? I mean to say, if you tell us where to invest, we'll follow your lead. You have the vision while we could carry it on. An expensive manager wouldn't be necessary. I must say, I'm rather taken with the idea. Very intriguing."

Sir Ephraim looked from one of his children to another, to another.

"I'm agreeably surprised by this conversation." Sir Ephraim took his time and weighed his words. "However, I have already decided on a course of action concerning the bank. I will tell you what it is tomorrow... when the others arrive. I'm rather tired now, and I still need my strength to finish dinner."

"Of course, Daddy," said Lady Anthea. "You must take good care of yourself."

Sophie hurried to the kitchen, carrying a silver serving tray. When she arrived, Mrs Barker immediately called out across the kitchen,

"Trifle's ready."

Sophie went to the table, where stood a large glass bowl of trifle. She looked at Mrs Barker and raised her eyebrows. Mrs Barker responded by giving a quick thumbs-up sign, causing Sophie to smile as she took the dessert to the dining room.

Mrs Barker had risen to the occasion. Sophie knew this for a fact because of the way the family had attended to their food. The plates from the table were coming back almost clean. The trifle looked so good, Sophie hoped the family refrained from demolishing it so she could sample some later.

"Lost my London cook," said Sir Ephraim, as the trifle was being served. "Wouldn't come out to the depths of Dorking. Still, whoever Fisher has found has prepared a tolerable meal."

"Better than tolerable," said Thomas, finishing his trifle.

"Yes, all in all, an excellent dinner," said Lord Philip. "I tell you who has an extraordinarily talented chef, a French chappie, and that's Lord Stokely."

"Oh, yes? He's been doing well for himself recently," said Stephen. "No matter what's going on, Stokely's in the middle of it. Wouldn't surprise me if he's prime minister one day."

"Which party would he lead?" asked Sir Ephraim, a strand of irritation in his voice. "No one knows. Bonar Law would make a good prime minister."

"I agree with Stephen about Stokely," said Lord Philip. "The man has vision. He rises above the narrower interests of competing parties. Bonar Law, like many others, is mired in party politics. This country needs to be united under a firm, fair leadership."

"I dare say," replied Sir Ephraim. "I'm afraid I must leave you to sort out Britain's future. Please excuse me, I'm rather tired."

He signalled to Sophie that he was ready to go back to his suite. She came over from her station to take Sir Ephraim away in his wheelchair. The rest of the diners stood up to bid him good night.

Sophie and Sir Ephraim waited in the hall for the footman to return with Sir Ephraim's valet and the nurse.

"If you will excuse my presumption, sir," said Sophie quietly. "I don't like Lord Stokely, either."

She had seen Sir Ephraim's reaction to the mention of the peer's name and wanted to draw him out.

"Have nothing to do with him," said Sir Ephraim. He thought for a moment. "Why don't you like him?"

"I have heard he will stop at nothing to get what he wants."

Sir Ephraim did not answer. Then the servants and Nurse Gleason arrived to carry him upstairs in a chair, his wheelchair to be brought up after him.

Barry, the Manningtree chauffeur, passed by an open door in the servants' area. He saw Ada arranging the now cleaned silver and fine china for Mrs Fisher to inspect and lock away in the silver room. He lounged against the doorpost.

"How are you settling in, my pretty maid?" asked Barry.

"The name's Ada, if you please. I'm settling in nicely, thank you, but I'm busy at the moment, as you can see."

She carried on with her work.

"That's a lot of silver. Makes you think, don't it?"

"Think of what?"

"Of being rich, of course. His Lordship has some gold plate. It never gets used, though. Now the Duke I was telling you about, he has a lot of gold plate."

"You want gold plate, too? What would you do with it...? I don't think you should be hanging around here. Mrs Fisher will catch you."

"So what if she does? It's a free country."

"Not in her silver room, it isn't."

"I'm outside the room... I've been thinking. I have to go to Dorking early tomorrow for supplies. Mrs Barker's right particular about what she wants. Gave me a list a yard long. Why don't you come with me?"

"Oh, yes, why not? I've the run of the place, I do."

"You look like a smart girl. You could work it if you wanted to."

Ada stopped to look at Barry.

"Maybe I could, but I'm only down here for the weekend. You have too much time on your 'ands."

"That's because chauffeuring's a cushy job."

"So it seems. What do you do, then?"

"Driving, of course. Looking after the cars, running errands. A lot of big names come over to Brayston. They need to be driven places." He hesitated for a moment. "I could tell you some interesting stories about his Lordship."

"Up to something, is he?"

"I'd say he was. But that's for me to know and you to wonder about."

"Why would I be interested? I'll never see him again. Still, I do like a good story."

"Ah, don't matter. I'll be off."

Barry moved quickly from the doorpost as they both had heard someone descending the stairs. Within a few seconds, Mrs Fisher entered the silver room.

"Ah, you're ready," said the housekeeper.

"Mrs Fisher, I noticed a side plate has a small chip under the rim. You can't see it from the top."

"It may have been there already. Show it to me."

CHAPTER 25

HIDDEN MESSAGES

"I'm exhausted," said Flora as she sat on her bed. "I just want to close my eyes."

Both she and Ada were in their bedroom, in their nightclothes. They both appreciated the warmth coming from the radiator.

"It's always like this," said Ada. "When I put my head on that pillow, I'll be off in a jiffy."

A soft knock came at the door, and Sophie entered. She had on her hat and coat, and carried a pad of paper, a black and silver torch, and an oilskin wallet.

"You make me feel slightly guilty," said Flora, "but it will pass."

"This won't take long. I've written up my part. Now, I need your reports."

Flora and Ada took turns in speaking while Sophie took down points of interest.

"Ada, I think Barry might just have been showing off a little - making himself interesting by making Lord Manningtree seem more interesting."

"That's what I thought, miss... Sophie. He legged it because Mrs Fisher was coming, but he 'ad a look on his mug like he had a big story to tell. I dunno. I might be wrong."

"It goes in the report," said Sophie. "If it comes to nothing, at least it can be seen how thorough we are."

"Everyone looks suspicious to me," said Flora. "After hearing Anthea, Thomas, and Stephen, I can readily imagine that each of them, or all of them together, might resort to killing Sir Ephraim."

"It's a possibility, I suppose. But do any of them also seem capable of pushing one brother in front of a train and shooting a second?"

"Phew... I can picture any of them doing the first, but I think the second is beyond them. They're too domesticated for that sort of behaviour," answered Flora.

"They could 'ire someone to do the shooting," said Ada. "The pushing, too, if it comes to it. Then there's that poisoning that got mucked up."

"Yes, the poisoning," said Flora. "They all seem capable of that... particularly Stephen. I could see him trying to poison his brother and making an utter mess of it."

"There is the possibility of another sibling being killed," said Sophie. "Let us suppose it happened. Suspicion would quickly shift to both of the remaining siblings... I fail to see why they would put themselves in such obvious jeopardy. If it came down to 'and then there was one', the police would arrest whoever remained. However, we have to keep our eyes open and observe the entire household as and when we can. It's not our job to interfere... I'm finding that part difficult to adhere to."

"I wouldn't like it if the master got done in," said Ada. "Well, none of them, really. It would look bad on us, an' all."

"Should we think something like that was about to happen, I'll telephone Inspector Morton immediately. He's only in Dorking so he can get here quickly."

"Is he?" said Flora. "He has nice eyes, you know."

"Shall I put that in the report?" asked Sophie. Ada giggled.

"Ah, please don't, thank you."

"Good, our work's finished for the day. We're making progress, but there's nothing conclusive here as yet. I've mentioned to Inspector Morton that Sir Ephraim has some significant news to impart tomorrow. I can't say why, but I have the feeling that nothing of consequence can happen until after the meeting. There's a definite tension in the air. The family is anxious. It makes one think there is more calamity to come."

Sophie took the pages of her report from her notepad and slid them into the wallet.

"Where are you going to hide that?" asked Ada.

"Behind a pillar at the front gate. I have to get it there before one or it will miss being picked up." She looked at her watch. "A quarter to twelve, plenty of time."

"I think it's still raining," said Ada. "I wouldn't like to be out in those woods at night."

"Do you want me to come with you?" asked Flora.

"No, I'll be fine. It's best nobody knows I'm leaving the house, so it's simpler if I go by myself. You rest - we have an early start in the morning."

———✠———

By the light of her torch, Sophie guided herself down the back staircase. Despite her caution, several treads creaked as she trod on them. Dim lights were on in both the first and ground floor hallways. The servants' area and connecting corridors were empty and dark. Having reached the side door, she slid the bolts back to let herself out.

Once outside, Sophie switched off her torch to save the bulb from burning out or the battery dying. She paused, allowing her eyes to become adjusted to the darkness. The air felt damp, but the rain had let up, so she began walking along the path.

A few lights were still on at the front of the house - the dim glow through Sir Ephraim's curtains, a guiding light from the hall downstairs, a soft light from Thomas' bedroom, and a narrow vertical strip of bright light between the heavy curtains of a lounge window. The last helped her to find the drive.

When she was safely away from the house, Sophie switched on her torch. The weak yellow beam was strong enough to reveal three paces in front of her. She hastened down the drive, the soggy night giving her no reason to linger.

From a distance in the dark, Sophie's torch gave her the appearance of a slowly moving firefly - attracting attention rather than illuminating her surroundings. The figure saw her little light. He began moving between the trees, keeping parallel with the drive. Moving stealthily and quickly, he kept up with her pace, despite obstacles in the dark.

The driveway was long, but Sophie soon reached the entrance. Switching off her torch, she listened. Hearing nothing in the stillness of the night, save for water dripping from the trees, Sophie switched on her torch once more and hid the wallet out of sight behind a pillar. She returned to the house, mindful of showing a light that might be seen.

When she had gone, another torch flashed on, its beam playing about the base of the pillars. The man found the oilskin wallet. Unwrapping it, he took out and read Sophie's report. Having finished, he re-wrapped the pages carefully and put the wallet back. The light went out.

At one in the morning, a car pulled up by the gates. Detective Sergeant Gowers got out to search behind the pillar for the oilskin wallet. Once found, he extracted the report and put the wallet back. He returned to Dorking.

———※———

The servants of Abinger Mansion arose, beating the dawn by a good forty-five minutes. Breakfast was a staggered affair. For several of the staff it began at 6:30 a.m., for the rest it was at 8:15 a.m., and at 9:30 a.m the family breakfasted.

Eat, clean, clean, clean was the servants' morning work, and it was a whirlwind of activity that did not subside until they sat down to their dinner at lunchtime, which came punctually at twelve. Everyone worked hard and, to some extent, helped one another.

Once more, Sophie appreciated how good Ada was at her job - any job. Everything she did she completed quickly, quietly, satisfactorily, without supervision, and usually ahead of schedule. She heard Mrs Fisher complimenting Ada, which was a rare moment for any housekeeper. It caused Sophie to wonder if Ada might be offered a job.

"Good morning, sir," said Ada to Stephen, as she pulled back the curtains and began tidying the room. "It's nine-thirty and breakfast is being served downstairs."

"What? Why are you waking me up?" Stephen pulled away the pillow from over his head. He slowly propped himself up.

"Master's orders. The rest of the family is at breakfast already. Mrs Frank Wright will arrive in an hour."

"You're cheerful," he said as he watched her move around the room, picking up his strewn clothes and putting the dressing table back in order. "It's a pleasure watching you," he added, smiling and running his fingers through his hair. "Ouch," he exclaimed suddenly. "Ooh, it's awful," he pressed a hand against his neck. "I have such a dreadful sharp pain..." He grimaced. "I wonder... I wonder, would you massage it for me?"

"Is it your neck, sir? I have the perfect cure for that. It's called a rope. Shall I go and fetch it?"

"Hilarious... It's going now, anyway."

"I'm pleased to hear it. I 'ave to leave, but I'll be back later to give your room a thorough airing, sir." She bobbed and quickly left the room before he could reply.

Lady Anthea's maid, Miss Rosina Murray, accosted Flora in a hallway when no one else was present.

"Excuse me, I want a word with you,"

"Yes, Miss Murray?"

"I dislike the way you read the bedtime story to Lady Mary. She is at an excitable age and needs to be calmed before she sleeps. She woke up pretending she was a rabbit this morning. This will not happen again."

"Do I not read to her again or is the prohibition against bunny rabbits only?"

"I shall find a more suitable book. You may read that to her."

"Very good, Miss Murray."

Sir Ephraim's library at Abinger Mansion comprised some two thousand volumes, although very few were recent acquisitions. The library represented a literary snapshot in time, dating to when the house was first built or shortly afterwards.

Flora was dusting the room when she found several old medical books left out on a table. One was an early edition of Grey's Anatomy. The others listed homoeopathic treatments or the identification of diseases. She saw the gap on the shelves and returned the books to their place. Flora reflected upon who it could be who had taken a sudden, late night interest in medicine.

The dining room table required polishing. After breakfast, Sophie, wearing an apron, set about the task. It was a long, mahogany table with a rich deep lustre that needed some light attention to bring it back to its full glory. While she was buffing the table, the front door was opened to admit Mrs Frank Wright - Millicent Wright. She was wearing mourning clothes with a thin, black veil over her hat. Her two children accompanied her. Sophie ceased working as soon as she saw them. Picking up the rags and tin of polish, she stepped back to a place out of sight from the hall.

Mrs Fisher greeted the widow and was very tender towards her. Millicent Wright spoke so quietly that Sophie had difficulty hearing what she said. She glimpsed the two children. The white-faced thirteen-year-old boy looked bewildered while the nine-year-old girl hung on her mother's hand as though she would never let go. The realization of the loss of Frank Wright, husband and father, suddenly caught at Sophie's heart. A surge of sympathetic emotion unexpectedly welled up inside her.

Barry came in, carrying luggage. He stopped to put the cases down, waiting while the two women finished their conversation. Sophie could see him clearly through the crack between a door and its post. While he waited for instructions, he smoothed his moustache. Within a few moments, Mrs Fisher spoke to him. Barry picked up the cases to follow the small party upstairs. Sophie returned to her polishing.

———⋈———

Lady Anthea entered the kitchen to speak to Mrs Barker.

"At what time will Sir Ephraim be having his luncheon in his room?"

"Ma'am, it will go up at half-past twelve."

"I'll take his meal to him. Make sure it doesn't go up before I come for it."

"Yes, ma'am."

Lady Anthea turned and left the kitchen. Mrs Barker glared after her until she had gone.

"That's not right," said the scullery maid, who was preparing vegetables. "Mrs Fisher should have told us, not her."

"There are a lot of things that aren't right in this world," said Mrs Barker. "Most you have to put up with quietly, my girl. How are those brussels coming along?"

"I've nearly finished, Mrs Barker."

"Good. Leave them in cold water and put the kettle on. We'll have tea while we're on the go. Can you use that there electric cooker?"

"I think so." The young woman turned to look at the cooker. "Hotpoint... You just turn the knob, don't you?"

"That's right. Turn it on High. Take the kettle off once it's boiling and don't forget to switch the knob back to Off. The top stays hot, you see... It's strange not seeing a flame. Don't you think so?"

"It is... I don't like electric. I can't really see how it will catch on."

"Well, neither do I. Electric might be handy for small saucepans as long as you're watching - I'll say that much for it. I wouldn't trust the oven, though. Give me a good gas oven any day... And I'm glad he has both here or I don't know what I would have done."

Sophie was trying to clean Sir Ephraim's rooms without disturbing him, which proved to be impossible. He was fussing over the slightest noise. While Sophie was working in an adjoining room, Sir Ephraim sent the nurse to find out what she was doing. He did this several times.

"Why is he like this today?"

"He had a slight turn last night and slept poorly," replied Nurse Gleason. "He's now convinced someone is going through his papers. I'm afraid it's the side effects of the medicine he's taking."

"What medicine is that?"

"Nitroglycerin. I telephoned the doctor about Sir Ephraim's condition and he said to halve the dosage next time. He'll be here tomorrow, so perhaps he'll change it again for something else."

"This must be very difficult for you, having the doctor in London."

"It is. I don't like it... I have atropine to use in case of a serious attack. If anything goes wrong, I'll be blamed."

"What could go wrong?"

"I can assure you, I shan't make a mistake. If there's an emergency and action needs to be taken immediately... well, I'm here and the doctor isn't. It's very easy to blame a nurse even if she is following instructions."

"Oh, dear, I see what you mean... I'm sure you'll be fine... Do you think Sir Ephraim has been given too much of the drug?"

"No, it's just something that can happen. Nitroglycerin can cause headaches. That's why he's irritable. A gentleman was asking about Sir Ephraim's medicine earlier."

"Really? Who was that? Perhaps he has medical training."

"No, he doesn't." Nurse Gleason smiled at her recollection. "It was Mr Thomas. I suppose he was just interested in his father's condition... Although, he asked for the exact quantity of atropine to be used in an emergency."

"That's interesting... Mind you, if it comes to that, I don't have a clue. Is it a pill or a tablespoon of powder?"

"It's a small amount of liquid in an ampoule. I have to inject it when needed."

"I'm so glad you have it under control."

"What are you talking about?" Sir Ephraim's faint, querulous voice came from the bedroom. "I feel nauseous."

"I must go," said the nurse.

Sophie returned to her cleaning and tidying.

CHAPTER 26

TENSION

Prudence Wright, Alfred's wife, should not have travelled to Abinger Mansion. She arrived after lunch. Had anyone with a modicum of kindness met her there, that person would have said either for her to lie down and rest, or to go home, lie down and rest. Being subject to Sir Ephraim's dictates, there was no respite for the poor lady.

During the Trefoil negotiations, Alfred Wright had been inexpressibly sad at the death of his brother Frank. She was, in her turn, devastated by the loss of her husband, Alfred. At thirty-five with no children, her dress was the blackest and least ornamented, her manner the most restrained, her veil the thickest, and, behind that veil, one imagined her eyes to be the reddest. When she spoke, which was infrequently, it was barely above a whisper. Mrs Wright, in her distracted state, needed continual reminders and gentle prompts. Mrs Fisher, kind though she was to Prudence, had her own urgent duties, which meant she had little time to spare for the grieving widow. The busy staff were not of her class, so could neither comfort nor comment, while the rest of the family preferred to let extreme grief keep its own company.

When lunch was over, the pressure of work for the domestic servants eased considerably. Sophie, Flora, and Ada had worked hard during the morning, getting all needful tasks accomplished to leave as much time as possible for surveillance. They all agreed they had to listen in on the private family meeting where Sir Ephraim would make his announcement.

"How are we going to manage it? He'll bung us out," said Ada.

"What a delicious phrase," said Flora. "I don't believe I've ever been bunged out of anywhere. I'm rather looking forward to it."

"Of course you have," said Sophie. "At school, we were always getting caught out of bounds and told to leave. We just never considered it as being bunged out."

"This meeting about the will or whatever it's supposed to be," said Ada. "Will they want tea?"

"Hmm, I don't know," said Sophie. "That's a good idea. Perhaps, I'll suggest it to Sir Ephraim... No, not him, he'll say no. I'll suggest it to Mrs Fisher instead and see what she says. I'll tell her it will help with our police work."

"Where is it being held?" asked Flora.

"I'm not sure... In the library, I should think. The study doesn't have enough chairs, and the upstairs office is too cramped."

"If he has it in the library and 'e's behind that big desk," said Ada, "there are a couple of places one of us could stand where he wouldn't see us."

"The family might see us," said Flora. "They would certainly exercise their bunging privileges on their own account."

"He'll want all servants out of the room while speaking of private matters. Now, if a window was open, I could listen from outside," said Sophie.

"Oh, it's raining," said Flora. "You don't want to get yourself wet."

"I don't want to, but we must know what happens. If we get that information, Inspector Morton will be so thoroughly impressed he'll give us more work."

"But if we don't, he won't," said Flora.

"They do say, if you put a wineglass against the wall, you can hear what's being said in the next room," said Ada.

"I've tried that, but it's very indistinct," said Flora.

"I know!" said Sophie. "We'll use the speaker from the gramophone."

"That's a grand idea! We should test it first, shouldn't we?" asked Flora.

"Yes, we should."

"What will you say if somebody sees you?" asked Ada.

There was a long silence.

"Shall we say we're looking for ghosts?" suggested Flora.

"Excellent! That's it! We'll tell them it amplifies the ectoplasm, and one can hear ghosts talking in the walls when the conditions are right."

"Bags, I do it! In a play, it would be a dead certainty I'd be cast for the part."

"Would you really say that to someone?" asked Ada, incredulously.

"If I say it with a straight face, they will either think I'm mad or it's true. Then, they'll want to listen."

"No, I just couldn't bring meself to do that, I'm sure."

Flora began speaking in a dramatic Russian accent. Her eyes flashed, and she made poignant, graceful gestures with her hands. "I shall be Madame Flora Danevetsky, the world-renowned medium and adept in ectoplasmic vibrations. You have heard of me, of course. I am famous in Paris, Vienna, Moscow, New York, and Dorking. What am I? A mere vessel... but the work I do - it is everything! You wish to receive a message from the other side? Pah, it is nothing to me. I shall summon the departed spirit of your choice for a measly tenner."

Ada and Sophie laughed while Flora maintained her grave dignity.

"I've never cared for this house. For goodness' sake, there's nothing to do once one is stuck out here," said Stephen, staring through the lounge window at the dismal woods.

"I'd keep horses," said Lord Philip from behind a newspaper.

"You can't ride them in the rain. It's too uncomfortable."

"You can, but I was speaking in a general sense, as an interest."

"Yes... Two hours until tea... It's a rum go, discussing wills in the library at tea-time."

Lord Philip put his paper down. "Better than traipsing out to some law office where the best you can hope for is a poor sherry and a dry biscuit."

"You're right about that. I wish I knew what he was up to."

"It's just two hours to wait, Stephen. Then he will explain everything."

"I know. I'm very concerned about him. It looks like a simple fright would carry him off. I don't think his nerves can stand another shock."

"I hope there isn't one... 'though I believe he's tougher than he looks."

"Yes, he is. But to lose two sons so close together... I don't know what to make of it all. Father says they were accidental deaths. I can see Frank's death being an accident, but Alfred's? It wasn't as though they were all out in the woods with their guns - he was standing on the terrace, for heaven's sake. That was no shooting accident; it was murder. I can't see why Alfred should be murdered, though. In the middle of those negotiations, too. How extraordinary is that...? The papers have said very little. Perhaps someone shot Alfred by mistake when they were really after someone else. Or something else was going on that we don't know about, and it's being hushed up. Now, that I can see."

"Maybe it's none of my business," said Lord Philip, "but you do not seem to be particularly upset at their loss."

"That's because I'm not. I'm sorry they've gone and all that sort of thing, and, of course, I wouldn't have wished it on either of them... You know, it's me being the outsider... Frank was Father's favourite, even when they'd had a bitter disagreement. He has never loved me. Made me realize early on - no matter what I did, it wouldn't make any difference to him."

"I think you're wrong. Sir Ephraim might have had his favourites, but you're here today and that alone is evidence of his affection for you. In a way, you mean more to him now. Sorry for being blunt. That's how I view the matter."

"Perhaps... It's all a bit too late now to patch things up, don't you think? I'll tell you one thing I am going to do, though..."

Sophie missed what he said next because voices and movement on the stairs caused her to abandon her post in some haste.

At 2:30 p.m., Mr Matthew Reese, private secretary to Sir Ephraim, arrived from London. He entered the house carrying a small suitcase and a large briefcase, which items were nearly the same size. He was immediately shown up to Sir Ephraim's suite with the briefcase while the footman took charge of the suitcase. Sir Ephraim told Sophie and Nurse Gleason to leave during his consultation with Mr Reese. The nurse, delighted, left for a walk about the house. When she had gone, Sophie listened at the closed door. Try as she might, she could make out nothing intelligible of the low and slow murmur of voices emanating from the bedroom.

With all the guests arrived, Barry had little to do. He sat for a while, reading newspapers in the servants' hall. Tiring of that, he smoothed his moustache, got up and went outside to smoke.

It had stopped raining. Barry paced up and down, sending quick puffs of smoke into the air. Ada watched him from a window. Broad-shouldered and quite tall, he looked smart in his close-fitting uniform. To her, he seemed restless. His pacing reminded her of the lions in Regent's Park Zoo just before feeding time. Deciding she had watched someone else do nothing for long enough, she carried on with her chores.

"Is there anything I can get for you, madam?" asked Sophie as she stood in Prudence Wright's bedroom.

"No, I don't think so. Will tea be delayed?"

"Tea will be served in the library at four o'clock. I can make a pot for you now if you wish."

"It doesn't matter, I can wait... Please call me at a quarter to four."

"Certainly, madam."

Sophie left the room quietly, trying not to make any noise that would disturb Mrs Wright's grief. She wanted to say something meaningful, but nothing presented itself. After she closed the door, Sophie noticed Thomas stealthily entering Sir Ephraim's rooms. Knowing he was unable to hear the conversation, she left him to it.

Mrs Fisher directed John, the footman, in arranging the seating in the library for the coming meeting. The large library was laid out as two rooms, with a wide archway between them. The meeting was being held at one end of it. After Mrs Fisher had left, John put six chairs in a semi-circle. He removed the chair behind the desk to make space for Sir Ephraim's wheelchair. He placed a seventh chair to one side of the desk for the use of Mr Reese.

John left. Flora brought in a tray of tea things. While arranging them at the far end of the library, Stephen came in and sat in Reese's chair. He dialled a telephone number and held the candlestick phone in one hand, while putting the receiver to his ear with the other. He raised his feet up onto the desk.

"Yes, I'll wait," he said to the operator. Stephen stretched himself out and lounged in the chair.

"Larry? Hello, old boy," he said, smiling. "What was the result?... Came in last? That's impossible. Was there a steward's inquiry?" Stephen sat bolt upright. "Yes... Yes, I understand... What's the total now...? How can it be that much...?" He brought his feet down suddenly. "Yes, I'll get the money for you this week. I promise I will. Yes... Goodbye."

Stephen crashed the receiver back on its cradle and thumped the phone onto the desk before stalking out of the room, wearing a thunderous look.

Flora went to the desk and put the telephone and chair back in their places.

After three o'clock, the house became so quiet it seemed deserted. Halls were empty of staff and the family stayed in their rooms. Lord Philip, in sole possession of the lounge, had his eyes shut and head propped by an arm. Reese had not emerged from Sir Ephraim's rooms. The Manningtree children were quiet and amused themselves in the old nursery while Rosina watched over them. Millicent Wright's children were in their mother's room. She read them a story to keep their minds from dwelling on their loss. Prudence Wright, dry-eyed, lay on her bed, staring at the ceiling.

The kitchen, as always, was a busy, separate world. It was now filled with the smell of fresh-baked cakes and scones. Mrs Barker, the kitchen maid, and a scullery maid were preparing for the afternoon tea. Mrs Barker was humming as she worked. The kitchen maid piled some small cakes on serving plates while others waited on wire racks. There was enough to feed the household twice over.

In this quiet before the meeting, Sophie, Ada, and Flora discussed matters in the morning room.

"I haven't been able to try the gramophone speaker yet," said Flora. "There's always someone in the lounge."

"We shan't worry about a test. Do what you can with it, Flora. We must use all means available to us to find out what Sir Ephraim will say. What about you, Ada?"

"I have the corner table set up with a long tablecloth over it and it's mostly hidden by the archway. Once you've tucked yourself underneath it, I'll put that big globe in front, so you should be safe."

"Excellent. Don't forget to call Prudence at a quarter to four, as I'll be hidden by then. Is there anything that rattles on top? I might bump the table accidentally."

"There's just a big empty bowl. Right colourful... It has all sorts of dear little fairies painted on it. It's beautiful."

"I saw that," said Sophie. "Yes, it is lovely. It's Wedgwood."

"Let's hope those little fairies are good ones and keep our secret," said Flora.

"Ada," said Sophie, "stay in the room if you can. If you're bunged out, stay outside to see if anyone else tries to listen in on the meeting."

"Er, I can only watch one door unless I stand right outside in the 'all."

"That would put them off. What to do? Allow someone to listen or prevent them?"

"I say prevent them," said Flora. "This is our eavesdropping show, after all. No one can push their way in when they're not wanted. Besides, I'll see if anyone approaches from the back because I'll be in the study next door."

"You can't do that. They'll see you with your giant ear trumpet against the wall."

"Not if I have the door only slightly ajar."

"I think you want to get caught so you can do your act."

"Oh, yes, you're perfectly right."

"Please, Flora, try not to be seen. We have to listen in and I might get caught, despite our precautions. Keep the door closed as far as possible. Ada, watch from the stairs or the dining room, whatever you think is best."

"Right-o. If you get caught, Miss Flora, could you try to hang it out so I can have a listen?"

"You'll be my audience? Oh, that is superb."

"Let's not lose sight of our reason for being here," said Sophie.

"Of course, we won't," said Flora. "There's no harm in a little fun along the way. Is there, Ada?"

"No, no. I like fun as well as you do," said Sophie, "but while we're here, it has to be the job first and last."

"Yes, Miss Burgoyne," said Flora.

CHAPTER 27

━ ✦ ━

KINDRED AND UNKINDRED SPIRITS

T he group at one end of the library settled into seats with an air of doomed resignation. Sir Ephraim sat back a little from his desk because the arms of the wheelchair did not fit under it. Reese sat on his right or to the left of those facing Sir Ephraim. Stephen was on the far left of the group. He was wearing a dark suit and a black armband. Next to him came Prudence Wright, her veil down, sitting very erect. Beside her sat Millicent Wright, so tense that she looked as though she were expecting a death sentence from a judge. Thomas had composed himself to look thoughtfully intelligent. Lady Anthea looked down at her lap and twisted the rings on her fingers. Lord Philip, on the far right, sat closest to the door. He looked relaxed. In the further room, beyond the archway, Sophie crouched hidden under a corner table that was draped with a long tablecloth. Her position was cramped, but she had her notepad and pencil at the ready.

Several files and envelopes were on the desk in front of Sir Ephraim. The old man reached forward to take a sheet of paper from the topmost file.

"Thank you all for coming," said Sir Ephraim. "Oh, ask that servant to leave, will you? We'll have tea afterwards."

Before anyone got up, Ada bobbed and left. She shut the door before going to the kitchen to request fresh tea be made.

"We have suffered grievous losses - husbands, brothers, and sons. I'm so sorry, my dears," he addressed Prudence and Millicent directly, "I wish I could comfort you, but I can't find comfort myself. If there's anything I can do, please tell me. We are in that awful grieving stage where the long, sad road ahead appears to have no end. It does have an end of sorts. You will both find it.

"As you know, I am not a well man. My own time to leave you is not so far distant. This meeting today concerns the new will I have written. All of you are well provided for and no one needs to be concerned about their financial future. You are all treated in a fair manner. However, there is about to occur a significant change. I wanted you to be aware of it so that it came as no surprise once I'm gone. Here you are, Reese. You read it."

Sir Ephraim passed to him the handwritten sheet. Reese adjusted his glasses and cleared his throat as he held the paper in front of him.

"Thank you, Sir Ephraim. This matter concerns the shares in Frobisher Bank. Sir Ephraim's current holdings are 63% of the ordinary voting shares. Thus, he has controlling interest in and, therefore, control of the bank. This means he can appoint whom he pleases to manage the company. Until today, as you know, Sir Ephraim has been the Managing Director.

"The change to this arrangement that is contemplated, discussed, and agreed to by both parties is the sale of 51% of the outstanding ordinary shares effective immediately. I hasten to point out how this percentage retains a controlling interest in all votes according to the company's by-laws.

"To be sold is a parcel of 408,000 shares for the sum of £165,000. The purchaser is Lord Manningtree. As soon as his cheque is honoured by his bank on Monday, the shares will belong to him. He can then do with the said shares as he sees fit. Lord Manningtree will have control of Frobisher Bank."

A long silence, like a pall, settled on the room as the news sank in. Lady Anthea grasped the significance, but was too angry to speak.

"I'm not good with figures," said Stephen, who addressed Reese rather than his father, "but I thought Frobisher's shares were about four pounds each. You're selling them for something around ten shillings. Is that right?"

"Frobisher shares are not publically traded. As of yesterday, each was valued in excess of £4 5s. The sale price in the agreement is eight shillings and ninepence."

Blank faces met this revelation.

"So I got the gist of it correct. Can I ask why, Father?"

"If I may answer that question," said Reese. "It is to pass control of Frobisher Bank to management that will continue the bank's tradition. The estate duty will be reduced by some £315,000, which otherwise would have been borne by the residue shared among you."

"So, to save three hundred thousand," Thomas addressed his father in a voice full of derision, "you give Manningtree here a million and a half profit? That's absurd. I fail to see the point of it!"

Sir Ephraim sat silent and the silence in the room lengthened.

"I can see why you would sell the shares." It was Lady Anthea who suddenly broke the silence, her voice brimming with anger and frustration. "What I dislike is not being forewarned of this action. Had I known, I could have raised the capital for such a purchase. I want an explanation." She turned upon her husband with a savage look. "Where did £165,000 come from!? Out with it."

"I will explain everything later, my dear. It is all for the best, I assure you."

Receiving no satisfactory answer from Lord Philip, Lady Anthea stood up and approached the desk.

"I suppose there is nothing I can say or do to alter this arrangement?"

Sir Ephraim looked at his daughter. It was a tender look.

"Some things are more important than money. The remaining sum is more than adequate. Be content with that, my daughter."

"It seems I must learn to be content." She said acidly before marching out of the room.

"Bit of a surprise, what?" said Stephen, also now standing. He sounded disappointed more than anything else. "May I see you after tea, Father?"

"Reese, if you please," said Sir Ephraim.

Reese picked up a large envelope and from it took a small package, one of several it contained. Saying nothing, he handed one to Stephen, which bore his name. Stephen examined the package, giving it a gentle squeezing.

"It's just a token amount for now," said Sir Ephraim to his son. "You will be amply provided for when the time comes."

"Thank you, sir," said Stephen.

"Will you be leaving now, my boy?" asked Sir Ephraim.

Stephen looked at him and smiled. "No, I'll stay the night, but I think I'll skip tea if you don't mind."

"No, I do not mind."

He watched Stephen as he left the library.

"There's something here for you, too, Thomas," said Sir Ephraim.

Thomas got up and approached the desk.

"I do not understand," he said.

"I know you don't. Leave it like that. Some say ignorance is bliss. I'm inclined to agree with that sentiment these days."

Thomas received his package from Reese and stared at it in his hands. It contained some hundreds of pounds, perhaps a thousand - it was thick enough - yet it brought him no joy. That was impossible, for he had just witnessed his parent give away half the Wright fortune to his brother-in-law. He supposed a similar transaction would have been made with Frank had he lived. And if not Frank, then Alfred. He stood holding a thousand in his hand and yet felt himself robbed of three or four hundred thousand pounds. He nodded, managed a lopsided smile, and left the library.

"I'll see you later," said Lord Philip in a quiet voice to Sir Ephraim. He closed the door behind him.

"I'm sorry you had to witness all of that," said Sir Ephraim to Millicent and Prudence. "It would have been worse later on." His breathing was easier, as if eased of a burden. "Please make any requests you have to Reese and he will take excellent care of you. I'm sorry, I'm rather tired. Please forgive me, but I'll go up soon."

"Thank you for your kindness," said Prudence.

"No, thank you... Thank you for loving my son and making his life one of contentment. Before I leave, there are a few things I'd like to say..."

———⊱✖⊰———

"What in the world are you doing?" asked John, the footman. He stood in the study's doorway.

"Shh, don't speak. The vibrations are difficult to discern." Flora held the great bell-like horn speaker against the wall with her ear close to the small end.

"That'll get you fired."

"Why would communing with the dead get me fired? And, please, be quiet."

"Oh, come off it. You're listening to a private conversation."

"Don't be silly. If I wanted to listen to a flesh and blood conversation, I'd do it at a door or through a keyhole, not through a thick wall. No, there's someone trying to communicate. They sound so distant, though... Did you know anyone called Jane?"

"Jane...? No, I don't think so... You can't really communicate with the dead, can you?"

"They're not dead. They have only departed to another place. You see, while they were alive on earth, these walls absorbed the vibrations from their voices. That created an anchor point that intersects between the unseen and visible worlds. Such strong magnetism draws them. They see their own vibrations like light in a dark place. They can also speak to other spirits. A message can be transmitted by any spirit to one with a tie to this place. I can only commune with them under exceptional circumstances. But I can hear what they say and they know I'm here... Was it Mary?"

"Ah, no... I had an aunt Marjorie who died."

"It must be her then."

"Does it... does it work...? I wonder... could I have a turn?"

"I don't see why not. As I say, the vibrations are weak and uncertain. Careful with the speaker, otherwise you'll hear nothing but the extraordinary noise it makes."

In a tentative way, John put his ear to the speaker and listened. "Funny, isn't it? It sounds like the sea and wind rushing about in a long tunnel."

"That's the sound of flowing ectoplasm. It will vibrate when the spirits are speaking and forming their words. It's quite simple."

"I can't say I hear any spirits speaking... except for them droning on next door."

"It's because two of us are trying to listen. Our combined presence creates an energy distortion which prevents the spirits being heard."

"Oh, yes, I suppose it would... I'm forgetting myself. There are things I've got to do," said John. "Reckon I'll give it a proper go later on."

"Yes, you do that. And thank you for reminding me. I have work to do as well. I had better put the speaker back before it's missed. Very few are as intelligent about these mysteries as you are."

"Here you go." He handed the gramophone speaker to Flora. "Are you a medium?"

"Sad to say I'm not. However, being a gipsy princess, disinherited because of the war you understand, I have received hidden knowledge of many things. This wisdom stretches back a hundred generations. It's passed down from mother to daughter. So don't tell anyone about this. Keep it a secret or the spirits will be very upset with you."

"Psst, you can come out now. They've all gone and the tea things have been cleared away." Ada began moving the globe aside from in front of the table.

"Uh, thank goodness. Could you give me a hand, please? My leg's gone to sleep."

"Upsadaisy," said Ada, as she helped Sophie to stand. "Did you hear anything?"

"Look... look at these pages! I got the lot, except for some things Prudence was saying at the end." Sophie fanned the pages of her notepad that were covered in shorthand. "I nearly sneezed at one point. There's dust under the table."

"Yes, you've got some on your dress. Hold still a mo." Ada brushed at Sophie's skirt. "That needs a proper doin', but it's good enough for the time being."

"Thank you. Did Flora hear anything?"

"I don't know because I didn't dare ask 'er, or I'd have broken up. She got John the footmen with that huge speaker stuck in 'is ear, up against the wall, listening to the ectoplasm. I couldn't stay cos I was cryin' with laughter. I had to go outside, so I missed the end. Miss Flora - she's a proper caution."

"I wish I'd been there," said Sophie, smiling. "What about you? Did you see anyone trying to listen at the door?"

"Only Rosina, Barry, Mrs Fisher, the two valets, Mr Fenton and Mr Barstow. Oh, and Annie, the scullery maid. It was like Clapham Junction out there at one point, what with one coming and chasing off the one ahead of them. To be fair, I think Annie was worried that the fresh tea was wanted. Mrs Fisher was the same. Doesn't matter, though, nobody heard nothing. I tried it and all I could hear was mumbling."

"Servants eavesdropping... I must remember this in the future. You know, Ada, Sir Ephraim has done something quite astonishing. I'll tell you everything as soon as I collect my thoughts but it's caused a lot of bad feeling. That's why the family didn't even touch their tea."

"Blimey, it must have been bad. About the tea, Mrs Barker blew her top with all her baking not being eaten. Don't go near the kitchen, that's all I'm saying."

"Oh, the poor thing. Well, I'm going to the kitchen to get tea and cakes. I've earned them. Come on, we'll both make a big fuss of her."

"All right, but I'm leaving if she starts off again... So, the master's upset 'em all, has he? It must be very serious."

"Yes, you'll never believe what he's done..."

CHAPTER 28

— ❖ —

ANGER AND SPITE

F lora reported to Sophie what she had been able to hear of
the conversation in the library. Her dubious listening method
allowed her only to hear distinctly Mr Reese in the beginning and
Anthea later when she raised her voice. What Flora recounted
agreed with what Sophie had taken down. All other voices, she
said, had sounded like the same person with a peg on their nose
and marbles in their mouth, whispering from the far end of a
tunnel.

Ada and Flora covered for Sophie's absence while she was
in her attic room, writing out a report for Inspector Morton.
As she transcribed her shorthand notes, Sophie's mind became
clearer concerning the Wright family situation. When she had
finished, she came downstairs to use the telephone, which she
managed without incident. Sophie arranged a six-thirty meeting
with Inspector Morton at the end of the drive.

Abinger Mansion was awash with bad feeling. Lady Anthea
smouldered with rage in her bedroom; Thomas was mute and
tense, listlessly wandering about the house; Stephen sat, de-
pressed, in the lounge. These various dispositions caused appre-
hension and some alarm among the servants. Mrs Fisher tried
to continue as though nothing had happened, but she, too, was
affected by the irritable gloominess settling on the place.

Sir Ephraim remained in private conference with Reese and
Lord Philip. They signed documents, transferring the shares.
Only Lord Philip looked pleased with the transaction. Sir Ephraim
possessed an air of relieved resignation while Reese, discharging

his duties with a weary efficiency, looked like he could hardly wait for the day to end.

The shouting started when Lord Philip went to see Lady Manningtree. Sophie had Flora go to the Manningtree's rooms to listen to their conversation if she could manage it. Flora faced a problem when she arrived. Rosina was already in the hall and listening at her mistress' bedroom door.

"What are you doing here?" whispered Rosina savagely as she pulled her ear away from the door and straightened up.

"The same as you," whispered Flora in return. "Move over so I can listen."

"I'll do no such thing."

Ignoring her, Flora put her ear close to the door. After a moment of annoyed hesitation, Rosina did likewise.

"You did it for five thousand!" exclaimed Lady Anthea.

"He was going to sell anyway," said Lord Philip. "It was always going to be Frank. Now it's someone else, but don't ask me who. At least this way we get five thousand pounds we wouldn't otherwise have seen. And we get it straight away."

"You traitor. Didn't you think to tell me?"

"Important people are involved in this. They demanded anonymity, and I gave my word. It's as straightforward as that."

"What a fool you've been. One and a half million going outside of the family."

"Please, I did not start this. It was your father's idea. Three days ago he asked me to act in the matter. I can't see the sense of it, either. If I had refused, another would take my place. That was made perfectly clear. At least we get five thousand... I know you're angry and it's a great disappointment, but there's plenty left in the estate."

"You betrayed me."

"I was sworn to secrecy by your father."

"Well, it's a pity you didn't think to break your promise. Who is behind this?"

"I'm not in a position to answer... Wait! Before you say more. I don't actually know. As I've explained, Sir Ephraim approached me first. He said an agent for the investor would contact me. This person did so at once. He was very cautious in his speech about who he represented, but he let slip it was a favour for somebody important. Honestly, I do not much care who it is. All I can say is we're five thousand better off, and that's all that matters. Come, my dear, you must surely see the sense of it... Well, you think about it and you'll see that I'm right."

With the conversation ending and discovery possible, Flora and Rosina rapidly made themselves scarce - and only just in time. Flora hurried upstairs to find Sophie, but she had already gone to her meeting with the Inspector.

The drive was well lit under the lowering cloud, but when Sophie got into the denser section of the woods, the light became a weak grey and details uncertain. The temperature drop caused a mist to develop. Where a break occurred in the undergrowth, a view of more distant trees showed hazy shelves and ledges of vapour forming around them.

An Austin coupe was waiting when she arrived at the gates carrying an envelope. Detective Sergeant Gowers opened the passenger door for her to get in. Inspector Morton was sitting in the back.

"Sorry for the cramped conditions," said Morton, "but it was all we could hire in Dorking."

"Pops along nicely, though," said a cheerful Sergeant Gowers.

"What is the information you couldn't repeat on the telephone?"

"This report's for you, Inspector. I'll give you the condensed version." She handed over the envelope. "The upshot of it is this. Sir Ephraim held 63% of all Frobisher shares, but he's selling 51% to Lord Manningtree for £165,000. Has sold them, I believe. This price for the shares is far below what they are worth. Essentially, he has given away over one and a half million to his son-in-law. From my observations, I doubt very much that this is Lord Philip's idea. Lady Anthea was unaware, so I firmly believe he's representing someone else."

"Nobody gives away money in the City. Why would he do that?"

"If the transaction had been with his son Frank, it would make sense to avoid hundreds of thousands in death duties. Instead, he has given away a large part of his fortune for no apparent reason," said Sophie.

"There's more to this than meets the eye. There has to be a link with the two murders," said Morton.

"Do you think he's being blackmailed?" suggested Gowers.

"Sir Ephraim doesn't have long to live... I wouldn't think it's that," said Morton. "Not in the normal sense, anyway."

"We'll try to discover how he's being coerced," said Sophie. "I must go. There's a dinner tonight and I have a lot to do."

"Of course. Thank you for this. Excellent work. Could you tell me how you acquired it?"

"Trade secrets, Inspector. Goodbye. I'll leave the daily report by the pillar. We might get fresh information tonight."

The two men said goodbye.

"That's good work," said Gowers, after Sophie had gone.

"Yes, it is. We wouldn't have known about this for weeks. Right, my lad. We'd better get busy. Pity it's the weekend. We need to take a very close look at Lord Manningtree. Where'd he get that kind of money from to buy those shares?"

The police car pulled away, heading for Dorking. It was much darker in the drive as Sophie returned. She drew level with a screen of undergrowth and did not perceive the motionless man behind it, watching her.

When she had passed, he stood up, adjusting the strap of the gun bag he carried. He stepped out to the side of the driveway, holding her in view until she neared the house. Then he moved back into the mist gathering under the trees.

When Sophie returned, Ada, passing her in a passage, made a sign because others were about. Crossed fingers on her left hand. Mrs Fisher was out for blood. Sophie raised her eyes and went to find the housekeeper.

"Miss Burgoyne, I have received a serious complaint about one of your staff."

The two women were standing in Mrs Fisher's office. The housekeeper looked as annoyed as she sounded.

"If you could please explain the complaint and which of my staff was involved?"

"It was Flora. Miss Murray found her listening at the door to Lord and Lady Manningtree's private room. She was found eavesdropping on their private conversation. I cannot for a minute tolerate this type of behaviour. She must leave immediately."

"I see. Have you spoken to Flora?"

"Yes. She replied with the preposterous story that both she and Miss Murray were eavesdropping at the door. I don't know if it's true or not. Miss Murray denies it. That's all beside the point."

"Let us set aside the question of truthfulness for the moment. Please consider why my staff is here. You are cooperating with the police against Sir Ephraim's wishes because you know something is terribly wrong. What have the police said about the two deaths?"

"They called both of them highly suspicious. They did not come right out and say that either was murder, but they left little doubt in my mind that this is how they view them. It is an awful situation."

"I feel much the same way. Mrs Fisher. I'm here to help find the murderer. Someone is wreaking vengeance on the Wright family and I mean to stop them. It is necessary to gather evidence. Flora was gathering evidence. I asked her to listen because I could not do so myself. A murderer will not declare his intentions. He has to be forced into the open and trapped."

"You asked her to listen?"

"Yes. Under the circumstances, I feel some things we count as normal decent behaviour must be suspended. Like you, I would not hesitate to dismiss a servant for eavesdropping out of unbridled curiosity or personal gain. Flora was doing neither. She was gathering information at my request so that it could be sent to the police."

"It can't possibly be Lord and Lady Manningtree... Are you suggesting the murderer is in the house? It's a preposterous idea that the murderer is here. I don't like this. The family is in uproar as it is... There's no peace, no stability."

"It is distressing. Flora listened because she was doing the very thing the police want. Ultimately, it's what you want, which is to restore peace and order to a wounded family. I believe Flora when she says Miss Murray was also listening. What were her motives? The usual ones, I suppose. It's common enough among servants, I don't doubt."

Mrs Fisher became quiet, upset by the atmosphere in the house and the visitation of death. "It goes against the grain," she said at last. "You must have an idea what has caused the agitation in the house."

"If that is a question, I can only give a partial answer, because we are not at the end of the matter."

"What is going on?"

"Sir Ephraim has sold controlling interest in Frobisher Bank to Lord Philip for a fraction of its value."

Mrs Fisher took some moments to digest this outlandish piece of news.

"Why would he do that?"

"Flora was trying to discover that very thing. I've yet to hear what she heard. Whatever it was, I'm sure it is of value to Inspector Morton."

"So, I must bite my tongue...? I see I have no choice. But if I receive a complaint from Lady Anthea, I will be forced to take steps."

"In my opinion, Lady Manningtree will never mention the incident because Rosina will never tell her."

"We shall see," said Mrs Fisher.

"Thank you for your patience," said Sophie. "I'm so sorry you're going through this."

CHAPTER 29

—— • ——

PLANNING

T he family ate dinner in near silence. Mr Reese was present while Sir Ephraim was unable or unwilling to join the family. Of those at table, Prudence and Millicent were the only ones in any way conversational, speaking lightly over a range of topics. The widows had found themselves all of a sudden free of the conventional barrier of sympathy towards those who mourn. At that moment, there were no averted eyes, no sympathetic smiles, or any of those hurried, precise comments people generally make before they can reasonably absent themselves to talk with others who do not grieve. The rest of the diners had forgotten this condescension while they themselves grieved over the loss of fortune. The widows ceased to be treated differently and, in the social vacuum around the table, found it easy to talk with each other. While the table mourned morosely, Prudence and Millicent laid down a stronger foundation of friendship for themselves. They made arrangements to travel back to London together. Prudence asked if she could help Millicent with her children. This prompted a heartfelt invitation from Millicent to Prudence to stay with her. Without hesitation, Prudence accepted.

———— ⋈ ————

Sophie went to Sir Ephraim's rooms to clear away his tray. Sir Ephraim was sitting at a small table alone.

"Tell the cook that her steak and kidney pudding was absolutely perfect. Just how I like it. What's her name?"

"Mrs Barker," answered Sophie.

"She's temporary, isn't she? Came down with you?"

"She did, sir."

"Would she stay on? She'd need Fisher's blessing, of course."

"She might. Perhaps, if you ask Mrs Fisher to speak to her, then they could arrange it between them."

"I'll do that... Would you stay on?"

"Sadly, I have other commitments, so I'm afraid it's out of the question."

"I knew you'd say that... Yesterday, you mentioned Stokely... Made me think. What exactly do you know?"

"I referred to his vindictiveness. I've also heard of his drive and ambition."

"Tell me, who are your people?"

"I'd rather not say because I don't wish them to know that I'm in service."

"Aha! You're a bit of a conundrum. You're not a maid. You're not just a manager of domestics, either. That's Fisher. She's very good at what she does. I'm good at sizing up people's characters. I have to be when I'm loaning money to them. You're what I would term a good risk... Yes, and a conundrum, because you don't like Stokely when everyone else is running after him. That takes insight on your part or your friends are insightful."

"What has he done to you, Sir Ephraim?"

"Ha, you prove my point... What has he done to me?" Sir Ephraim put his head back. "What has he not done to me?" There was pathetic sadness in his voice.

"He can't be brought to justice unless we take a stand against him," said Sophie.

"Stokely's too powerful and too cunning to be taken in the ordinary way. He'll never appear in court answering charges. His underlings might, but never Stokely himself. The only way he can be defeated is by turning his own weapons against him. I awoke to that fact much too late."

"How do you mean, Sir Ephraim?"

"See, you're no maid... He has to be ambushed. Taken in a trap... I hope he hasn't hurt you or anyone you care for."

"No, he hasn't. However, everyone he does hurt is dear to someone."

"Yes, I dare say. I feel a strong inclination to tell you the story, but I won't - for your own good and for the sake of others. We won't discuss him further."

"That is a pity. I might be the one who lays the trap for him." Sophie raised her eyebrows.

"Are you working for the police?"

"This is where I should tell a lie, but I won't. I was at Trefoil House last weekend. On Sunday, I was outside and within two hundred and fifty yards of the sniper when he fired the shot. I had no idea such a thing was going to happen. Several hours later, Stokely arrived. I met Alfred, you know. We had a brief conversation. He seemed a nice man. I found him to be very sad about his brother's death."

"You were there?" Sir Ephraim was stunned to silence. Comprehension began to dawn. He sighed. "Frank and Alfred were always very close... My dear boys. I can barely accept that they have gone. I seem unable to mourn them properly... You were there and now you're here... Are you pursuing Stokely?"

"I wasn't, but I suppose I am now. A few others are, too."

"You're such a puzzle. Not police, I think... I'll tell you this much - you'll hear it, anyway. I've taken a course of action and it would be a relief for me to know someone else understands. When you hear of this action, be assured of this: I have lost two children but I have also saved three... You're clever enough to work it out..." This last speech sapped Sir Ephraim's strength, but he continued.

"It's a great pity I didn't die before this business began... There's much more to it, but that's all I'll say - all I will ever say. Reese may have guessed, but he knows nothing as fact. He's a dry old stick - that doesn't make him stupid." Sir Ephraim paused for a long time while staring at the ceiling. "Always remember your own words. Stokely is vindictive." Sir Ephraim's breath came quick and shallow.

"I shall remember... Is there anything I can get for you, sir?"

"No, I don't think so. Fenton will take care of me."

Sophie took the tray from the room.

After clearing the dining room and other work had wound down, the agency held a meeting in an attic bedroom, discussing the important matters of the day. Sophie sat in a chair while Flora and Ada sat on their respective beds.

"I'm sorry I got us into trouble," said Flora.

"You were doing your job, and very well, too," said Sophie. "Mrs Fisher has come around to the correct perspective of the matter. In her mind, though, listening at doors is beyond the pale and the last thing she wants her temporary staff to be doing."

"That Rosina's got some cheek," said Ada, "causing trouble and lying like that."

"She must see me as a challenge to her authority," said Flora. "Also, she didn't like the way I read Peter Rabbit to Lady Mary. I suppose I'm not her cup of tea."

"Can't win 'em all."

"It's interesting that Lord Philip hadn't told his wife about the upcoming transaction," mused Sophie. "That must mean he knew she would try to stop him. He wanted to go ahead regardless of her wishes. Was it just for money, though?"

"Am I missing something?" asked Flora. "Surely, it was Sir Ephraim's idea."

"It's time for me to lay everything out so both of you can tell me what you make of it all. Ada is already aware of Lord Stokely's involvement, but I have mentioned nothing yet to you about him, Flora."

"Stokely? How is he involved with this?"

"I suspect he is behind it all."

"You do mean darling Lord Stokely, everybody's favourite?"

"Yes."

"Oh dear, is my hero tarnished?"

"He's encrusted with filth. I'll tell you, and what I'm about to relate is not mere idle chatter. The problem we all face is the danger of possessing this knowledge - so keep it all under your hats."

"We've already had to hide from one of 'is agents," said Ada. "Locked ourselves in a room, we did. It was quite funny in the end." She smiled.

Flora looked from Sophie to Ada and back again. "Tell me everything."

Sophie explained what had happened at Trefoil Hall. The only pieces of information she reserved were the identities of Superintendent Penrose, Sergeant Daniels, her cousin Archie, and the two foreign spies. Flora was a willing and amazed listener.

"I can definitely play a spy," said Flora. "There's so much more scope. Was there something else, or did I imagine it? Is the pay for spying better than being a police informant?"

"It was, but I don't know if that will hold true in the future. We're not to call ourselves informants. I don't like that - it sounds tawdry. Our remit is to observe and record... which makes us, um, either intelligence agents or secret agents... What shall we call ourselves? Let's vote on it."

"Oh, secret agents, miss," said Ada.

"Yes, I agree. Intelligence agent sounds unbelievably stuffy."

"Then it's unanimous," said Sophie. "We are, henceforth, secret agents working for a secret agency."

"Lovely!" said Flora. "We should drink a toast to the success of our new careers."

"It's under lock and key," said Sophie.

"I don't think that's a problem," said Ada. "But I wouldn't like to be stealing."

"You can pick locks?" asked Flora. "How marvellous. You must show me how you do it."

"We'll save our celebrations for when we return to London," said Sophie. "There are matters to deal with here. For example, the long reach of Stokely has fastened itself on Sir Ephraim. If my understanding is correct, Stokely's agents killed Alfred and Frank and would have killed again unless Sir Ephraim signed over the shares of Frobisher for a fraction of their value. He won't speak of it fully, but he's said enough for me to glean that much."

"Is that what all this is about?" asked Flora.

"Then there won't be any more killings," said Ada hesitantly.

"I'm not so sure," said Sophie. "I think it's possible that Stokely has not yet finished with Sir Ephraim. He leaves nothing to chance. If Sir Ephraim had not signed those papers today, what would happen next?"

"Another funeral for the Wright family," said Flora.

"Precisely. Which means there may be a killer in the house. Whether this person will act remains to be seen. The question is, what shall we do about it?"

"It depends on who it is," said Flora.

"Lord Philip," said Ada.

"He seems to be involved as far as his having purchased the shares is concerned," said Sophie, "but he received money from a Stokely agent, for he did not have it himself. The shares are destined to go elsewhere."

"Yes, that makes it sound like his Lordship is beyond reproach and was just earning a fee," added Flora.

"They had two of them to bump off poor Mr Alfred. That geezer with the rifle was one while the footman in the 'ouse was another."

"Yes!" exclaimed Sophie. "That careful arrangement of two attempts to ensure the killing of Alfred, preceded by the killing of Frank, makes me think it quite likely there is a murderer in the house at this very moment. If Sir Ephraim had not sold his shares, there would certainly have been another deadly lesson. That person... is here now."

"Who?" asked Flora and Ada simultaneously.

"Let us exempt Sir Philip for the moment, as his acting in the share purchase draws too much attention. That leaves Fenton, Sir Ephraim's valet, Lord Philip's valet Barstow, Barry the chauffeur, Thomas, Stephen, Mr Reese, and John the footman."

"In other words, almost everyone," said Flora.

"And they've all been acting peculiar... What about Mrs Fisher?" asked Ada.

"She is cooperating with the police and agreed to our being here. Although that would be good for camouflage."

"There's the nurse, too," said Flora.

"I wish it was Rosina," said Ada in a low, dark tone. "Handcuffs would suit 'er nicely."

"She exempts herself because she made a fuss about Flora over the eavesdropping. Again, she would not draw attention to herself like that. In the same way, Lady Anthea would not blow her top if she had been working according to a plan. They're both out."

"That running footman at Trefoil," asked Ada, "did he look like anyone 'ere?"

"I can't say he did... He had short hair... he was grimacing because he was running. He had a plainish face, clean-shaven, a lean, muscular build... I took him to be a policeman. I would say Thomas and Stephen are similar to him and, in a way, so are John and Barry, but Barry has a moustache."

"Not getting very close, are we?" said Flora. "We might be secret agents, but we're infants in the detective line."

"I've an idea! We'll get training," said Sophie brightly. "I'll look into that as soon as we get home."

"If I've got this right, one of four people might get bumped off and one of six might be a-doin' it. I don't reckon Mr Fenton; he looks like an 'armless old josser."

"No, I can't imagine him in the role."

"Two of the proposed bumpors are also bumpees," said Flora.

"Did you actually say bumpee...? I suppose Thomas or Stephen might be mad enough to go on killing, but for what reason? They were as shocked by Sir Ephraim's announcement as Anthea was."

"Let's get them off the list, otherwise we won't get anywhere... Who does that leave us with? Good heavens, it's not looking very good for my acolyte, John. And just when he's starting to learn how to commune with the departed, too."

"Oh please, Miss Flora, don't start me off again," said Ada, laughing.

"Right, here's the plan," said Sophie. "We don't know who in the family is the target or the murderer's identity. Our job is to make sure no one reaches one of the possible victims. Thankfully, they're all on the same floor. Sir Ephraim's suite and the Manningtree's rooms are in the right wing corridor while Thomas and Stephen's bedrooms are in the left wing."

"Um, Sophie, have you thought about how we are to stop a killer?"

"It really is more of a police job," said Ada. "Why don't we call them in?"

"I agree the police are better suited for such a task. However, if they were here, the killer wouldn't make a move. He might never be caught."

"I can see that," said Flora. "I'm reluctant to tackle a killer in the middle of the night on my own. I think there'd be an extra corpse in the morning, meaning me."

"Hm, yes, I see," said Sophie. "We really should have revolvers or one of those dear little automatics."

"Do you know, Ada, that Sophie's father is a vicar? I can't imagine where she gets it from. Mr Burgoyne is such a sweet gentleman."

"Although I am a vicar's daughter, I am not a vicar. In any event, murderous behaviour in a gentleman's country house is thoroughly reprehensible and outrageous. This person has been graciously welcomed as a guest and yet wishes to harm his host. This is a disgusting form of treachery that I cannot tolerate under any circumstances. We're in England, for goodness' sake. It happened at Trefoil and it must not happen again here."

"Bravo!" said Flora, clapping. "I'll tell you what I can do, O fearless leader. I'll keep watch in the corridors while remaining hidden. If I believe anything is about to happen, then I'll raise the alarm."

"I can do that, an' all."

"Yes, I suppose that's much more sensible and safe. We can take turns keeping watch. I think I'll ask Mrs Barker if she'll let us have some food. We need to keep our strength up."

———◇———

In the servants' hall just before ten, the staff was at ease. Fenton, a Tottenham Hotspur supporter, and Barstow, a Manchester City devotee, discussed football. They found their rivalry obstructed them from finding common ground save for their joint disdain of Burnley and, in particular, their contradictory admiration for and slight fear of Joe Anderson, Burnley's centre forward.

Barry was building a house of cards while waiting for the two daily kitchen maids to finish, at which point he would drive them home. Mrs Barker was reading recipes from Mrs Beeton's and scowling when she disagreed with them. Annie, the scullery maid, was writing a letter and asked how to spell the occasional word. John was in a shed where he had patched an inner tube for his bicycle tyre. Waiting for the adhesive to cure, he stood at the door smoking, staring into the thickening mist, wondering what dead people did all day. Mrs Fisher was in her office sipping a port and thinking of what she would do when Sir Ephraim died. With only four years of service, it was unlikely any great provision had been made for her in his new will. She considered Burgoyne's, but thought the agency must have an unsettled, disturbing atmosphere due to the peculiar work it did. She decided she would find a more stable establishment through which to find her next appointment.

Mr Reese, an early riser, had already gone to bed, glad the day was over. Rosina, waiting for when Lady Anthea would retire, was in her room, darning a stocking. Lady Anthea was in the lounge, talking with Thomas and Stephen. They talked in bored abstraction of commonplace things, with an inevitable return to the subject that was uppermost in their minds.

"He didn't come right out and say he had signed the new will," said Stephen.

"He sold the shares, so it doesn't matter," said Thomas, irritated by Stephen grasping at straws.

"Everything has been signed and witnessed," said Anthea. "It's all over as far as we're concerned."

"After all, we won't be paupers," said Thomas.

"It's not just the money. It's the condemnation that goes with it. That he trusted my husband while we three are thrown aside..."

"Who is his Lordship acting for? That's what I'd like to know. Any hints?" Stephen stubbed out his cigarette.

"None. Men can be so pigheaded. It would have been so simple to sell the shares to us."

"Let it go. I can still move my art gallery to the West End. You can prop up Brayston Hall, and Stephen can... What will you be doing with your share?"

"Oh, South of France for me. I'll have to brush up on my French... I might go to America."

"I wonder who gets this place?" asked Thomas. "If it's me, I'm selling it. Any buyers?"

"No, thank you," replied Stephen.

"It is rather annoying how everyone assumes I simply exist to pay for my husband's estate. I'm well aware that an important consideration when I married was that I received a title in exchange for the expectations I had under my father's will. My life does not begin and end there. My own plans have just suffered a large reduction in capital. That makes a great difference to me. I can survive, but I feel insulted and betrayed by everyone going behind my back. And I'm powerless to do anything about it."

"We're all in the same boat," said Thomas. "I take the view it is best to forget this outrage."

"How can we when our own father is the problem?" asked Stephen.

A little after ten, the secret agency, having received a generous invitation from Mrs Barker to help itself to food, was enjoying a picnic in the kitchen.

"Her bread's lovely," said Ada, cutting another slice.

"It is and what a pleasant surprise Mrs Barker's cooking has turned out to be." Sophie was thickly applying butter to a slice.

"Cheese is supposed to give you nightmares," said Flora as she ate some.

"Won't worry us tonight, will it? Here you are, miss, try some Pan Yan Pickle."

"I've never tried it before. We have Sharwood's chutney. Their works are just around the corner from the office.... Oh, this Pan Yan is so flavourful... I must take a jar home for Father. I haven't seen him for several weeks now."

"He's probably surviving," said Flora. "I should imagine that the leading ladies in the church are all making a fuss over Mr Burgoyne."

"Yes. There is one who's intent on marrying him. She literally flutters her eyelashes at him. I didn't know people did that in real life."

"That is an approved but somewhat dated tactic," said Flora. "It's simpler just to smile at a man. It makes him feel good about himself, whereas I feel the fluttering eyelid sends an uncertain message."

"Not if it's in Morse Code," said Sophie. "One could make one's meaning plain. I love you, in Morse is, dit-dit - dit-dah-dit-dit dah-dah-dah dit-dit-dit-dah dit - dah-dit-dah-dah dah-dah-dah dit-dit-dah."

"Heavens! You'd wear your eyelids out before you said anything," said Flora, laughing.

"Where did you learn Morse Code?" asked Ada.

"The Land Army... That seems to be my stock answer to most things. I have to say I enjoyed my time in service... Where was I? At one centre, we had to send and receive official messages in Morse. On long, boring nights, I used to chat with other operators. There were two women who used to exchange knitting patterns in code."

"That sounds like a recipe for disaster," said Flora.

"After my Nan lost the use of her legs, she started banging on the floor of the back bedroom when she wanted something. It's two bangs for tea and three's, I've had an accident. It's a good job she doesn't know Morse Code, or we'd 'ave no peace, for she's a talkative soul."

"How is your Nan these days?" asked Sophie, who had heard many tales of Nan before.

"She's still there in bed, but that's the problem. Half of us think she's puttin' it on 'cos sometimes you can hear her moving about quietly in her room even though she thinks nobody notices. An' the other half says she can't be able to walk because she'd never do such a thing as stay in bed for the rest of her life. Talks have been quite lively lately."

"Are there many in your family?" asked Flora.

"Do you mean both houses? Me dad bought our original house and we rent next door as there's so many of us an' we didn't all fit in the one... In both houses, I'd say there was eighteen and a couple more who come and go. The rented house is the quiet one. That's where I have my room. I keep a padlock on it, an' all. Nan's next door in the other house. She's such a dear, but she's an awful liar sometimes."

"How many brothers and sisters do you have?" asked Sophie, fascinated.

"Eleven plus the orphan. We think he's about five now and we call 'im Angel. Me dad found him wandering in the street one night and brought him 'ome and he really needed feeding up. We asked about and told the authorities but nobody was interested so we kep' him. Me mum likes 'im 'cos he's got green eyes and is a bit of company for her while she's in the kitchen."

"My goodness," said Flora.

"I know. For a moniker, Angel's a right hardship, but we'll call 'im something else before he goes to school."

Sophie and Flora exchanged a glance, both marvelling at Ada's story.

"Time for sentry duty," said Sophie, hurriedly. "As we agreed, I'm on until one-thirty, Ada until four-thirty, and Flora gets to rise bright and early. I'll clear up here."

"Can't we just sit and talk instead?" asked Flora.

"Off you go or you won't be fit for duty."

"Very well... You do realize I usually rise at ten."

"Ten!" said Ada. "What time do you start work?"

"The theatre keeps late hours. Unemployed actresses can keep any hours they please, at least for a while. We'd better go or our captain will have us flogged. Oh, yes, I almost forgot. I have to put the report behind the pillar. I hope I don't get lost in the fog. Goodnight, Sophie."

CHAPTER 30

— • —

MUCH CREEPING

The best and safest position for Sophie to remain unseen while observing the dimly lit left-hand corridor was at the extreme end, next to the back staircase. This corridor was where Stephen and Thomas had their rooms. Beyond the back staircase landing, the passage led to the bedrooms in the annexe.

In the main building, the right-hand corridor was a dead end. Between the two corridors protruded a bedroom, the walls of which fully obstructed the view along both passages and meant a detour to get to the opulent landing of the main staircase. This grand, marble staircase, sweeping up from the vast hall to the first floor, became a winding, wooden staircase from the first floor to the extensive attics above.

At first, Sophie had hoped that her ears alone could tell her when somebody was ascending the marble stairs. She discovered that little sound reached her position and anyone being stealthy coming up the main staircase might escape her notice entirely. She moved to a corner where she was screened from the left-hand corridor and the main staircase. The only certainties she could count on at present was that Sir Ephraim was in his bedroom and Nurse Gleason was in the adjoining dressing room, temporarily converted to serve as her bedroom.

Within five minutes, she heard footsteps on the wooden stairs. Sophie peeked, recognizing the lower half of Rosina's dress. In a fluster, she ran to the back staircase and stopped. Rosina, unwittingly, was following her. Sophie, driven before the lady's maid, climbed the backstairs to the attics. Then she threaded her way through the narrower passageways to reach the main staircase. She sat at the top, realizing that Rosina had to return the same way. While she sat, Sophie took off her shoes because, despite the carpets and the solidity of the house, the elfin tread she thought she possessed had sounded slightly elephantine to her.

For an hour, Sophie was hectically driven from place to place as the family retired to bedrooms, and while servants hurried on last missions for those they served or went to their own beds. By eleven-thirty, Rosina was in the attic, Lady Anthea and Lord Philip in their room, and Thomas in his room. Stephen was downstairs somewhere. The servants had gone up to the attics or their rooms in the annexe. Sophie was not entirely sure if they had all gone. In that scurrying hour, she had perfected a near noiseless, barefooted running style that, while not remarkably fast, put her beyond discovery by anyone walking.

With the household settled for the night, Sophie became less anxious. She again took up her prime position in the corner near the main staircase. However, the household was not yet a peaceful one. Peculiarities manifested themselves and they started just as she had determined everyone was in their rightful place and likely to stay put. It began with Thomas. He left his bedroom, which meant Sophie had to head for the attics again.

Sophie was not sure if he had seen her going up the main staircase. Her heart beat faster when Thomas entered the left-hand passage. As soon as he was out of sight, she cautiously descended the stairs. There was no knock or sound of a door opening. Sophie steeled herself and peeped around the corner, where she discovered Thomas standing outside Sir Ephraim's door. A second, longer look revealed he was talking to himself and making slight hand movements. Such behaviour puzzled her. She was unsure what to do. While she thought it over, footsteps sounded below on the tiled floor. Sophie withdrew upstairs to listen. Someone switched off the downstairs lights before trudging up the stairs.

"I thought you'd gone already," said Stephen in a slurred voice as he stepped onto the landing.

"I couldn't get to sleep," said Thomas.

"You need a stiff drink - that's the ticket. Does the trick for me... You know, you can't change a single thing, old boy, not a single dashed thing, so it's no use worrying about it. That's my advice, a stiff drink. Anyway, I'm off to the land of Nod. Goodnight."

"Goodnight," said Thomas.

A minute later, Thomas returned to his room. Sophie put her shoes away in her room and got her torch.

At midnight, with the ground floor in darkness, only a single light burned in each of the first-floor corridors. The house was still. Outside, no wind stirred the thick mist. Waiting in her dark corner, Sophie was thinking nothing could happen and was resigning herself to the boredom of her watch. Even though she rehearsed the events of the recent days, parading the faces of people present in Abinger Mansion before her mind's eye, she could not find a killer among them. She searched her memory for the little things that might betray the culprit. As she reviewed the recently met faces in their hazy outlines, she found no match for the running footman she had seen at Trefoil. Deep in thought, she nearly missed the faint noise coming from downstairs. After a minute of listening, during which she thought she must have imagined the noise, it occurred again - a light, metallic sound. She came from her corner to stand at the balustrade. There was another noise, a different one this time. She stole downstairs to locate the source of the sounds.

The mist had been thickening the whole evening until it could now rightly be called fog. The man moved through this disorientating blanket. He could see a couple of yards in front of him - less than that under the trees. The house lights no longer provided a bearing because the building had as good as vanished. His nearly useless torch only showed the ground under his feet. No breath of wind stirred the trees. Muffled sounds - little diffuse noises of creaks and drips - were only those common to a damp forest on a still night. In the distance came the sound of a car engine, but where it was, he could not tell. It grew neither perceptibly louder nor quieter, but existed as a steady buzzing in the yellow-grey envelope that his torch made of the fog-bound night. He switched it off and, in complete darkness, the scents of wet trees and woodland earth alone told him where he was.

264

As Sophie nervously approached the kitchen door, beneath which she could see a glow, the light went out. She began backing away. The door opened, causing her to freeze on the spot, not daring to breathe. As if floating by itself, a slow-moving hand appeared carrying a small, glimmering oil lamp.

"Fiddlesticks," said the man in exasperation, unable to see where he was going by the light he carried.

He bent down to put the lamp on the floor. Next, he placed something else that clattered on the tiles. Noiselessly, Sophie moved away, sliding her feet along the floor until well beyond the expected glow of the lamp when the wick was turned higher.

The flame of the oil lamp jumped once the wick was adjusted. The man stood. In that moment, as though a poignant subject in an old Dutch oil painting, Sophie beheld Fenton grasping the lamp in one hand and, in his other, a plate on which lay a wedge of Mrs Barker's beef pie. He was wearing a dark tartan dressing gown for his raid on the kitchen. Fenton began walking to the backstairs, but Sophie had slipped further along past the offices, and into the main hall.

Staying silent and still while everyone else was asleep had lost any novelty for Sophie by half-past twelve. It was too cold to sit on the marble staircase. Instead, she sat in the carpeted left corridor, her back against the wall. After several minutes, this proved uncomfortable. She did not know what to do with her legs. Sophie put them out straight and pulled them in again. While making these manoeuvres, she suddenly became trans-fixed - there had been another noise. Its origin was either the right corridor or downstairs, she could not tell. She got up, re-treating to the back staircase. As she held her breath, she listened and reasoned. Someone was down below or had gone to the lavatory. Which was it? She did not know.

Sophie returned to the top of the grand staircase, moving forward as fast as caution allowed. The stairs and hall lay in an inky pool of darkness, so she passed to the opposite corridor. Yet again, peeping around the corner, she found the passage desert-ed. Curiosity getting the better of her, she softly ran back along both corridors, to descend the back staircase, fully expecting to find another kitchen raider.

A quick play of her torch across the kitchen proved it to be unoccupied. She had assumed it would be, so attuned had she become to the presence of others in the dark. She started to move away from the kitchen, but then stood stock-still. Someone was moving ahead of her in the dark without a light. She thought he might have entered through the side door, and there was no mistaking his halting tread moving slowly further away. A slight swishing noise caused Sophie to guess the person was guiding himself by sliding a hand along the wall. For the first time, Sophie felt fear. This was no kitchen raider - he was going in the wrong direction and must have come from outside. The noise receded. When she thought the night-walker was at a sufficient distance, Sophie gulped and willed herself to follow.

It was a strange, slow chase in the dark. Sophie's senses were acutely aware of everything around her. She could smell polished wood in the downstairs passage and sensed the cooler, spacious air above the tiles in the main hall. Her quarry made very little noise as he moved. She then discovered she was gaining on this person before realizing he was stopping occasionally. It crossed her mind to find the light switch and start shouting, but she realized that, even if it were a murderer ahead of her, his simple, laughing denial of any imputed wrongdoing would be accepted without question if he was one of the household and had reason to be there. That was not how to catch him. Sophie weighed the risks even while she kept her fear in check. She must follow and catch him at a task that made his intentions obvious. She started up the stairs after him.

The insufficient glow from both corridors did not illuminate the landing. As Sophie took each slow step, she realized she had lost the man's position - unable to tell if he had stopped or had gone ahead into one or other of the passages. Unless he moved, she might bump into him. She stopped and listened to her own quick, strong pulse. A shadow moved ahead, making a slight noise, but at the angle she was standing, Sophie could not tell which passage he had entered. At least she could move again. Her quick stockinged feet padded lightly on the cold marble.

The crisis happened at the top of the stairs. There was no noise to be heard. Who was the killer after? She thought Anthea to be safe because her husband was present in the room. Her choice lay between Sir Ephraim to the right and Stephen or Thomas to the left. She chose left.

The dim light revealed an empty corridor. Although her quarry had the advantage of moving in the light while she delayed, forced to move noiselessly in the dark, had he had enough time to enter a room before she arrived? She thought so, by a small margin. She turned to the right-hand corridor.

Empty. She was certain he had not continued upstairs. Think, she told herself. And then it came to her. Sophie understood it was to Sir Ephraim's rooms she must go. According to Stokely's thinking, she reasoned, Sir Ephraim had now served his purpose by selling the shares and may as well die. Oh, why had she not seen it before?

Sophie opened the door to the darkened anteroom. It moved noiselessly, as though on oiled hinges and locks. She stepped across to the bedroom door, gripped the handle, and swung it open. The bedside lamp revealed a chilling sight that took her breath away. Barry was smothering Sir Ephraim with a pillow as he lay in bed. She looked on in horror, her shocked mind incapable of thought. Sophie had expected something, but not this. As the old man struggled, Barry whispered quiet, spiteful words - 'acknowledged' was one of them.

"Stop it!" cried Sophie involuntarily.

Barry whirled around at the sound of her voice. Hate and malevolent triumph had suffused his face. This subsided, giving way to a puzzled grimace.

"You're the running footmen," she said flatly.

Sophie took the blackjack from her pocket and advanced. She managed a good swing, but Barry jerked his head to one side so the blow landed on his shoulder, causing him to wince with pain. Sophie prepared to strike again, but he was on his feet, backing away, holding his shoulder. He looked like a cornered animal. Sophie changed position to cut off his retreat. He paused, and determination came into his face. He leapt at her. She had time to give a quick strike before the impetus of his charge sent her sprawling on the floor. It was a tepid blow on the head, yet swung with enough force to put Barry in a dazed condition.

Sophie scrambled to her feet. "If you move an inch," she said menacingly while shaking the blackjack at him, "I'll hit you again and then you won't get up."

She reached Sir Ephraim, who had removed the pillow from his flushed face, crowned with disordered, wispy hair. His breathing was rasping and irregular.

"Are you all right?"

"I don't know," he gasped.

"I'll get the nurse."

She tried to open the dressing room door, but found it locked. Sophie realized Barry had locked the nurse in.

"Give me the key," she demanded.

"No." Barry half groaned his defiance.

He was in no condition to do more harm. In the hall, Sophie hammered on bedroom doors, shouting for people to wake up and for the police to be called. The household roused itself. Soon, Barry was under guard.

While Nurse Gleason was being released, Sophie managed a quick word with Sir Ephraim.

She whispered in the old man's ear. "I heard him say 'acknowledge'. Is he a son of yours?" Sir Ephraim nodded. "There is a slight family likeness, I suppose. I won't say anything."

Sophie approached Barry, who was now sitting upright, clutching his head. Stephen was standing next to him, uncertain what to do with a prisoner. Sophie bent over and, without ceremony, pulled off Barry's moustache.

"Now it all makes sense. You had a moustache which you shaved off for last weekend's charade. Now you're wearing a false one until your own moustache grows back." Sophie stood up and put the article in her pocket.

Stephen stared at her with his mouth open. "Who are you?"

"Don't be so impertinent. Make sure he doesn't make a run for it. Who's telephoned the police?"

"I don't know."

"Of course you wouldn't." Sophie strode out of the room to go downstairs.

She was halfway down when someone fired a pistol outside. She halted. There came the crack of a second shot, closer to the door. A shotgun blast followed. Sophie just stared at the door in horrified amazement. The house was silent in the minute she waited. Then somebody began hammering for admittance. Sophie answered the knock.

"Who is it?" she asked.

"Open the door," said the man loudly.

"Not until you identify yourself." She thought it might be her guardian gardener from Trefoil.

"You identify yourself," he answered. "I'm carrying a wounded man and he weighs a ton."

"I don't believe you. It sounds like a trick."

"Open the door, blast you."

"You can blasted well stay put until the police arrive."

"I know who you are. King Edwards are better than Majestics."

"Oh... It is you... Why didn't you say that first?" Sophie threw back the bolts.

Framed in the doorway with fog behind him stood Ralph Yardley, appearing to Sophie as an ancient war chieftain carrying a vanquished opponent as proof of valour. His wet trench coat glistened and his broad-brimmed hat pulled down low. His eyes, shaded by his hat, fixed upon Sophie. Over a shoulder he carried a man in pain, whose trousers were rent and bloody. Sophie marvelled at the sight before her and stood to one side.

"Come in," she said.

"He took pot-shots at me, so I shot him in the backside. He'll live, unfortunately. May I put him down somewhere?"

"Ah, yes."

"You won't hit me with that thing?"

"Excuse me. I didn't realize I was still carrying it." Sophie hurriedly put her blackjack in her pocket. "We've also had a spot of bother. It was rather nerve-racking, but it's settled now."

The man looked at her quizzically, then at Sophie's shoeless feet. She smiled and shrugged.

"It sounds very interesting. I'll put him on the tiles... Can't have him making a mess anywhere."

"There's a nurse present who can attend to him."

"Don't hurry. This is the fellow who shot Alfred Wright. He probably killed Frank as well."

Sophie looked shocked. "I'm absolutely amazed... How do you know it's him?" She stared at the injured man. Although his wounds from shotgun pellets were extensive, they were not deep.

"Because it's the only theory that made sense to me. That's why I came to wait for him. Look, I'm very sorry, I'm in a hurry. Although I'd find it most delightful to stay and swap yarns, I have to be gone in the next two minutes." Yardley put down his burden carefully, but, despite his gentleness, the nearly insensible man groaned in pain.

"You'll need his pop gun. It has his fingerprints on it." From his pocket, Yardley produced a heavy object, wrapped in a handkerchief with one corner cut off.

"Oh, look at that. You've removed your monogram... How can I find out who you are when you leave me no clues?" Sophie smiled. "Well, mystery man, you look younger tonight than when you were a gardener."

"Clean living does that for a person. Be careful what you say in front of this fellow... Goodbye. I know we shall meet again." Yardley smiled. He picked up his shotgun, left propped outside the door, and departed.

"Goodbye," said Sophie. She continued to watch until the mist swallowed him up, then shut the front door. Had she stayed to listen, she would have heard a motorcycle starting a few minutes later.

"What in blazes was all that shooting?" demanded Lord Philip, striding into the hall, carrying a rifle. "Who's this?" he asked upon seeing the wounded man.

"I don't know his name. The police will want to talk to him, as he's a murderer."

"He is? Quite remarkable. That's two bagged in one night. I'm sorry I missed it all. I couldn't get the drawer unlocked where they keep the .22 cartridges... Who brought him here?"

"A large, taciturn man with a shotgun who did not state his name. His face was covered. I didn't recognize him or know how he came to be here. I didn't like to ask, as he frightened me so much."

"Of course, my dear. Quite understandable. Then that person just knocked on the door and left this fellow? How extraordinary."

"Excuse me, I must find Nurse Gleason to attend to this man's wounds."

"Yes, yes, please do." Lord Philip examined the man on the ground. "That's an embarrasin' place to get yourself shot."

Sophie left, carefully carrying the wrapped revolver in both hands. John came into the hall, and she sent him to find Nurse Gleason. In the library, she placed the revolver on the table while she prepared to telephone Inspector Morton. Using a telephone always made her nervous.

CHAPTER 31

— • —

PARTIES AFTER MIDNIGHT

Inspector Morton and Sergeant Gowers entered Abinger Mansion about ten minutes after a sergeant and constable from the Surrey police had arrived. Barstow let them in. The London police immediately encountered the highly novel sight to be found in the hall. The entire household was obviously awake and a large part of it was here in the hall in its nightclothes. Lord Philip, in a festive mood, was in command of the situation, wearing a burgundy dressing gown with long skirts, silk facings, having his family crest embroidered on a pocket. He wore this glorious article over his pyjamas, the trousers of which were tucked into the top of his Wellington boots. In one hand he carried the rifle, which had become his staff of office, while he held a large whisky and soda in the other. Against a wall, the unnamed and uncommunicative man lay face down on a camp bed, having been zealously bandaged by Nurse Gleason. Tied to a chair on the opposite side of the hall was Barry Chambers, Lord Philip's former chauffeur. With his one free hand, he was holding a wet compress against his head. Mrs Fisher was speaking to the police constable; Thomas was talking to the sergeant; Barstow, the valet, hovered around in the wake of his master; Stephen and Anthea stood together; and John the footman was whispering to Flora.

Mrs Barker was absent from the hall. Having made sure she had seen all that was to be seen, she retreated to her domain in the kitchen, saying, "Well, I never. What a ruckus," in tones of astounded delight. Once there, she made sandwiches and pots of tea, with Annie assisting her. Fenton and the nurse were upstairs with Sir Ephraim.

"Ah, come in, come in," said Lord Philip. "You must be the detectives."

"We are, sir. I'm Inspector Morton and this is Detective Sergeant Gowers."

"I'm Lord Manningtree. What are you drinking?"

"We're on duty, sir. Perhaps a cup of tea, if it could be managed."

"Barstow, tell cook two more for tea. Busy night, what? Did the fog hold you up?"

"It did rather. There were some very thick patches. Ah, what exactly has been going on here? I've been informed two murderers were apprehended. Are these the men?"

"Yes, they are. That one was my chauffeur until he went barmy and tried to smother poor old Sir Ephraim. Sir Ephraim's shaken up but unharmed, by the way. You'll not credit it, but they have this maid here and she's really quite amazing. Pretty as a picture, and you'd swear butter wouldn't melt in her mouth. What does she do? Brains me chauffeur with a cosh while he's attempting to kill Sir Ephraim. Astonishing, what? Hard to grasp, but there you have it.

"While all that excitement is going on, there's shooting outside. I'm barely into my dressing gown when some johnny knocks on the door and, as calmly as you please, drops that fellow off after having shot him. Says he's a murderer, too. Off he goes without another word. I hope that's all of them for tonight."

"Let's hope so, sir. Who is the wounded man?"

"Hasn't spoken a word. I firmly believe, if you poked him with a stick where it hurts, he'd tell you his name soon enough."

"Unfortunately, that sort of thing is against regulations, sir," said Morton, smiling. "Thank you for the information. I had better speak to the local boys and see what they're doing."

"By all means, Inspector. Glad I could help."

Before Morton had taken three steps, Sophie, now suitably shod, and Ada entered the hall, carrying trays of tea, sandwiches, and platefuls of Mrs Barker's fancy cakes. Of the household, they were the only ones fully dressed.

"I'd like a word with you," said Morton ominously to Sophie. "In private."

"Yes, Inspector Morton. Try the almond slices. They're very good, sir."

"I believe I will... Quite the social atmosphere... It's always the same with the gentry. They've absolutely no idea about how to behave normally."

"That's because their normal is different to ours. Lord Philip is thoroughly enjoying himself."

"I would say that you are also a part of this abnormality."

"Me, sir? I'm just a maid. Excuse me, I have to serve the others."

Inspector Morton soon had the situation under control and to his liking. Lord Philip had the rifle put away, somewhat reluctant to have his few minutes of glory come to an end. The Surrey police officers came under Morton's command as soon as they discovered the connection between the night's events and two ongoing murder investigations. A call to the Chief Constable, Captain Mowbray Sant, expedited matters even as additional Surrey officers arrived at the house.

Sir Ephraim was excited and had regained much of his composure. He called for Sophie to be sent to him and would answer no one's questions until he had spoken to her.

"Sit down, please."

"Are you feeling better?" asked Sophie, as she moved a chair closer to the bed.

"Yes, thank you... I owe you my life. My dear, it would have been better for Barry to finish me off because the danger would have passed. Now it's restored." The old man's slow, laboured breath paused often, as if he had to remind himself to breathe.

"You knew he was your son?"

"I did. I got him in as a chauffeur with Lord Philip after the war. Somehow, Stokely must have found him and induced Barry to turn against me and my family... Barry is named in my new will, one of several indiscretions who are now acknowledged. It was a condition Stokely put upon me. Upon reflection, I saw the justice of it." He sighed. "Being instructed in the matter, I knew no good could come of it. Tell me, what else did Barry do? I heard you speak of a footman."

"Barry masqueraded as a footman last week at Trefoil. He tried to poison Alfred's wine at dinner, but a gentleman by the name of Sir Reginald Fawcett drank it instead. He survived and has since recovered perfect health."

"I'm glad. Dear, dear, what a dreadful business this all is... An absolute nightmare."

"And it's over now," said Sophie softly.

"How can you say that? Stokely will not stop."

"I've considered the matter. Barry was included in these plans because of the wicked enjoyment Stokely would derive from you being killed by your own son. That is his vindictive nature asserting itself. He cannot now replicate that circumstance. On the other hand, the assassin with the rifle was employed to cover the potential failings of the more amateurish attempts by Barry. In concert, they were to keep the pressure on you to ensure Frobisher Bank came under Stokely's control. With the assassin and Barry now captured, even Stokely must think twice before attempting anything further."

"He could hire another assassin and kill off the rest of my children."

"He has nothing further to gain and would deem it too risky that he might end as being front-page news in his own newspapers. Then the entire nation would be aware of his murderous schemes. You could even confront him over the matter in an interview with a rival paper."

"It wouldn't get printed. The paper's legal advisers would be firmly against it on the grounds of libel."

"Perhaps... If you published the details of the extraordinary coercion to sell your shares and the murder of your two sons, with Stokely's name connected to the story, well, that is the sort of publicity he would hate. It would raise questions in the House of Commons... The best strategy is to publicize everything but, even if you don't, Stokely will believe you might. He values his public image too much to risk it. I think he will do no more. Have you considered cancelling the sale of shares? There's still time to talk to Lord Manningtree."

"No, I won't... Do you know what it's like to live in fear and be powerless to act...? Let him have the bank. I'm too weak to fight him."

"That's understandable. The assassin was here for a reason tonight."

"Why? To kill me if Barry failed?"

"Yes, I'm sure he would have done so. He had another objective, though. I'm sure of it now. He was going to kill Barry after Barry had killed you - to clean up all loose ends."

"Oh... Do you think so...? What complete wickedness."

"May I ask you something?"

"I'll answer if I can."

"Why has Stokely singled you out?"

"You're aware of so much, I may as well tell you. It's because of an old affair. There was a banking crisis in 1890. Barings Bank was over-extended in Argentina and had insufficient cash to withstand losses when that country went into recession. Many private banks in London could have failed if Barings failed. Well, Barings is still here because a banking consortium, willing to guarantee the bank's debts, saved it. Frobisher was part of the consortium. However, before the consortium formed, there was a lot of panic. Otherwise sensible men acted like fools.

"Peter Brownrigg, Stokely's uncle, lost his nerve. He owned 35% of Frobisher at the time and wanted out before the crash came. He was convinced the crash was unavoidable. I already held 20% when he offered me his shares. I bought them at a very steep discount with all the money I had. You see, talks of a consortium to bail out Barings had already begun. I took the risk because I trusted in the strength of British banking. Brownrigg... well, whatever he had heard, he was adamant about selling his shares. I just obliged him.

"That is one reason Stokely is interested in me. I presume he might have inherited those shares from his uncle... some of them, at least. Do you wonder how I know? The price per share Manningtree is paying me, 8s 9d, is the same price I paid Brownrigg all those years ago.

"The second reason is more recent. Stokely tried to get a loan from Frobisher during the war. In essence, he wanted the bank to take risks in a very shaky venture he was contemplating. He became annoyed when refused. Stokely came to see me to make a personal appeal. I told him in a kind way the venture was too risky for an old bank like Frobisher and under wartime conditions. A second refusal after a personal appeal…? I suppose he took against me then… Could I have some water, please?"

"Yes, of course. You don't need to say any more unless you feel up to it." Sophie filled a glass from the water jug and helped Sir Ephraim take some sips.

"Not much more to tell… He lost his temper and left my office. He found private money somewhere, but I heard the venture failed."

"I suppose he felt you owed him something… Do you have any idea why he wants control of a bank?"

"I can't say I do… Dividends will pay back his investment in a few years… I assume he wants cheap loans to finance new schemes. He's not interested in banking; he's interested in what a bank can do to further his personal ambition."

"That sounds dangerous… I wish there was a way to stop him."

"I can't do it, my dear. Three lives would be in peril. If he has the bank and I'm dead, he'll leave them alone. Of that I'm certain."

"Who was it you dealt with during these negotiations for the sale of your shares?"

"I don't know his name and I've never met him before."

"I shan't be telling any of this to the police. Can you give me his description?"

"Well, I would say he was forty-five to fifty. A big-framed individual, but not much above average height. His morning suit was impeccable. The curious thing was he had close-cropped hair as though just out of prison, but he looked healthy, like an outdoorsman. The set of his face was perhaps his most notable feature. It was a hard, unforgiving face. You couldn't tell what he was thinking."

"What did he sound like?"

"He had a deep, emotionless voice - very flat and very convincing. He began by stating I was to sell my Frobisher shares - gave me a typewritten note. Then he explained what would be the terms of my new will. He said I would comply because otherwise my children would start dying one by one. He said that, in the future, he would give all instructions over the telephone. Quite naturally, I thought it all nonsense. I remember him nodding and saying he understood my reaction but, when the first accident occurred, I would believe him then. He spoke as if it were all so reasonable... so reasonable.

"Frank died. I couldn't bring myself to accept the situation, even though I knew better. The man telephoned shortly afterwards, telling me what to do. I asked for time because I was in no state to do anything. He refused and hung up. I heard from him again after they shot Alfred. From then on, I did as he said. I had the will drafted and prepared sales documents for transferring the shares to Manningtree. Reese helped me with that. As instructed, we used a different lawyer for the will."

"How dreadful it all is... I'm so terribly sorry. I suppose Lord Manningtree knows nothing of this background?"

"No, he doesn't... I'm sure he doesn't. I explained the sale and gave him to understand that it was for the good of the country. Once he realized I was determined, he neither argued nor questioned further. He was happy with the fee I paid him. They contacted Manningtree to arrange the transfer of money into his account. I realized that if he did not do everything according to their plan, they might kill him, too."

"Yes, I can see that."

"Don't try to change Manningtree's mind about this or it won't stop."

"I thought to try, but your explanation has shown me I had better not. It's galling that Stokely will get away with it."

"He won't get away with it forever... Tell me, who was the man who shot the intruder?"

"I wish I knew... Someone else who is prepared to act, so that Britain does not fall into the hands of a megalomaniac."

"That gives me some hope... You've had a long and trying day. Get some rest, my dear."

"Yes, I will soon. I have to speak to a policeman first. Goodnight, Sir Ephraim."

"Goodnight... You won't tell them anything?"

"No. I'll keep it all straight and to the point. I'll not mention any of this, but they will be bound to discover Barry is your son."

"I know it."

CHAPTER 32

— • —

INSISTENT THOUGHTS

Sophie had already given her statement to Detective Sergeant Gowers, but afterwards, Inspector Morton wanted to review matters with her. They were sitting in Mrs Fisher's office with the door closed.

"Where to begin?" said Morton. He leaned his elbows on the desk and put his fingertips together. "First off, what were you doing creeping about the house in the middle of the night with a cosh in your pocket?"

"Observing people's movements. Not everyone sleeps soundly. I wanted to make sure they all behaved themselves."

"And the cosh?" he asked wearily.

"Self-preservation, of course. Are you annoyed, Inspector?"

"I'm not annoyed with the results of tonight's work. I am perturbed by your taking action against a suspect without informing me first."

"Well, I hardly had the time to do that! Was I to let Sir Ephraim be killed? Anyway, you might have said no to a night watch."

"I think you're missing the point and, ah, it's deliberate. You know very well what I mean. You were stalking the halls, trying to catch someone. You were hired to be eyes and ears for the police, not its boots and truncheon."

"That's very good. However, I had no intention of being such things. As soon as I had any information, I gave it to you. I had no particular suspicion against the chauffeur until I found him suffocating Sir Ephraim! Only then did I suddenly recognize him as the running footman at Trefoil. Remember, you weren't allowed in the house and you certainly wouldn't have come because I had a vague suspicion something might happen. All this is beside the point. There was nothing for me to tell you until I saw Barry Chambers in the very act."

"I grant you all of that, Miss Burgoyne. Nevertheless, you took far too much upon yourself in tackling a suspect."

"I agree with you there, but then I am rather new to this business. My powers of deduction are only just developing, otherwise I would have deliberated the case carefully and deduced the culprit's identity. Until my brainpower increases, I shall carry my blackjack wherever I go. Furthermore, what are the requirements for owning one of those little automatics? You know, the type that fits in a pocket or handbag?"

"I'm not telling you that." Morton laughed at the idea. "You were lucky tonight, and you could have been hurt or killed."

"Please don't be cross. Believe me, in retrospect, I fully appreciate how easily it might have gone wrong. However, you do have your man - both of them, actually."

"This is exactly my point. It also happens that it's you who opens the door to the mysterious stranger - he who magically appears from the mist carrying a suspect, all shot to pieces, over his shoulder. I can hardly credit it. Who is this stranger?"

"I have no idea. He was muffled up and wore a hat. He barely spoke a word except to say the man was the murderer of Alfred Wright. I believe him because he sounded believable. Now, I'll ask you a question. Who is the wounded man?"

Morton realized he was getting nowhere and sighed. "I don't know yet. I've an idea he's wanted in another matter. He fits the description of Frank Wright's assailant, but that's not enough to lay charges. At the moment, all I've got against him is trespass and a possible firearms charge."

"How did he travel out here? It must have been by car."

"If he came alone, we'll find it in the daylight."

"Then there might be a stolen vehicle charge, as well."

"We shall see."

"I apologize for taking action without your being aware of the circumstances. In the future, if Burgoyne's has a future, I will ensure nothing transpires without your first being alerted to the situation."

"That's all well and good, but my report is going to look like a dog's breakfast. How am I supposed to keep you out of it when you're slap bang in the centre of everything? Not only for here, but at Trefoil Hall, as well."

"Oh, not to worry... Um, get them both to confess? Would that help?"

"Chambers is scared and wants a lawyer, and the other is yet to say a word. They're both dodging murder or attempted murder charges. You do see the difficulties you've put me in?"

"Oh, come, come, it's not that bad, Inspector Morton. You'll think of something... Couldn't you get Barry Chambers to incriminate the other fellow? They must know of each other."

"I would say they don't. Which means someone else is behind these murder attempts."

"Who could that be? Do you have any ideas?"

"I have ideas, but it's evidence I'm wanting. Look, it's late and you're here until Monday afternoon. In the unlikely event anything else occurs, telephone me before you do anything. I mean, anything at all."

"I will do exactly as you ask."

"Thank you and goodnight, Miss Burgoyne."

"Goodnight, Inspector."

"Do you think we can close the file?" asked Gowers. He looked doubtful.

"No, I don't... I get a strong impression others are controlling the game while you and I are just means to their ends. I don't like it one bit."

"Takes two to play a game, sir. Who's on our side and who are we playing against?"

"I want to say Penrose for us... but I don't see him in this. Must be someone else. The man who dropped the wounded suspect on the doorstep - now, who in blazes is he? I'd like to have a word with him, for starters."

"Unless Miss Burgoyne can give us a better description, we don't have a chance of finding him."

"I think she knows who he is... Her having opened the door like that makes me suspicious... That's not normal behaviour for a woman... Many men wouldn't have opened the door, either... I'd say she was expecting him or she wasn't surprised by his arrival. Oh, yes, I believe she knows him all right."

"So she's keeping his identity a secret? And I thought she was a nice young lady."

Inspector Morton smiled. "She is a nice young lady, but she's too clever by half."

"Then who are we up against?"

"Someone powerful who wants a bank. Whoever gets it in the end, that's who's running this show. Proving anything against him, well, that's another matter."

"What about Lord Manningtree?"

"He doesn't fit the bill. You saw him tonight. Think he's behind it?"

"No, I can't say I do, sir. He doesn't seem to be the type."

"We'll get information on him, though. That sale of shares positively stinks. When we see who ends up with Frobisher Bank, that's when we'll know what this is all about. You mark my words."

"Yes, and what about Sir Ephraim's new will?" asked Gowers. "There's something fishy there, too."

"I'll ask him formally for the details. A pint says I get the runaround."

Sergeant Gowers smiled. "No, I'm not taking that one. Shall I tackle his secretary?"

"Yes." Morton stretched his arms and yawned. "Come on, let's go back to the hotel or we'll be fit for nothing in the morning and we have to up bright and early. I hope they feed us here tomorrow. I don't run well on no breakfast."

The Surrey police left, taking Chambers to jail in cuffs and sending the unidentified man to the hospital under guard. With the Scotland Yard men returning to Dorking, the household returned to bed. The night's excitement had ended, and the wretchedness of the late hour showed on tired, pale faces. John locked the doors and switched off the lights.

The household slumbered or rested. Sophie, although tired, turned the lamp on in her room because she was unable to sleep. She had been rehearsing the night's events in her mind, but that gave way to a nagging question. It was the type of thought that does not permit rest until resolved, if it can be resolved immediately. She put on her coat over her nightdress. In the coat pockets, she carried her torch, pencil, pad, and blackjack. The latter article had proved invaluable earlier, so she was loath to leave it - Abinger Mansion had proved to be such a surprising place.

She reached the library, shut the door, and turned on the light. Her question was primarily geographical in nature, so she took down an old atlas of the British Isles. Using a piece of paper as a ruler, Sophie marked off distances between two towns and London. She could not find Brayston Hall on the map, but thought it lay close to Ipswich. From there to Trefoil Hall, near Bedford, she calculated the distance to be ninety miles by road. Ipswich to London was nearly the same distance by road at eighty-five miles. The distance between London and Bedford was sixty-five.

Wishing she knew more about the speed of cars and her head hadn't started aching, she estimated travelling times until she arrived at a set of satisfactory answers. Barry Chambers could have driven the car directly from Brayston to Trefoil - a five-hour trip. There was no easy direct route. Much of the journey lay along sideroads and country lanes. Good county maps were a necessity for this.

The journey to and from London was different. It was a direct route over better, larger roads. She estimated Ipswich to London took three to four hours by car. The second leg from London to Bedford was two and a half hours. Entering London from the east and exiting to the north was a puzzling calculation. Sophie guessed two hours for that part. The total time via London was seven or eight hours. The same journey by trains, including switching between the Liverpool Street terminus to that of St. Pancras, had to be about six hours. Travelling to and from the station at either end added another two hours. By car or train from Ipswich to Bedford via London took the same amount of time.

Sophie sat back in her chair and tapped the end of the pencil on her chin. Barry Chambers, she decided, had to avoid being seen or remembered as being in Bedford. His shaved-off moustache might not be a sufficient disguise, although it had misled her well enough. Would his taxi driver remember him? Was Barry prepared to take that risk? Sophie assumed so if they had paid him enough to kill Alfred Wright. She recalled that Barry's foot-man's uniform was almost identical to those worn by the actual Trefoil footmen. That signified advanced planning. The planner of the attempted murder could not take the chance of Barry being remembered by a taxi driver or a station porter. She decided he had driven the direct route by car - it being the shorter, quicker journey.

This assumption returned her to the initial question that had kept her awake. Had Lord Philip loaned the car to Barry or even gone with him? She suddenly was certain he was involved due to the simple fact that Barry Chambers had been at Trefoil on Friday, when he tried to poison Alfred, and on Saturday, when she had seen him, and Sunday, when Paul Klest was looking through the bedrooms for him. Lord Philip would never have given his chauffeur a three- or four-day holiday and lent him his car. Similarly, if Barry had driven alone, he needed to park and hide the very noticeable and very glossy Sunbeam limousine - nearly impossible in the small village of Oxley, unless a confederate allowed the use of a barn or garage. Sophie now saw Lord Philip was up to his neck in the business. He could easily drop off Barry at night and the car be unnoticed in Oxley. If he drove to the gates in daylight, it might be unnoticed as there were several new, expensive cars at Trefoil and so one like the Sunbeam might be a common sight. His remark at dinner came to mind. She remembered he was a strong supporter of Stokely.

It was gone four, and she knew she could not sleep. Sophie went to the garage to inspect the Sunbeam, hoping it would reveal something.

The garage, a former carriage house and stable, was in a sep-arate block and hidden by mist. Sophie shivered as she walked in the disorientating, foggy darkness. Glad the building was no further away, she groped for, then opened the side door, entered the uninviting darkness, and switched on the light. Open stairs led to rooms above while the narrow passage she followed led her between former tack rooms and the few remaining but now disused loose boxes. She switched on the garage lights. They revealed a yawning, white-washed space converted from numerous stalls. It was startlingly bright and a stark, unwelcoming place. The air felt colder inside than outside.

The dark blue Sunbeam was one of four cars parked, which left space for three more. Sophie could smell oil and petrol as she shivered in the damp, still air.

The recently polished car was spotless. She pulled open the driver's door and began searching the sparse interior of the driver's compartment. There was little to examine, as there were no glove compartments or storage boxes present. The spaces underneath the bench seat were too tight for use. She looked thoroughly, but found nothing. Whatever else he may have done, Barry kept the car exceptionally clean.

The roomier passenger compartment was bare except for a small red oriental carpet. The leather bench seat looked comfortable while the rear-facing foldaway seats looked anything but. Sophie searched without result.

The wooden tool chest bolted to a running board was padlocked. The large trunk strapped to the back of the car contained an empty suitcase, two blankets, and a waterproof canvas bag containing maps and a map case. Sophie supposed the police had already searched the vehicle. Out of curiosity, she opened the map case to discover it contained some ten or twelve maps. These were maps of counties surrounding London and for Norfolk, Suffolk, and Cambridgeshire. She unfolded a newer Bedfordshire map.

She found no written notes or marks, but she noticed that someone had imperfectly folded the map. She refolded it along the newer creases and it fell into a front and back arrangement displaying large sections of Bedfordshire along a line between Bedford and the town of Sandy. She scrutinized the map under an overhead light and by torchlight. On the Bedford section, close beneath the name Oxley, was a small, faint scuff, as though the tip of a dirty finger had lightly grazed the map. It needed daylight to see it properly. This, she felt, was evidence to give to

Inspector Morton. She put everything away but took the canvas bag containing the maps with her back to the house.

In the kitchen, as Sophie made cocoa, she wondered if Lord Philip had alerted Stokely to the fact that his chauffeur-cum-footman had gone missing. Stokely had come to find Barry Chambers, Sir Ephraim's illegitimate son. It made dreadful sense to her. She looked for something to eat. The most readily available was cold beef pie. Sophie doubted it went with cocoa, but she risked the experiment, anyway.

CHAPTER 33

— ✦ —

DISAPPOINTMENT

"**M**iss, are you getting up today?" asked Ada when she put her head around Sophie's bedroom door.

"What time is it?" Sophie asked, sleepily.

"Quarter to seven."

"Huh, I didn't drop off until about an hour ago. I'll be down soon."

"Don't go back to sleep," warned Ada.

"I won't."

She nearly did, though. Whether it was sheer tiredness or a reaction to the events of the night, Sophie had to will herself to get up. At first it was hard to move, but the thought which brought complete wakefulness was her remembering that she had to telephone Inspector Morton. She washed, dressed, and started her duties, among which were the less onerous ones of eating breakfast and drinking cups of tea. By eight-thirty she began to feel human again and so made the call, but she got no answer.

The servants performed their daily tasks and if they were affected by an attempted murder in the house; they did not show it. They were quieter than usual among themselves, though. Despite the pretence of normality, there was an unsettled atmosphere in the house. If Sir Ephraim would rise and go downstairs, then perhaps things could be put right. He, ailing, could do no such thing. The person closest to acting in a somewhat carefree manner was Lord Philip, although he looked thoughtful on occasion when by himself.

Sophie wished to avoid Lord Philip, if possible, because she found herself in a quandary. She had always adhered to an unwritten code of conduct. Part of that code was that she, Sophie Burgoyne, should not be bringing such a dreadful accusation as she was contemplating against a peer of the realm. Elsewhere in that code was a clause that a peer of the realm should not be a murderer. To voice her suspicion and to present her reasonings, with the clues she had in support, would entail her crossing a line – and it was a thick and troubling line for her to cross.

In daylight, the more she pondered her theory, the weaker it seemed. By ten, she was changing her mind. She caught sight of Lord Philip crossing the hall and it seemed to be thoroughly impossible for him to be part of a murder conspiracy. He looked entirely natural, so unaffectedly innocent, that she doubted her ideas and lost confidence in her reasonings. It was not possible, was it?

Around this same time, as the thinning fog was lifting, a contingent of Surrey police arrived in two cars to search the grounds and surrounding roads. A little after ten, Morton and Gowers arrived at the house. As soon as they had entered, Ada passed the word of their arrival to Sophie, who retrieved the map case from her room and wrapped it in a towel before meeting them. Mrs Fisher had given the use of her office to the Scotland Yard men.

"Ah, good morning, Miss Burgoyne," said Morton. He looked at her closely. "I hope you managed to get some rest last night?"

"Good morning, Inspector, Sergeant Gowers. Very little, unfortunately. Did you sleep well?"

"We got a few hours. Many's the time we've had to work all night and the next day. Goes with the job, you might say."

"So I mustn't complain because I'll receive no sympathy from the police. Ah, where to begin... What kept me awake was an idea I had. I pursued it as far as I could. Now I'm not so sure. I'd better explain myself. You see, I could not imagine Lord Philip giving his chauffeur three days' holiday at the perfect time for Barry Chambers to be present at Trefoil Hall. I consulted some maps, and I think Chambers decided to drive to Trefoil rather than risk being seen and remembered by station staff and cab drivers. He'd have the inconvenience of luggage that needed to be hidden somewhere in Oxley. So, I doubt Chambers went to Trefoil by train. If by car, did he hire one or did Lord Philip lend him his Sunbeam? If the latter, it is a positively outlandish thing for him to have done. Let his chauffeur go on holiday and take the car? No, he would not do that. Which makes it all the more likely he accompanied Chambers."

"You're saying they were both at Trefoil or in the vicinity?"

"I suppose I am."

"Chambers states he was on holiday and stayed with friends in London who will vouch for him. He took a train. He even has a ticket stub from the return journey. So he has an alibi for his absence from Brayston Manor. Lord Manningtree confirms this. In other words, he's saying he never went near Trefoil Hall and all travel was by train."

"Anyone could have purchased that ticket," said Sophie. "And, if everything was above board, why the fake moustache?"

"Vanity. He says he was tired of it getting in his soup, so he shaved it off. Afterwards, he hated how he looked, so he used a fake one until his own grew back."

"That's nonsense. He's making it up. I'll give him credit for being plausible about the train ticket and his friends, but all that can be manufactured."

"What makes you so sure?" asked Morton.

"I'll show you, but first, what is Chambers saying about his attack on Sir Ephraim?"

"He says he was adjusting the pillows at Sir Ephraim's request when they got into an argument, being father and son. In the heat of the moment, Chambers says he lost his head and put the pillow over Sir Ephraim's face. Says it was only to scare him. Then you came in and started hitting him with a life preserver."

"I suppose he must say something to get off the charge. How can people speak such unbelievable rubbish? Anyway, I'll come to the point. This matter looked much more significant last night than it does now."

Sophie put the map case on the table and unwrapped it from the towel.

"I retrieved these maps from Lord Philip's car last night." She opened the canvas bag. "I looked them over and most are dated between 1911 and 1915. The Bedfordshire one was published in 1919. Now, to go directly from Brayston near Ipswich to Bedford requires the use of three maps. I believe Chambers drove to Cambridge without directions. It's a straightforward journey. Beyond Cambridge, he would need maps for Cambridgeshire and Bedfordshire because there are many alternative routes over minor roads."

Sophie opened up the Bedfordshire map and laid it on the table.

"Please notice this map has been refolded so it could be inserted into the case for ease of use. I shall refold it according to its new creases.

"Arranged like this, the map shows the sector around Sandy and the eastern border of Bedfordshire. On the other side, it displays the area around Bedford itself. Now it fits into the map case."

She put the map into the case where a section could be seen through the clear celluloid cover. She took it out again.

"Trefoil's just a few miles from Bedford," said Sergeant Gowers.

"Precisely so. It is next to the village of Oxley. Tell me, gentlemen, what do you make of that mark by the word Oxley?"

She placed the map in front of the men. They simultaneously tried to look, but Gowers gave way to his superior officer. In a matter of moments, Morton used a folding magnifying glass and his face was inches from the map. This action brought a smile to Sophie's face. She decided to buy herself a similar magnifier. Morton was silent as he studied the stain. He stood by the window for better light.

"What do you make of it?" he said to Gowers, holding out the map and his glass.

Gowers took them and examined the paper. At length, he said,

"That's a tiny spot of used oil or grease. Someone removed it with a clean finger or handkerchief but left a stain. The stain has small bits of grit stuck in it still, so it's recent. That's a good find, that is."

"I see it the same way... His Lordship's car was at Oxley, then. And you're suggesting he and Chambers drove together?" He returned to his chair.

"I can barely bring myself to believe it," said Sophie, "but, yes, that is what I'm saying. Otherwise, without an accomplice, Chambers would find it impossible to conceal such a car in a place like Oxley."

Morton was quiet for a moment before tapping on the table as he came to a decision. "Right, leave all this with us, Miss Burgoyne. We, ah, we shall pursue the matter." His clipped, brisk voice suggested his decision was an unpalatable one.

"Thank you, Inspector." She stood up and the two men rose with her.

"What are you thinking, sir?" asked Gowers after she had gone.

"That's a nice bit of work, but it's just made our job a lot harder. Dealing with peers is never easy at the best of times. Now we're after Manningtree. We have to tread softly on this one. Our best line of attack is to break Chambers' alibi. That way, we can put him in the car. Then his Lordship should - I say, should - naturally follow."

"At least we know we have to break his alibi. That's something to aim for. A few hours of questioning and we'll have Chambers singing like a bird."

"I hope you're right, for all our sakes."

Sir Ephraim's statement to the police was simple. His son Barry had attacked him and, if not for the maid's timely intervention, he would be dead. He was awake but with his eyes shut when a person entered the room. He assumed it was the nurse. Without warning, the person attacked him. When Barry pressed the pillow over his face, Sir Ephraim had been lying on his side and could still breathe despite the pillow. Barry realized this and repositioned the pillow to cut off his air supply completely. The weight of the young man pressing down immobilized Sir Ephraim. Some seconds later, he heard another voice, and the pressure relaxed. The maid had entered the room, striking at Barry.

When Sophie entered his rooms to tidy them, Sir Ephraim was reluctant to speak to her beyond a few commonplace remarks. Having said so much and suffered so much the day before, he acted as though all was best forgotten. She cleaned his rooms and ran an errand, but decided it was best for his health that she did not return to the taboo subject.

Early on in searching the grounds, the police found a stolen car with a London registration hidden behind a hedge. There was nothing inside that connected to the wounded man. He had still not given his name to the police, although he had spoken to the nurses and doctor attending him at the hospital.

———⋈———

At noon, Flora, Ada, and Sophie sat together at lunch. They all looked tired.

"What a flat, dull day it is," said Flora. With her elbows on the table, she propped up her head.

"I hate it if I don't get a good night's sleep. I 'ave to push myself to do anything."

"Who's acting strangely this morning?" asked Sophie.

"Everyone looks like they're sleepwalking," said Flora. "Rosina has gone very peculiar. For once, she might be mistaken for a human being. I suppose a murderer being in his Lordship's retinue has brought her down a peg or two."

"What about Lord Philip?" asked Sophie.

"I haven't seen him," said Flora. Ada shook her head.

"I saw him after breakfast. He looked pensive... I wouldn't say worried, exactly, just deep in thought. It could be he's wondering where his maps have got to. He might not know how to get home." All three girls laughed at Sophie's joke.

"What did the Inspector say about that?" asked Ada.

"Not a great deal. I don't think he relishes the idea of laying charges against an earl... It seems my discovery is insufficient evidence to do so."

"The Old Bill likes witnesses. If they can find someone who saw the pair of them, in the car, just outside of Bedford, on the day, then they'd be happy as sand-boys."

"I suppose they can look into that... By the way, what is a sand-boy?" asked Sophie.

"I don't know," said Flora. "My father uses that expression occasionally. I like it because it conjures up happy children at the seaside, but I've no idea, really."

"I know what it means," said Ada. "It was an old trade, but it died out. My granddad on me mum's side was a sand-boy when he was a nipper. Back then, they used to deliver sand by horse and cart. It was for the floors in taverns and other places. They'd cart away the old sand, it all mixed with slopped drink, muck, and what 'ave you. Then they put down fresh. Well, them being in so many pubs, you don't have to guess what 'appened. Sounds like they were happy all day long. But there's another bit an' all. They'd find a lot of dropped money amongst that old sand. The old josser me granddad worked for once found a purse with thirty gold sovereigns in it buried under the sand. I think he might have been the 'appiest sand-boy hever that day."

"A lucky find," said Flora. "They use sawdust in a few public houses, like they do in butcher shops. I've never seen sand being put down."

"Today feels as though we're cleaning out mucky sand without the hope of a farthing. I could do with a walk." Sophie got up from the table.

"I'll come with you," said Ada.

"Mrs Fisher told me to clean Stephen's room," said Flora, "so I had better get on with it."

"It's quite mild out," said Ada with some surprise, as she and Sophie emerged from the house.

"Not too bad. It's too damp in the gardens. Let's walk along the drive."

They left the side door area.

"Reckon we'll get more jobs from Inspector Morton?"

"That's hard to say... I think he's pleased with our work, but he seems rather intense, as though he'd rather we weren't involved and yet he's stuck with us."

"Oh... Men are so daft sometimes. They get all huffy if a girl can do what they can. My sister, Joan, she got a foreman's job in the shoe factory where she works. She supervises about thirty girls now. The other foremen don't like it much, her being female, and one of 'em won't ever speak to her. That's stupid."

"That's pride for you. Hopefully, attitudes will change over time. Oh, what's going on over there?"

The two women stopped at the front corner of the house. A uniformed officer, coming from the woods, carried a canvas gun bag. Behind him, several others were walking together in the easy attitude of those who had successfully completed a long task.

"Found something, eh?" called Lord Philip.

He was on the front steps. Sophie put a warning hand on Ada's arm. Stepping back out of sight behind a bush, they could still see and hear what was happening.

"Yes, my Lord," said the man carrying the bag. He slowed to a stop in front of Lord Philip. "I found this here .303 with its tellyscope propped up against a tree over thar'. Next the road." The constable pointed. "We reckon how the man as was shot last night, 'ee put it down and lost it in the fog. It wor' thick enow."

The other constables caught up and stopped.

"I see... How do you know it belongs to him?" Lord Philip asked sharply.

"Well, I don't know for sartin' but it's loikely, ain't it? The other fella, 'ee had 'isself a shotgun. 'Ee wouldn't be carryin' an arsenal around with him, would he, my Lord?"

"It's possible, though. When I go shooting, I usually take several rifles and shotguns with me."

"Ah, yes, you would. But... I don't know..."

"Just a thought. Seems obvious to me he would carry a shotgun and a rifle. Anyway, well done, my man. This is for you."

"Why, thank you very much, my Lord." The constable received the half-crown and gave a small salute.

"You men, go to the kitchen and ask the cook for some beer or whatever takes your fancy. Tell her I sent you."

The constables responded with a chorus of thank you. Lord Philip followed them into the house.

"Mrs Barker won't like that lot turnin' up in her kitchen all of a sudden."

"No, she won't... What did you make of Lord Philip?" asked Sophie.

"I would say he was not exactly happy they found the rifle."

"Exactly! If I'm correct, Lord Philip knows a lot more about all of this than he's letting on. Why would he just have been so quick to attempt to defend the intruder who was shot and arrested last night and whose fingerprints no doubt will be found on the revolver that was recovered? Do you know, I nearly approached Lord Philip to explain matters? I was even deliberating about mentioning Stokely's possible involvement. When will I learn? I've been told not to trust anyone and here's the proof of what they said before my eyes."

"Oh, dear me. I see what you mean. He knows about the sniper at Trefoil with the rifle. Now he's trying to cover for him by puttin' the rifle on the other fella, the one who shot the sniper. Well, well, what a wicked old git."

"Ada, please. I know it's shocking."

"Sorry, miss. I do try."

"I'm so thoroughly disappointed in him... It confirms all my suspicions about the map. Let's go back inside."

"It's funny, though. The way his Lordship carried on in the 'all last night, I'd never guess he'd be one of them."

"That's exactly the point that people like Auntie Bessie and Inspector Penrose have been making. Someone with evil intentions will also seem natural and believable."

"It's very difficult with strangers who behave nicely. You want to believe the best is in everyone. It's not always there, though, is it?"

"It seems it is not. We already knew that, but it's so easy to forget."

CHAPTER 34

— • —

A NEW WAY OF LIFE

B y Sunday evening, Abinger Mansion was quiet again. The police had gone. Morton and Gowers had returned to London.
Of the guests, Stephen had left early and then Thomas later in
the afternoon. The children and widows became more evident
- occupying the downstairs rooms. Prudence now looked less
afflicted than upon her arrival but both women were still bewildered as to why such affliction had visited them. Yet now that the
cause was identified, in the shape of a disgruntled, illegitimate
son, they could begin to understand and begin healing.

The police, not wishing to discuss the events at Trefoil Hall,
had not given complete explanations of their investigations to
the family and had omitted to mention Trefoil Hall. As far as
the Wrights understood the matter, Barry killed Frank, had an
accomplice shoot Alfred, and then made his attempt upon Sir
Ephraim.

The secret agents were neither consulted nor informed, once
Sophie had recounted her impression of Sir Philip possessing
knowledge of the sniper at Trefoil Hall. Sergeant Gowers was
extremely pleased over the discovery of the rifle, while Inspector
Morton looked relieved more than anything else. They had taken
the rifle with them for it to undergo a ballistics test to determine
if it was the same one as that used in the Trefoil shooting. On
their train ride back to London, Morton was glad that the case
was finding solid ground. Quietly staring out of the train window,
he did not see the countryside flashing past. Instead, he saw in
his mind's eye a young woman with light brown hair and a lovely
smile.

Sir Ephraim was better, but stayed in his rooms to speak with the family. He took an interest in the children - more so than was usual for him. He remained quite aloof with Sophie.

———✂———

On Monday, all the remaining guests left in the morning. Prudence and Millicent were now constant companions and departed for the station together. The Manningtrees left by car with Lord Philip at the wheel. Sophie considered whether her agency might supply a replacement chauffeur, but she refrained from suggesting her idea. It was inappropriate under the circumstances.

Mrs Fisher spoke to Sophie about Mrs Barker staying on as cook. They arranged the fee between them and Mrs Barker was to be paid twelve pounds a month, all found. Sophie subsequently met Mrs Barker, and they had an emotional meeting. Mrs Barker was so thoroughly happy it made Sophie cry, which occurrence caused Mrs Barker to cry. They required a pot of tea to restore themselves.

Sophie's final meeting with Sir Ephraim, just before she left in the afternoon, was brief.

"Thank you, Sophie, for all that you've done." Sir Ephraim was sitting in a chair. "I realize you were here on business against my express wishes, but none of that matters anymore."

"I'm glad I could help... Are you more at peace now?"

"In a way, I am. Then again, a greater realization has seized me. I look back over my life and, despite my success, it has all gone wrong. It has gone wrong in the things that matter most. My sins have caught up with me."

"The attacks were not your doing. It is the evil thoughts of others at work. Although calamity has fallen upon your house, you did not call it down. I'm very sorry about what has happened. I will remember Alfred until the day I die. He was peaceful when I met him. He was successful in the submarine negotiations. That's how I will remember him."

"Will you?" Sir Ephraim fell into a reverie.

"I'm sorry, but I must leave now. Goodbye, Sir Ephraim."

"Yes. Goodbye, my dear."

———⊠———

Bright and early Tuesday morning, Sophie was back at the agency, but she arrived after Miss Jones. They sat down together in Sophie's office.

"It was busy while you were away." Miss Jones' sharp face and tone suggested she hated the work. At other times, she seemed to hate the lack of it. "Fifteen typing assignments on Friday, four on Saturday, and twenty-three yesterday."

"My goodness. I had better get typing."

"No need. They are all completed and returned to the clients."

"Are they really? That is excellent work. What about the domestic servants?"

"We placed a footman and two maids in permanent positions on Friday. Yesterday it was two maids. I noticed you had a notation on some of your cards stating the type of environment in which they are likely to thrive. That is a commendable approach, Miss Burgoyne. We don't want square pegs in round holes. There are also several letters for your attention, which I believe are from prospective clients. One of them is from the Duke of Hampshire."

"The Duke of Hampshire... Excellent. That must be from Bunny Warren, his wife. I wonder what she wants."

"You're acquainted with the family?"

"Yes. I've stayed at Martingale twice. My father was up at Oxford with the Duke. They've stayed in touch, and I'm friendly with the youngest daughter."

This information visibly impressed Miss Jones, who raised her eyebrows.

"Can I ask you something, Miss Jones?"

"Of course."

"Do you enjoy working here?"

"Enjoy working here...? Why, I suppose I do. I like the office being so airy. I appreciate your trusting me with the management of your business while you were away."

"Would you consider continuing on? I have to warn you, though - there's a proviso attached to the suggestion."

"Yes, I would consider it."

"Very good. This is a new agency. I cannot guarantee work will come in with regularity. I was thinking, if you managed the office, I could find new clients. We'd send out letters advertising the services we provide. If I could concentrate on that, I believe it can do well. I can't do everything, though. So I need someone dependable to run the office."

"I've never worked for a lady before, but I've managed office staff, both male and female. As you are aware, the factory where I worked for the last ten years went bankrupt. My age is against me, so any work you provide would be most welcome."

"Then let's discuss a suitable per diem. If this rush of work holds, you'll have a full-time job. If it slows, you will probably get three days a week. I'll leave it to your discretion when to bring in temporary typists."

Miss Jones smiled, which was the first time Sophie had seen her do such a thing.

On Wednesday, Elizabeth Banks, about sixty years old, came to the office seeking employment. Sophie interviewed her.

"Thank you for filling out the card. Now, let me review your work experience."

She read that Miss Banks was formerly employed as a research assistant or secretary by several famous men - two of them had been cabinet ministers, one was an earl, and one was a shipping magnate. She had also worked at the British Museum.

"I'm afraid we don't receive requests for anyone with your type of experience."

"I can wash dishes or do laundry," said Miss Banks.

"Oh, dear... I wish I could think of something... Where did you get your training?"

"I studied history at Oxford in the eighties. I've organized and catalogued several important libraries. During the war, I researched Germany's economy, armaments, and military tactics... Now I can't pay the rent and I have two little cats. I'll do any available work."

This was not the first hard-luck story Sophie had heard and would not be the last. What struck a chord was the thought that she, herself, might be in the same position one day. To be genteel and poor was to possess a horror of destitution and the ultimate shame it threatened. Poor people suffer, but to be educated and then become poor is to suffer acutely in further hidden ways, beyond the realm of physical wants.

"Can you type?"

"Yes, but although accurate, I'm not quick."

"I see."

It was an awkward situation. Miss Jones, a fury on the typewriter herself, would never countenance a slow typist in the office. To impose Miss Banks upon Miss Jones would cause an unthinkable disruption to the recently established morale and organization of the office. There would be upset. As Sophie searched for a solution, the pipes thumped maniacally in the walls.

"You didn't jump," said Sophie with much surprise.

"No, I've dealt with that before. There is an airlock in your water pipes. Does it happen often?"

"Several times a day."

"There are three ways to cure it. First and most expensive is to replace the entire line unless one knows which pipe is improperly sealed. The second is to purge the line with air, but the noise will return later. The third is a simple trick. Where is your tap?"

"Allow me to show you at once." They went to the kitchenette. "Every time I turn on the tap, it does this spluttering thing. It's worse if it's been left for a long time."

Sophie looked on while Elizabeth examined the tap. She turned it on full. There followed a noisy discharge of water and air like a cannon blast, accompanied by small knocking noises in the pipe. After a brief hesitation, a healthy stream of water began flowing.

"The trick is to leave a slow drip." Elizabeth turned the tap so that it dripped once every four or five seconds. "By doing this, air cannot build up in the pipe. That air, when trapped, is being compressed by the water pressure in your line. When someone turns the tap on in an adjoining business, the sudden release in pressure causes the pipes to bang. London water is hard. Something should be put underneath, otherwise, there will be scale and stains on the enamel. A small bowl should be sufficient."

"Are you mechanically minded?"

"I suppose I am, although I've never considered myself so. I can manage a few car repairs, such as removing and cleaning a carburettor or adjusting the timing."

"You can repair a car as well? Now I'm doubly impressed. All I know is an engine is under the bonnet. If you told me it worked by magic, I would believe you."

Elizabeth gave a shy smile.

"Will you stay for tea? Or do you have somewhere to go?"

"I have nowhere to go."

"Then stay for tea. I'm sure there's work for you. Some typing... It doesn't pay a great deal. I'll tell you what does interest me, and that is your being experienced in research. Sometimes, situations arise and I wish I understood them better."

"Do you mean political situations?"

"Yes, both foreign and domestic. I think I need tutoring in some areas. Have you thought about tutoring?"

"Yes, I've been a tutor in several disciplines."

"There we are, then. I would like to understand the background of the Greek-Turkish war. While you're here, you could do the odd typing job at your own pace. Would six shillings a day be adequate?"

"Very adequate, Miss Burgoyne. When shall I start?"

"Would tomorrow be convenient?"

"Very convenient. What hours do you keep?"

"You only need to be present between ten and four."

They finished their meeting and their tea. Sophie hoped her offer had not sounded like charity. Outside, walking along Sack Lane, Elizabeth was beaming to herself and was feeling almost fit to burst with relief and happiness. She also very much looked forward to fulfilling the unexpectedly interesting duties of this new position. The prospect of conducting research again, even in a modest way, filled her with great pleasure. Elizabeth was truly grateful to the young lady and thought that Sophie had made a very creditable job of making the offer of tutor-cum-typist not seem too much like charity.

On Friday, two remarkable and transfiguring events occurred. The first was simple enough. A letter arrived at the office in the early morning post. Addressed to Sophie, it bore the inscription 'private and confidential' and a Dorking postmark. It contained a letter expressing heartfelt gratitude from Sir Ephraim, without reference to recent events. Enclosed was a cheque. As she held it, Sophie's hand shook with excitement and disbelief because she was, at that moment, precisely twenty-five hundred pounds richer than she had been the moment before. It made her feel quite giddy, which immediately brought Buloji to mind, which in turn made her laugh very merrily.

Pinned to the cheque was a curious note. It stated that she must never mention her having received the money. She supposed Sir Ephraim, or perhaps Mr Reese because it was in his handwriting, had decided it was best to keep secret any connection between Sir Ephraim and Burgoyne's Agency. At the very bottom of the note, in a weak scrawl, were the words, 'To carry on the fight.'

The second event, some hours later, took the form of Superintendent Penrose climbing the Agency stairs. From her desk, Elizabeth could hear him reading out loud the notices on the landing.

"Good morning," he said, after he had entered the office that was filled with the sound of typewriters being pounded. "Got trouble with the pipes?"

"No, they're behaving themselves. We've had no noise from the pipes since Wednesday."

"That's good. I might have been one of those who shrieked otherwise."

"Are you here to see Miss Burgoyne?"

"Yes, would you tell her Penrose is here, please?"

"I will at once. Please, take a seat."

"Thank you."

In short order, Elizabeth ushered Superintendent Penrose into Sophie's office.

"This is indeed an honour, Inspector. What can I do for you?" Sophie offered a chair to Superintendent Penrose.

"Nice place you've got here. I've come because a couple of small matters need discussing. Now don't worry, I had a pipe before I came in." He smiled at Sophie. "Before I forget - Inspector Morton, he's a taciturn chap, but I reckon he very much appreciated your work at Abinger Mansion."

"I got the impression that I was there under sufferance."

"That's just his way. He's used to giving orders. And you're what might be called a little on the independent side. Carrying a cosh made it seem like you were looking for trouble. With those attacks in the night, he thought he had put you in harm's way. You've confused the lad.

"The first matter is a kindness to you. Police are a closed-mouth lot, as a rule... for obvious reasons. I decided to let you know what be the state of affairs. Only you're to keep mum about it

"Thank you very much. That is perceptive of you. I have a hundred and one questions to ask."

"I knew you would. I doubt I have a dozen answers. First off, Barry Chambers is charged with the attempted murder of his father. He's going to plead guilty. The fellow who got shot in his hindquarters goes by the name of Gilbert Freemantle. We won't mention who did the shooting. Freemantle became more sociable after we found his prints on the rifle. It was the same rifle used to kill Alfred Wright. He's going to trial on that one. Morton is certain Freemantle also killed brother Frank, but we can't prove it, you see. Seems like he's done that trick before. The sooner he's out of the way, the better to my mind."

"Thank you for telling me... What about the other parties?"

Penrose lowered his voice. "Lord Philip is as guilty as sin, but Barry Chambers is sticking by him. Lord Philip received the share purchase money from a lawyer. He says he knows no more than that. The lawyer won't say who he's acting for. He did let slip the money came from another lawyer. In other words, what we want to know is tied up in knots and we can't undo them.

"On the bright side, Morton tore Chambers' alibi into tiny, little pieces. The man never was in London visiting friends that weekend. Chambers admits to the attack upon Sir Ephraim but won't incriminate anyone else. He says we've got his confession, and that's all he's giving out.

"Concerning the Sunbeam's journey, they've been trying to find witnesses all along the roads from Ipswich to Bedford, but have found nothing as yet. Chances are they won't. Wouldn't be enough, anyway. I reckon Chambers and Manningtree drove at night carrying spare petrol with them, so they did not need to stop. Can't prove it, though. We want both of them in Oxley, observed by a reliable witness or two. Surrey police knocked door to door, but no one had seen the car, let alone who was driving it. As for the other gentleman?" Penrose shook his head slowly and emphatically. "Not a chance. He's won this round. He has his bank and there's nothing we can do about it. If Sir Ephraim would talk, that would be different."

"It is so utterly annoying. There must be a way to beat the man."

"If you come up with something, tell me and I'll see what can be done."

"This is not right," said Sophie. "It would be better if we had Stokely and not the others."

Penrose smiled, took out his pipe, looked at it, then put it away again.

"If you want to smoke, you could open that window and blow the smoke outside."

"No, I'll manage, thank 'ee. Now, the other matter. There's a dinner coming up. A big swanky do in Mayfair. Reckon we need six people on the inside. Male or female, but I'd like it if you were one of them. We can set it up so's you're hired by the gentleman who runs the establishment."

"When is this taking place?"

"6th October. There'll be up to a hundred and fifty guests and better than fifteen resident staff. There's an illegal gambling den inside the house, and narcotics are sold while a harmless dinner and dance club for the socialites acts as the front. We won't touch it for the gambling; not yet, anyway. The drugs we're waiting on as well. What I'm looking for is a gang that's putting out counterfeit money. It started as a trickle. Now it's a steady stream that has to be dealt with. There's a French connection, but we're not sure that's where they're printed. They're excellent forgeries, too. Mostly pounds and fivers. A lot of these notes turn up at racecourses and places like the one we're thinking about in Mayfair."

"I'm very interested. What rate of pay are you considering for the night's work and the training?"

"Training?"

"Well, I've never gambled in my life. I must understand the games being played and how they manage the betting. Also, there's the floor plan of the house to study. The same for my staff. They must understand how to act and where they will be stationed. If you want us to cobble something together, it can be done. If you want Burgoyne's doing its exceptional best, then there needs to be training."

Penrose laughed. "I heard about the arrangement you had with Morton. Shall we say the same?"

"No, we shall not. That was for four people. This is for six. Pro rata would make it eighteen pounds a day for three days, including training and rehearsals. That's fifty-four pounds." Sophie smiled.

"No, it's too much. Training should be less than the pay for operations. Turn the numbers round. Forty-five."

"Fifty."

"Forty-seven is my last offer or I'll smoke my pipe elsewhere."

"Oh, please stay here and smoke it. Forty-seven it shall be."

"You drive a hard bargain. My poor budget is in tatters."

"Let me open the window for you. Then, pipe in hand, you can peacefully contemplate the wisdom of choosing Burgoyne's."

CHAPTER 35

— ⋅ —

FUTURE TROUBLES

H e was called Ferrers. No one addressed him by any other name, yet all agreed it was probably not the one he was born with. His was a large, tanned, carefully shaved, granite-hard face. This was a famous face in certain quarters, known for never betraying emotion. He wore a superb black cutaway coat, matching waistcoat over a white wing collar shirt and grey silk cravat, and striped trousers. He jauntily sported spats over his brilliantly polished shoes. His hat was a faultless silk topper, and he wore grey gloves. He appeared to be a fastidious and successful businessman in every respect. However, there were jarring notes that marred this image. The splendid clothes adorned a singularly massive frame and could not disguise his great bodily strength, even though he was not above the average height. Then there were his personal ornaments. He carried a heavy, polished black cane with a ruby set in the handle. This indeed looked very elegant and altogether nice until one found he could use it as a club, which he had several times, or he might resort to the long knife concealed within, that had also seen use. Under his jacket, in a holster which made no imprint in the smooth, expensive material of his coat, was a Webley snub-nosed revolver. He had other less frightful appurtenances to his costume. His watch fob was of oversized thick gold links, fire flashed from a big, brilliant-cut diamond tie pin, and a single, massive gold ring was on his little finger.

As he walked along the street, one noticed he had an odd gait - it was as though only his legs moved while his upper body remained utterly motionless. He mounted the steps to the white stucco-fronted Belgravia house in Lyall Place and pressed the electric doorbell.

A tall butler opened the door to admit Ferrers.

"Is he busy?"

"No, sir." The butler was nervous. "He's in the office."

Ferrers removed his top hat and gloves and handed them over.

"Take good care of those. Now, hop it," said Ferrers as he quickly ran a hand over his close-cropped, silvery hair.

"Yes, sir."

"Morning, Stokely."

"Morning, Ferrers."

Lord Stokely, dressed except for a jacket and wearing a blue silk dressing-gown, sat in a comfortable armchair with his legs stretched out, reading a letter.

"The job's done as far as I'm concerned. I don't like how it ended. I've lost a good man." Ferrers' voice was low, oscillating within a narrow range, and rhythmic. He sat down in a chair opposite.

Stokely was what some women would call a beautiful man. Men said he was good-looking, handsome. His every movement was made with an easy gracefulness. It was a pleasure just to watch him as one would watch a leopard. When he spoke, his words were rendered more important, more meaningful by the pleasantness of his tone and his sweeping cadence. He was tall, athletic, and had a brilliant mind. However, of the two men, he seemed the less consequential. Stokely might be dangerous in hidden, less obvious ways, while Ferrers looked savage and untamed. The peer was an elegant prince. By comparison, Ferrers was a brutal king over a violent kingdom.

"There are plenty of others out there." Stokely smiled at his companion.

"Yes, there are. Finding them and trusting them takes time. No more amateur hour for us. You've had your fun, got your bank, and now it's over."

"Yes, it turned out well. I am satisfied with the results. And my Greek agent has the submarine plans on their way to the Russians as we speak. That goodwill gesture should guarantee their support of us in the future."

"Let us hope so," replied Ferrers drily. "Is Manningtree going to cause trouble?"

"I think not. He's an ardent believer in changing Britain for the better. Even when he suddenly realized he was in the middle of a murder conspiracy, he saw the sense in playing along for his own safety. He didn't like it, but he won't be a problem."

"Well, if that changes, I'll deal with him."

"What about your sniper, Freemantle? Will he talk now the police have him on murder charges?"

"Oh, no. He has nearest and dearest. He knows perfectly well the harm that will come to them if he squeals. Freemantle's a professional after all's said and done. They'll hang him, but that's a risk he took. At least he has the knowledge his family's provided for *if* he keeps his mouth shut."

"I don't understand who it was who caught him."

"Like I said, we used an amateur, and it mucked up everything. To his credit, Chambers is playing a decent game. I'll give him that much. As to the party who shot Freemantle, I've no idea who it was. Might have been a copper. I don't think so, though, because I've asked around and they're keeping quiet about the shooting. I reckon someone with brains caught on to our game. We must be more careful in future. We'll cut out the fancy stuff and just do straight jobs as they need doing. That's the best policy."

"Oh, very well. I have to mention it, Ferrers. I would appreciate it if you used my title once in a while. Just for form's sake."

"I'm not a socialist. In fact, I hate them. I also hate this country's class structure. One day, I mean for you to be in power, with me making sure everything runs smoothly in the background. I cannot get there without you and you cannot get there without me. On the day I call you by your title, I'll put a bullet between your eyes. We're partners; we couldn't be more different, but we're equal. If we work together, we'll get what we want. If you don't like what I've said, we'd both better make other arrangements, and soon."

"Ha, and I believe you would do that. No, I am content with our partnership as it stands. In your way, you are the most straightforward and honest man I've ever met."

"Don't butter me up or I'll blush. What's next on the agenda?"

Sophie set down a fresh, bound notebook on the desk in front of her and opened it. She thought for some moments before dipping her pen in the inkwell. Upon the first page she wrote Secret Agency Casebook, hesitated, smiled, then added No. 1. Words flowed from her nib as she ordered her thoughts about recent events. It surprised her to record such things - to see her own name attached to these extraordinary affairs. She had a neat, legible hand, augmented with a few subtle flourishes. Upon reviewing what she had written an hour later, she made a few amendments and additions. Then she got up to open the cupboard where the office supplies were kept. Inside, she saw at once the tiny leather notebook she sought.

The title she gave to this little book was 'Serious Matters Requiring Urgent Attention.' The next page she entitled 'Matters of Justice' and underlined it. Her first entry was "Lord Stokely" and beneath, she included what pertinent details she had. Her second entry was for "Lord Manningtree", who received similar biographical attention. Upon completing her work, she hoped that no further peers would be similarly gazetted or it would start to look absurd - as though she was waging a vendetta against the peerage en masse.

With the names entered in her book, Sophie now had clearly defined targets, and this exercise had reduced all her swirling uncertainties and guesses into tangible objectives. The paths to completion were obscured, but writing their names had clarified what it was she intended to do, which was to bring the miscreants to justice. Sir Ephraim's generous gift would enable and help her to do just that. As she was ready to put the books away, a thought occurred. She opened her little book again and, turning to about the middle, wrote 'Matters of Interest.' Underneath she left a space and then wrote, "Who is the gardener?" She smiled once more, blotted her writing, and closed the book.

She opened the small Milner safe. Sophie placed the notebooks next to the cash box and ledgers of account, then shut the heavy door, threw the bolts, and spun the dial. As was her habit, she patted the top of the safe, saying, "Guard everything well, Milly." After that, with the day looking so nice, she decided upon something she had been planning but had never yet found the time to do.

In climbing the three hundred and eleven stairs of the Monument's circular staircase, Sophie got tantalizing glimpses through narrow windows. It was not until she arrived at the very top that the view took her breath away. Below lay Sack Lane and the roof of the agency building, but it was a tiny street in the great sprawling London metropolis. Up so high, it was windy, requiring Sophie to hold on to her hat as she walked around the platform. The wide Thames was busy with the traffic of ships, barges, and every type of small craft. Tower Bridge, Westminster Abbey, Houses of Parliament, and numerous other landmarks and large buildings formed great citadels of power and influence. In every direction, the scenes were novel but, between the landmarks, always composed of parks, rooftops, churches, spires, trees, and smoke. So many people, so much activity. She smiled to herself. The young woman from the sleepy country village had carved her own niche in the city and, if everything continued as she hoped it would, a busy, productive, and exciting life ahead of her.

Looking towards Scotland Yard and the Foreign Office, Sophie found she could distinguish neither in the distance, but that did not stop her wondering which institution she would hear from first.

ALSO BY G J BELLAMY

If you have enjoyed this book, it would be a great help if you could leave a good review

Other books by G J Bellamy
SOPHIE BURGOYNE SERIES - 1920s
Secret Agency
Lady Holme
Amazon USA https://www.amazon.com/dp/B0B99ZFC67

Amazon UK https://www.amazon.co.uk/dp/B0B99ZFC67
Dredemere Castle
Chertsey Park
Primrose Hill

BRENT UMBER SERIES
Death between the Vines
Death in a Restaurant
Death of a Detective
Death at Hill Hall
Death on the Slopes
Death of a Narcissist

FREE NOVELLA - The Village of the Sevenfold Curse.
A murder mystery set in ancient Britain.
A great choice is to sign up for the newsletter to learn about upcoming new releases and receive your free book.

https://gjbellamy.com/newsletter-landing-page/

Made in the USA
Monee, IL
25 January 2024

8d79f712-8ee2-4358-ad34-058a99e423bfR01